TALES OF GOOD AND EVIL

NICOLAI GOGOL

was born in the Ukraine in 1809. He settled in Petersburg in 1828 where he published four volumes of short stories between 1831 and 1835 and where his famous comedy *The Government Inspector* saw its first performance in 1836. The rest of his life Gogol mostly spent abroad, where he wrote *The Overcoat* and *Dead Souls*. He died in Moscow in 1852.

Tales of
GOOD AND EVIL

Nicolai V. Gogol

Translated with an Introduction
by DAVID MAGARSHACK

JOHN LEHMANN
MCMXLIX

FIRST PUBLISHED IN 1949
BY JOHN LEHMANN LTD
6 HENRIETTA STREET, LONDON W.C.2
MADE AND PRINTED IN GREAT BRITAIN BY
PURNELL AND SONS LTD
PAULTON (SOMERSET) AND LONDON

INTRODUCTION

NICOLAI GOGOL was born in the Ukrainian township of Sorochintsy, Poltava province, on 19th March 1809. His father was a small landowner and the author of a number of Ukrainian comedies which were performed at the country house of a local grandee and a former Cabinet Minister, a distant relative of the Gogols. It was at the house of this rich landowner that Gogol first came into contact with the world of art, for there he found a large library, a picture gallery, and a theatre. Gogol was sent to school in 1819. He went first to a preparatory school in Poltava and then to a grammar school in Nezhin. Already as a schoolboy he made up his mind to leave a mark on the history of his country. In a letter to a school-fellow Gogol speaks scornfully of the people in Nezhin. "They have buried the high destiny of man," he writes, "under the rubbish heap of their ridiculous self-complacency. And among these people who merely vegetate I have to spend my days ! I dread the thought that fate may cast me into some God-forsaken hole and make me play the part of a nobody in the world." Living among "people who merely vegetate", and being conscious of his future greatness, it is no wonder that Gogol, though fond of laughter and merry pranks, gave way to fits of depression and made few friends. "I have suffered more unhappiness than you think," he writes to his mother shortly before leaving school. "I doubt if any other human being has ever experienced so much ingratitude or so much cold contempt. . . . You say I am a dreamer. No, I know people too well to be a dreamer. The lessons I have learnt from them I shall never forget."

His father died when Gogol was sixteen, and three years later, on leaving school, he went to seek his fortune in Petersburg. But literature was not Gogol's chosen career when he arrived in Petersburg towards the end of 1828. It is true that he had already written an "idyll" in verse, but what had brought him to Petersburg was a grandiose idea he cherished of reforming the laws of his country and thus bringing about a new era of prosperity and happiness for his people. He had already seen too much injustice in the world and he had reached the conclusion that "injustice is the greatest evil of mankind." He therefore hoped to enter the Ministry of Justice and, by taking a hand in the framing of the laws of his country, "be of use to humanity." But it seemed that it was not so easy to convince the officials of the Ministry of Justice of his talents as a legislator. Gogol could not get a job in the Civil Service, and his first year in Petersburg was a year of hunger and privations. He did, however, succeed in publishing his idyll under the pseudonym of Alov. Curiously enough, considering how typically Russian all Gogol's heroes are, the hero of this juvenile poem bore the German name of Hans Kuechelgarten. Hans is a dreamer who leaves his home and his beloved Louise to wander all over Europe in search of "the beautiful." In his wanderings he visits Greece and on the ruins of Athens comes to the conclusion that people everywhere are "contemptible creatures." Realising how empty his dreams are, Hans returns home and marries his Louise.

Gogol's first literary effort is interesting in that it shows that even as a schoolboy Gogol was realist enough to prefer a common-sense ending to the romantic nonsense of the popular literature of his day. *Hans Kuechelgarten*, however, was a dismal failure and, characteristically, Gogol at that early phase of his literary career did what he was later to do in more tragic circumstances: he destroyed his book of verse and went abroad. He took ship for the German port of Luebeck, intending to emigrate to America ("the fantastic country of happiness and rational productive labour"), but came back within a month. "The moment I found myself at sea," Gogol writes in his *Confessions*, "on board a foreign ship among foreigners (the ship was English and there was not another Russian on board), I felt terribly depressed; I was so sorry to leave the friends of my childhood whom I had always loved that even before I felt the firm ground under my feet I was thinking of going back. I spent only three days abroad, and, notwithstanding the fact that I was beginning to be interested in the strange new things I saw, I hastened to return home on the same ship, fearing that otherwise I might not return at all."

In Petersburg Gogol at last succeeded in getting a small and miserably paid job in the Civil Service, eking out his salary with translations of articles. In April 1830 he was transferred to a better-paid post in another department and spent his leisure time in the summer of that year in attending a course of painting at the Petersburg Academy of Art. Through influential friends he also got lessons in rich houses, and in 1831 he gave up his "idiotic" and "nonsensical" work in the Civil Service and got a job as teacher in the Petersburg Institute for Young Ladies. All his free time he now devoted to writing. In September 1831 the first volume of *Evenings in the Hamlet near Dikanka* appeared and was universally acclaimed. At the age of twenty-two Gogol was a literary figure in Petersburg. He became a close friend of Pushkin and the Russian poet and translator Zhukovsky and other famous literary men. His financial position, too, had improved. The second volume of *Evenings in the Hamlet near Dikanka* was published in March 1832. This volume, which included the story *The Terrible Vengeance*, established him finally as a writer of genius.

In *The Terrible Vengeance*, which was first published with the subtitle *An Old Legend*, the conflict between good and evil, which is so characteristic of Gogol's writings even in what was later to become known as his "naturalistic" period, finds its most perfect expression. In it he seems to penetrate into the most hidden places of the human mind and reveal the most secret stirrings of the human heart, and, while never overstepping the borders of the supernatural world, uncover the world of truth that is usually concealed and shows its power over man only in his dreams. The two heroic figures in the story, the ideal hero Danilo and his ideal wife Katherine, are helpless against the evil machinations of Katherine's father, the sorcerer, who in his person embodies the two evils most dreaded by mankind : murder and incest. But the sorcerer himself is merely the instrument of a still greater evil : man's treachery to his friends.

The whole story is a remarkable example of Gogol's creative genius. Not a single fact in it stands up to rational analysis. Even Katherine's age presents the most insuperable difficulties, for, according to the story, she is at most eighteen, while if other facts, such as her father's long absence, his murder of her mother, her own memories of her mother, and so on, are pieced together, she would be at least forty. And yet the more incredible each single circumstance is, the more credible does the whole story become, for it contains a world in itself, a world in which facts as we know them do not exist, a world in which the earth, the sun, and the stars, the wood-demons and the water-demons, the quick and the dead, form one magic tapestry in which man's life is interwoven with the life of everything on earth—the rivers and the woods, the mountains and the valleys, the birds and the clouds. The whole story is sheer magic, a poet's dream, a fantasy that transcends reality. And the most remarkable thing of all is that against this background of supernatural forces, the forces of good spring to life with such an intensity that they make everything acceptable and credible.

The final triumph of good over evil in this story does not, however, solve the problem of just retribution: the "terrible vengeance" is so terrible because it is based on man-made justice; and if God acquiesces in it, He does so reluctantly, for it lacks the essentials of mercy.

After publishing the second volume of *Evenings in the Hamlet near Dikanka*, Gogol paid a visit to his mother's estate, only stopping for a short time in Moscow, where he made a number of friends among the local literary celebrities, including Sergey Aksakov, the famous author of *A Family Chronicle*, who was to become one of his lifelong friends. He returned to Petersburg in the autumn of 1832. In spite of his fame, he still refused to regard literature as his proper career. It was history that now began to occupy his mind to the exclusion of everything else. "World history is everything," he writes in a letter to a friend; "the rest does not matter." He planned to write "a general history and a general geography." At the same time, however, he also decided to try his hand at writing plays. "I have gone crazy over comedy," he writes in a letter. "While in Moscow I thought of a plot and now it just won't get out of my head. I have even thought of a title for it, but the moment I started writing it I realised how hopeless the whole thing was, for my pen insists on putting down things the censorship will never pass." His enthusiasm for history, however, put an end to all his literary plans. He began writing a history of the Ukraine, and in July 1834 he got himself appointed Reader in Medieval History at the University of Petersburg. Gogol's career as a don was perhaps one of the greatest failures of his life. Turgenev, who studied history at Petersburg University at the time, described Gogol's position in the lecture room as extremely comic. All the students, Turgenev declared, were convinced that Gogol knew nothing about history. It was easy to see that Gogol himself was bored and that he realised that his students, too, were bored. Gogol complained that his students refused to listen to his lectures. "I read my lectures," he wrote "but no one listens to me. Oh, if only one student would take the trouble to understand me !" Gogol gave up his lectureship at the end of 1835. "Unrecognised I entered the lecture room and unrecognised I left it," he wrote. "But in these eighteen months—inglorious months, for everyone agrees that I have undertaken something I have no ability for—I have learnt a great deal. . . . Long live comedy ! At last I have made up my mind to put one on the stage !"

The comedy was *The Government Inspector*. For balked in his ambition to achieve fame as a historian, Gogol spent all his leisure time writing. In addition to *The Government Inspector*, he was working on his collection of short stories and critical essays *Arabesques*, published in 1835, and on his other collection of short stories, published in the same year under the title of *Mirgorod*.

The only literary work that seems to owe its origin to his lectures on English medieval history is the dramatic fragment *Alfred the Great*.

The miscellany *Arabesques* included Gogol's story *The Portrait*, which again deals mainly with the conflict between good and evil. In its original version the supernatural mechanism, so characteristic of Gogol's first stories, was given full play. But in the second version (included in this volume), published in 1842, Gogol had removed most of the "demonic" elements. Thus the artist-recluse declares in the new version of the second part, "I know the world denies the existence of the devil, and will therefore not speak of him." But while Gogol eliminated most of the fantastic features of the story, he could not very well change its main feature, namely, the existence of evil outside man and man's helplessness against it. Its influence on Chartkov's career, however, is confined only to supplying him with the means of his spiritual and ultimately physical self-destruction—money. The story, therefore, deals mainly with evil as expressed in man's lust for money and the dire effect this lust has on art, though the mysterious disappearance of the portrait of the moneylender does carry the idea of evil as a separate entity to its logical conclusion.

The Portrait is also interesting as showing Gogol's own ideas on art. Gogol condemns art that copies life too faithfully and at the same time demands that art should exert a beneficent influence on humanity ("It is essential," Gogol wrote towards the end of his life, "that life should take a step forward in the work of a creative artist"). A remarkable anticipation of the modern methods of psychiatric treatment is to be found in this story. The doctor who attends on Chertkov is looking for some connecting link between his patient's dreams and the facts of his life, regarding this as the only way of curing his madness.

Nevsky Avenue, which was also published in the miscellany *Arabesques*, marks a transition stage in the development of Gogol's art. Here the conflict between good and evil is shifted from man's blind subjection to the forces of evil to the incompatibility of man's idealised conception of life with reality. The idealist artist who falls in love with a girl he meets on Nevsky Avenue, whom he afterwards discovers to be a common prostitute, refuses to accept reality and prefers to live in a dream world of his own where the girl he loves appears as the direct opposite of what she is—with the inevitable tragic results.

But this story is also important because in it Gogol emerges as the great realistic writer he was afterwards to become. The artist is still a romantic figure, though he is no longer treated romantically, but his friend, Lieutenant Pirogov, is one of the most realistic portraits Gogol ever painted, and it is its realism Dostoyevsky admired so much. "This naïve impudence and self-conceit of a fool," Dostoyevsky writes in *The Idiot*, "are marvellously depicted by Gogol in his wonderful portrait of Lieutenant Pirogov."

A highly significant feature of *Nevsky Avenue* as well as of *The Portrait* is Gogol's extraordinarily effective way of using the mechanism of dreams for uncovering the hidden motives of a man's conduct. Writing of the artist's dream in *Nevsky Avenue*, Belinsky observes that "reality and fantasy are so inextricably blended in it that the reader is surprised to learn that the whole thing is only a dream." Gogol's treatment of dreams was to have a great influence on the Russian novel, as can be seen from the works of Dostoyevsky and Tolstoy.

The publication of *Arabesques* and *Mirgorod*, the latter collection including the first version of *Taras Bulba*, brought Gogol recognition as the greatest living writer in Russia. Belinsky, the dictator of letters in Gogol's lifetime, was the first to acknowledge Gogol's pre-eminence as a creative writer and declared that he had stepped into the shoes of the immortal Pushkin. And there could be no greater praise than that. So it seemed that it was not as a lawgiver or historian but as a writer that Gogol was to leave his mark on Russian history. Having at last realised that it was in literature that his "high destiny" lay, Gogol took two decisions. First of all, he made up his mind to get out of Russia. At the very beginning of his literary career during his short visit to his mother's estate, Gogol wrote: "Now I live in the country. . . . What hasn't the countryside here got? Corn, fruits of every kind, everything under the sun in plenty! And yet the people are poor, the estates are ruined, and the landowners are in debt!" A rich country ruined by men who were satisfied "merely to vegetate." To save it—and that was what his "high destiny" meant to Gogol—he had to see it as a whole, which was only possible if he saw it from a distance. "Twice," Gogol wrote in his *Confessions*, "I returned to Russia in the past six years, once with the intention of staying there for good. But the strange thing was that while in Russia I was unable to see Russia. It was only when I left Russia that I was able to see it again as a whole and the desire to know it better reawakened in me."

Secondly, since it was clear now that his true vocation in life was the pursuit of literature, he must dedicate himself to the task of becoming a writer. So far he had used his pen merely as a diversion, as an escape from failure. He had become famous as a writer almost in spite of himself. It was different now. To begin with, therefore, he would have to rewrite a number of his works. There was *The Portrait*, about which Belinsky had been so sniffy. "*The Portrait*," Belinsky wrote, "is Mr. Gogol's failure in the fantastic genre. The first part cannot be read without admiration, but the second part is absolutely worthless. You don't see Gogol in it." Very well. He would scrap the second part and write an entirely new one. Then there was *Taras Bulba*, his historical novel. Belinsky, it was true, had acclaimed it as a great epic, but Gogol knew better. He had written it in too great a hurry. The whole thing would have to be rewritten. The same must be done with *The Government Inspector*. The play was a success, but it was not the impeccable masterpiece Gogol wanted it to be. Then there were two more masterpieces to be written. The subject for the first one had been suggested to him by Pushkin; and while on a short visit to the Crimea in the summer of 1835, Gogol wrote to the poet to tell him that he had begun work on *Dead Souls*. The subject for the second work had also been suggested to him. It all happened quite by chance. He was visiting some literary friends and one of them told an amusing story of a poor civil servant who had a passion for shooting wild fowl. The trouble was that he had no money to buy a shotgun. So for years he stinted himself, saving up all he could from his meagre salary till one day he had enough money to buy the gun he had so passionately desired to possess. But on his first shooting excursion in the Finnish Bay he dropped the gun into some reeds and could not retrieve it. The poor man took the loss of his gun so much to heart that he fell ill. He was saved from death by the generosity of his colleagues at the office who made a collection among themselves and bought him a new gun. The story made everybody laugh, everybody, that is, except Gogol. To the amazement of the whole company, Gogol lowered his head, looking sad and dejected; he felt pity for the civil servant. The plot of *The Overcoat* was already stirring in his mind.

So that was the programme. Gogol did not set about carrying it out all at once. First he travelled in Germany, Switzerland, and France, staying in Paris for some time. In March 1837 he arrived in Italy and settled in Rome, where he began to work in earnest, leaving for another short trip to Germany and Switzerland in the autumn of the same year, and for a short trip to Moscow in 1839 to settle his family affairs. In August 1841 he was once more in Moscow to see the first part of *Dead Souls* through the press. By 1842 the whole of his programme had been carried out; at least, all he was to write had been written.

Taras Bulba, entirely rewritten, so that in its final form it emerged as a new work, was published in 1842. Gogol had devoted three years to the task of writing the new version of his historical novel, being occupied with it from 1839 to 1841. It deals with the same historical period of the wars between the Cossacks and the Poles in the fifteenth and sixteenth centuries as *The Terrible Vengeance*, but it does not rely on the supernatural structure of the earlier work. Taras and his two sons, Ostap and Andrey, are no longer giant figures towering against a background of cosmic forces; they are carefully conceived and brilliantly executed human characters that have their feet firmly planted on the ground. They are larger than life only in the sense that all creative art is larger than life. Like *The Terrible Vengeance*, *Taras Bulba* deals with the conflict of good and evil, but the forces of evil Taras fights against are no longer elemental forces (and it is in this respect, perhaps, that *Taras Bulba* does not exert the same immediate impact on the reader's imagination as *The Terrible Vengeance*); what Taras fights against is the suppression of a people's right to freedom, the aping of the manners of a foreign nation, treachery to one's own kinsfolk, etc. The good he stands for is loyalty, justice, love of one's own country, self-sacrifice and death—all, according to Gogol, steps of the ladder leading to salvation.

But if it is the national aspirations of a people that in *Taras Bulba* form the background of the conflict between the forces of good and evil, it is the inalienable right of the human personality to freedom and happiness that is the theme of *The Overcoat*. Akaky's mild expostulations against the baiting of his colleagues at the office makes at least one of them hear in those pathetic words the unspoken protest of all persecuted men against inhuman treatment: "I am your brother !"

Gogol draws the character of the inoffensive little civil servant with a compassion, simplicity, gentle humour, and seeming casualness of style that makes the story one of the greatest achievements of his genius. With this story Gogol began a new chapter in Russian literature, a chapter in which the underdog and social misfit is treated not as a nuisance, or a figure of fun, or an object of charity, but as a human being who has as much right to happiness as anyone else. "Through the gentle humour which pervades the whole story," a modern Russian critic writes, "through the compassion to man who is every other man's brother, however lowly, absurd, or mentally undeveloped he may be, Gogol expresses his protest as a moralist against 'man's inhumanity to man,' and at the same time exposes the suffocating atmosphere of the bureaucratic world of the Russia of his day."

As regards what Gogol himself called "the fantastic ending" of the story, another Russian critic justly observes that "it has not been dictated by any desire to fire the imagination of the reader, but solely by the desire not to miss a single feature that might fully delineate the character of Akaky." The fantastic element in the story, unlike the fantastic elements in Gogol's earlier stories, does not in fact enforce a "suspension of disbelief" on the reader. Indeed, Gogol's contemporaries seemed to have interpreted the robbing of the overcoat from the Very Important Person by Akaky's ghost as the fate awaiting the Russian ruling class if it did not repent of its ways, an interpretation that most certainly did not occur to Gogol but that seems to have been justified by the events of less than a hundred years later.

The last ten years of Gogol's life were years of bitter frustration. Gogol's literary career only covers a period of about eleven years, the first volume of *Evenings in the Hamlet near Dikanka* having been published in 1831 and the first part of *Dead Souls* in 1842. After these years of feverish activity his genius seemed to have burnt itself out. Gogol himself admits as much in his *Confessions*. "Several times, accused of idleness," he writes, "I took up the pen trying to force myself to write a short story or any other literary work, but I could not produce anything. Almost every time all my efforts ended in sickness, suffering, and, finally, such attacks that as a result of them I was forced to put off all my work for a long time. What was I to do? Was it my fault that I was no longer able to repeat what I had written in the days of my youth? And if every man is subject to these inevitable changes as he passes from one age to another, why should a writer be an exception to this rule? Is not a writer also a man? I never turned aside from my path. I always walked along the same road. My subject was always the same: my subject was life, and nothing else."

Gogol's illness, incidentally, which has puzzled many of his biographers because the doctors could find nothing organically wrong with him, seems to have been a flight from reality, from the thought that his writing days were over; it was an escape into sickness rather than a real illness. For his sense of dedication to literature was too strong to make him give it up. He still had to finish *Dead Souls*, and he went on working on it. His methods of work remained the same. As a young writer he got his mother to supply him with the details of everyday life in the Ukraine (no detail was too small for him, and indeed it is these small realistic details that lend such tremendous force to his most fantastic tales), while he himself collected Ukrainian legends and songs. Out of all this material he built his stories. "I only succeeded in those things which I took straight from life, from data known to me," Gogol wrote. "My imagination has never presented me with any remarkable character or created a single thing which I had not myself seen in nature. . . . I never painted a portrait in the sense of a simple copy: I created a portrait, but created it as a result of careful observation rather than relying solely on my imagination." When working on the second part of *Dead Souls* he therefore appealed frantically to his friends to send him details of everyday life in Russia. The required information came to him by every post, but the work on the book did not seem to progress. In the summer of 1845 he burnt all the chapters of the second volume and started work afresh. In the meantime the feeling that the "high destiny" of which he had dreamt as a boy, had not yet been fulfilled, for his works had not effected the slightest improvement in the lives of the people of Russia, made him publish in 1846 his *Correspondence with Friends*, a collection of essays in the form of letters in which he discussed politics, religion, and literature in the manner of a man laying down the law. He had published a similar collection of essays before in *Arabesques* which provoked Belinsky to an outburst of such contempt for Gogol's "learned essays" that anyone but Gogol would never have attempted anything of the kind again. "I can't understand," Belinsky wrote, "how a man can compromise his literary name so thoughtlessly. If these essays are meant to show Mr. Gogol's learning, then may the Lord save us from this sort of learning. We have plenty of it as it is." But this time Gogol's *Correspondence with Friends* produced a veritable storm in Russia. From his deathbed Belinsky hurled a thunderbolt at Gogol's head, accusing him of black reaction and calling him "a preacher of the whip, an apostle of ignorance, a defender of obscurantism, and a panegyrist of Tartar customs." Belinsky's *Letter to Gogol*, which was immediately suppressed by the authorities, was directly responsible for Dostoyevsky's arrest and imprisonment in Siberia, Dostoyevsky having read it to what was later to be known as "Petrashevsky's group" in Petersburg. Gogol's efforts to save his country certainly had the most unpredictable consequences. But the unkindest cut of all to Gogol was that his political supporters in Russia had also turned against him. To them Gogol's rather naïve blending of religious mysticism and politics at a time when the whole of Europe was in a revolutionary ferment was a political blunder of the first order, and they told him to mind his own business and leave politics to those who knew something about them. Gogol replied to the criticisms of *Correspondence with Friends* by publishing his *Confessions* in 1847, but no one listened to him any more. At last the truth dawned on him, and in a letter to Zhukovsky he ruefully admits that "as a matter of fact, preaching is not my business. My business is to speak with living images and not with arguments. I must present life as it is and not write essays about it."

Unhappily Gogol could no longer "present life as it is." He was essentially a visual artist and, when his keen inner sight was gone, his natural predisposition to melancholy and his mystical bent grew apace till they took entire possession of him. He had always been a valetudinarian and a melancholic. Now he became obsessed with his imaginary illnesses, rushing all over Europe in an effort to find a cure for them. He finished up by going on a pilgrimage to the Holy Places in Palestine, but to his horror he discovered that even during the divine service in the Church of the Holy Sepulchre his thoughts wandered and the spirit of grace did not once descend upon him. He returned to Moscow in 1848, still pegging away at the second volume of *Dead Souls*. When his confessor, Father Matthew Rzhevsky, demanded that he should renounce his literary work and enter a monastery, Gogol replied, "Not to write means the same to me as not to live." And he meant it. For when on the night of 12th February 1852 he burnt for the second time the completed chapters of the second volume of *Dead Souls* he pronounced by this act a sentence of death on himself. Indeed, he immediately proceeded to starve himself to death. Neither the exhortations of priests nor the efforts of doctors were of any avail. He died on 21st February 1852.

D.M.

CONTENTS

THE TERRIBLE VENGEANCE

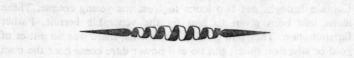

I

THE OUTSKIRTS of Kiev resounded to the din of a wedding feast. The Cossack Captain Gorobetz was celebrating the wedding of his son. A great many people had come as guests to the Captain's house. In the old days they liked to eat well, they liked even more to drink, and most of all they liked to enjoy themselves. The Dnieper Cossack Mikitka was among the guests. He arrived on his sorrel horse straight from a wild orgy in the Pereshlyaye Plain where for seven days and seven nights he had been regaling the Polish king's gentlemen with red wine. Among the guests, too, was Danilo Burulbash, the Captain's sworn brother, who came with his young wife Katherine and his year-old son from the other side of the Dnieper where his farmstead lay tucked away in a fold between two hills. The wedding guests marvelled at the fair face of Katherine, her eyebrows black as German velvet, her handsome dress of fine cloth and blouse of blue silk, her boots with silver-shod heels; but they marvelled still more that her old father had not come with her. He had been living for no more than a year in the Cossack country beyond the Dnieper. For twenty-one years there had been no news of him, and he returned to his daughter only after she was married and had borne a son. He would no doubt have told many wonderful stories of his adventures. He had been away so long in foreign parts that it would be strange indeed if he had no tales to tell! Everything is different there; the people are different, and there are no Christian churches . . . But he had not come. They gave the guests a strong drink of vodka and mead with raisins and plums and on a large dish a round white loaf of fine bread made with butter and eggs. The musicians tried the loaf first, concentrating their attention on the lower crust, for there were coins baked in it; and, falling silent for a while, they

19

put aside their cymbals, fiddles and tambourines. Meanwhile the young matrons and girls, having wiped their mouths with their embroidered kerchiefs, stepped out again into the middle of the room; the young men, arms akimbo and looking proudly about them, were ready to dash forward to meet them—when the old Captain brought out two icons to bless the young couple. Those icons had been given to him by the venerable hermit, Father Bartholomew. They had no rich ornaments, there was no glitter of gold or silver on them; but no evil power dare come near the man in whose house they were. Having raised the icons, the Captain was about to utter a brief prayer, when all at once the children who were playing on the floor became frightened and began to cry loudly, and after them the people in the room shrank back, and they all pointed their fingers in alarm at a Cossack who was standing among them. No one knew who he was. But he had already danced through a Cossack reel to everybody's delight and he had raised many a laugh among the people who gathered round him. But when the Captain lifted up the icons, the Cossack's face underwent a sudden transformation: his nose grew longer and twisted to one side, his eyes began to roll wildly and their colour changed from brown to green, his lips turned blue, his chin shook and became pointed like a spear, a long tusk grew out of his mouth, a hump raised itself from behind his head, and in a twinkling the Cossack turned into an old man.

"That's him! That's him!" shouts were raised in the crowd as they all huddled together.

"The sorcerer has appeared again!" the mothers cried, snatching up their children.

Solemnly and with great dignity the Cossack Captain stepped forward and, turning the icons towards the sorcerer, said in a loud voice, "Vanish out of sight, image of Satan! There is no room for you here!"

With a hiss and a snap like a wolf, the mysterious old man vanished. A hubbub of voices rose in the room, like the roar of the sea in a storm, each expressing his own opinion or hazarding his own guess.

"What sorcerer is this?" young and ignorant people asked.

"There's going to be trouble!" the old men were saying to each other, shaking their heads.

Everywhere, in every corner of the Cossack Captain's spacious

20

forecourt, the people gathered in small groups and listened to the story of the mysterious sorcerer. But almost every other man was telling a different tale, and no one knew anything certain about him. A cask of mead was rolled out into the yard, and there were gallons of Greek wine besides. Everybody grew merry again. The musicians struck up a dance tune; the girls, the young matrons and the brave Cossacks in their bright Ukrainian coats were soon caught up in the dance. The ninety-year-olds and the hundred-year-olds, having had a drop too much, jigged about too, not satisfied idly to remember the years that had passed. They feasted far into the night, and feasted as people no longer feast nowadays. By and by the guests began to disperse, but only a few went home. Many of them stayed to spend the night in the Captain's large courtyard, and many more Cossacks dropped to sleep, uninvited, on the floor, or under the benches, or by their horses, or near the barn: wherever a Cossack's head, heavy with drink, dropped, there the Cossack lay, snoring for all Kiev to hear.

II

A soft light shone all over the world: that was the moon which had appeared from behind a hill. It covered the hilly bank of the Dnieper as with a costly damask muslin, white as snow, and the shadows drew back further into the dense pine woods.

A large boat was gliding in midstream. Two Cossack oarsmen sat in front, their black Cossack caps cocked on one side, and from beneath the oars spray flew in all directions like sparks from a flint. Why did the Cossacks not sing ? Why did they not speak about the Catholic priests who went about the Ukraine, converting the Cossack people into Catholics ? Why did they not tell about the hard-won battle with the Tartars at the Salt Lake which had gone on for two days ? But how could they be expected to sing or to speak of acts of bravery when their master Danilo sat brooding, the sleeve of his crimson coat trailing in the water ? Their mistress, Katherine, was gently rocking her child, and not for one moment did she take her eyes off it, while the spray like grey dust descended upon her fine dress, unprotected by a boat cover.

How beautiful the high hills, the broad meadows, and the green woods are when seen from the middle of the Dnieper ! Those hills are not hills : they seem to float in the air, sharp-pointed above as below, and under them and above them is the towering sky. Those woods on the hills are not woods: they are the hair which grows on the shaggy head of the wood-demon; under the wood-demon's head his beard is being rinsed in the water, and both under his beard and over his head is the towering sky. Those meadows are not meadows: they are a green girdle encircling the round sky, and the moon is taking a stroll in both the upper and lower halves.

Danilo gazed neither to the right nor to the left; he gazed on his young wife.

"Why are you so sad, my dearest Katherine?"

"I am not sad, Danilo. The strange stories about the sorcerer have filled my heart with dread. They say that when he was born he was a terrifying sight . . . and no small child would play with him. Listen, Danilo. They tell such dreadful things about him. They say he always imagines people are laughing at him. If he meets a man on a dark night, he immediately thinks the stranger is grinning at him. Next day that man is found dead. As I listened to those stories, I was filled with dreadful forebodings, Danilo; I felt frightened," said Katherine, taking out a kerchief and wiping the face of the child who slept peacefully in her lap.

Not a word from Danilo, who was scanning the dark bank of the river where, in the distance, an earthen mound could be seen rising like a black shadow from behind the wood, and behind the mound rose the dark pile of an old castle. Three deep wrinkles suddenly appeared above Danilo's eyebrows; his left hand stroked his handsome moustaches.

"It isn't that he is a sorcerer that worries me," he said. "What worries me is that he is here for some evil purpose. What did he want to come here for at all? I'm told the Poles intend to build some kind of fortress to cut off our way to the Dnieper Cossacks. There may be some truth in it. . . . I shall destroy his devilish lair if any rumour reaches me that he is using it as a hiding-place for our enemies. I shall burn the old sorcerer himself so that there won't be anything left of him for the crows to pick. I wonder if he has any gold or other treasures, though. Look, that's where the old devil lives! If he has gold . . . We shall soon row past some crosses —that's the cemetery where the bones of his wicked forebears are rotting. I'm told all of them were ready to sell themselves to Satan for a groat—soul, and tattered old coat, and all. If he really has gold, there's no time to lose: it's something you can't always get in war. . . ."

"I know what you're thinking of. I fear no good will come of it if you meet. But what's the matter? Why are you breathing so hard? Why are you looking at me so fiercely? Why are you frowning on me so?"

"Hold your tongue, woman!" Danilo said angrily. "Have anything to do with you, and before I know where I am I'll be talking and acting like a woman myself! I say, one of you lads, let me have a light for my pipe, will you?" he addressed one of the oarsmen, who knocked some hot ash from his pipe into his master's. "Not trying to frighten me with a sorcerer, are you?" Danilo went on. "A Cossack, thank God, fears neither devil nor Catholic priest. Much good would it do us if we started listening to our wives. Am I not right, lads? The best wife for us is our pipe and our sharp sword!"

Katherine made no reply. She turned away and began watching the sleepy river. The wind raised a ripple on the water and the Dnieper gleamed like a wolf's coat at night. The boat turned and kept close to the wooded bank. A cemetery came into sight; the tumbledown crosses stood huddled together. No guelder-rose grows among them, nor does green grass grow under them; the moon alone sheds its ghostly light upon them from high up in the sky.

"Do you hear the shouts, lads? Someone's calling for our help!" said Danilo, turning to his oarsmen.

"We can hear the cries, sir. They seem to be coming from over there," the oarsmen replied in one voice, pointing to the cemetery.

But everything grew quiet again. The boat turned and began to go round the bend of the projecting bank. Suddenly the oarsmen dropped their oars and stared before them without moving. Danilo stopped, too; his blood ran cold with horror.

A cross on one of the graves swayed giddily and a withered corpse rose slowly from it. A beard to the waist; long nails on the fingers, longer than the fingers themselves. The dead man raised his hands slowly upwards. His face twitched and was twisted. One could see that he was suffering terrible agonies. "Give me air! Air!" he moaned in a wild, inhuman voice, which cut one's heart like a knife. Then, suddenly, the dead man disappeared under the earth. Another cross swayed and again a dead man rose up from the ground, taller and more terrible than the one before. He was

23

covered with hair all over. His beard reached to the knees, and his claws were even longer. "Give me air !" he cried still more wildly, and disappeared under the ground. A third cross swayed; a third dead man rose up. It seemed as if only bare bones rose up high over the earth. His beard reached down to his heels; the long nails of his fingers pierced the ground. Terribly did he extend his hands upwards, as if he wished to seize the moon, and he shrieked, as if someone were sawing his yellow bones.

The child, asleep in Katherine's lap, screamed and woke up. The oarsmen let fall their caps in the river. Even Danilo himself could not suppress a shudder.

Suddenly it all vanished, as if it had never been; but it was not for some time that the oarsmen took up their oars again. Burulbash looked anxiously at his young wife, who, terrified, was rocking the screaming child on her lap, and he pressed her to his heart and kissed her on the forehead.

"Don't be frightened, Katherine ! Look, there's nothing there !" he said, pointing in every direction. "It's the sorcerer who wants to frighten people so that no one should go near his foul nest. He'll scare none but women by these tricks of his ! Come, let me take my son !" With these words, Danilo picked up his son and kissed him. "Well, what do you say, Ivan ? You're not afraid of any sorcerers, are you ? Now say, 'Daddy, I'm a Cossack !' There, there; stop crying ! We shall be home soon, then your mother will give you your porridge, put you to bed in your cradle, and sing:

'Lullaby my own dear heart,
Lullaby my own dear darling,
Grow up, my son, to be our joy,
To be the Cossacks' pride and glory,
And our enemies to destroy !'

Listen, Katherine," he addressed his young wife; "it seems to me that your father does not want to live at peace with us. When he arrived he looked harsh and sullen, as though he were angry with us. . . . Well, if he's not pleased, why come at all ? He would not drink to the freedom of the Cossacks. He has never dandled the baby ! In the beginning I would have confided all my secrets to him, but for some reason I couldn't bring myself to do it: the words stuck in my throat. . . . No, Katherine, he hasn't a Cossack's heart. When Cossack hearts meet, they almost leap out of the breast to greet each other. Well, lads, how far is the bank ? Don't worry about your caps. I shall get you new ones. You, Stetsko, I'll give you one made of velvet and gold. I took it off a Tartar, together with his head. Got all his trappings, too. The only thing I let go was his soul. Well, let's land here. Look, Ivan, we're home and you're still crying ! Take him, Katherine !"

They all got out. From behind a hill a thatched roof came into view: that was Danilo's family mansion. Beyond it was another hill, and beyond that the open plain, and there you might walk a hundred miles and not meet a single Cossack.

III

Danilo's farmstead lay between two hills in a narrow valley that ran down to the Dnieper. His country seat was not large. His cottage looked like the cottage of any humble Cossack, and there was only one big room in it ; but he and his wife and their old maidservant and ten picked young men lived there without feeling cramped. There were oak shelves high up on the walls, on which were piled bowls, pots and pans, silver goblets and drinking cups mounted in gold, both gifts and war booty. Lower down hung costly muskets, sabres, harquebuses, spears. They had come to him, willingly or unwillingly, from Tartars, Turks, and Poles. That was the reason why many of them were notched and dented. Each mark on the steel served to remind Danilo of some bitter encounter with an enemy. Along the bottom of the wall were smooth oak benches. Beside them, in front of the low stove, the cradle hung on cords from a ring fixed in the ceiling. The entire floor of the room was levelled smooth and smeared with clay. Danilo and his wife slept on the benches ; the old maidservant on the low stove ; the child played and was lulled to sleep in the cradle ; and the fighting men slept one beside the other on the floor. But a Cossack likes best to sleep on the bare ground in the open air. He needs neither feather-bed nor pillow. He spreads a pile of fresh hay under his head and stretches at his ease upon the ground. He feels happy when on wakening in the middle of the night he looks up at the lofty sky studded with stars, and shivers at the chill of night which brings fresh vigour to his Cossack bones. Stretching and muttering through his sleep, he lights his pipe and wraps himself more closely in his warm sheep-skin.

Burulbash did not waken early after the merry-making of the night before. When he woke, he sat on a bench in a corner, sharpening a new Turkish sabre he had exchanged for something or other; and Katherine set to work embroidering a silk towel with gold thread. All of a sudden Katherine's father came in, angry and frowning, with an outlandish pipe between his teeth. He went up to his daughter and began questioning her sternly why she had come home so late the night before.

"You'd better question me and not her about such matters," said Danilo, going on with his work. "Not the wife, but the husband is responsible. If you don't mind, this is our way here. In some infidel country perhaps it isn't so—I don't know."

The colour came into his father-in-law's stern face and his eyes flashed ominously.

"Who if not a father should look after his daughter?" he muttered to himself. "Well, I ask you. Where were you gadding about so late last night?"

"Ah, that's better, dear father-in-law! I can easily answer that. You see, I am no longer a baby. I can sit on a horse. I can hold a sharp sword in my hands. And I can do something else: I can refuse to answer to any man for whatever I do!"

"I can see, Danilo, that what you want is to pick a quarrel with me. A man who has something to hide is quite certainly hatching some dastardly plot in his head."

"Think as you please," said Danilo, "and I shall think as I please. Thank God, I've never been a party to any dishonourable action so far. I've always stood up for the Orthodox faith and for my country, not like some vagabonds I know who gad about heaven knows where while good Christians are fighting to the death, and then drop from the sky to reap the harvest they have not sown. They're much worse than the Uniats, I'm sure, for they never visit the church of God. It's such people who should be made to give an account of themselves."

"Ah, what a pity, Cossack, I'm such a bad shot; my bullet only pierces the heart at two hundred yards. I'm afraid I'm not much of a swordsman, either; I always leave some bits and pieces of my man behind, although it's quite true they are not bigger than the grits they use for porridge."

"I'm ready," said Danilo, making the sign of the cross smartly in the air with his sabre, as though he knew what he had sharpened it for.

"Danilo!" Katherine cried aloud, seizing him by the arm and hanging on it. "Think what you're doing, you madman! See against whom you're lifting your hand! Father, your hair is white as snow, and you're as hotheaded as a foolish boy!"

"Wife," Danilo exclaimed angrily, "you know I brook no interference! You mind your woman's business!"

The sabres clashed terribly: steel struck against steel, and the Cossacks sent sparks flying like dust. Weeping, Katherine went to another room, flung herself upon the bed and covered her ears that she might not hear the clash of the sabres. But the Cossacks did not fight so badly that she could smother the sound of their blows. Her heart was ready to break. Each sound made by the sabres seemed to go right through her. "No, I can't bear it; I can't bear it. . . . Red blood is perhaps gushing out of his body this very minute. My dear one may even now be bleeding to death, and I'm lying here!" And, pale as death, scarcely breathing, she went back.

The Cossacks fought a terrible, but well-matched battle. Neither got the better of the other. Now Katherine's father pressed home his attack, and Danilo gave way; now Danilo attacked, and the dour old man yielded ground; and again they were equal. But their blood was up. They swung their sabres, slashing out at each other with all their might, and, with a noise like thunder, the blades broke off at the handles and flew out of their hands.

"I thank you, I thank you, O Lord!" cried Katherine, but she screamed again when she saw that the Cossacks picked up their muskets.

They set the flints, drew the triggers. Danilo fired and missed. Katherine's father took aim. . . . He was old; he could not see as well as a young man, but his hand did not falter. A shot rang out. Danilo staggered. Red blood stained the left sleeve of his Cossack coat. "No," he cried, "I shan't sell myself as cheap as that. Not the left, but the right hand is master. There on the wall hangs my Turkish pistol; never before has it failed me. Come down from the wall, old comrade! Do your friend a service!"

Danilo stretched out his hand to take the gun.

"Danilo!" cried Katherine in despair, clutching his hands and flinging herself on the floor at his feet. "Not for myself do I beseech

27

you. There can be only one end for me: unworthy is the wife who outlives her husband. The cold Dnieper will be my grave. . . . But look at your son, Danilo; look at your son! Who will cherish the poor child? Who will fondle him? Who will teach him to outstrip the wind on his black stallion, to fight for faith and freedom, to drink and be merry like a true Cossack? Oh, my son, you must perish, you must perish utterly! Your father does not care for you. Look how he turns away his head. Oh, now I know you! You're a wild beast and not a man! You have the heart of a wolf and the mind of a crafty serpent. I thought that there was a drop of pity in your veins, that there was human feeling in that heart of stone of yours! What a fool I was! I suppose it will make you happy, your bones will dance in the grave with joy, when you hear the dastardly brutes of Poles throwing your son into the flames, when your son shrieks under the knife and the burning pitch. Oh, I know you! You would be glad to rise from your grave and fan the flames under him with your cap!"

"Stay, Katherine. Come, my precious Ivan; let me kiss you! No, my child, no one shall touch a hair of your head. You shall grow up to the glory of your country; you shall fly like a whirlwind at the head of the Cossacks, with a fine velvet cap on your head and a sharp sabre in your hand. Give me your hand, Father! Let us forget our quarrel. If I have wronged you, I am sorry. Why do you not give me your hand?" said Danilo to Katherine's father, who stood without moving, showing no sign either of anger or reconciliation.

"Father," cried Katherine, embracing and kissing him, "please don't be so merciless. Forgive Danilo. He will never offend you again."

"For your sake only I forgive him, daughter," he replied, kissing her, a strange glitter in his eyes.

Katherine shuddered faintly; the kiss and the strange glitter in his eyes seemed uncanny to her. She leaned her elbows on the table, at which Danilo was bandaging his wounded arm, wondering if he had done right and like a Cossack in asking forgiveness for something for which he was not to blame.

IV

Day dawned, but there was no sunshine: the sky was overcast and a drizzling rain was falling on the fields, the woods and the broad Dnieper. Katherine woke up, but she did not feel happy: her eyes were tear-stained, and she was restless and vaguely alarmed.

"Oh, dear husband," she said, "I have had such a strange dream!"

"What kind of dream, my darling Katherine?"

"Oh, such a queer dream, and it was as plain as though it were really happening. I dreamt that my father was the very same monster whom we saw at the Captain's house. But please don't pay any attention to this dream. People dream all sorts of silly things! I dreamed that I was standing before him, shivering and frightened, my whole body tortured by every word he spoke. Oh, if only you had heard what he said. . . ."

"What did he say, my precious Katherine?"

"He said, 'Look at me, Katherine! Am I not a handsome man? People talk nonsense when they say that I am ugly. I should make you a fine husband! Look at me, Katherine! Look at my eyes! Can't you see anything there?' Then he looked at me with those fiery eyes of his, and I screamed and woke up."

"Yes, there's much truth in dreams. However, do you know that things aren't so quiet beyond the hills? I shouldn't be surprised if the Poles didn't show up again. Gorobetz has warned me to keep my eyes open. But he needn't have troubled. I am not asleep as it is. My lads have been felling trees during the night and put up a dozen barricades. We shall welcome the soldiers of the Polish king with lead plums and we shall make his gentlemen dance with our sticks!"

"And Father . . . Does he know about this?"

"What do I care whether your father knows about it or not? I'm damned if I can make him out even now. I suppose he must have committed many sins in foreign lands. How else can you explain the way he behaves? He has lived with us for over a month and not once has he made merry like a true Cossack. He would not drink any mead! Do you hear, Katherine, he would not drink the mead I extorted from those cowardly Jews in Brest! Here, lad," exclaimed Danilo, "go down to the cellar, there's a good fellow, and bring me some of that Jewish mead ! He won't even drink vodka ! The devil take it, I do believe, Katherine, he doesn't even believe in the Lord Jesus. Eh ? What do you say ? "

"The Lord forgive you, Danilo ! What are you saying ?"

"It certainly is strange, my dear," Danilo went on, taking the earthenware beaker from the Cossack. "Even the damned Catholics are partial to vodka. It's only the Turks who do not drink. Well, Stetsko, did you have a good sip of mead in the cellar ?"

"I just tasted it, sir."

"Tasted it, did you ? You lie, you son of a dog ! See how the flies have fallen upon your moustache. I bet you've had at least half a bucketful. I can see it in your eyes, my lad. Oh, these Cossacks ! What desperate rogues ! Ready to share everything with a comrade, except the bottle; they'll drain that to the last drop themselves ! You know, Katherine, it's a long time since I was really drunk. Eh ?"

"A long time indeed ! Why, last . . ."

"All right, all right ! Don't be alarmed ! I won't drink more than a beakerful. Here's that Turkish abbot barging through the door !" he muttered through his teeth, seeing his father-in-law stooping to get through the door.

"What's the matter, daughter ?" the father said, taking off his cap and adjusting his belt, on which hung a sabre set with precious stones. "The sun's already high and your dinner isn't ready !"

"Dinner's ready, Father. It will be served in a minute. Bring the pot with the dumplings !" Katherine said to the old maid-servant, who was wiping the wooden bowls. "Wait, I'd better take it out myself," she went on. "You call the men !"

They all sat down on the floor in a ring: Katherine's father facing the corner with the icons, Danilo on his left, Katherine on his right, and ten of Danilo's most trusty men in blue and yellow coats.

"I don't like these dumplings," said Katherine's father, after eating a little, laying down the spoon. "There's no flavour in them."

"I daresay you like Jewish stew better," thought Danilo. "Why do you say there's no flavour in the dumplings ?" he went on aloud. "They're not badly made, are they ? My Katherine makes dumplings such as our hetman himself does not often taste. And there's no need to despise them. It's a Christian dish. All God's saints and holy men have eaten dumplings."

Katherine's father was silent. Danilo, too, kept his peace. They served wild boar with cabbage and plums.

"I don't like pork," said Katherine's father, helping himself to some cabbage with his spoon.

"Why don't you like pork?" said Danilo. "It's only Turks and Jews who do not eat pork."

Katherine's father knit his brows, looking more angry than ever. He ate nothing but some buckwheat pudding and milk and, instead of vodka, he sipped some black liquid from a flask he kept inside his coat.

After dinner Danilo had a good sleep and only woke at dusk. He sat down at the table to write letters to the Cossack army, while Katherine sat on the low stove, rocking the cradle with her foot. As he sat there, Danilo kept his left eye on his writing and looked out of the window with his right; from the window he could see far in the distance the shining hills and the Dnieper. Beyond the Dnieper stretched the blue ridge of the woods. Overhead glimmered the clear night sky. But it was not the far-away sky or the blue woods that Danilo was admiring: he was watching the spit of land which jutted out into the river and on which the dark mass of the old castle could be made out. He thought he could see a light gleaming in the narrow little window of the castle. But all was quiet. He must have imagined it. All he could hear was the hollow murmur of the Dnieper down below and, from three sides, the resounding thuds of the waves which suddenly came to life. The river was not in its defiant mood. Like an old man, it was merely growling and grumbling. Nothing pleased it. Everything about it had changed. Softly it was waging a war against the hills, the woods and the meadows on its banks.

Now the dark outline of a boat appeared on the wide expanse of the Dnieper and again a light gleamed and disappeared in the castle. Danilo gave a low whistle, and his faithful servant ran in at the sound.

"Stetsko," said Danilo, "grab a sharp sabre and a musket and follow me!"

"Are you going out?" asked Katherine.

"Yes, I'm going out. I have to inspect everything. See that everything's in order."

"But I'm afraid to be left alone. I'm so sleepy, I can't keep awake. What if I should have the same dream again? I am not even sure it was a dream. It seemed so real."

31

"The old woman will be staying with you and there are Cossacks asleep in the passage and in the courtyard."

"The woman is asleep already and, somehow, I have no confidence in the Cossacks. Listen, Danilo. Lock me in and take the key with you. Then I shan't be afraid. And let the Cossacks lie before the door."

"All right," said Danilo, wiping the dust off his musket and scattering some powder on the gun-lock.

The faithful Stetsko stood already dressed from head to foot in the Cossack harness. Danilo put on his lambskin cap, closed the window, locked and bolted the door, walked quietly out of the courtyard, threading his way among the sleeping Cossacks, and made straight for the hills.

The sky was almost completely clear again. A fresh breeze blew gently from the Dnieper. But for the distant wail of a gull, everything seemed to be dead silent. But soon his ear caught a faint noise. . . . Burulbash and his faithful servant hid quietly behind some bramble bushes which concealed one of the barricades of felled trees. Some one in a scarlet coat, with two pistols and a sabre at his side, was coming down the hillside.

"It's my father-in-law," Danilo murmured, watching him from behind the bushes. "Where is he going to at this hour of the night, I wonder? And what is he up to? Don't gape, Stetsko; keep your eyes open and see which way your mistress's father takes!"

The man in the scarlet coat went down to the bank of the river and then turned towards the spit of land.

"I thought so," said Danilo. "Gone straight to the sorcerer's den, Stetsko!"

"Yes, sir. Couldn't have gone anywhere else or we should have seen him on the other side. He disappeared near the castle, sir."

"All right, let's get out and follow him. There's something wrong here. Well, Katherine, I warned you that your father was a wicked man. No wonder he never behaves like a true Christian."

Danilo and his trusty servant went quickly across the tongue of land. In another moment they were out of sight. The pitch-black wood around the castle hid them. A soft light appeared at the upper window of the castle. The Cossacks stood below, wondering how to reach it. They could see neither gate nor door. There must be a door in the courtyard; but how were they to get into it? They could hear in the distance the clanking of chains and the dogs running about in the yard.

"Why am I losing time?" said Danilo, seeing a big oak-tree by the window. "You stay here," he said to Stetsko, "and I'll climb up the oak; from it I could look straight into the window."

He took off his belt, threw his sabre on the ground, so that it might not clatter, and, catching hold of some branches, lifted himself up. There was still a light at the window. He sat down on a branch close to the window, and, holding on firmly to the tree, he peered in: there was not even a candle in the room and yet it was bathed in a soft light. There were mystic symbols on the walls. Weapons of all kinds were hanging there, but all were strange; neither Turks, nor Crimeans, nor Christians, nor the gallant Swedes ever bore such weapons. Large bats flitted to and fro under the ceiling and their shadows darted over the floor, the door and the walls. Presently the door opened without a sound. Some man in a scarlet coat walked in and went straight up to the table which was covered with a white cloth.

"It is my father-in-law," Danilo murmured, lowering himself a little and clinging closer to the tree.

But his father-in-law was too busy to look whether anyone was watching him through the window. He came in, frowning and out of humour, pulled the cloth off the table, and at once a transparent blue light spread gently through the whole room; but the waves of the pale golden light with which the room had been filled before did not mingle with the blue light, but eddied and dived as in a blue sea and spread out in streaks as though in marble. Then he set a pot on the table and began throwing some herbs into it.

Danilo peered more closely and saw that he was no longer wearing the scarlet coat; instead he was wearing a pair of wide Turkish breeches with pistols in his belt and a strange-looking head-dress inscribed with letters that were neither Russian nor Polish. And even as he looked at his face, his face, too, began to change: his nose grew longer and hung over his lips; in one instant his mouth stretched to his ears; a tooth peeped out from his lips and bent sideways; and he saw before him the same sorcerer who had appeared at the wedding at the Captain's house.

"Your dream was a true dream, Katherine," Danilo thought.

The sorcerer began pacing round the table; the mystic signs on the walls were now changing more rapidly and the large bats

B 33

flitted more swiftly up and down and to and fro. The blue light grew dimmer and dimmer and at last went out altogether. A tenuous rosy light now filled the room. It seemed to spread through the room to the accompaniment of the soft ringing of bells; then, suddenly, it vanished and darkness covered everything. Nothing was heard but a faint murmur like the gentle whispering of the wind in the peaceful hours of evening as, circling over the mirror-like surface of the water, it bends the silvery willows lower and lower into the waves.

It seemed to Danilo that the moon was shining in the room and the stars were twinkling, and now and then he thought he could catch a glimpse of the dark-blue sky, and he even felt a puff of the cold evening air against his face. Then Danilo imagined (here he even pulled at his moustache to make sure he was not dreaming) that it was not the sky he could see in the room, but his own bed-chamber. There on the walls hung his Tartar and Turkish sabres; round the walls were the shelves and on the shelves the pots and bowls and goblets; on the table stood bread and salt; the cradle hung from the ceiling. . . . But where the icons were, hideous faces stared; on the low stove . . . but a dense mist hid everything, and it was dark again, and once again a rosy light spread through the room to the accompaniment of the wonderful ringing of bells, and again the sorcerer stood motionless in his strange turban. The sounds grew louder and richer, the faint rosy light became brighter, and something white, like a cloud, hovered in the middle of the room. And it seemed to Danilo that the cloud was not a cloud at all, but that a woman was standing there. But what was she made of ? Not of air, surely ? And why did she stand there without touching the floor or leaning on anything ? Why did the rosy light shine through her ? Why were those dancing signs on the wall still visible ? Now she moved her transparent head: her pale blue eyes shone softly; her hair fell in curls over her shoulders like a light-grey mist; her lips glowed faintly like the scarcely perceptible red glow of dawn over the white transparent morning sky; her eyebrows were just two faint dark lines. . . . It was Katherine ! Danilo felt his limbs stiffen. He tried to speak, but his lips moved without uttering a sound.

The sorcerer still stood motionless in the same place.

"Where have you been ?" he asked, and the ethereal figure which stood before him trembled.

"Oh, why did you call me up ?" she moaned softly. "I was so happy. I was in the place where I was born and where I lived

34

till I was fifteen. Oh, how wonderful it was there ! How green and fragrant was the meadow where I used to play as a child ! And the sweet wild flowers were the same as ever, and our cottage and the garden ! Oh, how my dear mother embraced me ! How much love there was in her eyes ! She caressed me, kissed my lips and cheeks, combed my fair hair with a fine comb . . . Father," here she fixed her pale eyes on the sorcerer, "why did you murder my mother ?"

The sorcerer shook his finger at her menacingly. "Did I bid you speak about it ?" he asked, and the ethereal beauty trembled. "Where is your mistress now ?"

"My mistress Katherine has fallen asleep, and I was so glad I took wing and flew away. I have yearned to see my mother for such a long time. I was suddenly fifteen again. I felt so light, like a bird. Why have you summoned me ?"

"You remember all I said to you yesterday ?" asked the sorcerer in so soft a voice that Danilo found it hard to catch his words.

"I remember, but what would I not give to forget it ! Poor Katherine, she doesn't know as much as her soul knows, does she ?"

"It is Katherine's soul," thought Danilo, but still he dared not stir.

"Repent, Father ! Is it not terrible that after every murder you commit the dead rise up from their graves ?"

"Don't mention that to me again !" the sorcerer interrupted her menacingly. "I shall insist that you carry out my wish. I shall make you do what I want. Katherine shall love me !"

"Oh, you are a monster and not my father !" she moaned. "No, it shall never be as you wish. It is true that by your evil spells you have the power to summon a soul and torture it, but only God can make it do what He wills. No, never shall Katherine consent to such an ungodly deed while I am still in her body ! Father, a terrible judgment is near at hand ! Even if you were not my father, you would never make me betray my husband whom I love and who is true to me. But even if my husband was not true and dear to me, I would not be false to him, for God abominates souls who are faithless and false to their vows."

Here she fixed her pale eyes on the window under which Danilo was sitting and fell silent, still as death.

"What are you looking at ? Whom do you see there ?" cried the sorcerer.

The wraith of Katherine trembled violently. But already Danilo was on the ground and with his faithful Stetsko was on his way to his native hills.

"Terrible, terrible," he murmured to himself, fear gripping his Cossack heart.

He soon reached his own courtyard where his Cossacks slept as soundly as ever, all but one who sat on guard, smoking a pipe.

The sky was all studded with stars.

V

"Oh, I'm so glad you wakened me !" said Katherine, rubbing her eyes with the embroidered sleeve of her nightgown and observing her husband closely as he stood before her. "What a terrible dream I've had ! I could hardly breathe. Oh, I thought I was dying !"

"What sort of dream ? Not this one by any chance ?" and Burulbash started telling his wife all that he had seen.

"But how did you know it ?" Katherine asked in amazement when he finished his story. "But no, no ! You told me many things I did not know. No, I certainly did not dream that my father had killed my mother. I did not dream anything of the dead rising from their graves, either. No, I did not dream anything of the kind. Danilo, you're making it up. Oh, what a terrible man my father is !"

"And it is no wonder you did not see everything in your dream. You don't know a tenth part of what your soul knows. Do you know that your father is the Antichrist ? Last year when I was getting ready to go against the Crimean Tartars with the Poles (at that time those faithless people were still my allies) the Abbot of the Bratsky Monastery—and he is a holy man, my dear, if ever there was one—told me that the Antichrist had the power to summon the soul of every living man ; for when the body is asleep, the soul wanders where it pleases and flies with the archangels about the abode of God. I disliked your father's face from the first. I would not have married you, had I known what kind of a father you had. I should have left you and not taken upon my soul the sin of marrying into the Antichrist's family."

"Danilo," Katherine said, burying her face in her hands and bursting into tears, "what wrong have I done to you ? Have I been unfaithful to you, my dear husband ? Why then are you so angry with me ? Have I not served you truly ? Have I ever said a cross word to you when you came home merry from some gay feast ? Have I not borne you a black-browed son ?"

"Don't cry, Katherine. I know you now and I shall never leave you. It is not you, but your father who has sinned so grievously."

"Please, don't call him my father ! He is not a father to me ! God is my witness that I disown him ; I disown my father ! He is the Antichrist. He has renounced God. If he were perishing, if he were drowning, I would not stretch out a hand to save him. If he were dying of thirst after eating some magic herb, I would not give him a drop of water. You are my father !"

VI

The sorcerer sat in a deep cellar at Danilo's house behind a door with three locks and with iron chains on his hands and feet. In the distance above the Dnieper his devilish castle was in flames, and the waves, glowing red as blood, surged and broke against the ancient walls. But it was not for sorcery or any ungodly act that the sorcerer lay imprisoned in the deep cellar. God was his judge. It was for an act of secret treachery that he was imprisoned, for plotting with the enemies of the holy Russian soil to sell the Ukrainian people to the Catholics and burn Christian churches. The sorcerer was cast down. Thoughts black as night filled his head. He had only one more day left to live : tomorrow he would have to take leave of the world ; tomorrow his punishment was awaiting him. It would be an act of mercy if he were boiled alive in a cauldron or if his sinful skin were flayed off him. The sorcerer was cast down ; his head was bowed. Perhaps he was already repenting in his last hour, but his sins were not such as God would forgive him. Above him was a narrow window, interlaced with iron bars. Clanking his chains, he went up to the window to see if his daughter were passing. She was meek and gentle as a dove ; she bore no malice against any man. Would she not take pity on her father ? But there was not a soul to be seen. Below the window was the road ; no one passed along it. Below the road was the Dnieper ; but the river cared for no one : it raged and the monotonous sound of its waves made cheerless music for the prisoner.

Then someone appeared on the road. It was a Cossack. The prisoner heaved a deep sigh. Again the road was deserted. In the distance someone was coming down the hill. A woman's coat was fluttering in the wind. A gold head-dress glittered on her head. It was she! He pressed still closer to the window. Now she was coming nearer. . . .

"Katherine, my daughter, have pity on me! Help me, help me!"

She made no reply. She would not listen to him. She did not even turn her eyes towards the prison. She had already passed. She was gone. The whole world was empty. Dismally the Dnieper murmured. Sadness stole into the heart at that sound. But did the sorcerer know anything of such sadness?

The day was drawing to a close. The sun had set. In another moment the last gleam of light in the sky was gone. Now it was evening. It was cool. Somewhere an ox was lowing. Sounds of voices floated from somewhere: people returning from the fields and laughing happily. A boat appeared for a brief moment on the Dnieper and was gone again. . . . No one gave a thought to the prisoner. The silver crescent gleamed in the sky. Somebody was coming along the road from the opposite direction. It was hard to tell in the darkness who it might be. It was Katherine coming back.

"Daughter, for Christ's sake spare one glance at your guilty father. Why, even the savage wolf cubs will never tear their mother to pieces!" She paid no attention to him and walked on. "Daughter, for the sake of your unhappy mother . . ." She stopped. "For the sake of your unhappy mother come here and listen to my last words!"

"Why do you call to me, you renegade? Don't call me daughter! I have disowned all kinship with you. What do you want of me for the sake of my unhappy mother?"

"Katherine, my end is near. I know that your husband means to tie me to the tail of a mare and let me be dragged along the fields until I'm dead. He may even think of a more dreadful punishment for me. . . ."

"But is there a punishment in the world bad enough to atone for your sins? Prepare yourself for it; no one will intercede for you."

"Katherine, it is not the punishment that frightens me, but the torments that await me in the next world. . . . You are innocent, Katherine. Your soul will fly in paradise near the abode of

38

God, but the soul of your renegade father will burn in the everlasting fire that will never be quenched; no drop of dew will descend on it, nor will the wind breathe on it. . . ."

"That punishment I have not the power to abate," said Katherine, turning away.

"Katherine, one more word. You can save my soul. You have no idea how good and merciful God is. You must have heard of the Apostle Paul, what a great sinner he was, but afterwards he repented and became a saint."

"What can I do to save your soul?" said Katherine. "It is not for a weak woman like me to think of it!"

"If only I could get out of here, I'd give up everything. I will repent. I will retire to a cave, put on a rough hairshirt, and spend day and night in prayer. I will give up not only meat, but I will not even taste fish. I shall sleep on bare boards, and I shall pray, pray all the time. And if God in His great mercy will not forgive even a hundredth part of my sins, I'll bury myself up to the neck in the earth, or immure myself into a stone wall. I will take neither food nor drink, and I shall die. All my treasures I will distribute among the monks that they may sing a requiem for me for forty days and forty nights."

Katherine thought it over. "Even if I unlocked the door," she said, "I couldn't possibly take off your chains."

"My chains!" he said scornfully. "You think they have chained me hand and foot, don't you? Oh, no. I threw a mist over their eyes and held out a dry piece of wood instead of hands. Here, have a look: there is not a chain on me now!" he said, stepping into the middle of the cellar. "Even these walls would not have stopped me and I would have gone through them. But your husband does not know what walls these are. They were built by a holy hermit and no evil power can release any one from this prison without unlocking the doors with the very same key with which the saint used to lock his cell. Just such a cell I shall build for myself, great sinner that I am, when I am free again!"

"Listen, I will let you out; but what if you deceive me?" said Katherine, stopping before the door. "What if, instead of repenting, you again become the devil's own accomplice?"

"No, Katherine. I have not long to live. My end is near even if I am not put to death. Do you really believe I shall consign myself to eternal perdition?"

The locks rattled. "Farewell, my dear child. May the merciful God keep and preserve you !" said the sorcerer, kissing her.

"Don't touch me, you abominable sinner ! Go, go quickly !" said Katherine.

But he was no longer there.

"I let him out," moaned Katherine, terror-stricken and looking wildly at the walls. "What shall I say to my husband now ? I am undone. I'd better bury myself alive !" And bursting into tears, she almost fell on the block on which the prisoner had been sitting. "But I have saved his soul," she said softly. "I have done a good deed which cannot but please God. But my husband . . . I have deceived him for the first time. Oh, how terrible ! How hard it will be to lie to him ! Someone's coming. . . It is he ! My husband !" she exclaimed in despair and fell senseless on the ground.

VII

"It's me, you poor darling ! It's me, my sweet child !" Katherine heard when she came round.

She looked up and saw her old maidservant. The old woman was bending over her, muttering something, and, stretching out her withered hand, sprinkled cold water over her.

"Where am I ?" Katherine said, sitting up and looking round her. "I can hear the Dnieper in front of me and behind me I can see the hills. Where have you brought me, you old hag ?"

"I haven't brought you anywhere. I took you out of that stuffy old cellar, I did. Locked it up with the key so that you don't get into trouble with your husband Danilo."

"But where is the key ?" said Katherine, looking at her girdle. "I can't see it."

"Why, my poor child, your husband has taken it off to have a look at the sorcerer."

"At the sorcerer ? Oh dear, I'm undone !" Katherine cried.

"May the Lord preserve us from such a calamity, my poor darling. Just keep quiet and no one will know anything about it."

"He's escaped, the cursed Antichrist ! Do you hear, Katherine, he has escaped !" said Danilo, coming up to his wife.

His eyes blazed angrily; his sabre shook and rattled at his side. Katherine was paralysed with fear.

"Has someone let him out, dear husband?" she asked in a shaking voice.

"He has been let out all right! The devil has let him out! Look, a log is chained to the wall instead of him. Oh, why did not God make the devil fear a Cossack's strong hands? If any of my Cossacks had only thought of doing it and I got to know about it . . . I'd find no punishment bad enough for him!"

"And if I . . ." The words were out of Katherine's lips before she knew what she was saying, and she stopped, aghast.

"If you had taken it into your head to do such a thing, you'd no longer be my wife. I'd have sewn you up in a sack and drowned you in the middle of the Dnieper!"

Katherine caught her breath and she felt her hair stand on end.

VIII

At a roadside inn near the frontier the Poles had gathered, and for the past two days they had been carousing there. The inn overflowed with the vermin. They had met, no doubt, for some raid. Some had muskets; spurs were jingling, sabres rattling. The Polish gentlemen made merry and bragged, told tales about their marvellous feats of arms, mocked at the Orthodox Christians, called the Ukrainian people their serfs, twirled their moustaches with an air of importance, and with the same arrogant air sprawled on the benches, their noses turned up. They had a Catholic priest among them. He drank and revelled with them and uttered obscene speeches with his foul mouth. The servants were no better than their masters. They turned back the sleeves of their tattered coats and strutted about, as if they were persons of some importance. They played cards, and struck each other on the nose with the cards. They had brought with them other men's wives. Shrieks, fights. . . . The Polish gentlemen, too, ran wild and played all sorts of silly tricks: they pulled the Jewish innkeeper by the beard, painted a cross on his impious brow, fired blank shots at the women, and danced the Cracovienne with their blaspheming priest. Even the Tartars had never behaved in so disgraceful a manner on Russian soil. God must have willed it that Russia should suffer such indignities for her sins! In the general hubbub people could be heard talking of Danilo's homestead beyond the Dnieper and of his beautiful wife. . . .

The band of cut-throats were not there for any good!

41

IX

Danilo sat at the table, his head propped up on his hand, thinking. Katherine sat on the low stove, humming a song.

"I don't know why, but I'm feeling sad, Katherine," said Danilo. "My head aches and my heart aches. Oh, I'm so weary, weary! I think my death must be near."

"Why don't you come and put your head on my bosom, dear husband? Why do you harbour such black thoughts?" Katherine thought, but she dared not speak her thoughts aloud. She was too conscious of her guilt to accept her husband's caresses.

"Listen, Katherine," said Danilo, "promise me not to desert our son when I am gone. God will never grant you any happiness either in this world or in the next if you forsake him. Hard will it be for my bones to rot in the damp earth, but harder still will it be for my soul."

"What are you saying, dear husband? Was it not you who laughed at us, weak women? And now you talk like a weak woman yourself. It's much too early for you to talk of death!"

"No, Katherine, I feel that I have not long to live. I don't know, my life is no longer what it used to be. Everything is so sad. Oh, the years of my adventurous youth, how they come back to me! But they have gone for good, never to return. He was living then, the pride and glory of our army, old Konashevich, the Ukrainian hetman! I can still see those Cossack regiments, as though they were passing before my eyes now. Oh, what a glorious time it was, Katherine, what a glorious time! The old hetman sitting on a black horse, his golden mace gleaming in his hand, the soldiers of his regular army standing around him and the red sea of the Dnieper Cossacks astir on every side! The hetman began to speak and every man in that vast army of foot and horse stood still as if rooted to the ground. The old man wept when he told us of the old days and battles of long ago. Oh, if you only knew, Katherine, how valiantly we fought the Turks in those days! You can still see the scar on my head which I received in those battles. Four bullets pierced me in four places, and not one of the wounds has quite healed. The gold we took in those days! The Cossacks filled their caps with precious stones. What horses, Katherine, oh, what fine horses we drove away with us in those days! Never, never shall

I fight like that again ! Not that I have grown old or that my body has grown feeble, but the Cossack sword drops out of my hand. There seems nothing more left for me to do, and I don't know what I live for. There is no order in the Ukraine: the colonels and the captains fight each other like dogs. There is no recognised chieftain over them all. Our gentry are aping the Polish fashions and they have also grown crafty as the Poles. They have even sold their souls, accepting the Uniat faith. The Jews are oppressing the poor. . . . Oh, those days, those days, the days that are gone ! Where are you, the years of my youth ? Here, lad, go to the cellar and bring me a jug of mead. Let me drink to the happy times that have gone and to the years that will never come back ! "

"How shall we receive our guests, sir ? The Poles are approaching from the direction of the meadow !" said Stetsko, entering the room.

"I know what they are coming for," said Danilo, rising from his seat. "Saddle the horses, my faithful followers ! Put on your harness ! Out with the sabres ! Don't forget your rations of lead ! We must prepare a great welcome for our guests !"

But before the Cossacks had time to mount their horses or load their muskets, the Poles covered the hillside as leaves from the trees cover the ground in autumn.

"Oho, there are certainly enough of them here to avenge our injuries !" cried Danilo, looking at the fat Polish gentlemen, who were swaying haughtily on their gold-harnessed horses in the front ranks of the advancing Poles. "It seems that once again I shall be having good sport ! Make the best of it, Cossack soul, for the last time. Enjoy yourselves, lads ! This is the day we've been waiting for !"

Oh, what sport there was in the hills ! What gay revelry ! The swords were gambolling, the bullets flying, the horses neighing and prancing. The shouting dazed the brain, the smoke blinded the eye. Everything was in confusion. But a Cossack knew unfailingly where his friend or where his enemy was. A bullet whistled and a gallant rider dropped from the saddle ; a sabre flashed and a head rolled in the dust, muttering incoherent words.

But the red top of Danilo's cap could always be seen in the crowd ; the golden belt on his blue coat gleamed bright ; the mane of his black stallion fluttered in the breeze. He darted hither and thither like a bird, exhorting his followers, waving his Damascus sabre, and cutting down the enemy right and left. Cut them down, Cossack ! Have a merry time, Cossack ! Cheer your brave heart ! Don't look at the gold trappings and the rich coats : trample underfoot the gold and jewels ! Spear them, Cossack ! Have a merry time, Cossack ! But look back ! The godless Poles are already setting fire to the cottages and driving away the frightened cattle. And like a whirlwind Danilo turned round, and the cap with the red top was darting now near the cottages and the crowd round him was fast dwindling.

For many hours the Poles fought with the Cossacks. There were not many left of either. But Danilo showed no signs of slackening: with his long spear he knocked Poles out of their saddles and his mettlesome horse trampled more of the enemy underfoot. His courtyard was almost cleared of the enemy; the Poles were taking to their heels; the Cossacks were beginning to strip the dead of their gold coats and rich trappings; Danilo was about to set off in pursuit of the beaten enemy and looked round to call his men—when suddenly he flew into a terrible rage: for he caught sight of Katherine's father. There the sorcerer stood on the top of a hill, aiming his musket at him. Danilo urged his horse straight towards him. . . . Cossack, you go to your doom ! . . . There came the crack of a shot, and the sorcerer vanished behind the hill. Only the faithful Stetsko caught a glimpse of the scarlet coat and the strange hat. The Cossack staggered and fell to the ground. The faithful Stetsko rushed to his master, but his master lay stretched on the ground, his bright eyes closed. The dark-red blood spurted from his breast, but he must have become aware of his faithful servant's presence, for he raised his eyelids and there was a gleam of recognition in his eyes. "Farewell, Stetsko. Tell Katherine not to forsake her son, and don't you, my faithful servants, forsake him, either !" He fell silent. His gallant soul flew from his noble body; his lips turned blue. The Cossack slept, never to awaken.

His faithful servant burst out sobbing and waved a hand to Katherine.

"Come, my lady, come. Your master has had a drop too much. Here he lies on the damp earth, drunk as a lord. It'll be a long time before he's sober again !"

Katherine wrung her hands and fell like a sheaf of corn on the dead body.

"Oh, my husband, is it you lying here with closed eyes ? Get up, my dearest darling; stretch out your sweet hand ! Stand up !

Please, look at your Katherine just for once. Open your lips, say just one little word to me ! But you're silent, you're silent, my noble lord ! You have turned blue like the Black Sea. Your heart beats no more. Why are you so cold, dear husband ? Are not my tears hot enough to warm you ? Is not my weeping loud enough to wake you ? Who will lead your regiments now ? Who will ride like a whirlwind on your black steed ? Cry in a mighty voice and wave a sabre in front of the Cossacks ? Oh, Cossacks, Cossacks ! Where is your pride and glory ? Your pride and glory is lying with closed eyes on the damp earth. Bury me in the same grave as him, bury me with him, I pray ! Heap earth upon my eyes ! Press the maple boards upon my white breasts ! I need my beauty no more !"

Katherine wailed and mourned; but a cloud of dust was rising over the road in the distance: old Captain Gorobetz was galloping to the rescue.

X

The Dnieper is beautiful on a calm day when it glides along in full flood, unconstrained and unruffled, through woods and hills. There is not a ripple; not a sound. You look and you cannot tell whether its majestic expanse is moving or not moving, and you almost fancy that it is all made of glass and that, like a blue, mirror-surfaced road, measureless in breadth and endless in length, it winds and twists over a green world. On such a day even the bright sun likes to have a peep at it from its great height and dip its hot beams into its cool glassy waters; and the woods along the banks appear to enjoy nothing better than to see themselves reflected in its waves. Smothered in green foliage, they, and the wild flowers, too, crowd together along the margin of the flowing waters and, bending over, gaze into them, never for a moment tiring of this pastime, never for a moment averting their admiring, radiant glances from the stream, and they smile at it and they greet it, waving their branches. But they dare not look into the Dnieper in midstream; none but the sun and the blue sky gaze into it there. Rarely will a bird fly as far as that. Glorious one ! There is no river like it in the world.

Beautiful, too, is the Dnieper on a warm summer night when every living creature is asleep—man, beast, and bird. God alone majestically surveys heaven and earth and majestically shakes His robe of gold and silver, scattering a shower of stars. The stars shine and twinkle over the world and are all reflected together in the Dnieper. The mighty river finds room for them all in its dark bosom. Not one star will escape it, unless indeed it is extinguished in the sky. The black woods, dotted with sleeping crows, and the mountains, rent asunder long ago, which overhang the flowing river, try their utmost to cover it up, if only with their long shadows, but in vain ! Nothing in the world could cover up the Dnieper. Blue, deep, deep blue, it flows on and on in a smooth flood at midnight as at midday, and it can be seen far, far away, as far as the eye of man can reach. Playfully snuggling up to the banks, as if seeking for warmth in the chill of the night, it leaves a silvery trail behind, gleaming like the blade of a Damascus sword; but the river, the deep blue river, falls asleep again. The Dnieper is beautiful even then, and no river in the world is like it. But when dark clouds scud like uprooted mountains across the sky, when the black woods sway wildly and are bent to their roots, when the mighty oak is riven asunder, and lightning, zigzagging through the clouds, suddenly lights up the whole world—then the Dnieper is truly terrible. The mountainous billows roar as they dash themselves against the hills, and when, flashing and moaning, they rush back, they wail and lament in the distance. So the old mother of a Cossack laments when she sees off her son as he leaves for the army. A high-spirited, but good lad, he rides off on his black stallion, arms akimbo and cap at a rakish angle; but she, sobbing, runs after him, seizes him by the stirrup, catches his bridle, and wrings her hands over him, shedding bitter tears.

Among the contending waves weird, dark shapes of burnt tree-stumps and boulders can be seen on the projecting tongue of land. And a boat is dashed against the bank, rising and falling as it comes in. What Cossack was so reckless as to take out a skiff when the old Dnieper was raging ? Did he not know that the river swallows men like flies ?

The boat reached the bank, and out of it stepped the sorcerer. He looked unhappy; bitterly did he resent the funeral the Cossacks had given their slain master. The Poles, too, had paid heavily: forty-four Polish gentlemen in their costly armour and rich coats and thirty-three serfs were left cut to pieces on the battlefield, while the rest were captured with their horses, to be sold to the Tartars.

The sorcerer went down some stone steps between the burnt tree-stumps to a small hut he had dug deep in the earth. He went in softly without making the door creak, put a pot on the table that was covered with a cloth and began throwing some magic herbs into it with his long hands; he then took a pitcher made of some rare wood, scooped up some water with it, and poured it into the pot, moving his lips and muttering some incantations. The room was filled with a rosy light. In this light his face looked horrible: it seemed covered with blood except where the deep wrinkles left lines upon it, and his eyes seemed to blaze with an infernal fire. Villainous sinner! His beard was grey, his face lined with wrinkles; he was all shrivelled, yet he still persevered in his godless design. A white cloud hovered in the room, and something like joy gleamed in his face. But why did he stand rigid all of a sudden with gaping mouth, not daring to stir? Why did the hair of his head stand up? A strange face appeared in the cloud; unbidden and un-invited, it had come to his subterranean home. As the minutes passed, its features grew more and more distinct and its motionless glance more penetrating. The features—eyebrows, eyes, lips—were unfamiliar to him. Never before had he seen them. Nor was there anything fear-inspiring about that face, and yet it filled him with horror. The strange unfamiliar face gazed upon him from the cloud, steadily, unblinkingly. The cloud had vanished, and yet the unfamiliar features of that face showed up more sharply than ever, and the piercing eyes looked hard at him. The sorcerer turned white as a sheet. He uttered a wild scream and overturned the pot. . . . The vision vanished.

XI

"Do not worry, dear sister," said old Captain Gorobetz; "dreams seldom come true."

"Lie down, my dear," said his young daughter-in-law. "I'll fetch a wise woman: no evil power can withstand her. She will drive your fears away."

"Fear nothing," said his son, grasping his sabre. "No one shall hurt you."

Sombrely and with dull eyes Katherine looked at them, not knowing herself what to say. "I have brought this misfortune upon myself," she thought. "It was I who let him out." At last she said: "He gives me no peace. Here I have been ten days with you in Kiev, but I am as unhappy as ever. I thought that at least I would be able to bring up my son in peace to avenge his father's death, but . . . Oh, if you knew how terrible he looked when he appeared to me in a dream! God grant you will never see him! My heart is still pounding. 'I'll kill your son, Katherine,' he shouted, 'if you do not marry me!'" and, bursting into tears, she rushed to the cradle, and the frightened child stretched out its little hands and cried.

The Captain's son boiled with rage when he heard these words and his eyes flashed with anger.

Captain Gorobetz could no longer contain himself. "Let him try coming here, the accursed Antichrist. He'll soon find out if there is still any strength left in an old Cossack's hands. God is my witness," he said, lifting up his keen eyes, "that I hastened to Danilo's help as soon as I learnt of his plight, but I came too late. It was God's will no doubt that I should find him on his cold bed upon which many, aye, many Cossacks have been laid. But, come, don't you think we gave him a worthy funeral? And did we let a single Pole escape with his life? So calm yourself, my dear child. So long as I am alive, or my son, no man will dare harm you!"

Having finished speaking, the old Cossack went up to the cradle, and the child, seeing his red pipe, set in silver, and his pouch with the glittering flints, hanging from a strap, stretched out his arms towards him and laughed.

"He takes after his father," said the old Captain, taking off the pipe and giving it to the child. "He's not out of the cradle, but he already wants to smoke a pipe!"

Katherine sighed softly and began rocking the cradle. They agreed to spend the night together, and after a short time they were all asleep. Katherine, too, fell asleep.

All was quiet in the courtyard and the cottage. Everyone slept except the Cossacks who were keeping watch. Suddenly Katherine woke with a scream, and the others woke, too.

"He's dead! He's been murdered!" she cried and rushed to the cradle.

All surrounded the cradle and they were paralysed with horror when they saw that the child in it was dead. Not a sound did any of them utter, not knowing what to think of so shocking a crime.

XII

Far from the Ukraine, beyond Poland and the populous city of Lemberg, there rise range upon range of immense mountains. Mountain after mountain, they encompass the earth to the right and to the left, as if with chains of stone, and box it up with a wall of rock to protect it from encroachment by the wild and turbulent sea. These mountain ranges stretch into Wallachia and across the Semigrad region, and their enormous pile stands like a horse-shoe between the Galician and the Hungarian peoples. We have no such mountains in our country. The eye is quite powerless to survey them; and on some of their summits no human foot has ever trod. Their aspect is quite amazing: had, one wonders, the frolicsome sea broken away from its wide shores in a storm and thrown up its monstrous waves to a tremendous height, and had they then turned to stone and remained motionless in the air? Or had the heavy stormclouds come tumbling from the sky and blocked up the earth? For they, too, are grey, and their white crests flash and sparkle in the sun.

Until you reach the Carpathian mountains, you may still hear Russian speech, and even beyond the mountains you may here and there hear echoes of our native tongue, but beyond neither speech nor faith is the same. The country there is inhabited by the numerous Hungarian people, and they, too, ride, fight and drink like so many Cossacks; nor are they niggardly with the golden coins in their pockets for their horses' harness or costly coats. There are great and wide lakes among the mountains. They are as still as glass and, like glass, they reflect the bare mountain-tops and their green slopes below.

But who rides through the night on a huge black horse whether the stars shine or not? Who is this giant of superhuman stature who gallops over the mountains, above the lakes, who is reflected with his gigantic horse in the still waters, and throws his vast and terrifying shadow across the mountains? His chased coat of mail glitters; across his shoulder is a pike; his sword clatters against his saddle; his helmet is tilted up; his moustaches are black; his eyes are closed; his eyelashes are drooping—he is asleep! And, asleep, he holds the reins. Behind him sits a young page, and he, too, is asleep, and even in his sleep he holds on to the giant. Who is he? Whither rides he? And why? Who knows? Not one day nor two

49

has he been riding over the mountains. Day breaks, the sun rises, and he is seen no more. Only from time to time do the mountain-people notice a large shadow flitting over the mountains while the sky is clear and no cloud passes across the sun. But as soon as night descends and darkness falls, he becomes visible again and is reflected in the lakes and, quivering, his shadow gallops after him. He has crossed many mountains, and at last he rides up to the top of Krivan. There is no mountain in Carpathia higher than this one. It towers like a monarch over the other mountains. There the rider and his horse stop. The knight sinks into an even deeper slumber and the clouds descend and hide him from view.

XIII

"Hush, woman; don't make such a noise! My baby's asleep. My son cried a long time and now he is asleep. I'm going for a walk in the woods now. . . . What are you looking at me like that for ? Oh, how hideous you look: iron pincers are coming out of your eyes ! Such long pincers, too, and they are red hot ! You must be a witch ! Go away, go away, if you are a witch ! You will steal my son ! How ridiculous that old Cossack Captain is ! He thinks I like living in Kiev. No, my husband and my son are here. And, besides, who's going to look after our cottage ? I went out so quietly that neither the dog nor the cat heard me. Would you like to grow young again, old woman ? It isn't a bit hard : all you have to do is to dance. Like that. See ? Just as I'm dancing. . . ." And, having uttered those incoherent sentences, Katherine, her arms akimbo and looking wildly about her, began to dance. With a shriek she tapped with her feet, her silver heels beating spasmodically and out of time. Her black plaits came undone and tossed wildly about her white neck. She darted about the room without stopping, like a bird, waving her hands and nodding her head, and it seemed that she must either collapse on the ground from sheer exhaustion or fall dead.

The old nurse stood mournfully, tears rolling down her wrinkled face; the hearts of the faithful Cossacks were heavy as they looked at their mistress. At last she became exhausted and went on tapping languidly with her feet on the same spot, in the belief that she was dancing the slow Ukrainian turtle-dove dance.

"I have a lovely necklace, boys," she said at length, stopping.

"You haven't got one, have you? . . . Where's my husband?" she screamed suddenly, drawing a Turkish dagger from her girdle. "Oh, this is not the knife I need!" she said, tears gushing out of her eyes and her face becoming overcast by a great sadness. "My father's heart is far away: it will not reach it. His heart is wrought of iron. It was forged by a witch in the fire of hell. Why doesn't my father come? Doesn't he know it is time he was stabbed to death? I suppose he expects me to go for him. . . ." And, breaking off, she laughed queerly. "Listen, I've just remembered such a funny thing: I've remembered how my husband was buried. He was buried alive, you know. Oh, it did make me laugh. . . . Listen, listen!" And instead of speaking, she began to sing:

"The cart on the road is covered in blood,
    In the cart a brave Cossack's lying;
They cut him down and shot him, and now he's dying.
    In his right hand a spear he's holding,
    A river of blood from that spear's flowing,
    Over the river a plane-tree's growing,
    Above the plane-tree a raven's croaking.
    A mother for the Cossack's weeping.
    Don't weep, Mother, tears you ne'er need shed,
    For your son a pretty lady's wed,
    A pretty lady, a young bride.
    In a field a little cottage stands,
    Without doors and without casements long,
    And that's the end of my song. . . .
    A crayfish with a fish was dancing,
    If you don't love me, your mother in an ague'll be shaking!"

It was such fragments of songs that she strung together in a medley of words.

For the past few days she had been living in her cottage. She would not hear of Kiev; she would not say her prayers; and she shunned everybody. From morning till night she wandered about the dark woods. Sharp twigs scratched her white face and shoulders; the wind tousled her loose plaits; the dead leaves rustled under her feet—she looked at nothing. At the hour when the glow of sunset fades from the sky, but before the stars have appeared or the moon is up, people are afraid to walk in the woods. Unbaptised children claw at the trees and clutch at the branches, sobbing and laughing, turn somersaults on the roads and the wide patches of nettles. Maidens who have drowned themselves in the Dnieper and whose souls are for ever damned come out of its waves in shoals; their hair streams from their green heads over their shoulders; with a loud ripple the water pours from their long hair to the ground; and a maiden shines through the water as though through a crystal dress; her lips smile enigmatically, her cheeks blaze, her eyes enchant the soul: she looks as if she might pine away with love, as if she might kiss her lover to death. . . . Run, Christian! Her lips are ice, her bed—the cold water, her caress deadly: she will drag you into the river. But Katherine looked at no one; in her frenzy she did not fear the water maidens. She ran about with her knife far into the night, searching for her father.

In the early morning a visitor arrived, a handsome man in a scarlet coat, and he inquired after Danilo. He heard their story, wiped the tears from his eyes with his sleeve and shook his head. He said he had fought side by side with Burulbash; side by side they had engaged in mortal combat with the Crimean Tartars and the Turks. Never had he thought that Danilo would meet with such an end. The visitor told them many other things and expressed a wish to see Katherine.

At first Katherine would not listen to anything the visitor told her. But by and by she began to listen to his speeches as though she understood them perfectly. He told her how Danilo and he had lived together like brothers, how once they had hidden under a dam from the Crimeans. . . . Katherine listened and did not take her eyes off him.

"She will recover," the Cossacks thought, looking at her. "This man will cure her! She is listening like one who has already recovered her senses!"

Meanwhile the visitor began describing how Danilo once in confidence had said to him, "Look here, Kuprian. If by the will of God I should die, you take Katherine for your wife. . . ."

Katherine gave him a piercing look. "Ah," she shrieked, "it is he! It is my father!" and she sprang at him with her knife.

For a long time he struggled to snatch the knife from her; at last he did snatch it away, raised it—and a terrible deed was done: the father killed his crazed daughter.

The thunderstruck Cossacks rushed at him, but the sorcerer had already leapt upon his horse and vanished out of sight.

XIV

Outside the city of Kiev an extraordinary miracle happened. All the gentlemen and the hetmans flocked to witness it: suddenly it became possible to see far away to the ends of the earth. Afar could be seen the blue waters of the mouth of the Dnieper, and beyond that the Black Sea was plainly visible. Men who had travelled in foreign lands recognised the Crimea, rising like a mountain out of the sea, and the marshy Sivash. On the right could be seen the Galician land.

"And what's that?" people asked the old men, pointing to the white and grey crests, which loomed far away in the sky, looking more like clouds than anything else.

"Those are the Carpathian mountains!" replied the old men. "Among them there are some that are covered with eternal snow, and the clouds cling to them and spend the night there."

Then a new miracle happened: the clouds which hid the summit of the highest mountain dispersed and on it appeared a horseman in full knightly armour, with his eyes closed. He was plainly visible to all, as though he were only a few yards away.

It was then that one man among that marvelling and frightened multitude leapt on a horse and, looking wildly about him, as though afraid that he might be pursued, he quickly rode off at a gallop. That was the sorcerer. Why was he so panic-stricken? Looking in terror at the strange knight, he recognised the face which had appeared to him unbidden while he was working his spells. He could not have said why he was filled with such dismay at this sight; and, looking apprehensively about him, he rode madly on until he was overtaken by night and the stars began to come out. Then he turned homewards, perhaps to ask the Evil One what that miracle meant. He was just about to leap with his horse over a narrow stream, which ran right across his path, when his horse suddenly stopped in full career, looked round at him and—wonder of wonders!—laughed aloud, both rows of teeth gleaming uncannily in the darkness. The sorcerer's hair stood on end. He uttered a wild scream, wept like one possessed, and turned his horse towards Kiev.

He felt that he was being pursued on all sides. The trees that surrounded him like a dark forest shook their beards and stretched forth their long branches, as though alive, trying to strangle him;

53

the stars seemed to be running ahead of him and pointing to the sinner; the road itself seemed to be racing after him.

The frantic sorcerer hurried to the holy places in Kiev.

XV

A hermit sat alone in his cave before a dimly burning lamp, and he did not take his eyes off the holy book. He had retired to his cave many years ago and he had already made himself a coffin in which he lay down to sleep instead of a bed. The holy man closed his book and began to pray. . . . Suddenly a man of a strange and terrible aspect ran into his cave. The holy man was startled at first at the sight of such a man and he drew back from him. He was trembling all over like an aspen leaf. His eyes rolled wildly and blazed with panic. His misshapen face made one shudder.

"Father, pray! Pray!" he shouted desperately. "Pray for a lost soul!" and he sank to the ground.

The holy hermit crossed himself, took up his book, opened it and, drawing back in horror, dropped it. "There is no mercy for you, terrible sinner that you are! Go, I cannot pray for you!"

"No?" the sinner cried, distraught.

"Look, the holy letters in the book are dripping with blood. . . . There has never been such a sinner in the world!"

"Father, you are mocking me!"

"Go, accursed sinner! I am not mocking you. I am overcome with fear. It is not good for a man to be with you!"

"No, no. You are mocking. Don't pretend. . . . I see you're laughing at me! I can see your old teeth gleaming white!"

And, mad with fury, he sprang at the old hermit and—killed him.

A deep moan rose in the cave and it echoed through the woods and the fields. From behind the woods a pair of gaunt, withered arms with long claws rose in the air, trembled and disappeared.

And now he felt no fear. He felt nothing. Everything was confused. His ears rang, his head spun round as though he were drunk, and everything before his eyes seemed covered with spiders' webs. He leapt upon his horse and rode straight for Kanev, intending to ride from there through Cherkassy direct to the Crimean Tartars, although he hardly knew himself why. He rode one day and another and still Kanev was not in sight. He was on the right road and he ought to have reached it long ago, but there was no sign of Kanev. In the distance he could see the gleaming cupolas of churches. But that was not Kanev. It was Shumsk. The sorcerer was amazed to find himself in quite a different part of the country. He turned back towards Kiev and a day later a city appeared. It was not Kiev, though, but Galich, a city more distant from Kiev than Shumsk. At a loss what to do, he again turned back, but he had the curious feeling that he was still riding in the opposite direction, and always farther and farther away from where he wanted to go. No one in the world could tell what was in the sorcerer's mind; if anyone had seen and known what was there, he would never again have had a quiet night's sleep, neither would he have laughed again for the most of his life. It was not spite, or anger, or fierce resentment. There is no word in the world to describe it. His blood boiled; he was mad with rage; he would have gladly trampled upon the whole world with his horse, seized the whole country from Kiev to Galich, with all the people and everything in it, and drowned it in the Black Sea. But it was not from spite or malice that he would do it. No, he did not know himself why he wished to do it.

A cold shudder ran through his veins when he saw the Carpathian mountains quite near him, and lofty Krivan capped with grey cloud. His horse still galloped on and was already racing among the mountains. The clouds suddenly lifted, and there before him was the horseman in all his terrible majesty. . . . The sorcerer tried to stop; he tugged at the rein; his horse neighed wildly and, its mane flying, it continued to race towards the horseman. As he saw the motionless horseman stir and suddenly open his eyes, the sorcerer felt everything die within him. But when the dreadful knight saw the sorcerer racing towards him, he laughed, and his wild laugh echoed like thunder through the mountains and resounded in the sorcerer's heart, shaking him to the very core of his being. He felt as if some mighty creature had crawled into him and was walking within him, hammering away at his heart and veins . . . so dreadfully did that laugh resound in him !

The horseman seized the sorcerer with his mighty hand and lifted him into the air. In a trice the sorcerer was dead. He opened his eyes after his death, but he was dead and gazed like a dead man. Neither the living nor the risen from the dead have such a terrible look in their eyes. He rolled his dead eyes from side to side and saw dead men rising up from Kiev, from Galicia and the Carpathian mountains, and they all looked like him.

Pale, terribly pale, one taller than another, one bonier than another, they thronged round the horseman who held his awful prey in his hand. Once more the knight laughed and then he dropped the sorcerer down into the abyss. And all the dead men leapt into the abyss, seized the dead man as he was falling and fastened their teeth into him. Another, taller and more terrible than the rest, tried to rise from the ground, but he could not, for he had not the strength to do it, so huge had he grown in the earth; and if he had risen out of the earth he would have overturned the Carpathian mountains, and the whole of the Semigrad and Turkish lands. He only moved a little and he set the whole earth in a tremor, and many cottages were overturned and many people crushed to death.

A roar is often heard in the Carpathian mountains as if a thousand water-mills were churning up the water with their wheels. It is the sound of dead men gnawing a dead man in the bottomless abyss which no living man has ever seen, for no man dares to go near it. It sometimes happens that the earth trembles from one end to the other: that is, learned men will tell you, because there is a mountain somewhere near the sea from which flames issue and fiery streams flow. But the old men who live in Hungary and Galicia know better and they say it is the dead man who has grown so huge in the earth, trying to rise and shaking the earth.

XVI

A large crowd gathered round a bandore-player in the town of Glukhov, and for the past hour they had been listening to the blind man's playing. No bandore-player sang so well or such wonderful songs. First he sang about the rule of the hetmans, of Sagaydachny and Khmelnitzky, the famous chieftains of the Dnieper Cossacks. Times were different then: the Cossacks were at the height of their glory, they trampled their foes underfoot, and no one dared to hold them up to scorn. The old bandore-player sang merry songs, too, and he turned his sightless eyes upon the crowd as though he could see, and his fingers, with the little sheaths of bone fixed to them, darted about like flies over the strings and the strings seemed to play by themselves; and the people, old men with their eyes fixed upon the ground and young men with their eyes staring at the old singer, dared not even whisper to one another.

"Now," said the old man, "I will sing you about what happened long, long ago."

The people pressed closer and the old man began:

"In times long past when Stephen, famed far and wide as Prince of Semigrad, was king of the Poles, two gallant Cossacks, Ivan and Petro, lived together in amity and love like brothers. 'Whatever you, Ivan, in battle or raid shall obtain, we shall divide in equal parts; when good fortune smiles upon you, I, too, shall be merry; but when dire misfortune befalls one of us, then we both shall share it; if one of us gains rich booty in battle, it shall be shared between us; if the cruel foe takes one of us captive, the other shall sell his goods and chattels for ransom, or else himself go into captivity.' And so it came to pass that whenever they seized cattle and horses from strangers, each of them received his equal share.

"It so fell out that when King Stephen waged war against the Ottoman, he could never prevail in battle, although for three full weeks he stoutly fought the infidel hordes. The Sultan had a Pasha who with only ten of his janissaries put to flight a whole regiment of Poles. The king therefore proclaimed that if a man should be found among his troops who, singlehanded, should bring that Pasha to him dead or alive, he would, as recompense, receive the entire pay of his army. 'Come, brother, let us take the Pasha prisoner,' said Ivan to Petro. So the two Cosacks set off, one one way, one the other.

"Whether or not Petro would have captured the Pasha, there is no telling, but meanwhile Ivan led the Pasha to the king with a rope round his neck. 'Brave fellow!' said King Stephen, and he commanded that Ivan alone be given the pay of the whole army. The king also ordered that Ivan be given any land he might desire, wheresoever it might chance to be, and as many heads of cattle as he should wish. No sooner did Ivan receive the king's reward than he gave half of it to Petro. Petro took his half, but the honour Ivan received from the king rankled in his breast, and in his heart the thought of revenge was planted deep.

"The two knights rode off to take possession of the land beyond the Carpathians that the king had granted to Ivan. The Cossack

Ivan had set his little son behind him on the horse, tying him for safety with a rope passed round his own waist. Dusk fell, but they continued on their way. The young child fell asleep; Ivan, too, began to doze. Do not slumber, Cossack, the mountain paths are treacherous ! But the Cossack's horse is endowed by nature with a sixth sense, and he can find his way in darkness wherever he may happen to be; nor will he stumble or step off the path. There is an abyss between the mountains, a bottomless chasm, unplumbed by man; as many miles as there are between heaven and earth, are also between the top and the bottom of that great chasm. A narrow path skirts perilously the chasm's edge, so narrow a path that two people can barely ride abreast upon it, but three never. Warily the horse picked his way along that perilous path with the slumbering Cossack on his back, and Petro, in a quiver of excitement and breathless with joy, rode beside him. He looked round, cast a glance into the chasm and thrust his sworn brother over the edge. Horse and Cossack and small child hurtled to their doom together.

"But in his fall the Cossack chanced to grasp a branch, and the horse alone fell to the bottom of the abyss. With his son on his back, Ivan started on his dangerous ascent up the treacherous slope of the precipice; but barely had he reached the top when, looking up, he saw Petro pointing his pike at him to push him back over the precipice. 'Just and merciful Heaven,' Ivan cried, 'far better I had never lifted my eyes than that I had seen my own brother holding his pike ready to thrust me back to my destruction. Stab me, dear brother, stab me with your pike, if God so wills that I should perish here, but spare my child ! Take him ! Take him, I implore you, for what has an innocent child done to deserve such a cruel death ?' But Petro laughed and thrust at him with his pike. Cossack and child fell to the bottom of the chasm. Petro seized his brother's land and cattle and lived like a lord for the rest of his human span. No man had such droves of horses as he, nor flocks of sheep and rams. And Petro died.

"No sooner was Petro dead than God summoned the souls of the two brothers to appear for judgment before His throne. 'This man, O Ivan,' said God, 'is so great a sinner that it will take me too long to choose a fit punishment for him. Choose thou his proper punishment thyself !' Ivan pondered long what punishment to choose. At length he said, 'This man has done me a great injury. Like Judas, he betrayed his brother; he brought my honourable line to an end and robbed me of all hope of posterity. For a man without an honourable line and without progeny is like a seed that falls upon the ground and perishes in the earth; there is no green shoot to tell the whole world that a seed has been dropped there.

"'Therefore, O Lord, make it so that no issue of his loins may know happiness on earth. Let, I beseech Thee, the last man of his line be the wickedest man on earth, and let each wicked deed of his disturb the peace of his fathers and forefathers in their graves, and, suffering torments unknown in the world before, let them rise from their tombs ! But let Judas Petro not have the strength to rise and let him thereby suffer worse torment, and may he bite the earth like one possessed, and may he writhe in agony beneath the ground.

"'And when the hour of retribution comes, when the villainous career of that evil man has in full measure been consummated, raise me, O Lord, from that deep abyss on to the highest mountain, where I may sit mounted on my stallion, and let him come to me, and from that mountain I shall hurl him into the deepest abyss, and let all his dead, all his ancestors, come creeping from every corner of the earth, wherever they lived in their lifetime, to that abyss to gnaw his bones and so repay him for the torments his crimes had made them suffer, and may they gnaw him for ever and for ever. Thrice happy will I be to watch his sufferings ! But do not let Judas Petro ever rise from under the ground; let him strive in vain to gnaw the bones of his great-great-grandchild, but let him instead gnaw his own bones, which, growing longer and longer as the years pass, shall make his pains more unbearable still. This will, I am sure, be the worst torture for him, for greater torment knows no man than to long for vengeance, but to be powerless to avenge.'

"'Terrible is the punishment thou hast devised, O man,' said God, 'but be it as thou hast spoken; but thou too shalt sit on that mountain-top for ever, and never shalt thou enter the Kingdom of Heaven whilst thou sittest there on thy horse !' And so it befell as it was spoken, and to this very day the wondrous knight, horsed and accoutred, stands on the highest peak of the Carpathian mountains, watching dead men gnawing the bones of a dead man in the bottomless abyss, and feeling how a dead man's bones are growing larger and larger under the earth, and how he, suffering dreadful agonies, gnaws at his own bones and sets the whole earth shaking fearfully. . . ."

The blind man had long finished his song and he began again thrumming the strings, singing amusing rhymes of Khoma and Yeryoma and Sklyara Stokoza; but his listeners, old and young, did not heed him, and for a long time they stood with bowed heads, their thoughts still full of the dreadful events that happened in the days long gone by.

THE PORTRAIT

Part One

NOWHERE WAS there so great a crowd of people as before the little art dealer's shop in Pike's Yard, one of the many markets in St. Petersburg. This little shop had indeed a most varied assortment of curiosities: the pictures were mostly painted in oils, covered with a dark-green varnish, in dark-yellow, tawdry frames. A winter landscape with white trees, a red evening sky, looking like the reflection of some conflagration, a Flemish peasant with a pipe and a broken arm, looking more like a turkey with frills than a human being—those were their usual subjects. To these must be added a few engraved portraits: the portrait of Hozreva-Mirza, the Persian prince and special envoy, in a lambskin cap, and portraits of generals with crooked noses in three-cornered hats. In addition, the doors of such shops are usually hung with all sorts of illustrated popular ballads, printed on large sheets of paper, which bear witness to the native talent of the Russian. On one of them was the fairy princess Miliktrissa Kirbityevna, on another the City of Jerusalem, with houses and churches unceremoniously bedaubed with red paint, which also covered part of the street and two praying Russian peasants in mittens. As a rule, not many people purchased any of these works of art, but hundreds were eager to look at them. Some shiftless footman would be quite sure to stop and gape at them, holding in his hands dishes from the restaurant with the dinner for his master, whose soup would be cold by the time it was served. An old soldier in a greatcoat would be gazing at them, this king of hawkers with a few penknives for sale; or a market woman from Okhta with a basketful of shoes. Each one would show his admiration in his own way: the peasants usually poked their fingers; the hawkers examined them with a serious air; servant lads and apprentices laughed and teased each other about the coloured caricatures; old footmen in frieze overcoats looked at them simply because they had to gape at something; and the market women, young Russian peasant women, hurried towards such a shop by instinct, eager to hear what the people were gossiping about and to look at what the people were looking at.

At this time Chartkov, a young artist, who happened to be passing by, involuntarily stopped before the shop. His old overcoat and far from fashionable clothes showed that he was a man who had devoted himself to his work with self-denying zeal and had not time to worry about clothes, which always have a mysterious attraction for the young. He stopped in front of the shop and at first began laughing inwardly at those grotesque pictures. At last he began wondering unconsciously what sort of people wanted such pictures. That the Russian people should gape at cheap prints of Yeruslan Lazarevich, or popular figures of fun like Foma and Yeryoma, or "The Glutton" or "The Drunkard," did not strike him as particularly strange; the subjects were, after all, familiar and intelligible to the people. But who were the purchasers of those ridiculous, clumsily painted, dingy oil paintings? Who wanted these Flemish peasants, these red and blue landscapes, which showed some pretensions to a higher level of art, but which merely succeeded in expressing the depth of its degradation? They did not even seem to be the works of a precocious child, for, if they were, one would have perceived in them a certain intensity of feeling in spite of the caricature of an art which the whole picture conveyed. But all one found in them was a total lack of talent, the dull-witted, feeble, decrepit incompetence of a born failure that impudently thrusts himself among the arts, whereas his true place is among the meanest of the crafts, a failure that is true to his calling, however, and introduces the tricks of his trade even into the world of art. The same colours, the same mannerisms, the same unimaginative, bungling and clumsy hand, which one would have thought belonged to an automaton rather than to a living man ! . . .

He stood before those grimy pictures a long time without even thinking of them any more, while the owner of the shop, a drab little man in a frieze overcoat and with a face that had not been shaved since Sunday, talked to him for some time, bargaining and discussing prices before even finding out what his prospective customer fancied and what he was likely to buy.

"For those peasants, sir, and for the little landscape painting I'd take two pounds. What wonderful brushwork! It fairly hits you in the eye! Just got them from the warehouse. The varnish isn't dry yet. Or take that one, sir—the winter landscape! Thirty bob. The frame itself is worth more. What a lovely winter landscape, sir!" Here the art dealer struck a light blow on the canvas as further proof of the fine quality of the winter landscape. "Shall I tie them up together and take them to your place? Where do you live, sir? Here, boy, give me some string!"

"Wait a moment; not so fast!" said the artist, recovering with a jolt as he saw the enterprising dealer beginning in good earnest to tie up the pictures with a piece of string. Feeling a little ashamed, though, not to take anything at all after standing so long in the shop, he added, "Wait a moment. I'll have a look round. Perhaps there is something I'd like to have."

Stooping, he began picking up from the floor the faded, dusty old paintings, thrown together in a heap, which the shopkeeper apparently did not consider to be of any great value. There were among them old family portraits of people whose descendants could most probably no longer be traced anywhere; pictures of quite unknown people on torn canvases and frames that had lost their gilding; in fact, all sorts of trash. But the artist began examining them carefully, thinking to himself, "I might find something worth while here." He had heard many stories of the discovery of paintings of the great masters among the rubbish of popular print shops.

The art dealer, seeing that his customer was likely to be busy for some time, stopped fussing over him and, assuming his usual attitude and proper gravity of demeanour, again took up his position at the open door of his shop, inviting the passers-by to come in, waving his hand towards his pictures. "Come right in, sir! Have a look at my pictures! Lovely pictures! Come in, come in! Just got them from the warehouse!" he shouted until he was hoarse and generally in vain. Then he had a long talk with a rag merchant, standing opposite at the door of his little shop, and at last remembering that he had a customer in his shop, turned his back on the people in the street and went inside.

"Well, sir," he addressed the artist, "have you found anything?"

The artist had been standing without moving for some time before a portrait in a huge and once magnificent frame, upon which,

63

however, only a few gleaming spots of gilt remained. It was the portrait of a man with a face the colour of bronze, rather haggard and with high cheekbones; the features of his face seemed to have been caught by the artist in a moment of a sudden spasmodic movement and there was a terrific force in them that could not possibly belong to a man of a northern latitude. The fiery tropical sun was clearly imprinted upon them. A wide oriental robe was draped round him. However damaged and dusty the portrait was, Chartkov could see the unmistakable hand of a great artist as soon as he removed the dust from the face. The portrait had apparently been left unfinished; but the firmness of hand with which it had been painted was astonishing. The eyes were particularly striking; the artist seemed to have applied to them the full power of his brush and all his painstaking care. They seemed to glare at you, glare at you out of the portrait, destroying its harmony by their uncanny vitality. When Chartkov carried the portrait to the door, the eyes stared at him with even greater intentness. They produced almost the same impression on the people in the street. A woman who stopped behind him cried, "He looks at you as if he was alive!" and drew back. A curious, uncomfortable feeling, a feeling which he could hardly explain to himself, took hold of the young artist, and he put the portrait down on the floor.

"Well, sir, won't you take this portrait?" asked the owner of the shop.

"How much?" said the artist.

"Well, I don't want to make a profit on it, sir. Shall we say six shillings?"

"No."

"Well, what would you offer me for it, sir?"

"One and sixpence," said the artist, preparing to go.

"Dear me, what a price to offer! Why, the frame alone is worth more than one and sixpence! Seems to me you don't really want to buy it. Come back, sir, come back! Just add another sixpence. No? All right, all right! Take it for one and six. It's practically giving it away, but seeing that you are my first customer today . . ." He made a gesture which seemed to say, "Ah well, so be it! It's giving a fine picture away!"

It was thus that Chartkov quite unexpectedly became the owner of the old portrait, and almost at the same instant he could not help reflecting, "Why have I bought it? What do I want it for?"

But there was nothing he could do about it. He took one and sixpence out of his pocket, gave it to the art dealer, took the portrait under his arm and went home. On the way he remembered that the one and sixpence he had given for it was the last one and sixpence he had in the world. His thoughts at once took on a gloomy cast. He cursed himself for being such a fool, and at the same time he felt a listless void inside him. "Damn, what a rotten world it is !" he said, expressing the typical feeling of a Russian whose affairs have just about touched rock bottom. And he walked on mechanically with hurried steps, feeling totally indifferent to everything. The red glow of sunset still lingered over half the sky ; the houses which faced that way were faintly illuminated by its warm light, while the cold, bluish radiance of the moon was getting stronger. Light, half-transparent shadows, cast by the houses and the feet of pedestrians, fell upon the ground in long, narrow bars. The artist was already glancing more and more frequently at the sky, which was irradiated by a kind of faint, translucent, uncertain light, and almost at the same moment there burst from his lips the words, "What a delicate tone !" and "Damn it, what a nuisance !" The portrait kept slipping from under his arm and he was continually putting it back and quickening his pace. Dog-tired, and covered with perspiration, he at last dragged himself home to Fifteenth Row of Vassilyev Island. With difficulty he climbed up the stairs, wet with slops and adorned with the footprints of cats and dogs, and he was out of breath by the time he reached the door of his flat. There was no reply to his knock at the door : his servant, whose name was Nikita and who always wore a blueshirt, was not at home. He leant against the window, resigned to wait patiently for the return of Nikita, whom he employed as his Jack of all trades : his model, his paint grinder and his sweeper of floors which he usually dirtied immediately with his boots. At last he heard the lad's footsteps behind him. While his master was away, Nikita spent all his time in the street. It took him a long time to get the key into the key-hole which he could hardly see because of the darkness. At last the door was opened. Chartkov entered the hall, which was terribly cold, like all the halls of artists' flats, not that it seems to matter to them much. Without handing his overcoat to Nikita, he went into his studio—a large, square room, though with rather a low ceiling, with window-panes covered with hoar-frost, filled with all sorts of artist's lumber : bits of plaster-of-Paris arms, frames covered with canvas, sketches begun and discarded, draperies hung on chairs. Feeling terribly tired, he threw off his overcoat, put the portrait absent-mindedly between two small canvases, and flung himself on a narrow sofa, of which it could hardly be claimed that it was covered with hide, because the row of brass nails which had once fastened the hide to the frame of the sofa had long since detached themselves, leaving the upholstery also detached, so that Nikita pushed dirty socks and shirts and all the dirty linen under it. Having stretched as much as it was possible to stretch on so narrow a sofa, he at last called for a candle.

"There is no candle, sir," said Nikita.

"What do you mean, there is no candle?"

"We had no candle yesterday, either," said Nikita.

The artist remembered that they had indeed had no candle the night before, and he calmed down and fell silent. He let Nikita help him with his undressing, and put on his worn, old dressing-gown.

"The landlord's been here again, sir," said Nikita.

"Oh? Came for his money I suppose. I know," said the artist, dismissing the subject with a wave of the hand.

"But he wasn't alone, sir," said Nikita.

"Who was with him?"

"Dunno, sir. Looked like a policeman to me."

"What did he want to bring a policeman for?"

"Dunno, sir. He said, sir, it was because your rent had not been paid."

"Well, what about it?"

"Dunno what about it, sir. Only he says, 'If he can't pay,' he says, 'he'd better clear out of the flat.' They'll be coming again tomorrow, both of 'em, sir."

"Let them come," said Chartkov with mournful indifference, feeling completely out of humour with the whole world.

Chartkov was a talented young man of great promise; there were odd moments when his brush seemed suddenly to show that he possessed keen observation, intense perception, and a quick impulse to get closer to nature.

"Take good care, my dear fellow," his art master used to say to him; "you have talent, and it would be a thousand pities if you ruined it. The trouble with you is that you're so confoundedly impatient. If you get interested in something, if you happen to take

66

a fancy to something, you get so entirely absorbed in it that everything else is just of no account to you; you don't want even to look at it. Take care you don't become a fashionable artist. Even now your colours seem to be getting out of hand. Much too slick those colours of yours are, if you don't mind my saying so. Your drawing, too, lacks strength. Sometimes it is very weak. No lines. Running after fashionable light effects. You seem to be mainly working for effect. Watch out or one day you'll find yourself a mere imitator of the English school. And another thing. You're getting too much attracted by the fashionable world. I have seen you sometimes wearing an expensive scarf round your neck, a beautifully polished hat. Mind, I don't say it isn't a tempting prospect. Start painting fashionable pictures, become a fashionable portrait painter, and all your money worries are at an end: you'll get lots of money. But remember, my dear fellow, that is the way to ruin your talent, not to develop it. Take great care over every picture you paint. Take your time over it; think it over carefully. Forget about fine clothes. Let others rake in the money; your time will come !"

The professor was partly right. There were indeed moments when our artist wanted to enjoy himself, to show off, in fact to display in some way his youthful exuberance. But in spite of that he could take himself in hand. At times, as soon as he got hold of his brush, he could forget everything, and he would only put it down reluctantly, as one waking from a beautiful dream. It is true that he was as yet incapable of understanding the whole depth of Raphael, but he was already under the spell of the swift, mighty brush of Guido, lingered before the portraits of Titian, was enraptured by the Flemish painters. He was still unable to see through the darkened surface of the old painters; but he already saw something in them, though in his heart he disagreed with his professor's view that the art of the old masters was unattainable by the modern painter. It seemed to him that in some ways the nineteenth century had got ahead of them; that the imitation of nature had somehow or other become more brilliant, more vivid, and more close. He was reasoning in this instance as youth always reasons, youth that has already achieved something and realises it in the pride of its inner consciousness. Sometimes he could not help feeling annoyed when some foreign painter, a Frenchman or a German, created a general stir, although he was not always even a professional painter, but just a showman, who by the smartness of his brushwork and the brightness of his colours amassed a fortune in no time. He did not think of this when absorbed in his work, for then he forgot food and drink and the whole world; but when he felt the pinch of necessity, when he had not enough money to buy paints and brushes, when the importunate landlord came ten times a day to demand the rent for the flat. It was then that the lot of the rich fashionable painter appealed so powerfully to his hungry imagination; it was then that the thought, which often flashes through the mind of a Russian, also flashed through his mind: give it all up and take to drink just out of sheer vexation of spirit and spleen. And now he was almost in that mood.

"Yes, have patience, have patience!" he muttered, irritably. "But there is an end even to one's patience! Have patience! And where will I get the money for my dinner tomorrow? No one will lend me any. And if I were to take all my drawings and paintings to an art dealer, he wouldn't give me more than sixpence for them. I suppose they have been of some use to me. I realise that. None of them has been a waste of time. Each of them has taught me something. But what's the use of it? Sketches, rough drafts. It can go on for ever. And who'd buy any of my pictures never even having heard my name? And who wants studies from the antique or from life? Or my unfinished Psyche's Love, or the interior of my room, or Nikita's portrait, a damn sight better though it is than the portraits of some of the fashionable painters? Why take all this trouble; why waste my time, like a beginner, on the elementary rules of my art, when I could easily do something that will make me as famous as the rest of them and earn as much money as they do into the bargain?"

Having said this, the artist suddenly shuddered and grew pale; a horribly contorted face was looking at him from behind one of his canvases. Two terrible eyes were gazing intently at him as though about to devour him; the lips seemed sternly to enjoin silence. Terrified, he was about to cry out and call Nikita, whose loud snoring he could hear from the hall; but suddenly he stopped and laughed. The feeling of terror disappeared in an instant. It was the portrait he had bought and completely forgotten. The moonlight which filled the room fell upon the portrait and invested it with an uncanny vitality. He began examining and wiping it. Dipping a sponge in water, he rubbed it over the portrait a few times, washed off almost all the accumulated and encrusted dirt, hung it on the wall before him and admired more than ever its extraordinarily fine technique; almost the whole face seemed to have come to life, and the eyes looked at him in a way that made him shudder involuntarily and retreat a few steps, exclaiming in an astonished voice, "By Jove, it looks at you with human eyes !" He suddenly remembered the story he had heard from his professor a long time ago of a portrait of Leonardo da Vinci's. The great master had worked on it for several years and still regarded it as unfinished, but in spite of that it was, according to Vasari, generally acclaimed as a finished masterpiece. The most finished thing about it was the eyes which amazed Leonardo's contemporaries; even the tiniest, hardly visible veins in them were not overlooked and were reproduced on the canvas. But here, in the portrait that now hung on the wall before him, there was something uncanny. This was no longer art; it destroyed the harmony of the portrait itself ! Those eyes were living, human eyes ! They seemed to have been cut out of a living man and put in there. Here there was no longer any of that sublime feeling of joy that encompasses the soul at the sight of the work of an artist, however terrible the subject chosen by him might be; the sensation he received from looking at this portrait was rather one of joylessness, painfulness and anxiety. "What's the matter ?" the artist could not help asking himself. "After all, it is only something copied from life, a picture painted from a model ! Then why on earth should it give me this strangely unpleasant feeling ? Or is a faithful, slavish imitation of nature such an offence that it must affect you like a loud, discordant scream ? Or if you paint a thing objectively and coolly, without feeling any particular sympathy for it, must it necessarily confront you in all its terrible reality, unillumined by the light of some deep, hidden, unfathomable thought ? Must it appear to you with the reality which reveals itself to a person who, searching for beauty in man, picks up a scalpel and begins to dissect a man's inside, only to find what is disgusting in man ? Why is it that simple, lowly nature appears in the work of one artist as though illumined by some magic light and you never get the sensation of anything low ? On the contrary, you seem to derive a certain enjoyment from it, and life afterwards seems much more placid and calm. And yet the same kind of subject appears in the work of another artist as low and sordid, though he is no less true to nature. The truth is that there is nothing in it that sheds a lustre upon it. It is just like a landscape in nature; however beautiful it may be, something seems to be missing in it, if there is no sun in the sky."

He again went up to the portrait to examine those wonderful eyes more closely, and to his horror he noticed that they were actually looking at him. That was no longer a copy from nature; it was the kind of life that might have lit up the face of a dead man risen from the grave. Whether it was the moonlight which brought with it the phantasmagoria of a dream world and clothed everything in shapes so different from what it appeared in broad daylight, or whether there was another reason for it, he became suddenly (he himself hardly knew why) frightened of remaining alone in the room. He walked slowly away from the portrait, turned away from it and tried not to look at it, but, try as he might, he could not help looking at it now and again furtively out of a corner of an eye. At last he even became frightened to walk about in the room; he had the odd feeling that at any moment somebody else would be walking behind him, and he began casting apprehensive glances over his shoulder. He was not a coward, but his imagination and his nerves were extremely sensitive, and that evening he could not have explained to himself what he was so afraid of. He sat down in a corner of the room, but even there he could not help feeling that someone would any minute be peering over his shoulder into his face. Even Nikita's loud snoring which came from the hall did not dispel his fear. At last he rose quietly from his place and, without raising his eyes, went behind the screen, where he undressed and went to bed. Through a chink in the screen he could see the whole room, which was flooded with moonlight, and straight in front of him he saw the portrait hanging on the wall. Those eyes were fixed upon him steadily, more terribly and more significantly than ever, and it seemed they would not look at anything but him. Feeling strangely ill at ease, he decided to get up and cover up the portrait. He jumped out of bed, snatched up a sheet and, walking up to the portrait, covered it up entirely. That done, he went back to bed in a more composed frame of mind.

He could not sleep and his thoughts turned upon the miserable lot of a painter, the thorny path which lay before him in this world. Meanwhile his eyes looked involuntarily through the chink in the screen at the portrait wrapped in the sheet. The moonlight emphasised the whiteness of the sheet, and it seemed to him that the terrible eyes were gleaming through the cloth. Panic-stricken, he began to peer more keenly at the portrait, as though wishing to convince himself that it was all imagination. But . . . good gracious, what was that? He could now see plainly, very plainly indeed, that the sheet had vanished and . . . the portrait was all uncovered and, without paying the slightest attention to anything round it, it was looking straight at him—no, not at him, but into him, right into him! . . . His heart began to pound violently. The next thing he saw was that the old man began moving, and presently he pressed both his hands against the frame. Then he raised himself on his hands and, thrusting out his legs, jumped out of the frame . . . Through the chink in the screen he could now see the empty frame. He could hear footfalls in the room, footfalls which were drawing closer and closer to the screen. The artist's heart began pounding even more violently. Panting, and hardly able to breathe for fear, he expected to see the old man glancing from behind the screen any minute. And almost immediately he did indeed glance from behind the screen, his bronze face looking not a bit different, and rolling his big eyes. Chartkov tried to scream, but his voice failed him; he tried to move, but his limbs were paralysed. With a gaping mouth he gazed breathlessly at this terrible phantom of enormous height, wearing a curious kind of flowing oriental robe, and waited to see what it would do next. The old man sat down almost at his feet and pulled something out from between the folds of his wide robe. It was a bag. The old man undid it, and, picking it up by the bottom, shook it. Heavy packets in the shape of large rolls of coins fell on the floor with a dull thud; each roll was wrapped in blue paper, and each was clearly marked: 1,000 sovereigns. Thrusting his long, bony hands out of his wide sleeves, the old man began unwrapping the rolls. There was a gleam of gold. However deeply the artist had been disturbed in his mind, and however terror-stricken he was, he could not help looking with avidity at the gold, staring motionless as it came out of the paper in the bony hands of the old man, gleaming and ringing dully and faintly, and as it disappeared when the old man wrapped it up again. Then he noticed one roll of coins that had rolled farther away than the rest and was lying near the top of the bed where he could easily reach it with his hand. He grasped it almost convulsively and glanced in terror at the old man to see whether he had noticed it or not. But the old fellow seemed to be too busy to see anything. He collected all his packets, replaced them in the bag and, without even looking at him, retired behind the screen. Chartkov's heart beat wildly as he listened to the sound of the retreating footsteps in the room. He clasped the little packet more firmly in his hand, quivering in every limb, and suddenly he heard the footsteps coming back, nearer and nearer, to the screen: the old man must have discovered that one of the rolls was missing. And in another moment Chartkov saw him looking in again from behind the screen. In despair he clasped the packet in his hand with all the strength at his command, exerted every effort to make some movement, uttered a scream and . . . woke up.

He was bathed in a cold sweat; his heart was pounding away as fast as could be, his chest tightened, as though his last breath was about to leave it. "Was it only a dream?" he said, clasping his head with both his hands; but the amazing vividness of that apparition was not like a dream. For it was *after* he had awakened that he saw the old man disappearing inside the frame of the portrait, and he even caught a glimpse of the skirt of his wide robe, and he could still feel that only a minute ago he had been holding some heavy packet in his hand. Moonlight filled the room, and from the dark corners it picked out in one place a canvas, in another a plaster-of-Paris hand, in a third a piece of drapery left on a chair, in a fourth a pair of trousers and dirty boots. It was only then that he became aware of the fact that he was no longer lying in bed, but was standing in front of the portrait. How he had got there he could not for the life of him say. What surprised him even more was that the portrait was all uncovered and there was certainly no sheet to be seen anywhere. Paralysed with terror, he stood motionless before it and, as he gazed at it, he saw a pair of living human eyes fixing him with their stare. Cold sweat broke out on his brow; he wanted to run away, but his feet seemed to be rooted to the ground. And he could see that it was no longer a dream, for the old man's face began to stir and his lips began to protrude towards him, as though they wished to suck him dry. . . . With a loud shriek of despair he leapt back—and woke up.

"Was this, too, a dream?" His heart was beating so violently that it seemed about to burst. He groped round him with his hands. Yes, he was lying in bed in precisely the same position in which he had fallen asleep. There was the screen before him; moonlight flooded the room. He could see the portrait through the chink in the screen, covered with the sheet as he had left it before going to bed. So this, too, was a dream! But his clenched fist still felt as though something had been inside it. His heart was beating strongly, almost terrifyingly; the weight on his chest was unbearable. He fixed his eyes on the chink in the screen and looked steadily at the sheet. And now he could see clearly that the sheet began to unfold as though a pair of hands were struggling behind it, trying to throw it off. "Good Lord, what is all this?" he cried, crossing himself in despair, and woke up.

So this, too, was a dream. He jumped out of bed, half-crazed and bewildered, and he could not explain what was happening to him: whether he was suffering from the after-effects of a nightmare, or whether he had become the victim of the devil; whether he was feverish or delirious, or whether he had seen a real apparition. In an attempt to calm his overwrought nerves and to still his throbbing blood which pulsated feverishly through his veins, he went up to the window and opened the little ventilating pane. The cool breeze, blowing across his face, revived him. Moonlight was still lying on the roofs and white walls of the houses, though little clouds were now scudding more frequently across the sky. All was still; only at rare intervals could he hear the faint, distant creaking of a cab, the driver of which must have fallen asleep on his box in some out-of-the-way lane, lulled by his lazy nag while waiting for a belated fare. He went on gazing for a long time, his head thrust out of the window. Signs of the approaching dawn were already perceptible in the sky; at last he felt drowsy, shut the ventilating pane, left the window, went back to bed and was soon sound asleep.

He woke up very late. He had a splitting headache and he felt sick like a man suffering from coal-gas poisoning. It was a dull, dismal day; a thin drizzle of rain was falling outside and the moisture was coming through the crevices of the windows against which pictures and primed canvases were piled. Sullen and disgruntled like a wet cockerel, he sat down on his tattered sofa, without an idea in his head what to do or how set about doing anything. At last he remembered his dream. The more of it he recalled, the more depressingly real it became in his imagination, and he even began to wonder whether it had been a dream or a hallucination. Had it not been something more than that? A vision perhaps? He pulled down the sheet and examined the dreadful portrait in the light of day. The eyes, it was true, were rather strikingly alive, but there

73

was nothing in them to make him feel nervous; all that had remained of his terrors of the night was quite an unaccountable feeling of uneasiness. Yet even now he was not sure that it had only been a dream. He could not help feeling that among the different incidents in his dream there was some appalling fragment of reality. There was, for instance, something in the look of the old man and in the expression of his face which seemed to say that he had paid him a visit during the night; his hand still felt the weight of the heavy packet, as though someone had only snatched it away a minute ago. He had the odd feeling that if only he had held on to it more firmly the packet would have remained in his hand after he had awakened.

"Lord, if only I had a little bit of that money!" he murmured, fetching a deep sigh, and in his imagination he could see those packets again, each inscribed alluringly: 1,000 sovereigns, tumbling out of the bag. They opened up, the gold gleamed, then they were wrapped up again. . . . He was sitting on his torn sofa, his eyes staring vacantly at nothing, unable to tear his thoughts away from so fascinating a vision, like a child sitting in front of some particularly delectable sweet with his mouth watering as he watches others at the table eating it.

Presently there came a knock at the door which brought him back to reality with a disagreeable bump. His landlord came in, together with the district police inspector, whose appearance, as is well known, is more disturbing to people of small means than the face of a petitioner is to the wealthy.

The landlord of the small house where Chartkov lived belonged to the class of persons who are commonly owners of houses somewhere in Fifteenth Row in Vassilyev Island, in the Petersburg district, or in some remote corner of Kolomna—persons who are to be found in great numbers all over Russia and whose character is as difficult to describe as the colour of a threadbare frock-coat. In his young days he had been a captain in the army, and was also often employed in civil affairs, a big bully and a great believer in flogging; he was rather efficient in a way, though stupid, and a bit of a dandy. But in his old age all those striking peculiarities of his character became merged into a kind of uniform dullness. He had been a widower for some time; he had been in retirement for some time; he was no longer a dandy; and he had even left off bragging and bullying. All he cared for now was his cup of tea and an opportunity of gossiping over it. He used to spend his time pacing his room, snuffing the candle end, calling upon his tenants punctually at the end of each month for the rent, and, key in hand, would go into the street to have a look at the roof of his house. He routed the caretaker several times a day out of his den where he usually sneaked off to sleep; in short, he was a retired army officer who, after a gay and dissolute life and after years of being jolted about in post-chaises, was left with only a few insipid, conventional habits.

"You can see for yourself, sir," said the landlord to the police officer with a deprecatory wave of the hands. "He just doesn't pay his rent. Just doesn't pay!"

"What do you expect me to do if I have no money," said Chartkov. "Can't you wait a little longer? I'll pay you."

"I'm afraid, sir, I can't wait," said the landlord crossly, waving the key in his hand. "I'm used to decent tenants, sir. Lieutenant-Colonel Potogonkin has been living in my house for seven years; Anna Petrovna Bukhmisterova has rented the coach-house and the stables with two stalls, keeps three servants—that's the kind of tenants I have. I am not in the habit, sir, of having trouble with my tenants about the rent, and that's the truth. Will you please be so good as to pay at once or look for another place!"

"Well, sir, if you've undertaken to pay, you have to pay," said the police inspector with a slight shake of the head, pushing a finger between the buttons of his uniform.

"But what am I to pay him with? That's the question. You see, I haven't got a penny."

"In that case, sir, you'd better satisfy Ivan Ivanovich by giving him some of your pictures," said the police officer. "He might agree to be paid in pictures."

"No, sir, thank you very much! No pictures for me. I might have considered it if this gentleman's pictures were anything decent, something you could hang on a wall, such as a general with a star, or a portrait of Prince Kutuzov, but look at those pictures of his! There, if you please, is a portrait of a peasant, a peasant in a shirt, a portrait of his servant, the young feller who grinds his paints for him. Now fancy painting a portrait of that oaf! I shall give him a good thrashing one day; he's been removing all the nails from my bolts, the rascal! . . . Look at the kind of things he paints. There's a picture of his room. Now what I'd like to know, sir, is why if he must paint his room he doesn't tidy it up first. Look at that! Painted it with all the filth and rubbish on the floor! See what a mess he's made of my flat? I tell you, sir, some of my tenants have been living in my house for over seven years! Gentlemen, sir, colonels! Anna Petrovna Bukhmisterova. . . . No, sir, there's no worse tenant in the world than an artist. Lives like a pig and doesn't pay his rent! It's just a scandal, sir!"

And the poor artist had to listen patiently to all this. Meanwhile the police inspector amused himself by an examination of the pictures and sketches, showing at once that he had a much more sensitive imagination than the landlord and that his soul was not altogether impervious to artistic impressions.

"Ah," he said, poking a finger into a picture of a nude, "nice bit of goods that. . . . And what's that black mark doing under the nose of this fellow here? Been taking too much snuff, or what?"

"Shadow," Chartkov muttered gruffly, without looking at the policeman.

"But you should have put it somewhere else, sir," said the police officer. "Shows up too much under the nose. And whose portrait is that?" he went on, going up to the portrait of the old man. "Looks a bit of a horror, don't he? Wonder if he really did look so terrifying. Good gracious me! Seems to look through you, don't he? Makes your flesh creep. Who was your model?"

"Oh, some man . . ." said Chartkov.

He stopped short without finishing the sentence, for at that moment there was a loud crack. The police inspector must have grasped the frame of the portrait too firmly between his fingers, and, a policeman's grip being notoriously clumsy, the moulding at the side broke and fell into the hollow frame with the exception of one piece, which dropped out together with a packet wrapped in blue paper, which fell with a heavy thud on the floor. Chartkov's eyes immediately caught the inscription on the roll: 1,000 sovereigns, and he flew like mad to pick it up. Seizing it, he clasped it convulsively in his hand, which sank with the weight.

"I could have sworn I heard the jingling of money," said the police officer, who had heard the noise of something falling on the floor, but was not quick enough to see what it was owing to the lightning rapidity with which Chartkov picked up the roll of gold coins.

"What has it got to do with you whether I have anything or not?"

"All it's got to do with me, sir, is that you have to pay your landlord at once the rent you owe him. You seem to have the money, but you don't want to pay him. Isn't that so ?"

"All right, I'll pay him today."

"But why didn't you pay him before, sir ? Why give your land-lord all this trouble ? Why waste the time of the police, sir ?"

"I didn't want to touch that money. I shall pay him in full this evening and I'm leaving his flat tomorrow. I don't want to stay with such a landlord !"

"Well, it seems he'll pay you all right, sir," said the police officer, turning to the landlord. "But if he doesn't satisfy you in full this evening, he'll have to take the consequences, artist or no artist."

Having delivered this warning, the police inspector put on his three-cornered hat and walked out into the passage, followed by the landlord, whose head was lowered as though he were sunk in deep meditation.

"Thank God they've gone at last," said Chartkov as he heard the front door closing behind his visitors.

He looked out into the passage and, wishing to be left entirely alone, sent off Nikita on some errand. Then he locked the front door, and returning to the studio, began unwrapping the packet with trembling hands and a wildly beating heart. The packet contained gold sovereigns, all new and red hot. Almost beside himself, the painter sat down in front of the heap of gold, asking himself all the time whether he were not seeing it in a dream. There were exactly one thousand sovereigns in the roll, which before he had unwrapped it looked exactly as he had seen it in his dream. He turned the coins over in his hand for some time, examining them, and unable to regain his composure. Stories came crowding into his mind of hidden treasures, cabinets with secret drawers, left by grandfathers to their spendthrift grandchildren in the firm belief that the money would restore their fortunes. It occurred to him that some grandfather might have wished to leave his grandson a present and had hidden it in the frame of a family portrait. Full of such wildly romantic ideas, he wondered whether there were not some mysterious connexion here with his own fate, whether the existence of the portrait was not in some way connected with his own existence, and whether the very fact of its acquisition by him was not due to some kind of predestination. He began examining the frame of the portrait with particular interest. There was a hollowed-out space at the side of the frame, so skilfully and neatly closed up by a little board that if the heavy hand of the police officer had not smashed through it, the gold coins would have remained undisturbed for ever. Looking closely at the portrait, he was again struck by the high quality of its workmanship and the extraordinary treatment of the eyes : they no longer frightened him, and yet every time he looked at them he could not help experiencing a curiously unpleasant sensation. "Well, sir," he apostrophised the portrait mentally, "I don't know whose grandfather you are, but I'm going to put you behind glass all the same and I'll get you a fine gilt frame for having been so good to me." Then he put his hand on the heap of gold coins which lay before him, and his heart began beating fast at the touch.

"What shall I do with them ?" he thought, looking at the big pile of gold sovereigns on the table. "Now I have nothing to worry about for at least three years. I can shut myself up in my room and work. I have enough money to pay for my paints, my dinners, my teas, my rent, everything ! No one will worry me or interfere with my work ; I can buy myself an excellent lay-figure, order a plaster torso, model some legs and feet, set up a Venus, get myself copies of the most famous pictures. And if I go on working for the next three years, without hurry or fuss, without caring a hoot whether my pictures sell or not, I can knock the whole lot of them into a cocked hat, and I can become an excellent painter into the bargain !"

That was what he was saying to himself at the prompting of his reason ; but within him another voice was making itself heard louder and louder. And when he looked at the gold again, his twenty-two years and his ardent youth said something quite different to him. For now everything he had hitherto been looking upon with such envious eyes was within his reach ; now he could have everything that had made his mouth water in the past, everything he had only been able to admire from a distance. Oh, how his young heart began to throb at the mere thought of it ! To be dressed in the height of fashion, to be able to afford a real feast after so long a fast, to be able to rent a fine flat, to go to the theatre any time he liked, or to a pastrycook's, or to . . . and so on and so forth. He picked up the money, and in another instant he found himself in the street. The first thing he did was to go to a fashionable tailor and get himself dressed in the smartest clothes, dressed like a man of fashion from head to foot ; and having got himself fitted out, he kept admiring himself incessantly, like a child. Next he bought all sorts of scents and pomades ; then he rented the first magnificent flat on

Nevsky Avenue he came across, without haggling over the price. He further acquired (quite by the way) an expensive *lorgnette* and (also quite by the way) a huge quantity of various cravats, many more than he would ever be likely to use. He then visited a hairdresser's and had his hair curled; drove twice in a carriage through the main thoroughfares of the city without rhyme or reason; went into a pastrycook's and gorged himself on sweets; and, finally, treated himself to a dinner at one of the most select French restaurants in town about which the rumours that had reached him were as vague as the rumours about the Chinese Empire. There he had dinner in grand style, looking rather disdainfully at the other diners and constantly arranging his curled locks in the mirror. He drank a bottle of champagne which till now he had also known chiefly by hearsay. The wine went to his head and he left the restaurant in high feather, as though he were Old Nick's best friend, as the Russian saying has it. He strutted along the pavement, ogling everyone through his *lorgnette*. On the bridge he caught sight of his old professor and darted past him with his nose in the air, leaving the poor professor quite flabbergasted, rooted to the spot, an interrogation mark frozen on his face.

The same evening all his things, everything he possessed in the world—his easel, his canvases and his pictures—were moved to his new magnificent flat. Putting the best of them in the most conspicuous places and the worst in some obscure corner, he walked about for hours from one handsome room to another, continually looking at himself in the mirrors. His soul yearned with an irresistible desire to become famous overnight and show the world what a fine fellow he was. He could already hear the cries, "Chartkov, Chartkov, Chartkov! Have you seen Chartkov's latest? What sureness of touch! What intense perception of truth! What amazing speed! What genius!" He paced the rooms in a state of growing exultation, carried away by the wonderful vistas that opened up before him. Next day, taking ten gold sovereigns with him, he went to see the editor of a popular daily whom he intended to ask for his kind assistance. The journalist received him very cordially, immediately addressed him as "my dear fellow," pressed both his hands, made a careful note of his name and address, and on the very next day there appeared in the paper, below a notice of some newly invented tallow candles, the following article under the heading:

79

Chartkov's Remarkable Genius

"We are sure that every cultured reader of our paper will be glad to hear of the wonderful acquisition our capital has just made, an acquisition that is highly desirable from every point of view. No one, we venture to think, will deny that we have among us many handsome men and many beautiful and charming ladies, but so far we have lacked the means of immortalising them in paint so that posterity may admire them as much as we do. We are now glad to be able to state that this omission has been made good. An artist has at last been found who combines everything that is required for so high and responsible a task. No beautiful lady need any longer despair of being depicted in all her grace and charm, light, airy, lovely, and bewitching as a butterfly fluttering over spring flowers. The respectable head of a large family can now behold himself surrounded by all its members. The merchant, the warrior, the citizen, the statesman —everybody can now pursue his work or profession with fresh zeal. We would like to give them one word of advice, though: *Do not delay your visit to the studio of this remarkable artist !* Go there immediately, wherever you are or whatever you happen to be doing, whether you are out for a drive in your carriage, or on your way to visit a friend or a cousin, or doing some shopping in one of our large emporia. The artist's magnificent studio (Nevsky Avenue, number so-and-so) is filled with portraits from his brush, portraits that we do not hesitate to say are worthy of a Van Dyck or a Titian. It is hard to know what to admire most: the truth with which a likeness has been caught, the resemblance to the original, or the quite extraordinary and amazing brightness and freshness of the painting as a whole. We congratulate this artist: all glory to him ! We wish you every success, Andrey Petrovich ! (The journalist must have cultivated a familiar style.) May you make yourself and your country famous ! We for one know how to value you, and we are sure that great popularity and with it also great riches—much as some of our fellow-journalists seem to despise the latter—will be your reward."

The artist read this notice with unconcealed delight. His face brightened; he was beginning to be talked of in print—that was quite a new experience to him, and he re-read the notice a few times. He felt greatly flattered by the comparison with Van Dyck and Titian. He also liked the phrase, "We wish you every success, Andrey

Petrovich !" To be addressed in print by his Christian name was an honour that he had never known before. He began pacing the room quickly, ruffling his hair, sitting down in a chair for a minute and then jumping up again and sitting down on the sofa. He tried to imagine how he would receive the ladies and gentlemen who came to sit for him, and he walked up to a canvas and began making all sorts of grand gestures with the brush over it in an attempt to discover which of them lent more grace to his hand. On the following day his doorbell rang. He ran to open the door. A lady, preceded by a footman in a livery with a fur lining, entered, followed by a girl of eighteen, her daughter.

"Are you Mr. Chartkov ?" the lady asked.

The artist bowed.

"The papers have been writing such a lot about you. I'm told your portraits are simply marvellous!" Having said this, the lady raised her *lorgnette* to her eyes and went quickly to look at the walls, on which, however, there was nothing to be seen. "But where are your portraits ?"

"Oh, I've had them removed," said the artist, somewhat taken aback. "I've only just moved into this flat and—er—I'm afraid they're still on the way. . . . Haven't arrived yet."

"Have you been to Italy ?" asked the lady, eyeing him through her *lorgnette*, having found nothing else to look at.

"No, ma'am, I haven't been to Italy. I—er—wanted to go, but I've had to put it off for the time being, I'm afraid. . . . Won't you sit down ? Here are arm-chairs. You must be tired. . . ."

"No, thank you. I've been sitting a long time in the carriage. Ah, there it is ! At last I can see one of your works !" cried the lady, running to the opposite wall and looking through her *lorgnette* at his sketches, studies, interiors and portraits which were standing on the floor. "*C'est charmant, Lise. Lise, venez ici !* Look, an interior in the style of Teniers. Do you see ? Everything in a most frightful disorder : a table, a bust on the table, a hand, a palette. Look at the dust, my dear ! How wonderfully the dust has been painted ! *C'est charmant !* And there's a painting of a girl washing her face—*quelle jolie figure !* Oh, Lise, Lise, look at that jolly young peasant ! A peasant in a Russian shirt ! Look, my dear, a peasant ! So you don't confine yourself to portraits, do you ?"

"Oh, that's nothing. . . . Just a few studies. Been amusing myself. . . ."

"Tell me, what is your opinion of our modern portrait painters ? It's true, isn't it, that we haven't got anyone today who can be even compared with Titian ? They haven't the same strong colours . . . that . . . that . . . I'm afraid I can't express it in Russian." (Chartkov's first visitor was a great admirer of painting and had rushed through all the art galleries in Italy with her *lorgnette*.) "But M. Zéro; ah, what a wonderful painter ! What marvellous genius ! I find there is even more subtlety in his faces than in Titian's. Haven't you heard of M. Zéro ?"

"I'm afraid I haven't."

"M. Zéro ! Oh, what a genius ! He painted a picture of my daughter when she was only twelve. You must come to see us. Lise, you must show Mr. Chartkov your album. You know, we came to see you today so that you could start on her portrait at once."

"Why, yes . . . of course . . . I . . . I can start at once."

And in a twinkling he pulled out the easel to the middle of the room, put a canvas he had ready on it, picked up his palette and fixed his gaze on the pale face of his visitor's daughter. If he had been a judge of character, he would have at once discerned in it the dawning of a childish passion for balls, the first signs of boredom during the long periods of waiting before and after dinner, the eagerness to show herself in a new dress in public, the heavy traces of her uninspired application to the various arts which her mother insisted that she should study to improve her mind and refine her feelings. But all the artist saw in this delicate little face was an almost porcelain transparency of skin, so irresistible to the brush; a charming, faintly perceptible languor; a slender, lovely, gleaming neck; and an aristocratic slenderness of figure. And he was already triumphing beforehand as he thought how he would show off the lightness and brilliance of his brushwork, for until now he had painted only the harsh features of coarse models, or the severe lines of ancient sculptures, or made copies of some classical masters. He could see already in his mind's eye how this sweet little face would look on canvas.

"You know," said the lady with quite a rapturous expression on her face, "I'd very much like to . . . You see, she's wearing an ordinary dress now. . . . Well, I don't mind telling you that I shouldn't like her to be painted in a dress which we're so used to. I should like her to be dressed quite simply and to sit in the shade of a tree, with fields in the background or just a wood. You see, I don't want anything that might suggest that she is about to go to a ball or some fashionable party or something of the sort. . . . Our balls, you know, have such a devastating effect on the spirit; so deadening, I mean. . . . They destroy all that remains of our feelings. . . . What I want is simplicity, as much simplicity as possible."

(Alas ! From the faces of both mother and daughter it could be clearly perceived that they had spent so much of their energy in dancing at balls that they had almost turned into wax figures.)

Chartkov set to work. He put his sitter in the best possible position, got a rough idea what he was going to do, waved the brush in the air, making a few rapid mental notes, different points of composition, screwed up his eyes a little, retreated a few steps to look at the girl from a distance, and in one hour finished the rough sketch of the portrait. Feeling satisfied with it, he began painting in earnest, feeling carried away by his work. He seemed to have forgotten everything, even that he was in the presence of two aristocratic ladies, and lapsed sometimes into certain artistic mannerisms, such as ejaculating all sorts of sounds, humming a tune from time to time, as is usual with an artist who becomes engrossed in his work. With one movement of his brush and without the slightest ceremony he made his sitter raise her head, which she at last could hardly keep still for a moment, for she was beginning to show unmistakable signs of fatigue.

"That'll do," said the mother. "That's quite enough for the first sitting."

"Just another touch," pleaded the artist, completely forgetting himself.

"No, thank you so much. It's really time we went. Lise, three o'clock !" she said, taking out a watch, suspended on a gold chain from her waist and exclaiming, "Goodness, how late !"

"Please just give me one more minute !" said Chartkov in the innocent and imploring voice of a little boy.

But the lady was not at all disposed to humour his artistic demands on this occasion and promised to stay longer another time instead.

"What a pity," Chartkov thought to himself. "I was just getting into my stride !"

And he could not help remembering that no one ever interfered with him or stopped him in his studio on Vassilyev Island. Nikita used to sit for hours in the same pose without moving—he could have gone on painting him for ever; he would even fall asleep in the same pose. And feeling rather out of humour, Chartkov put down his brush and palette on a chair and stopped rather vaguely before the canvas. A compliment paid him by the society woman roused him from his reverie. He flew to the door to see them off; on the staircase he received an invitation to dinner for the next week. He returned to his flat looking very cheerful. He thought the woman of fashion exceptionally charming. He had always looked upon such beings as something unapproachable, beings born for the sole purpose of driving along the street in magnificent carriages with liveried footmen and gorgeous coachmen and casting glances of cold indifference on some poor devil trudging along on foot in a cheap, shabby cloak. And suddenly one of those beings had actually been to see him in his rooms; he was painting a portrait of her daughter; he had been invited to dinner to an aristocratic house. He felt so pleased and delighted that he celebrated his first success by an excellent dinner, an evening show and another ride in a carriage through the city for no particular purpose.

During the following days it never occurred to him to carry on with his ordinary work. He was only making ready for the next visit, waiting impatiently for the bell to ring. At last the aristocratic lady with her charming, pale daughter arrived. He made them sit down, pulled out the easel with a certain bravado and an affectation of social airs and graces, and set to work on the girl's portrait. The sunny day and the bright light helped him a great deal. In the sweet face of his sitter he saw much that, if only he succeeded in catching it and putting it on canvas, would lend great distinction to the portrait. He perceived that he could make an exceptionally good job of it if only he could carry out fully his present conception of what his picture should be like when finished. His heart even began beating a little faster when he felt sure that he would be able to bring something out that no one seemed to have noticed in a face before. He became so absorbed in his work that he was aware of nothing but his painting, completely oblivious of the fact that his sitter was a person of quality. With ever mounting excitement, he saw how marvellously well he managed to bring out those subtle features and the almost transparent flesh tints of the seventeen-year-old girl. He caught every shade, the slight sallowness, the almost imperceptible blueness under the eyes, and he was even about to put in the little pimple on her forehead, when he suddenly heard her mother's voice over him, "Gracious me, you're not going to put that in, surely? That's quite unnecessary," she said. "And in a few places you got it a little too yellowish, don't you think? Here, for instance; and there it looks as if she had some dark spots on her skin. . . ." The artist tried to explain that the dark spots and the yellow tint blended so well because they brought out the soft, pleasing tones of the face. But he was told that they did not bring out any tones and did not blend at all, and that he was merely imagining it.

"But," said the artist good-naturedly, "please let me add just a touch of yellow here. Just in this one place."

But he was not allowed to do anything of the sort, it being announced that Lise was a little indisposed that day, that she never was sallow and that her complexion had indeed always been remarkably fresh. Sadly he began removing what his artistic instinct had made him put on the canvas. Many almost imperceptible touches disappeared and with them the resemblance to the original partly disappeared also. Apathetically he began imparting to the portrait that conventional colouring which is daubed on mechanically and which transforms even faces drawn from life into those coldly ideal faces one finds only in the sketches of art students. But the society woman was pleased that the unflattering tints had been completely eliminated. She merely expressed her surprise that the work was taking so long, adding that she was told that he usually finished a portrait in two sittings.

After they had gone, Chartkov stopped for a long time before the unfinished picture, gazing stupidly at it, while his head was full of those soft, feminine features, those shades and ethereal tones, he had observed and which his own brush had so pitilessly removed. Being full of them, he took the portrait off the easel and began looking for the head of Psyche he had sketched roughly on a canvas a long time ago but had put away somewhere. He found it. It was a lovely girlish face, cleverly drawn but completely idealised, with the cold conventional features which did not seem to belong to any living body. Having nothing else to do, he now began going over it, retracing on it everything he had happened to observe in the face of his aristocratic sitter. The features, shades and tones caught by him appeared on it in a refined form in which they occasionally appear on the paintings of an artist who, having made a close study from nature, moves away from it and creates a work of art which is like it and yet independent of it. Psyche began to come to life and the as yet faintly dawning idea began gradually to be clothed into a visible body. The type of the face of the young society girl was unconsciously transferred to Psyche's face and through this it received a unique individuality which entitles a work of art to be considered as truly original. He seemed to have made use of certain idiosyncrasies of his sitter and of the whole impression of her as created in his mind, and he kept working on it, and for the next two days did nothing else.

It was while he was working on this picture that the ladies arrived again. He did not have time to take the picture off the easel and, seeing it, the two ladies uttered a cry of joy, throwing up their hands in amazement.

"Lise ! Lise ! Look, how extraordinarily like you ! *Superbe! Superbe!* What a clever idea to dress her in a Greek costume. Oh, what a pleasant surprise !"

The painter did not know how to disillusion them, seeing that they were so pleased with being deluded. Feeling rather ashamed, he said, without looking at them, "This is Psyche. . . ."

"You mean you painted her as Psyche ? *C'est charmant!*" said the mother with a smile, and her daughter smiled, too. "Don't you think, Lise, you look really lovely as Psyche ? *Quelle idée délicieuse!* But what a work of art ! It's . . . it's a Correggio ! I have of course read and heard about you, but to tell you the truth I never thought you had such a talent. You simply must paint my portrait, too !"

It was quite evident that the mother also wanted to be painted as some kind of Psyche.

"What am I to do with them ?" thought the artist. "If they have set their hearts on it, let Psyche be what they imagine it to be." And aloud he said, "Would you mind posing for a few more minutes ? I want to touch up a few things."

"Oh, I'm afraid you might. . . . I mean, the picture looks so like her now !"

But the artist realised that she was afraid he might add some yellow tints on the face, and he reassured her, saying that he would only add a little more brilliance and expression to the eyes. To be quite just, he felt rather ashamed of himself and he wanted to impart just a little more similitude to the portrait for fear that otherwise he might be accused of being guilty of a barefaced fraud. And the features of the pale young girl did in the end appear more clearly in Psyche's face.

"That's enough!" said the mother, who was beginning to fear that the portrait might show too close a resemblance to her daughter.

The artist was generously rewarded: smiles, money, and compliments were showered upon him. He had his hand pressed in real gratitude; he was invited to dinners; in short, he was overwhelmed with a thousand flattering encomiums.

The portrait created a sensation in town. The society woman showed it to her friends, and everybody was in raptures over the art with which the painter had succeeded in preserving the likeness of the original and at the same time adding beauty to it. The last remark was of course made not without a touch of malice. The artist was suddenly snowed under with work. It seemed as though the whole town wanted to be painted by him. His door-bell rang continuously. This might, on the one hand, have turned out to be rather a good thing for him, for it provided him with endless opportunities for practice by the sheer diversity and multiplicity of the faces of the sitters. But, unfortunately, they all belonged to a class of people whom it was very difficult to manage, people who were always in a hurry, always busy, or who belonged to the polite world and, consequently, were more busy than anyone else and therefore impatient to excess. They all demanded that his work should be both good and quick. The artist realised that it was absolutely impossible to finish any portrait and that he would have to substitute cleverness, rapidity and superficial brilliance for everything else. To capture merely the general expression as a whole and not to probe with his brush into the finer details—in fact, he found it almost impossible to follow nature to the bitter end. Moreover, nearly all his sitters made all sorts of stipulations of one kind or another. The ladies demanded that as a rule only soul and spirit should be shown on their portraits, that in certain circumstances the rest should be completely ignored, that all the angularities should be rounded off, all the defects touched up and even, if possible, eliminated altogether. What they wanted, in fact, was that their faces should be generally admired, if not indeed that men should fall in love with them at first sight. As a result, many ladies, when posing, assumed expressions that quite startled the artist. One tried to give her face a melancholy cast; another tried to look dreamy; a third was quite determined to make her mouth look as small as possible and she screwed it up so much that it finally turned into a point not bigger than a pinhead. And in spite of all that, they all wanted their portraits to be like them, demanding, moreover, that he should make them look artless and natural. The men were no whit better than the women. One insisted that his profile should express strength and energy; another wanted his eyes to be raised and to look inspired; a Lieutenant of the Guards demanded that Mars should be plainly visible in his eyes; a civil servant was absolutely set on having more frankness and nobility in his face and that one of his hands should rest on a book bearing the clearly legible inscription: "He Always Upheld Truth."

At first all these demands threw the artist into a cold sweat: he felt that all that had to be carefully considered and thought over, and yet he was given precious little time to do it in. At last he realised what it was all about and found the whole thing as easy as anything. Two or three words were enough to give him a pretty good idea what his sitter wanted to be portrayed as. If one showed a partiality for Mars, he thrust Mars into his face; if someone else had an ambition to look like Lord Byron, he obliged him with a Byronic pose and profile. If the ladies wished to be shown as Madame de Stael's heroine Corinne, or Lamotte-Fouqué's heroine Undine, or as Aspasia, he was only too glad to please them all, throwing in a plentiful supply of good looks on his own account, which, as the whole world knows, can do no harm and will make up for any want of resemblance. Soon he began to marvel himself at the amazing rapidity and smartness of his brush. And it is unnecessary to add that all his sitters were in raptures about his portraits and proclaimed him a genius.

Chartkov became a fashionable painter in every sense of the word. He was invited to dinners; he escorted society women to picture galleries and even went for drives with them. He was always immaculately dressed, and was heard again and again to express the opinion that an artist must belong to society, that he had to uphold the honour of his profession, that artists as a rule dressed like cobblers, that their manners were atrocious, that they had no idea of good taste, that they lacked every social refinement, and that they were, in fact, utter boors. At home, in his studio, everything was now very tidy and spotlessly clean. He employed two magnificent footmen; he had a large following of well-groomed pupils; he changed a few times a day into all sorts of morning coats; he had his hair waved regularly; gave a great deal of attention to improving his deportment with different types of callers; devoted much time to beautifying his appearance in every possible way so as to make the best and most pleasing impression upon the ladies; in short, very soon it was quite impossible to recognise in him that modest and unassuming artist who had once worked so obscurely in his miserable little flat on Vassilyev Island. About art and artists he now expressed very decided opinions; he affirmed that too much merit had been allowed the old masters and that all the painters could paint before Raphael was herrings and not human figures; that the idea that in them one could feel the presence of some divine spirit existed merely in the imagination of their admirers; that many works of Raphael himself were far from perfect and that the fact that they were still considered masterpieces was due merely to the influence of tradition; that Michael Angelo was a cheap braggart because he merely wanted to show off his knowledge of anatomy, that there was not a jot or tittle of grace about him, and that real brilliance, real power of subtle drawing, real splendour of hue, could be found only among the modern painters. And here, quite naturally, he thought it necessary to make a few personal observations. "I can't understand," he used to say, "why some artists are so keen on slaving and drudgery. In my opinion a man who wastes several months on a picture isn't an artist at all. He is simply a hack. I can't believe he really possesses any talent at all. A genius works boldly, rapidly. Take myself, for instance," he declared, usually addressing one of his visitors. "This picture took me only two days to paint; that little head I did in one day; that one in a couple of hours; and that one in just over one hour. No, I must say quite frankly that I do not recognise anything as art that is produced laboriously, stroke by stroke. That's not art; that is craft !" So he harangued his visitors, and his visitors marvelled at the strength and cleverness of his brush, uttered cries of surprise on hearing how little time it had taken him to produce his pictures, and afterwards told each other, "That man's got talent, real talent ! Just look at him when he's speaking ! How his eyes flash ! *Il y a quelque chose d'extraordinaire dans toute sa figure !*"

The artist was flattered to hear such opinions expressed about him. When a notice praising his work appeared in some journal, he was as pleased as Punch about it, though this praise had been bought with his own money. He carried the press cutting about with him wherever he went, showing it with assumed casualness to his friends and acquaintances, as though it were something of no importance to him, and this really pleased him in a sort of good-natured, ingenuous way.

His fame spread, his works and orders multiplied. He was even beginning to weary of the same kind of portraits and faces, whose profiles and poses he now knew by heart. He lost all zest in his work, painting portraits without any particular enthusiasm, drawing a rough sketch of a head and leaving the rest to his pupils. Before then he had tried at any rate to find some kind of new pose for every sitter; he did his best to startle and stun his public by the forcefulness of his style of painting and by the ease with which he achieved his effects. But now even that gave him no more pleasure. His brain was weary of planning and thinking. He just could not go on doing it and, anyway, he had not the time: his rather dissipated mode of living and the polite society in which he tried to play the part of a man of the world—all that distracted him too much and left him no leisure either for thought or work. His hand lost its cunning, his paintings became cold and lifeless, and without noticing it himself he lapsed into monotonous, well-defined and long-worn-out forms. Monotonous, cold, eternally neat and tidy and, as it were, buttoned-up faces of Civil Servants and army officers did not give much scope to his brush, which was beginning to forget how to draw magnificent draperies, forceful movements and passions. As for composition, dramatic effect and its lofty purpose—not a trace of it remained. All he saw was a uniform or a corsage or a frock-coat, before which art wilts and imagination withers. His work lost even all ordinary distinction, and yet it was still popular, although real art experts and artists merely shrugged their shoulders when they saw his latest paintings. Some who had known Chartkov before were puzzled, for they could not understand how his talent, the signs of which were quite unmistakable at the beginning, could have vanished so completely, and they tried in vain to solve the mystery of how a man could have lost his gifts in the heyday of his power.

But the self-satisfied artist, intoxicated by his success, did not hear this criticism. He was already approaching the age when his mind and his habits were settling down into a rut: he began to put on flesh and was visibly expanding in girth. In the papers and journals he was already coming across the adjectives *distinguished* and *honoured* coupled with his name: "Our honoured Andrey Petrovich. . . . Our distinguished Andrey Petrovich. . . ." He was already being offered important posts in the Civil Service, invited to serve on boards of examiners and on committees. He was already beginning, as is usual when a man reaches the age of discretion, to take the part of Raphael and the old masters, not because he had convinced himself entirely of their transcendent merits, but because he enjoyed throwing them in the teeth of the younger artists. He was already beginning, as is the habit of men of his age, to accuse all young people indiscriminately of immoral and vicious trends of thought. He was already beginning to believe that everything in the world was achieved by simple methods, that there was no inspiration from above, and that everything must be subject to one strict rule of precision and uniformity. He had, in fact, reached the age when anything showing the slightest flash of inspiration is condemned and frowned upon, when even the mightiest chord reaches the spirit feebly and does not pierce a man's heart with its sound, when the touch of beauty no longer fans the virgin forces into fire and flame, but all burnt-out feelings respond more easily to the jingle of gold, hearken more attentively to its seductive music and little by little allow themselves unconsciously to be lulled to sleep by it. Fame cannot give pleasure to a man who has stolen it, to one who does not deserve it; it never fails to produce a thrill only in those who are worthy of it. For this reason all his feelings and desires became obsessed with gold. Gold became his passion, his ideal, his terror, his joy, his aim. The bundles of banknotes grew in his coffers, and, like every one who succumbs to the dreadful fascination of money, he became a bore; he was no longer interested in anything that did not bring in money; he became a miser for no reason at all, a vicious hoarder. He was in danger of becoming one of those strange human beings one meets in such large numbers in our callous world: human beings who are regarded with horror by men full of life and passion, to whom they seem to be walking coffins with a corpse where their hearts should be. But one event which occurred just then gave him so powerful a shock that all his dormant vitality was reawakened.

One day he found a note on his table in which the Academy of Art invited him, as one of its distinguished members, to go and give his opinion on a new painting sent from Italy by a Russian artist who had been pursuing his art there. The painter was one of his old fellow students who had from his earliest years devoted himself passionately to art and who had been working at it like a slave, his fiery spirit entirely dedicated to it. He had left his friends and relations, abandoned the mode of life to which he had become accustomed and which was dear to him, and hurried off to the country under whose beautiful skies art comes to full fruition, to the lovely city of Rome, the very name of which makes the ardent heart of an artist beat faster and more vigorously. There he buried himself in his work like a recluse and allowed no diversions to distract him. He did not care whether people discussed his character or not; whether he did or did not cut a figure in society; whether his manners were polished or not; whether his poor, shabby clothes brought the profession of an artist into disrepute. He cared even less whether his fellow artists were angry with him or not. He scorned everything. He gave himself up entirely to his art. He never wearied of visiting the art galleries, and he would stand for hours before the works of the great masters, studying every aspect of their genius and following every movement of their magic brush. He never finished anything without comparing his work several times with the work of these great teachers and without drawing from them a silent, yet eloquent lesson for himself. He never took part in noisy discussions and controversies; he neither defended nor condemned the purists. He gave every man his due and extracted from everything what was beautiful and true. He ended up by taking for his teacher one great master only—the divine Raphael, like a great poet who, after reading many works of every kind, full of many wonderful and sublime passages, leaves Homer's *Iliad* on his table as his constant book of reference, having discovered that it contains everything one can wish, and that there is nothing in the whole world that cannot be found in it expressed to perfection. And so he had gained from the study of his great master's works a sublime conception of creative art, an intense beauty of thought, and the superb loveliness of a divinely inspired brush.

When Chartkov entered the room, he found a large crowd of people already gathered before the picture. A profound silence, so rare among a large crowd of art lovers, this time pervaded the room. He hastened to assume the grave air of a connoisseur and approached the picture. But, dear God, what was it he saw?

Pure, perfect, lovely as a bride, the work of the artist stood before him. Modest, divine, innocent, and simple as genius itself, it towered over him. It was as though those heavenly figures, amazed at the multitude of eyes turned upon them, had modestly lowered their lovely eyelashes. The art experts studied the work of the new, unknown artist with a feeling of sheer astonishment. All seemed united in it: a study of Raphael, which was reflected in the high nobility of the composition, and a study of Correggio, which was expressed in the finished perfection of the artist's brush. But what appeared more powerfully than anything was the firmness of conception that emanated from the very soul of the artist himself. Every detail of the picture was pervaded by it: in everything law and innate strength was evident. Everywhere could be discerned that liquid roundness of lines, which nature alone seems to possess, which only the eye of the creative artist can see, and which in a copyist merely becomes angular. The artist, it could be plainly seen, had first of all absorbed everything he had received from the outside world and stored it up in his mind, and it was from there, from that living fountain of his spirit, that he had drawn it, transforming it into one harmonious, triumphant song. Even the uninitiated could now see how measureless is the gulf that separates creative art from a mere copy from nature. It is almost impossible to describe the unusual stillness which had fallen against their will upon all those whose eyes were fixed on the picture. Not a murmur could be heard, not a sound. Meanwhile the picture seemed every minute to assume grander and grander proportions; it seemed to become a thing apart, growing more brilliant and more and more wonderful until at last it was transformed into one flash of inspiration, into a blinding instant of time, the fruit of a thought that had descended to the artist from heaven, an instant compared with which the whole life of man is but a preparation. Involuntary tears filled the eyes of the visitors who had crowded round the picture and were about to roll down their cheeks. It was as if all tastes, all the arrogant, wrong-headed aberrations of taste had blended into one silent hymn of praise in honour of a divine work of art.

Chartkov stood motionless and with parted lips before the picture, and when at last the visitors and the art experts burst into talk and began discussing the merits of the painting, when at last they turned to him with a request to tell them what he thought of it, he came to himself. He tried to assume an air of indifference, tried to repeat the usual platitudes of dry-as-dust artists, something like, "Of course I don't want to run him down. The man certainly has talent and there is something in the picture which shows that he had certain ideas he wanted to express, but so far as the chief thing is concerned . . ." And then, needless to say, to utter the few words of praise which have damned many an artist. He wanted to do this, but the words died on his lips, and instead tears burst from his eyes, discordant sobs broke from his lips and he rushed out of the room like one distracted.

For a moment he stood motionless in the middle of his magnificent studio. All his senses seemed numbed. His whole being, every living part of him, had been awakened all at once, as though his youth had come back to him, as though the dead embers of his genius had burst into flame again. The scales suddenly fell from his eyes. O Lord, and to have ruined, so pitilessly ruined, the best years of his life, to have stamped out, to have quenched the spark of divine fire that perhaps glowed in his breast and that would perhaps by now have developed into greatness and beauty which, too, might have wrung tears of admiration and gratitude. And to have ruined it all, to have ruined it all without pity ! It seemed as though at that moment all those impulses and strivings he had once known had revived in his soul all of a sudden. He snatched up a brush and approached a canvas. Beads of perspiration came out on his brow. One desire took hold of him and only one thought filled his brain: he longed to paint a fallen angel. No idea could have been more in harmony with his present frame of mind. But, alas, his figures, attitudes, groupings, and thoughts looked forced and disconnected as they appeared on the canvas. For his painting and his imagination had too long conformed to one pattern, and his feeble attempts to escape the limits and fetters he had laid upon himself merely showed up his faults and blunders. He had disdained the long and wearisome stairway of the gradual accumulation of knowledge of the fundamental laws of art—the stairway to future greatness. He felt irritated, dejected, dismayed. He ordered all his latest works to be taken out of his studio, all those lifeless fashionable pictures, all those portraits of hussars, society women and state councillors. He then shut himself up in his studio, gave strict orders that no one should be admitted, and became absorbed in his work. He set to work with infinite patience, as though he were a young art student. But how mercilessly, how thanklessly did his brush expose his shortcomings ! At every step he was pulled up by his ignorance of the most elementary rules; his failure to master a simple and quite unimportant mechanical process damped all his enthusiasm and stood like an insurmountable obstacle in the way of his imagination. His hand unconsciously returned to the trite and commonplace forms to which it was so well accustomed: hands folded in one set way, head not daring to depart by an inch from the usual angle, even the folds of the garment following conventional lines and refusing to obey and drape themselves round a body in an unfamiliar position. And he knew it, he knew it! He felt it! He saw it all himself!

"But, good Lord, did I ever possess any talent?" he said at last. "Was I not mistaken?" And as he pronounced these words, he walked up to his old paintings which he had produced in so pure and unmercenary a spirit in that wretched flat of his in the lonely Vassilyev Island, far from the noisy crowds, far from all splendour and abundance, far from all sorts of cravings. He went up to them now and began examining them carefully. As he did so, all the details of his former poor existence came back to him. "Yes," he exclaimed in despair, "I had talent! I can see the traces of it everywhere! Everywhere there are signs of it!"

He stopped dead and suddenly trembled all over: his eyes met the motionless stare of the old man whose remarkable portrait he had bought in Pike's Yard. The old man's eyes seemed to be staring at him, boring through him! The portrait had been covered up all that time, concealed behind a stack of other pictures. He had forgotten all about it. But now after all the fashionable portraits and pictures which had filled the studio had been removed, it emerged, as though by design, together with the other pictures of his youth. As he recalled every detail of that strange incident of his life, as he recalled that in a way it was that strange portrait that was the cause of his transformation, that the hoard of money he had received in so miraculous a manner had awakened in him all those vain desires and passions which had destroyed his talent—as he recalled all that, he almost went off his head. He immediately ordered the hateful portrait to be taken out. But his mental excitement was not allayed by the mere fact of the removal of the portrait: his whole being, all his emotions were shaken to their foundations, and he suffered that dreadful torture which sometimes appears as a rare exception in nature when a man of small talent tries to fill a space too big for him and fails miserably; the kind of torture which in a young man may lead to greatness, but which in a man who should long ago have left the phase of idle dreams behind him is transformed into futile yearning; that terrible torture which renders a man capable of the most frightful crimes. He became obsessed with a horrible envy, an envy that bordered upon madness. His face became contorted with hatred when he saw a work that bore the stamp of genius. He ground his teeth and devoured it with a basilisk glance. A plan, the most monstrous plan ever conceived by man, was devised in his mind, and he threw himself into carrying it out with all the energy of a man possessed. He began buying up all the best works of art that came into the market. Having spent a fortune on a picture, he took it up carefully into his studio and there he flung himself upon it with the fury of a tiger, slashing it, tearing it, cutting it to pieces, stamping on it, and roaring with delighted laughter as he did so. The vast wealth he had amassed provided him with all the means for gratifying this fiendish passion. He opened his bags of gold. He unlocked his chests. No monster of ignorance ever destroyed so many wonderful works of art as were destroyed by this fierce avenger. At his appearance at an auction, everyone despaired of obtaining any work of art. It seemed as if the heavens in their wrath had sent this awful scourge into the world expressly for the purpose of depriving it of all harmony. This horrible passion threw a most horrible shadow upon his face: he now always looked at the world with jaundiced eyes. Scorn of the world and everlasting denial were stamped on his features. It was as though the terrible Demon of Pushkin's poem had been reincarnated in him. Words of venom and bitter reproof poured from his lips unceasingly. He walked through the streets like some harpy and, seeing him from a distance, all his acquaintances did their best to avoid him, for to meet him was enough to poison the whole day for them.

Fortunately for the world and for art, such a highly strung and violent life could not last long: the intensity of his passion was too abnormal and vast for his feeble strength. He began suffering more and more from fits of raving madness which, finally, took the form of a most dreadful disorder. A high fever combined with a galloping consumption took hold of him with such fierceness that in three days he was reduced to a shadow of his former self. To this were added all the symptoms of incurable madness. Sometimes it took several men to restrain him. He began to be haunted by the long-forgotten, living eyes of the strange portrait, and in those moments his insane fury was truly horrible. All the people who stood round his bed seemed to him like dreadful portraits. The portrait was doubled and quadrupled before his eyes; all the walls seemed to be hung with portraits, and their unmoving, living eyes were gazing fixedly upon him. Terrible portraits glared at him from the ceiling and from the floor; the room widened and lengthened endlessly to make room for more and more of those staring eyes. The doctor who had undertaken to treat him, and who had heard something of the strange story of his life, tried hard to find some connexion between the hallucinations of his brain and the events of his life, but without success. The sick man understood nothing and felt nothing except his own frightful agonies, and only uttered bloodcurdling screams or babbled incoherently. At length his life came to an end in a final —and this time silent—paroxysm of suffering. His corpse looked horrible. Nothing could be found of his great wealth; but the discovery of the savagely torn-up masterpieces, which must have cost millions, made people realise the terrible purpose they had served.

Part Two

Many carriages, chaises and cabs were standing before the entrance of a house in which an auction was taking place of the possessions of one of those wealthy art lovers who have an easy, comfortable life and gaily tread the primrose path of dalliance, acquiring quite innocently the reputation of art patrons and very amiably spending millions on works of art of all kinds, millions accumulated by their well-to-do, business-like fathers and grandfathers and, as often happens, even by their own hands during the early days of their life. Such patrons of the arts, needless to say, no longer exist; for our nineteenth century has long ago acquired the dull physiognomy of a banker whose sole delight is his millions, and those, too, in the shape of figures in ledgers. The long drawing-room was filled with a most miscellaneous crowd of people who had swooped down like birds of prey on an abandoned corpse. Here was a regular flotilla of Russian merchants from the Arcade as well as from the less fashionable markets, all in dark-blue coats of German cut. Their looks, the expression of their faces, were somehow more grave, more independent; they showed no trace of that excessive and rather extravagant servility which is so characteristic of a Russian shopkeeper in the presence of a customer in his shop. Here they were not so eager to parade their courtesies, in spite of the fact that in the same room were many of those aristocrats before whom, in any other place, they were ready to kowtow and sweep away the dust they themselves had brought in on their boots. Here they were completely at ease, fingered books and pictures without the slightest ceremony in their eagerness to find out the quality of the goods, and boldly outbid the noble art experts.

Here were many inveterate frequenters of public auctions who seemed to have made it a rule of their lives to be present at an auction every morning instead of having lunch at home; aristocrats who fancied themselves as art experts, and who deem it their duty never to miss a chance of adding to their collections and who anyway have nothing else to do between twelve and one o'clock; finally, the gentlemen whose clothes were as poor as their pockets were empty and who appear every day at an auction without any mercenary aim but just out of curiosity, to see who will bid more and who less, who will outbid whom, and to whom the goods will be knocked down. A large number of pictures were scattered all over the room without any attempt at classification, among pieces of furniture and books with the monogram of their former owner who most probably never had the laudable curiosity to look into them. Chinese vases, marble table-tops, modern and antique furniture with curved lines, adorned with the paws of griffons, sphinxes and lions, gilt and not gilt, chandeliers, sconces—all this lay about in confused heaps on the floor, not arranged in order as in shops. It was a veritable chaos of the fine arts. The feeling we generally get at an auction is rather uncomfortable: it all looks too much like a funeral procession. The room in which it takes place is rather gloomy; the windows are obstructed with furniture and pictures and give very little light; the silent faces and the funereal voice of the auctioneer, who keeps knocking with his little hammer and chanting a requiem for the poor arts which have met here under such strange circumstances. All this seems to emphasise even more the general unpleasant atmosphere of the place.

The auction was apparently in full swing. A whole crowd of eminently respectable people were huddled together in one spot and seemed to be very excited about something, each one trying to outbid the other. From every side came the words, "Rouble, rouble, rouble." They did not even give the auctioneer time to repeat the last bid which had already grown to four times the original offer. The crowd was excited about a portrait which could not but attract the attention of anyone with the most rudimentary knowledge of painting. The hand of a master was clearly discernible in it. The portrait had quite clearly been restored several times as well as revarnished, and showed the features of some oriental gentleman in a wide robe and with an unusual, strange expression on his face, though the people who crowded round it were most

98

of all struck by the remarkable vitality of his eyes. The longer a person looked at them, the more did they seem to bore right through him. This peculiarity, this extraordinary whim of the artist, attracted the attention of almost everyone. Many of the bidders for the picture had had to withdraw from the sale, for the price offered for it was quite incredible. There remained only two well-known aristocrats, great collectors of paintings, who seemed equally determined to secure the picture. They were both in a ferment of excitement and they would have most certainly gone on outbidding each other till the picture was knocked down for quite a fantastic price, if one of the men who had been examining it had not said, "Allow me, gentlemen, to interrupt your competition for a while. You see, I perhaps more than anyone else have a right to the picture." These words immediately drew the attention of everybody in the room to the speaker. They were uttered by a tall and slender man of about thirty-five, with long black hair. His pleasant face, full of a kind of gay light-heartedness, showed a character free of all worldly care; there was no pretence to fashion in his dress: everything about him indicated the artist. He was, in fact, the artist B., whom many people in the room knew personally.

"However strange my words may sound to you," he went on, seeing that everybody in the room was looking at him, "you will, I think, admit, if you will be so kind as to listen to my little story, that I had every right to speak them. Everything convinces me that this is the portrait I am looking for."

A quite natural curiosity took possession of almost everybody in the room, and even the auctioneer himself stopped short, openmouthed and with raised hammer, prepared to listen. At the beginning of the story many people quite involuntarily turned again and again to have a look at the portrait, but as the story got more and more interesting everyone's gaze was directed only at the artist.

"I suppose you all know that part of the town which is called Kolomna," he began. "Everything there is quite unlike any other part of St. Petersburg. There we are no longer in a capital city, and not even in the provinces. Indeed, as you walk through the streets of Kolomna, you seem to feel all the desires and passions of youth leaving you. There the future seems never to bother to look in; there everything is quiet, silent, dead; there everything is suggestive of retirement from active life, everything is in strange and striking contrast to the movement and noise of a capital city. The people who live there are for the most part retired Civil Servants, widows, poor people, people who seem at one time or another to have had some acquaintance with the Supreme Court and who have therefore sentenced themselves to life imprisonment in that district; cooks no longer in service who spend the whole day in the street markets, gossiping in the small grocers' shops with the shopkeepers, and who every day spend a few pence on a little coffee and a quarter of a pound of sugar, and, lastly, that class of people who can be summed up by the word ashen-grey, people whose clothes, faces, hair, and eyes have a kind of dingy, ashen appearance, like a day which is neither sunny nor stormy, but something betwixt and between: a slight mist covers everything and robs every object of its sharp outlines. Here, too, we may add the retired titular councillors and the retired military men with an eye missing and a swollen lip. These people are entirely apathetic. They go about without looking at anything; they are silent and yet do not seem to be thinking of anything. You won't find much in their rooms, except perhaps sometimes a bottle of pure Russian vodka, which they go on sipping all day without any particular enthusiasm and without any strong rush of blood to their heads that follows too much drinking, such as the young German artisan likes to indulge in on a Sunday, that dare-devil of the slums who is the sole monarch of the pavement after midnight.

"Life in Kolomna is terribly dull; you rarely come across a carriage in its streets, except perhaps one carrying the actors to and from the theatre, which alone breaks the universal silence by its clatter and loud din. Here almost every one goes on foot, and a cab very often crawls along at a snail's pace without a fare, but with a bundle of hay for its bearded nag. You can easily find a flat there for ten shillings a month, with morning coffee thrown in. Widows with pensions form the aristocracy in that part of the town; they behave with the utmost propriety, sweep their rooms at fairly frequent intervals and discuss with their lady friends the dearness of beef and cabbage; very often they share their rooms with their young daughters, silent, mute, though sometimes quite good-looking creatures, with disgusting lap dogs and clocks with dismally ticking pendulums. Then there are the actors whose meagre pay does not allow them to live in any other part of the town, free and easy folk, living, like all artists, as they please. At home they sit about in their dressing-gowns, repairing a pistol, or gluing together out of

100

cardboard all sorts of things that might come in useful in the house, or playing draughts or cards with their friends, and so spend the whole morning and do almost the same thing in the evening, except occasionally with the addition of a glass of punch. Besides these grand seigneurs and aristocrats of Kolomna, there is the usual small fry. It is as difficult to name or number them as it is to enumerate the multitude of insects in stale vinegar. Among them you will find old women who are constantly saying their prayers; old women who are constantly drinking; old women who both pray and drink; old women who eke out a miserable existence by means that pass all understanding, who, like ants, drag all sorts of things on their backs, such as old clothes and linen, from Kalinkin Bridge to the old junk market to sell them there for tuppence-half-penny; in fact, you will find there the very dregs of humanity whose position even a benevolent economist would find it hard to improve.

"I mention all this just to let you see how often these poor people are driven by necessity to obtain some immediate, temporary help by resorting to borrowing; for the presence of such people usually attracts a certain type of money-lender who settles among them and supplies them with small loans on any kind of security at a high rate of interest. These small money-lenders are a hundred times more hard-hearted than any big money-lender, for they live in the slums among a poverty-stricken population clad in rags that the rich money-lender who only deals with people who drive about in carriages never sees. This is why every human feeling dies in them so soon.

"Among these money-lenders there was one. . . . But perhaps I'd better tell you straight away that the events I am about to relate occurred in the last century in the reign of the late Empress Catherine II. You will, of course, realise that since then the very appearance of Kolomna and the life of its inhabitants have greatly changed. Well, among these money-lenders there was a certain person, a remarkable man in every respect, who had settled in that part of the town a long time ago. He went about in a flowing oriental robe. His dark complexion revealed his southern origin; but what his nationality actually was, whether he was an Indian, a Greek, or a Persian, no one could say for certain. His great, almost gigantic height; his dark, haggard, scorched face with a complexion that was indescribably repulsive; his large eyes blazing with an unnatural fire; his thick, beetling eyebrows, set him rather sharply apart from all the ashen-grey inhabitants of the capital. His very house was different from the small wooden houses of that district. It was a stone building of a type which the Genoese merchants had at one time built in large numbers, with irregular windows of different sizes, iron shutters, and bolts and bars. This money-lender differed from every other money-lender in that he was willing to advance any sum to anybody, from a poor old lady to the most extravagant courtier. Very often splendid equipages used to stop in front of his house, and sometimes the head of some gorgeously dressed court lady would look out of their windows. As usual, it was rumoured that his iron chests were filled to the very top with gold, jewellery, diamonds and all sorts of pledged articles of great value, but at the same time he was not by any means as greedy of gain as other money-lenders. He lent money very readily, and seemed to fix the dates of repayment very fairly; but by some curious methods of arithmetic he made the repayments work out at enormous rates of interest. So at any rate it was rumoured. But what was really strange and what amazed many people was the fate of all those who borrowed money from him: for all of them came to an unhappy end. Whether it was simply the sort of thing people said about him, or some absurd superstitious talk, or rumours spread with the intention of harming him, was never discovered. But a few facts which occurred within a short time of each other and for everybody to see, were certainly very remarkable and could not easily be forgotten.

"Among the aristocracy of that day one young man rapidly attracted general attention. He belonged to one of the best families and had distinguished himself in the service of his country while still very young. He was a warm admirer of everything that was true and noble, a patron of learning and the arts, a man who had in him the making of a Mæcenas. Soon he was worthily rewarded by the Empress who had appointed him to an important office which corresponded exactly with his wishes and in which he could do much for learning or any other worthy cause. The young statesman surrounded himself with artists, poets and men of learning. He wished to give work to all, to encourage all. He undertook a large number of useful publications at his own expense, placed many orders, offered many prizes to encourage art and science, spent thousands on it all, and in the end found himself financially embarrassed. But, full of noble impulses, he would not give up his work. He raised money by borrowing wherever he could and finally came to the Kolomna money-lender. Having obtained a considerable loan from him, this man within a short time changed completely: he became an embittered persecutor of art and learning, venting his spite particularly on young scholars and artists. He could only see the bad side of whatever was written or published, and he twisted every word round to mean something the writer never intended it to mean. Unfortunately the French Revolution happened just at that time. He used it as an excuse for all sorts of wickedness. He began discovering revolutionary tendencies in everything; he began suspecting subversive intentions in everything. His suspicions grew so much that finally he began suspecting even himself; he began fabricating terrible and unjust accusations against innocent people and brought unhappiness and ruin upon thousands. It goes without saying that such acts in the end came to the ears of the Empress herself, who was terribly shocked, and full of the nobility of mind and spirit which is so great an ornament of crowned heads, she uttered words which unhappily were not recorded at the time and preserved for us, but the deep sense of which impressed itself upon the hearts of many. The Empress observed that it was not under a monarchical form of government that the high and noble aspirations of the human mind were trampled upon, and the finest achievements of the human mind, poetry and the arts, despised and persecuted; on the contrary, it was the monarchs and the monarchs only who had been their patrons; that the Shakespeares and Molières flourished under their gracious protection, while Dante could not find a corner for himself in his republican birthplace; that real geniuses arose during the time when kings and kingdoms were at the topmost pinnacle of their power and glory and not at the time of ugly political disturbances and republican terror which had so far not given a single poet to the world; that poets must be held in honour, for they brought peace and sweet contentment to the heart of man, and not troubles and discontent; that scholars, poets, and all those who were actively engaged in the arts were the diamonds and pearls in the crown imperial, for it was by them that the reign of a great monarch was glorified and made immortal. In a word, the Empress, when speaking those words, was divinely beautiful. Old men, I remember, could not recall that speech without tears. All took an interest in that affair. To the honour of our national pride be it said that in the Russian heart there always abides a fine impulse to take the side of the persecuted. The statesman who had forfeited the confidence of his Sovereign was punished in an exemplary manner and dismissed his post. But he could read a much worse punishment in the faces of his fellow countrymen: utter and universal scorn. Nothing could adequately describe the sufferings of his vain spirit; his pride, his disappointed ambitions, his ruined hopes, all combined to torture him, and his life came to an end in dreadful attacks of raving madness.

"Another striking example of the baneful influence of the money-lender also occurred in the sight of all. Among the many lovely women of our northern capital at that time, one was universally acclaimed as the loveliest of them all. Her beauty was an exquisite blend of our northern beauty with the beauty of the south, a gem that makes its appearance only rarely in the world. My father used to tell me that he had not seen any woman to equal her in his life. Everything seemed united in her: riches, intelligence, and great charm of soul. Many men sought her hand in marriage, and foremost among them was Prince R., one of the best and most honourable of all young noblemen of that time, handsome of face and of a noble, chivalrous character, the ideal hero of novels and women, a Grandison in every respect. Prince R. was passionately, madly in love, and his love was fully reciprocated. But the girl's parents did not consider him a good match for their daughter. The ancestral estates of the prince had ceased to be his property long ago; his family was in disfavour at court, and the bad state of his affairs was known to all. Suddenly the prince left the capital for a time, as though for the purpose of improving his affairs, and after a short time he returned a rich man who could now afford to live in great style and luxury. Splendid balls and parties made him known at court. The father of the beautiful girl gave his consent and one of the most fashionable weddings in town soon took place. What was the real reason of so sudden a change in the affairs of the bridegroom, and where he had obtained such great wealth no one could say for certain; but it was whispered that he had entered into some kind of agreement with the mysterious usurer and received a loan from him. Be that as it may, the wedding was one of the great social events of the season. The bride and the bridegroom were the objects of general envy. Every one knew how deeply in love they were, and how constant their love was, and how much they must have suffered during their long separation, and how great their virtues were.

Romantic ladies already painted in rosy colours the great happiness that was in store for the young people. But everything fell out quite differently. In one year a terrible change took place in the husband. His character, until then so fine and noble, was poisoned with suspicion, jealousy, intolerance and all sorts of insane humours. He became his wife's tyrant and torturer and, what no one could have foreseen, was guilty of the most abominable acts of cruelty, going so far as to beat her. In only one year people found it difficult to recognise the woman who so recently had been such a radiant beauty and had had crowds of the most devoted admirers. At last, unable to bear her treatment any longer, she first broached the subject of a divorce. Her husband flew into a terrible rage at the mere mention of it. In his first outburst of fury he forced his way into her room with a knife and he would without a doubt have stabbed her there and then, if he had not been seized and restrained. In a fit of raving madness and despair he turned the knife against himself —and ended his life in the most horrible agonies.

"In addition to these two instances, which occurred before the eyes of the whole world, many more instances were told of similar happenings among the lower classes, all of which had ended tragically. In one instance, an honest, sober man became a drunkard; in another a shopkeeper's assistant robbed his employer; in a third a cabby, who had for years plied his trade honestly, murdered his fare for a few pence. It was of course impossible that such happenings, sometimes retailed with all sorts of embellishments, should not have struck terror in the hearts of the humble inhabitants of Kolomna. No one doubted that the usurer was possessed of the devil. It was said that he often made such demands that the poor wretches who came to him for a loan fled from him in horror, not daring to repeat them to anyone afterwards; that his money possessed the power of becoming incandescent and burning through things, and that it was all marked with strange symbols. All sorts of fantastic tales were told about him. And perhaps the most remarkable thing of all was that the entire population of Kolomna, the entire world of poor old women, low-grade Civil Servants, small-part actors, and all the small fry we have mentioned earlier, would rather suffer any hardships and privations than apply to the terrible money-lender for a loan. There were even cases of old women who had actually died of starvation, preferring to starve to death rather than destroy their souls. Any one meeting him in the street shrank back in horror and threw frightened glances over his shoulder a long time at the receding, immensely tall figure. In his appearance alone there was so much that was uncommon that people could not help ascribing supernatural powers to him. Those powerful features, so deeply chiselled that no living man has ever had any features like them; that torrid bronze complexion; that excessive thickness of the eyebrows; those unbearable, terrible eyes, even the long folds of his oriental robe—everything seemed to say that the passions of other men paled before the passions that stirred in his body. My father always used to stand motionless when meeting him and each time he could not help saying to himself, 'A devil, a real devil!' But I'd better introduce you to my father who, by the way, is the real subject of my tale.

"My father was a remarkable man in many ways. He was an artist the like of whom you do not often meet, a self-taught artist, who without the help of teachers or a school had discovered in his own soul the rules and laws of art, driven only by his passion for perfection and walking (for reasons which he himself perhaps did not know) along one path only, the path along which his spirit led him. He was one of those born geniuses whom our contemporaries so often contemptuously dismiss by the word 'amateur' and who are never disheartened by sneers or failure, whose strength and zeal are, on the contrary, constantly renewed, and who in spirit go far beyond those works which had earned them the title of 'amateur.' By his own innate, lofty instinct he perceived the presence of an idea in every object; he grasped the meaning of the words: historic painting; he grasped why a simple drawing of a head, a simple portrait of Raphael, Leonardo da Vinci, Titian, and Correggio could be called historic painting, while a huge canvas of an historical subject was still nothing more than a *tableau de genre*, despite all the artist's pretensions to historical painting. Both inner inclination and personal conviction guided his brush to religious subjects, the highest and the very last step of the sublime in art. He did not know the meaning of personal ambition or bad temper, so inseparable a part of the character of many a painter. He was a man of great firmness of character, honest, frank, even rude, with somewhat rough manners, but with more than a touch of pride in his soul, who always spoke of people both indulgently and critically. 'Why should I care what they think?' he used to say. 'It isn't for them I am working. I'm not painting my pictures for a drawing-room. He who understands me will thank me. It's no use blaming a man of the world for understanding nothing about painting: instead he understands everything about cards, is a good judge of wine or a horse—what more does a gentleman want? I daresay if he tried one thing and then another and started getting clever he'd become a confounded nuisance! To each his own: let each man mind his own business. So far as I'm concerned, I prefer a man who tells me frankly that he doesn't know anything about art rather than one who plays the hypocrite and pretends to know what he doesn't know and only succeeds in making trouble and being a damned nuisance generally!'

He worked for very little pay, that is to say, for a pay which was just sufficient to keep his family and to permit him to carry on with his work. Moreover, he never refused to help anyone who was in real need, and especially to hold out a helping hand to a poor brother artist. He believed with the simple, reverent faith of his fathers, and that was perhaps why a lofty, exalted expression appeared as though by itself on all the faces he painted, an expression which even the most brilliant artists of his time never succeeded in reproducing, however hard they might try. At last, by unremitting labour and perseverance in the path he had marked out for himself, he even began to win the respect of those who had before decried him as an amateur and as a self-taught, 'home-made' artist. He was always getting commissions for pictures from churches, and he was never without work. One of his pictures in particular occupied all his thoughts. I can't remember what its subject was; all I know is that he had to introduce the Prince of Darkness into it. He pondered long what kind of a face to give him, for he wanted that face to express all that weighs down and oppresses man. While thinking about it, the face of the mysterious money-lender would occasionally flash through his mind and he could not help saying to himself, 'That's the man I ought to take as my model for the devil.' Imagine his surprise, therefore, when one day, while working in his studio, he heard a knock at the door and almost immediately the terrible usurer entered. A cold shiver ran down my father's spine in spite of himself.

"'You're a painter?' the money-lender asked my father without ceremony.

"'Yes,' said my father, bewildered and wondering what was to come next.

"'All right. I want you to paint my portrait. I don't know, but I may possibly be dead soon. I have no children and I don't want to die completely. I want to live. Can you paint a portrait that will look alive in every detail?'

"My father thought, 'Couldn't be better. The fellow is asking me himself to use him as a model of the devil for my picture!' So he agreed. They came to terms and arranged the times of the sittings, and the very next day my father, taking his palette and brushes, was already at the usurer's place.

"The high wall surrounding the courtyard, the dogs, the iron doors, the bolts and bars, the arched windows, the chests covered with strange rugs, and, last but not least, the extraordinary master of the house himself who sat motionless before him—all that produced a strange impression upon my father. The lower part of the windows was, as though on purpose, covered and blocked up, so that the light came in only from the top. 'Damn it, how wonderfully his face is lighted up now!' my father said to himself, beginning to paint breathlessly, as though afraid lest the favourable light should vanish. 'What terrific power!' he went on speaking to himself. 'If I'm successful in getting him even half as well as he is now, he'll kill all my saints and angels: they'll all pale into insignificance before him! What devilish power! He'll simply jump out of my canvas, even if I am only just a little true to nature. What amazing features!' he went on repeating to himself, working away with redoubled zeal, and soon he was able to see himself how certain features were already beginning to be transferred to the canvas. But the closer he got to them, the more he became oppressed by a strange, uncanny feeling of dread, which he could not himself explain. However, he decided in spite of it to pursue, with the most scrupulous exactitude, every inconspicuous feature and expression. First of all he applied himself to portraying his eyes. There was so much force in those eyes that it seemed absurd even to attempt to reproduce them as they were. But he made up his mind to discover their minutest feature and shade and thus to solve their mystery. . . . However, as soon as he began painting them and delving deeper and deeper into them as he proceeded with his work, there arose in his heart such a strange revulsion, he felt such an inexplicable prostration of soul, that he was forced again and again to lay down his brush for a time and then start afresh. But at last he could endure it no longer. He felt that those eyes pierced his very soul and filled it with indescribable alarm. This feeling became much stronger next day and the day after. He became frightened. He threw down his brush and told the money-lender bluntly that he did not intend to go on with the painting of his portrait. The change that came over the sinister usurer at those words had to be seen to be believed. He fell at my father's feet, imploring him to finish his portrait, pleading that his fate and his continued existence in the world depended on it, saying that my father had already caught with his brush his living features and that if he would reproduce them faithfully his life would in some supernatural way remain in the portrait and because of that he would not die completely, and finally urging that it was absolutely necessary for him to remain in the world. My father was terrified by these words: they seemed so utterly inexplicable and horrible to him that he dropped his brushes and his palette and rushed out of the usurer's house.

"He was worried about it all that day and the following night, but next morning he got the portrait back from the money-lender. It was brought by a woman, the only human being the usurer kept as a servant, who told my father that her master did not want the portrait, that he did not intend to pay anything for it, and that he was therefore returning it. On the evening of the same day my father learnt that the money-lender had died and was about to be buried according to the rites of his religion. All that seemed inexplicably strange to him. But from that day a marked change showed itself in my father's character: he grew restless and ill at ease, and he was unable to understand the reason for it. Shortly afterwards he did something which no one would have expected of him. For some time the paintings of one of his pupils had begun attracting the attention of a small circle of art experts and art lovers. My father always considered that he had talent and for that reason he did all he could to help him. But suddenly he felt jealous of him. The general interest taken in his work and the discussions which it provoked became unbearable to him. Then to his utter annoyance he learnt that his pupil had been commissioned to paint a picture for a rich church which had been recently rebuilt. That was the last straw! 'No, I shan't let that youngster triumph over me!' he said to himself. 'It's a bit too soon for you, my boy, to lick your elders. Thank God, there is still some strength left in me. Let's see who will lick whom!' And this straightforward and honourable man began scheming and intriguing, a thing he had hitherto abhorred, until at last he succeeded in getting the church authorities to declare an open competition for the picture, so as to give other artists a chance of sending in their pictures. Then he shut himself up in his studio and began working feverishly at his picture. It seemed as if he wished to give all he had, to sacrifice his last ounce of strength, to it. And indeed it turned out one of his best works. No one doubted that he would win the competition. All the pictures were sent in, and, compared with my father's picture, all the others were as day is to night. Then suddenly one of the members of the committee of judges (I think he was a person in holy orders) made a remark which rather surprised everybody. 'There is doubtless a great deal of talent in the picture of this artist,' he said, 'but there is no saintliness in the faces; on the contrary, there is even something demonic in their eyes, as though some evil feeling has guided the hand of the artist.' All looked at the picture, and they could not help agreeing with the justice of these words. My father rushed up to his painting, as though anxious to make sure whether what he considered an offensive remark was justified or not, and perceived with horror that he had given the usurer's eyes to almost every face in his picture. They all gazed with such demon-like intensity that he could not help shuddering himself. His picture was rejected, and to his great mortification he learnt that his pupil's picture had been accepted. It is impossible to describe his fury when he returned home. He nearly assaulted my mother, drove all his children away, broke his brushes and smashed his easel, took the picture of the money-lender off the wall and ordered a fire to be lit in the fireplace, intending to cut it up and burn it. But just as he was about to destroy the picture a friend of his came in, an artist like my father, a very jovial fellow, who was always in high spirits, never hankered after fame, worked away happily at anything that happened to come his way, and was never happier than at a dinner or a party.

"'What are you doing? What do you want to burn?' he said, going up to the portrait. 'Why, man, this is one of your best works! It's the money-lender who recently died, isn't it? It's a real masterpiece! You certainly hit him straight between the eyes! Gosh, got right into them, haven't you? I bet in real life his eyes never looked like that!'

"'Well, let's see what they'll look like in the fire!' said my father, and he seized the portrait and was about to throw it in the flames.

"'Wait a minute, for God's sake!' said his friend, restraining him. 'If it's got on your nerves so much, give it to me!'

"At first my father would not agree, but at last he let himself be persuaded, and his jovial friend took the portrait away with him, pleased as anything with his new acquisition.

" After he had left, my father suddenly felt much happier, as though with the removal of the portrait a heavy load had been taken off his mind. He was now himself surprised at his spite and jealousy and the quite apparent change in his character. Thinking over his behaviour towards his pupil, he felt deeply grieved at heart and said, not without a feeling of inward anguish, 'It was God who punished me; my picture deserved to be rejected. It had been planned with the idea of ruining a fellow artist. A fiendish feeling of envy stimulated my brush, so is it any wonder that a fiendish feeling was also reflected in it?' He immediately went in search of his former pupil, clasped him to his heart, asked his forgiveness, and did his best to make amends. He went on working as happily as before, but his face grew much more pensive. He said his prayers more frequently, became more taciturn, and never spoke disparagingly about people again; even the rather coarse exterior of his character somehow became softer and more gentle. Something else soon gave him another shock. He had not seen the friend who had carried off the portrait for some time. He was thinking of going to find out how he was, when his friend quite unexpectedly entered his studio. After the usual greetings his friend said:

"'I say, old man, now I understand why you wanted to burn that picture. Damn it, there's certainly something uncanny about it. . . . I don't believe in witchcraft, but, say what you like, there certainly is some evil power in it. . . .'

"'What do you mean?' asked my father.

"'Well, ever since I hung it up in my room I've felt so unsettled, so worried, so depressed, as though I was contemplating murder or something. I never knew what insomnia meant, but now I began to suffer not only from insomnia. . . . I have had such awful dreams. . . . I really hardly know if they were dreams or something quite different. It was as if the devil himself was trying to strangle me, and all the time that damned old fellow was sure to bob up somewhere. My dear chap, I simply can't tell you the sort of state I was in. Nothing like it ever happened to me before. All that time I was walking about like a madman : obsessed with fears, expecting something awful to happen to me any moment. I felt I couldn't say a friendly word to anyone, speak frankly to any man, just as though some spy was at my elbow all the time. And it was only after I had given the portrait to my nephew, who kept asking for it, that I felt as if a heavy weight had been lifted from my shoulders. I was a happy man once more, and I still am, as you see. Well, old chap, you certainly dished up the devil himself this time !'

"My father listened to his story with rapt attention and then asked, 'Has your nephew still got the portrait?'

"'Heavens, no ! He couldn't stand it, either,' replied the jovial artist. 'I tell you the soul of that usurer must be in that portrait: he seems to be jumping out of the frame, walking about the room and, according to my nephew, doing all sorts of uncanny things. I'd have thought he had gone off his head, if I hadn't had a somewhat similar experience myself. He sold it to a collector, who I understand couldn't put up with it, either, and got rid of it to someone else.'

"This story made a deep impression upon my father. He was now worried in good earnest, became oppressed with melancholy thoughts, and at last persuaded himself that his brush had been the tool of the devil and that part of the usurer's life had somehow or other really passed into the portrait and was now plaguing and tormenting people, instilling all sorts of devilish ideas into their minds, leading an artist astray, inflicting terrible tortures of envy and jealousy, and so on and so forth. Three severe blows that he experienced one after another a short time later—the sudden deaths of his wife, his daughter, and his little son—he looked upon as a punishment from above and he made up his mind to retire from the world immediately. As soon as I was nine years old, he placed me at the school of the Academy of Art and, after settling his debts, he withdrew to a lonely monastery where he soon took monastic vows. There he amazed the monks by the austerity of his life and his strict observance of all the monastic rules. The Father Superior, having learnt about his skill as a painter, demanded that he should paint the principal icon in the monastery church, but the humble brother categorically refused, saying that he was unworthy to touch his brush, that it had been contaminated, and that he had first to purify his soul with hard work and mortification of the flesh to be once more worthy of undertaking such a task. They did not want to force him to paint the picture, while he increased the rigors of his monastic life as much as possible until even such a life did not satisfy him, for he did not consider it sufficiently austere. So with the blessing of the Father Superior he went into the wilderness to be entirely alone. There he built himself a hut with the branches of trees, fed only on raw roots, hauled large stones from one place to another as a penance, stood on the same spot with his hands raised to heaven from sunrise to sunset and recited his prayers all the time. He seemed in fact to have applied himself to finding and experiencing every possible degree of suffering and attaining to that state of self-immolation, examples of which can be only found in the Lives of the Saints. In this manner he mortified his flesh a long time, for several years, strengthening it only by the living grace of prayer. One day at last he returned to the monastery and said to the Father Superior, 'Now I'm ready. If God wills, I shall bring my labour to an end.' He selected as the subject of his picture the Birth of Jesus. He worked on it for a whole year, without leaving his cell, and barely sustaining himself on the coarse monastic fare, and praying incessantly. At the end of the year the picture was ready. It was indeed a miracle of art. I need hardly tell you that neither the Father Superior nor the monks knew much about painting, but even they were struck by the singular holiness of the figures. The feeling of divine humility on the face of the Blessed Virgin as she bent over the Child; the profound intelligence in the eyes of the Holy Child, as though they already saw something from afar; the solemn silence of the Magi, amazed by the Divine Miracle and prostrating themselves at His feet; and, finally, the indescribably holy stillness which pervaded the whole picture— all this was presented with such harmonious strength and great beauty that its effect was magical. All the brethren fell on their knees before the new icon and the Father Superior, deeply moved, said, 'No, man could never produce such a picture with the aid of human art alone; a holy, divine power has guided your brush and the blessing of Heaven rested upon your labours.'

"Just at that time I finished my course at the Academy, was awarded a gold medal and with it the joyful hope of a journey to Italy—the greatest ambition of a twenty-year-old artist. All I had to do was to take leave of my father, whom I had not seen for the past twelve years. I don't mind confessing that I had even forgotten what he looked like. I had of course heard some talk about the austerity and holiness of his life and was prepared beforehand to meet a recluse of a forbidding exterior, a man who had renounced the world and become a complete stranger to it, a man who knew nothing except his cell and his prayers, a man exhausted and shrivelled from eternal fasts and vigils. Imagine my surprise therefore when I saw before me a fine-looking, almost inspired old man !

There was no trace of exhaustion on his face: it shone with the brightness of heavenly joy. A beard, white as snow, and thin, almost ethereal, hair of the same silvery hue fell picturesquely over his chest and the folds of his black frock, almost to the rope with which his poor monastic garb was girded; but still more remarkable to me was to hear from his lips such words and thoughts which, I don't mind telling you, I shall treasure in my heart for the rest of my life and I sincerely hope that every one of my fellow-artists will do the same.

"'I was waiting for you, my son,' he said when I went up to him for his blessing. 'There is a path before you which you will henceforth follow all through your life. Your path is plain; do not turn away from it. You have talent; talent is one of the most precious of God's gifts—do not destroy it. Examine, study carefully everything you see, pursue your art and master it, but in everything try to find its inward meaning, and most of all endeavour to obtain an understanding of the high mystery of creation. Blessed are those who possess it, for there is nothing in nature too low for them. Indeed, a creative artist is as great in little things as in great things; in things that are despicable, he finds nothing to despise, for the beautiful spirit of Him who made them shines invisibly through them, and whatever is despicable is in fact clothed in glory, for it has gone through the purifying fire of His spirit. It is in art that man finds an intimation of heavenly paradise, and for this reason alone art is higher than anything. And as a life spent in the calm contemplation of God is higher than a life spent in the turmoil of the world, so is creation higher than destruction. As an angel is by the pure innocence of his bright soul alone higher than all the vast power and proud passion of Satan, so is a great work of art greater than anything else in the world. Sacrifice everything to it and love it with all your heart, not with the passion of earthly lust, but with a gentle, heavenly passion; for without it man is powerless to raise himself above the earth and incapable of uttering the sweet sounds of contentment and peace. For a great work of art comes into the world to bring peace of mind and reconciliation to all. It is incapable of sowing the seeds of discontent in the soul of man, but everlastingly aspires to God like an uttered prayer. But there are moments in a man's life, dark moments . . .' He paused and I could not help noticing that his bright countenance became suddenly overcast, as though obscured for a moment by a cloud. 'There is one incident in my life,' he said, 'I cannot explain. Even to this day I cannot understand what that strange being was whose portrait I painted. It surely must have been some manifestation of the devil. I know the world denies the existence of the devil, and I will therefore not speak of him. I will only say that it was with repugnance that I painted him, that at the time I felt no love for my work. I tried to force myself to be true to nature by stifling every human emotion in me. No, that was not a work of art, and it is because of that that the feelings aroused by it in all who look at it are unruly feelings, riotous, restless, turbulent feelings, not the feelings of an artist, for even in times of general alarm an artist remains tranquil and at peace. I am told this portrait is passing from hand to hand, spreading feelings of dissatisfaction and discontent, giving rise in an artist to a feeling of envy, jealousy and black hatred towards his fellow artists, to wicked desires to persecute and oppress. May the Almighty keep and preserve you from these evil passions ! There is nothing more dreadful than they. Far better to endure all the anguish of the worst persecution than to inflict even a semblance of persecution on any man. Keep your heart pure, my son. He who has a spark of genius in him must be purer in soul than the rest of mankind. For much will be forgiven an ordinary man that will not be forgiven him. A man who goes out of his house dressed in bright holiday clothes has only to be splashed by a spot of dirt from under a wheel for people to crowd round him, point a finger at him, and talk of his slovenliness, while the same people do not even notice the great number of spots on the week-day clothes of other passers-by. For stains on week-day clothes are never seen !'

"He blessed me and embraced me. Never in my life was I so deeply moved or felt so uplifted in spirit. I clung to his breast with reverence rather than with the feeling of a son and I kissed the scattered strands of his silvery hair. A tear glittered in his eye.

"'My son,' he said to me at the moment of parting, 'I want you to do one thing for me. I expect that one day you will come across the portrait I told you of. You will have no difficulty in recognising it by the remarkable eyes and their unnatural expression. Destroy it, I beg you, destroy it at all costs !'

"I promised him solemnly to do as he wished. What else could I have done ? For fifteen years I have never happened to come across anything that remotely resembled the description of the portrait my father had given me, when all of a sudden at this auction . . ."

Here without finishing his sentence the artist turned to the wall to have another look at the portrait. The crowd of listeners did the same at the same instant, searching for the strange portrait with their eyes. But to their amazement it was no longer on the wall. A low murmur went through the crowd, followed almost immediately by the word "stolen" pronounced distinctly by several people. Someone had succeeded in filching it, taking advantage of the fact that the attention of the listeners had been distracted by the story. And for a long time the people in the auction room looked perplexed, wondering whether they had really seen those uncanny eyes, or whether it was merely an illusion, a vision that had flashed across their eyes tired by the long examination of old pictures.

NEVSKY AVENUE

THERE IS nothing finer than Nevsky Avenue, not in St. Petersburg at any rate; for in St. Petersburg it is everything. And, indeed, is there anything more gay, more brilliant, more resplendent than this beautiful street of our capital? I am sure that not one of her anaemic inhabitants, not one of her innumerable Civil Servants, would exchange Nevsky Avenue for all the treasures in the world. Not only the young man of twenty-five, the young gallant with the beautiful moustache and the immaculate morning coat, but the man with white hair sprouting on his chin and a head as smooth as a billiard ball, yes, even he is enthralled with Nevsky Avenue. And the ladies . . . Oh, for the ladies Nevsky Avenue is a thing of even greater delight! But is there anyone who does not feel thrilled and delighted with it? The gay carriages, the handsome men, the beautiful women—all lend it a carnival air, an air that you can almost inhale the moment you set foot on Nevsky Avenue! Even if you have some very important business, you are quite certain to forget all about it as soon as you are there. This is the only place in town where you meet people who are not there on business, people who have not been driven there either by necessity or by their passion for making money, which seems to have the whole of St. Petersburg in its grip. It really does seem that the man you meet on Nevsky Avenue is less of an egoist than the man you meet on any other street where want and greed and avarice can be read on the faces of all who walk or drive in carriages or cabs. Nevsky Avenue is the main communication centre of the whole of St. Petersburg. Anyone living in the Petersburg or Vyborg district who has not seen a friend on the Sands or the Moscow Tollgate for years can be sure to meet him here. No directory or information bureau will supply such correct information as Nevsky Avenue. All-powerful Nevsky Avenue! The only place in St. Petersburg where a poor man can combine a stroll with entertainment. How spotlessly

117

clean are its pavements swept and, good gracious, how many feet leave their marks on them ! Here is the footprint left by the clumsy, dirty boot of an ex-army private, under whose weight the very granite seems to crack; and here is one left by the miniature, light as a feather, little shoe of the delightful young creature who turns her pretty head towards the glittering shop-window as the sun-flower turns to the sun; and here is the sharp scratch left by the rattling sabre of some ambitious lieutenant—everything leaves its imprint of great power or great weakness upon it. What a rapid phantasmagoria passes over it in a single day ! What changes does it not undergo in only twenty-four hours !

Let us begin with the early morning when all St. Petersburg is filled with the smell of hot, freshly baked bread and is crowded with old women in tattered clothes who besiege the churches and appeal for alms to the compassionate passers-by. At this time Nevsky Avenue is deserted: the stout shopkeepers and their assistants are still asleep in their fine linen shirts, or are lathering their noble cheeks, or drinking coffee; beggars gather at the doors of the pastrycooks' shops where the sleepy Ganymede, who the day before flew about like a fly with the cups of chocolate, crawls out with a besom in his hand, without a cravat, and flings some stale pasties and other leavings at them. Workmen are trudging through the streets: occasionally the avenue is crossed by Russian peasants, hurrying to their work in boots soiled with lime which not all the water of the Yekaterinsky Canal, famous for its cleanness, could wash off. At this time it is not proper for ladies to take a walk, for the Russian workman and peasant love to express themselves in vigorous language that is not even heard on the stage. Sometimes a sleepy Civil Servant will walk along with a brief-case under his arm, if the way to his office lies across Nevsky Avenue. It can indeed be stated without fear of contradiction that at this time, that is to say, until twelve o'clock, Nevsky Avenue does not serve as a goal for anyone, but is merely a means to an end: it is gradually filled with people who have their own occupations, their own worries, their own disappointments, and who are not thinking about it at all. The Russian peasant is talking about the few coppers he earns; old men and women wave their hands about or talk to themselves, sometimes with picturesque gestures, but no one listens to them or even laughs at them except perhaps the boys in brightly coloured smocks who streak along Nevsky Avenue with empty bottles or mended boots. At this time you can please yourself about your dress. You can wear a workman's cap instead of a hat, and even if your collar were to stick out of your cravat no one would notice it.

At twelve o'clock Nevsky Avenue is invaded by tutors and governesses of all nationalities and their charges in cambric collars. English Johnsons and French Coques walk arm in arm with the young gentlemen entrusted to their parental care and explain to them with an air of grave decorum that the signboards over the shops are put there to tell people what they can find inside the shops. Governesses, pale misses and rosy-cheeked mademoiselles, walk statelily behind slender and fidgety young girls, telling them to raise a shoulder a little higher and to walk straighter. In short, at this time Nevsky Avenue is a pedagogic Nevsky Avenue. But the nearer it gets to two o'clock in the afternoon, the fewer do the numbers of tutors, governesses, and children grow, until finally they are crowded out by their loving fathers who walk arm in arm with their highly-strung wives in gorgeous, bright dresses of every imaginable hue. These are by and by joined by people who have by that time finished all their important domestic engagements, such as talking to their doctors about the weather and the small pimple that has suddenly appeared on their nose; or enquiring after the health of their horses and the children, who, incidentally, seem always to be showing great promise; or reading in the papers the notices and important announcements of the arrivals and departures; or, lastly, drinking a cup of tea or coffee. They are soon joined by those upon whom enviable fate has bestowed the blessed calling of officials on special duties as well as by those who serve in the Foreign Office and who are particularly distinguished by their fine manners and their noble habits. Dear me, what wonderful appointments and posts there are! How they improve and delight the soul of man ! But, alas, I am not in the Civil Service myself and so am deprived of the pleasure of appreciating the exquisite manners of my superiors. Every one you now meet on Nevsky Avenue is a paragon of respectability: the gentlemen in long frock-coats with their hands in their pockets; the ladies in pink, white and pale blue redingotes and hats. You will meet here a most wonderful assortment of side-whiskers, a unique pair of whiskers, tucked with astonishing and extraordinary art under the cravat, velvety whiskers, satiny whiskers, and whiskers black as sable or coal, the latter, alas, the exclusive property of the gentlemen from the Foreign Office. Providence has denied black whiskers to those serving in any other ministry, and to their great mortification they have to wear red whiskers. Here you come across moustaches so wonderful that neither pen nor brush can do justice to them, moustaches to which the best years of a lifetime have been devoted—the objects of long hours of vigil by day and by night; moustaches upon which all the perfumes of Arabia have been lavished, the most exquisite scents and essences, and which have been anointed with the rarest and most precious pomades; moustaches which are wrapped up for the night in the most delicate vellum; moustaches for which their possessors show a most touching affection and which are the envy of all who behold them. Thousands of different sorts of hats, dresses, multicoloured kerchiefs, light as gossamer, to which their owners sometimes remain faithful for two whole days, dazzle every eye on Nevsky Avenue. It looks as if a sea of butterflies have risen from flower stalks and are fluttering in a scintillating cloud above the black beetles of the male sex. Here you meet waists such as you have never seen in your dreams: slender, narrow waists, waists no thicker than the neck of a bottle, waists which make you step aside politely whenever you meet them for fear of injuring them by some awkward movement of your elbow; your heart is seized with apprehension and terror lest these most delightful products of art and nature should be snapped in two at the merest breath from your lips. And the ladies' sleeves you meet on Nevsky Avenue! Oh, what lovely sleeves! They remind you a little of two balloons, and it really seems as though the lady might suddenly rise in the air were she not held down by the gentleman walking beside her; for it is as delightfully easy to lift a lady in the air as it is to lift a glass of champagne to the lips.

Nowhere do people bow to each other with such exquisite and natural grace as on Nevsky Avenue. Here you meet with a unique smile, a smile which is perfection itself, a smile that will sometimes make you dissolve with pleasure, sometimes make you bow your head with shame and feel lower than the grass, and sometimes make you hold up your head high and feel higher than the Admiralty spire. Here you meet people who talk about the weather or a concert with an air that is the acme of good breeding and with a dignity that is full of the sense of their own importance. Here you meet a thousand of the oddest characters and witness a thousand of the oddest incidents. Oh dear, the strange characters one meets on Nevsky Avenue! There are, for instance, many people who when they meet you will be quite sure to stare at your boots and, when you have passed, turn round to have a look at the skirts of your coat. I have not discovered the reason for it yet. At first it occurred to me that they must be bootmakers, but I was wrong, of course: they are for the most part Civil Servants from different ministries, many of whom are very able men who can draw up excellent reports from one ministry to another, or they are people who spend their time taking walks or reading the papers in cafés; they are, in fact, highly respectable people. In this thrice-blessed hour between two and three o'clock in the afternoon when the entire capital seems to be taking a walk on Nevsky Avenue, it becomes the greatest exhibition of the best productions of man. One displays a smart overcoat with the best beaver, another a nose of exquisite Grecian beauty, a third most excellent whiskers, a fourth a pair of most ravishing eyes and a perfectly marvellous hat, a fifth a signet ring on a most charming little finger, a sixth a foot in a delightful little shoe, a seventh a cravat that arouses your admiration, an eighth a moustache that takes your breath away. But at the stroke of three the exhibition closes and the crowds begin to dwindle. . . .

At three o'clock there is a fresh change. Spring suddenly descends on Nevsky Avenue: it is covered with Civil Servants in green uniforms. Hungry titular, court and other councillors walk as fast as they can. Young collegiate registrars, provincial and collegiate secretaries do their best to promenade along Nevsky Avenue with a dignified air which seems to belie the fact that they have been sitting in an office for six solid hours. But the elderly collegiate secretaries and titular and court councillors walk along quickly with bowed heads: they cannot spare the time to gaze at passers-by; they have not yet completely torn themselves away from their office worries; their thoughts are still in a terrible jumble; their heads are full of whole archives of business begun and still unfinished; instead of signboards they see for a long time a cardboard file with papers or the fat face of the head of their department.

From four o'clock Nevsky Avenue is empty and you will scarcely meet a single Civil Servant there. Some sempstress from a shop will run across Nevsky Avenue with a box in her hand; or some unfortunate victim of a philanthropic court registrar, thrown upon the mercy of the world in a frieze overcoat; or some eccentric visitor to whom all hours are alike; or some tall, thin Englishwoman with a reticule and a book in her hand; or some workman, a Russian, in a high-waisted coat of twilled cotton, with a very narrow beard, who lives from hand to mouth all his life, a man of tremendous energy, his back, arms and legs working away as he walks deferentially along the pavement; or sometimes a humble artisan—you will meet no one else on Nevsky Avenue at that time.

But once let dusk fall upon the houses and streets, and the policeman, covered with a piece of matting, climb up his ladder to light the street lamp, and engravings which do not venture to show themselves in daylight appear in the low shop-windows, and Nevsky Avenue comes to life again and everything begins to stir; it is then that the mysterious time comes when the street lamps invest everything with an alluring, magic light. You now meet a great many young men, for the most part bachelors, in warm frock-coats and overcoats. There is a certain purposefulness or something that resembles some purpose in the air at this time. It is something that is very difficult to account for: everybody seems to be walking much faster, everybody seems to be strangely excited. Long shadows flit over the walls and the road, their heads almost touching the Police Bridge. Young collegiate registrars, provincial and collegiate secretaries walk up and down the Avenue for a long time; but the elderly collegiate registrars, and the titular and court councillors mostly sit at home, either because they are married and have families, or because their German cooks who live with them are masters of the culinary art. You meet here the same elderly gentlemen who at two o'clock in the afternoon were walking along Nevsky Avenue with such admirable decorum and dignity. Now you will see them vying with the young collegiate registrars in overtaking some lady to peep under her hat, a lady whose full lips and cheeks plastered with rouge many of the strollers find so irresistibly attractive, especially shop managers, handicraftsmen, and merchants in frock coats of German cut, who walk in groups and usually arm in arm.

"I say," cried Lieutenant Pirogov on such an evening, catching hold of the arm of the young man who was walking beside him in a cut-away coat and cloak, "did you see her?"

"Yes, I did. What a lovely creature! A perfect Bianca of Perugino!"

"Who are you talking about?"

"Why, that girl, the girl with the dark hair and those wonderful eyes. Oh, what lovely eyes! What poise, what a glorious figure, what a perfect profile!"

122

"I'm talking about the blonde who passed her in that direction. Why don't you go after the dark one if you like her so much ?"

"What do you mean ?" exclaimed the young man in the cut-away coat, reddening. "As if she was one of the women who stroll about Nevsky Avenue in the evening ! She must be a woman of high society," he went on with a sigh. "Why, her cloak alone must be worth eighty roubles !"

"Don't be an ass," said Pirogov, giving him a violent push in the direction in which the brightly-coloured cloak was fluttering. "Go on, you idiot, or you'll miss your chance ! I'll go after the blonde !"

The two friends parted company.

"We know what you are, all of you !" thought Pirogov to himself with a conceited and self-confident smirk, convinced that no woman in the world could resist him.

The young man in the cut-away coat and cloak went rather nervously and tremulously in the direction in which the brightly coloured cloak was fluttering in the distance, lit brilliantly every time it drew near a street lamp and shrouded in darkness the moment it receded from it. His heart beat fast, and he unconsciously quickened his pace. The thought that he might have some claim on the attention of the beautiful girl who was disappearing in the distance never occurred to him; and still less could he accept the horrid implication of the coarse hint thrown out by Lieutenant Pirogov. All he wanted was to see the house of that ravishing creature who seemed to have flown down on Nevsky Avenue straight from heaven and who would most probably fly away no one could tell where. Oh, if only he knew where she lived ! He walked so fast that he continually pushed dignified, grey-whiskered gentlemen off the pavement.

This young man belonged to a class of people so rare in our country as to be looked upon as phenomenal. These people are no more citizens of St. Petersburg than the people we see in a dream are part of the world of reality. This quite exceptional class of people is particularly uncommon in a city where the inhabitants are either Civil Servants, shopkeepers, or German artisans. He was an artist. A strange phenomenon, is it not ? A St. Petersburg artist ! An artist in the land of snows ! An artist in the land of the Finns, where everything is wet, flat, monotonous, pale, grey, misty ! . . . These artists are not at all like the Italian artists, proud and fiery,

123

like Italy and her skies; on the contrary, they are mostly inoffensive, meek men, shy and easy-going, devoted to their art in an unassuming way, drinking their tea with a couple of friends in a small room, modestly discussing their favourite subject, and satisfied with the minimum of food and comfort. They employ some old beggar woman for their model, keeping her posing for six full hours just to transfer her impassive, numb and miserable expression on the canvas. They like to paint interiors of their rooms with every kind of litter lying about: plaster-of-Paris hands and feet, coffee-coloured with dust and age, a broken easel, a discarded palette, a friend playing the guitar, walls covered with paint, and an open window through which you can catch a glimpse of the pale Neva and poor fishermen in red shirts. Everything they paint has a greyish, muddy tint—the indelible imprint of the north. But for all that they labour over their pictures with real enjoyment. They are very often men of talent, and if they were breathing the air of Italy their talent would probably have opened up as freely, as widely, and as splendidly as a plant that has been taken out into the open air after being kept indoors for a long time. They are generally rather timid folk: a star and a fat epaulette throw them into such confusion that they automatically reduce the prices of their pictures. Sometimes the desire for smart clothes proves too strong for them, but for some reason a handsome coat never seems right on them, looking like a new patch on old clothes. Very often they will wear an excellent cut-away coat and a dirty cloak, or an expensive velvet waistcoat and a frock-coat covered with paint: just as on one of their unfinished landscapes you will sometimes see a nymph drawn with her head upside down; not finding any other place, the artist painted it on the old priming of another of his works on which he had once spent so many happy hours. An artist of this sort never looks you straight in the face, and if he does look at you it is with dull, rather vacant eyes. He does not transfix you with the keen stare of an observer, or with the penetrating hawk-like glance of a cavalry officer. This is because while looking at your features he at the same time sees the features of some plaster-of-Paris Hercules which stands in his room; or he may be thinking of a picture he is planning to paint. This often makes it extremely difficult to make any sense of his replies, which at times indeed are quite incomprehensible; and the fact that he is constantly thinking of several things at once merely increases his natural shyness.

The artist Piskarev, the young man we have described, belonged to this class of people. He was a very shy and inoffensive fellow who carried within his breast the seeds that at a favourable opportunity might one day have blossomed into flower. He sped after the girl who had struck him with such wonder, with a secret dread in his heart, and he seemed surprised at his own impertinence. The unknown girl, upon whom all his thoughts and feelings were now concentrated and whom he did not for a moment lose sight of, suddenly turned her head and looked at him. Oh, dear God, what heavenly features ! Her enchanting forehead of such dazzling whiteness was framed by hair as lovely as an agate. They curled, those wonderful tresses, and some of them, straying from under the hat, brushed against her cheek, suffused with the most delicate, fresh colour, brought on by the chill of the evening. Her lips held the delightful promise of ineffable bliss. Whatever remains of the memories of childhood, whatever excites the imagination and gives birth to a gentle mood of inspiration in a room lighted only by a glimmering lamp, seemed to have become fused, blended and reflected on the sweet lips of the unknown beautiful girl. She looked at Piskarev, and his heart fluttered in dismay at that look : there was anger in her eyes and indignation on her face at so impertinent a pursuit ; but even anger was enchanting on her lovely face. Overcome with shame and shyness, he stopped dead, his eyes fixed on the ground. But no ! He just could not give up that divine creature without even knowing where the shrine was to which she had come down to dwell !

These were the thoughts that passed through the head of the young dreamer, and he made up his mind to follow her. But to make sure he did not annoy her again, he kept at a great distance from her, looked idly about him, stared hard at the signboards, without however losing sight of a single movement of the fair stranger. There were fewer people about now, and the street became much quieter. The beautiful girl looked round again, and this time it seemed to him as if a ghost of a smile had flitted across her lips. He trembled all over, unable to believe his eyes. No, it just could not be true ! It must have been the deceptive light of the street lamp which had produced that illusion of a smile on her face ! Or was it his own imagination that was making a fool of him ? He could scarcely breathe for excitement ; everything in him was transformed into a kind of half-realised, tremulous agitation. All his feelings seemed to have caught fire suddenly, and a mist seemed to spread itself before his eyes. The pavement, he felt, was moving at a terrific speed under him; the carriages with their galloping horses stood still; the bridge stretched and was about to break in the centre of its arch; the houses were upside down; a sentry-box came reeling towards him; and the halberd of the constable, together with the gilt letters of some signboard and the scissors painted upon it, flashed across his very eyelash. And all this was produced by a single glance, by one turn of a pretty head. He saw nothing, he heard nothing, he heeded nothing: he only followed the light footprints of her lovely feet, trying in vain to slow down the rapid pace of his own feet, which flew in time with the beating of his heart. Sometimes he was overwhelmed with doubt: did that expression on her face really mean that she did not object to his following her? And then he would stop for a moment, but the beating of his heart, the irresistible force and the tension of all his feelings drove him on and on. He did not even notice the four-storied building which loomed suddenly in front of him, or the four rows of lighted windows that glared at him all at once, and he was brought to a sudden halt by the iron railings of the front steps which seemed to rush violently at him. He saw the unknown girl run up the steps, turn round, put a finger against her lips, and make a sign to him to follow her. His knees shook; his feelings, his thoughts, were aflame; joy like a flash of lightning pierced his heart, bringing with it the sensation of sharp pain. No, it was certainly not a dream! Oh, how much happiness could be crowded in one brief moment! What a lifetime of ecstasy in only two minutes!

But was it not all a dream? Was it possible that she who with one glance could make him sacrifice his life for her, that she who made him feel so overpoweringly happy if he so much as went near the house where she lived—was it possible that she was really being so nice and kind to him? He flew up the stairs. No earthly thought troubled him; no earthly passion blazed within him. No! At that moment he was pure and without stain, like a chaste youth who still yearned for some vague, spiritual love. And what in a dissolute man would have awakened lust, made his desires even more holy. The confidence that such a weak, beautiful creature reposed in him, that confidence meant that he must treat her as a knight used to treat the lady whose favour he wore in the lists, and that he must obey her commands like a slave. All he longed for at that moment was that her commands should be as hard to carry out as possible and preferably be fraught with great danger, so that he might fly to carry them out with greater zeal. He did not doubt that an event both mysterious and of the highest moment compelled the unknown girl to place her trust in him, and that he would most probably be asked to perform some important service, and he felt sure he possessed the necessary strength and determination for anything.

The staircase went round and round and his thoughts whirled round and round with it. "Mind the step !" A voice like a heavenly harp sounded above him and sent a fresh thrill through him. On the dark landing of the fourth floor the unknown girl knocked at a door; it was opened and they went in together. They were met by a rather attractive-looking woman with a candle in her hand, who gave Piskarev such a strange and impudent look that he could not help dropping his eyes. They entered a room, and the artist saw the figures of three women in different corners. One was laying out cards; another was sitting at the piano and strumming with two fingers a pitiful travesty of some ancient polonaise; the third was sitting before a mirror and combing out her long hair, and made no attempt to discontinue her toilette at the entrance of a stranger. A sort of disagreeable disorder, to be found only in the untidy room of a bachelor, reigned everywhere. The furniture, which was fairly good, was covered with dust; a spider had spread his web over the ornamental moulding in one of the corners of the ceiling; through the door of another room that was ajar he caught a glimpse of a shiny spurred boot and the red braid of a uniform; a man's loud voice and a woman's laugh resounded without any restraint.

Good God, where had he got to ? At first he refused to believe it, and he began scrutinising the different objects that filled the room. But the bare walls and the uncurtained windows did not indicate the loving care of a housewife, and the faded faces of these wretched creatures, one of whom sat down right in front of him and examined him as coolly as if he were a dirty spot on someone's dress —all that convinced him that he had got to one of those foul places where vice begotten of the spurious education and the terrible overcrowding of a big city takes up its abode, a place where man sacrilegiously crushes and holds up to scorn all that is sacred and pure and all that makes life beautiful, and where woman, the beauty of the world and the crown of creation, becomes a strange and equivocal creature, losing with the purity of her heart all that is womanly and adopting in a way that can only arouse disgust the impudent manners of man, and so ceasing to be the weak and lovely creature that is so different from ourselves.

Piskarev looked at the girl with amazement, as though still wishing to convince himself that it really was the same girl who had so bewitched him and who had made him follow her from Nevsky Avenue to this place. But she stood before him as beautiful as ever; her hair was as lovely; her eyes seemed no whit less heavenly. She was fresh: she was only seventeen! It could be seen that it was not long that abominable vice had had her in its clutches, for it had as yet not dared to touch her cheeks; they were so fresh and suffused with such a delicate rosy bloom—oh, she was beautiful!

He stood motionless before her and was almost on the point of letting himself be deceived again in a kind of well-meaning, good-natured way as he had let himself be deceived a short while ago, had not the beautiful girl, bored by his long silence, given him a meaning smile, looking straight into his eyes. That smile of hers was full of such pathetic impudence that it was as strange and out of place on her face as a look of piety is on the vicious face of a corrupt official or a ledger in the hands of a poet. He shuddered. She opened those sweet lips of hers and said something, but it was all so stupid, so vulgar. . . . Just as if the loss of innocence must needs bring with it the loss of intelligence, too. He did not want to hear any more. Oh, he was so absurd! He was as simple as a child! Instead of making the best of the circumstance that the girl seemed to like him, instead of being glad of such an opportunity, as doubtless many a man would have been in his place, he fled out of that house, leaping down the stairs like a frightened wild animal, and rushed out into the street.

With his head bent low and his hands lying lifelessly in his lap, he sat in his room, like a beggar who has found a priceless pearl and almost immediately dropped it into the sea. "Such a beautiful girl! Such divine features! And where? In what kind of a place? . . ." That was all he could bring himself to say.

And, indeed, we are never so moved to pity as at the sight of beauty touched by the corrupting breath of vice. If ugliness were the companion of vice, it would not matter so much, but beauty, sweet beauty which in our thoughts we associate only with purity and innocence !

The beautiful girl who had so bewitched poor Piskarev was indeed a most extraordinary and singular phenomenon. Her presence in that ghastly place and among those contemptible people seemed even more extraordinary. Her features were so faultlessly formed, the whole expression of her lovely face was marked by such nobility, that it was impossible to believe that vice had already got its terrible claws into her. She should have been the priceless pearl, the whole world, the paradise, the dearest possession of a loving and devoted husband; she should have been the lovely, gentle star of some small family circle, where her slightest wish would have been anticipated even before she opened her sweet lips. She should have been the belle of the crowded ball-room, on the shining parquet, in the glitter of candles; she would have been divine when surrounded by the silent adoration of a crowd of admirers, prostrate at her feet. But alas ! Instead she had been flung into the abyss to the accompaniment of loud, demonic laughter, by some terrible whim of a fiendish spirit, eager to destroy the harmony of life.

Overcome by a feeling of poignant pity, the artist sat disconsolately before a guttered candle. It was past midnight, the clock on the tower struck half-past twelve, and he still sat motionless, neither asleep, nor fully awake. As if taking advantage of his immobility, sleep was beginning to steal gently over him. The room had almost entirely disappeared, only the flickering light of the candle still penetrating the world of dreams into which he was fast sinking, when a sudden knock at the door made him shudder violently and sit up. The door opened and a footman in a rich livery walked in. Never before had a rich livery made its appearance in his lonely room and at such an unusual time, too. . . . He did not know what to make of it, and he eyed the footman with impatience and ill-disguised curiosity.

"The lady you visited a few hours ago, sir," said the footman with a courteous bow, "asked me to say that she wished to see you and sent her carriage to fetch you."

Piskarev was speechless with amazement. "A carriage, a footman in a livery ! No, it can't be ! There must be some mistake. . . ."

"I'm afraid you must have come to the wrong place," he said rather shyly. "Your mistress must have sent you to fetch someone else and not me."

"No, sir, I've made no mistake. Did you not, sir, accompany a young lady to a house in Liteynaya Street, to a room on the fourth floor?"

"Yes, I did."

"Well, in that case, sir, will you please come quickly? My mistress is most anxious to see you and she begs you to come straight to her house."

Piskarev ran down the stairs. Outside a carriage was indeed waiting for him. He got into it, the door was slammed, and the carriage sped noisily over the cobbled road. A panorama of lighted shops with bright signboards passed swiftly across the windows of the carriage. Piskarev was wondering all the time what the explanation of this adventure could be and was unable to find an answer to the mystery. A house of her own, a carriage, a footman in a rich livery. . . . All this could hardly be reconciled with the room on the fourth floor, the grimy windows and the discordant piano. The carriage stopped in front of a brightly lighted entrance, and he was immediately struck by the long row of carriages, the talk of the coachmen, the brilliantly lit windows and the strains of music. The footman in the rich livery helped him out of the carriage and escorted him deferentially to a hall with marble columns, with a doorkeeper smothered in gold braid, fur-coats and cloaks lying about, and a brightly burning lamp. An airy staircase with shining banisters, fragrant with all sorts of perfumes, led to the rooms upstairs. Already he was ascending it, already he had gone into the first large room, when he grew frightened and drew back at the sight of such crowds of people. The extraordinary diversity of faces completely bewildered him: it seemed as though some demon had chopped up the whole world into thousands of pieces and then mixed them all indiscriminately together. The gleaming shoulders of the women, the black frock-coats, the chandeliers, the lamps, the airy floating gauzes, the ethereal ribbons, and the fat double-bass which peeped out from the railings of the magnificent orchestral gallery—everything looked splendid to him. He saw all at once so many highly respectable old gentlemen and middle-aged gentlemen with stars on their evening coats, or ladies stepping with such grace, pride and poise over the parquet floor, or sitting in rows; he heard so many English and French words; moreover, the young gentlemen in black evening dress were so full of noble airs, spoke with such suave dignity or kept silent with such grave decorum, that they seemed quite incapable of saying anything *de trop*; they made jokes with so grand an air, smiled so respectfully, wore such superb whiskers, knew so well how to display their elegant hands while straightening their cravats. The ladies were so ethereal, so utterly and divinely vain, so full of rapture, they so enchantingly cast down their eyes that . . . But Piskarev's humble look as he leaned against a column was enough to show that he was utterly confused. At that moment the crowd surrounded a group of dancers. They were whirling round, draped in transparent creations of Paris, in garments that seemed to be woven out of air; their lovely feet touched the floor without any apparent effort and they could not have looked more ethereal if they had walked on air. One among them was lovelier, more dazzling and more gorgeously dressed than the rest. An indescribably subtle taste was expressed in her whole attire, and yet she did not seem to be aware of it herself, as though it all came to her naturally and of its own accord. She looked and did not look at the crowd of spectators who surrounded the dancers; she lowered her long, lovely eyelashes indifferently, the dazzling whiteness of her face still more dazzling; and as she bent her head a light shadow fell across her ravishing brow.

Piskarev tried hard to push through the crowd to have a better look at her, but to his intense annoyance a huge head of curly black hair kept getting continually in his way; moreover, he was wedged so tightly in the press of people that he did not dare either to move forward or to step back for fear of treading on the toes of some Privy Councillor. But at last he did succeed in forcing his way to the front. He glanced instinctively at his clothes to make sure that they were tidy, and to his horror he saw that he was wearing his old coat which was stained all over with paint. In his haste to leave he must have forgotten to change into proper clothes. He blushed to the roots of his hair and stood there with downcast eyes, praying for a chance to get away. But there was no possibility of getting away, for Court Chamberlains in resplendent uniforms formed an impenetrable wall behind him. He wished he were miles away from the beautiful girl with the lovely brow and eyelashes, and he raised his eyes fearfully to see whether she were looking at him, and, good Lord, she stood facing him ! . . . But what was that ? What was that ? "It is she !" he cried almost at the top of his voice. And, indeed, it was she. It was the girl he had met on Nevsky Avenue. The girl he had followed to her house.

Meanwhile she raised her long eyelashes and looked at everybody in the room with her bright eyes. "Oh, how beautiful she is, how beautiful!" was all he could utter with bated breath. Her eyes roamed slowly round the circle of men, each of whom seemed eager to attract her attention, but she soon withdrew them with a bored and fatigued air and, as she did so, her eyes met Piskarev's eyes. Oh, what bliss! What heavenly joy! His happiness was so overwhelming that it threatened to destroy him, to kill him outright! She made a sign to him: not with her hand, nor with an inclination of her head; no, it was in her eyes, in those entrancing eyes of hers, that he read this sign, and so subtle and imperceptible was it that no one could see it, no one but he. Yes, he saw it! He understood it! The dance went on for a long time; the languid music seemed at moments to fade and die away entirely, but again and again it burst forth in shrill, thunderous notes; at last —the end. She sat down, her bosom heaving under the light cloud of gauze; her hand (goodness, what a divine hand!) dropped on her knees, crushing her ethereal dress under it, and the dress under her hand seemed breathing music, and its delicate lilac hue made her lovely hand look more dazzlingly white than ever. Oh, all he wanted was just to touch it, and nothing more! He had no other desires; they would be sheer impertinence! . . . He stood behind her chair, not daring to speak, not daring to breathe.

"Were you bored?" she said. "I was awfully bored, too. You hate me, don't you?" she added, lowering her eyelashes.

"Hate you? I . . . Why . . ." Piskarev, completely taken aback, was about to say, and he would no doubt have poured forth a stream of quite meaningless words, if at that moment a Court Chamberlain with a beautifully curled shock of hair had not come up and engaged her in conversation, his talk sparkling with wit and compliment. He displayed rather charmingly a row of good teeth, and every witticism he uttered knocked a sharp nail into the young artist's heart. Fortunately, a stranger at last approached the Court Chamberlain with some sort of question.

"Oh, what a frightful nuisance this is!" she declared, raising her heavenly eyes at him. "I think I'd better sit down at the other end of the room. I'll wait for you there!"

She swept through the crowd and disappeared. He pushed his way after her like a man possessed, and in a twinkling he was there.

Yes, it was she. She sat like a queen, fairer and lovelier than all, and her eyes were searching for him.

"You're here?" she asked softly. "I'll be frank with you. I expect the circumstances of our meeting must have seemed strange to you. Did you really imagine I could belong to that contemptible class of human beings among whom you met me? I suppose you can't help thinking my actions rather strange, but I will reveal a secret to you. Will you promise," she said, looking straight into his eyes, "never to betray it?"

"Yes, oh yes, I promise!"

But at that moment an elderly gentleman walked up, began speaking to her in a language Piskarev could not understand, and offered her his arm. She cast an imploring glance at Piskarev and indicated to him by a sign that she wanted him to remain there and wait for her; but he was much too impatient to obey any command, even one that came from her lips. He went after her, but the crowd parted them. He lost sight of her lilac dress and he rushed from room to room in great agitation, pushing every one he met unceremoniously out of his way. But in every room important-looking gentlemen were sitting at card tables, plunged in dead silence. In a corner of one room some elderly people were engaged in an argument about the superiority of military to civil service; in another a group of people in magnificent dress-coats were making disparaging remarks on the voluminous labours of a hard-working poet. Piskarev became suddenly aware that a distinguished-looking gentleman had button-holed him and was submitting an eminently fair observation he had made to the artist's criticism; but Piskarev pushed him rudely away without even noticing that he wore a very high order round his neck. The artist rushed into another room, but she was not there; into a third—she was not there, either. "Where, oh where is she? Give her to me! Oh, I can't live without another look at her! I must, I simply must know what she wanted to tell me!" but all his search was in vain. Worried and exhausted, he stood desolately in a corner and watched the crowds; but his eyes had become strained by then and everything seemed blurred and indistinct. At last the walls of his room became clearly visible to him. He raised his eyes. Before him stood the candlestick with the light flickering in the socket; the whole candle had burnt out and the melted tallow had spread all over the table.

So he had been asleep! Oh, dear, what a wonderful dream that was ! And why had he wakened ? Why had he not waited another minute ? She would quite certainly have come again ! The cheerless dawn shed its dull, unpleasant light through his window. The room was in such a terrible, untidy mess. . . . Oh, how disgusting reality was ! How could it even be compared with a dream ? He undressed quickly and got into bed, wrapping himself up in a blanket, anxious to recapture even for an instant the dream that had vanished. And he did fall asleep almost immediately, but the dream he dreamed was not the one he longed for: one moment Lieutenant Pirogov appeared with his pipe, another the Academy caretaker, then some Regular State Councillor, then the head of the Finnish woman who had sat to him for a portrait, and the like absurdities.

He lay in bed till midday, trying to fall asleep and see her again in his dreams; but she did not appear. Oh, if only he could have seen her lovely features for one minute; if only he could have heard again the faint rustle of her dress; if only he could have caught a fleeting glimpse of her bare arm, white and dazzling like driven snow !

Dismissing everything, forgetting everything, he sat there looking utterly crushed and forlorn, full only of his dream. He never thought of touching anything; his eyes stared lifelessly and without a glimmer of interest at the window that looked out into the yard where a dirty water-carrier was sprinkling water that froze in the air, and the bleating voice of the rag-and-bone man resounded stridently, "Ol' clo' for sale ! Ol' clo' for sale !" Everyday life and reality fell jarringly upon his ear. He sat like that until evening, and then he went eagerly back to bed. He struggled long with sleeplessness, but at last he got the better of it. Again a dream; a stupid, horrid dream. "O Lord, have mercy upon me ! Show her to me for one minute ! Just for one minute, O Lord, I beseech Thee !" Again he waited for the evening; again he fell asleep; again he dreamed of some Civil Servant, who was a Civil Servant and a bassoon at the same time. Oh, this was intolerable ! At last she appeared ! Yes, yes. . . . Her sweet little head, her curls. . . . She was looking. . . . But oh, only for a moment, for the briefest possible moment ! Again a mist, again some silly dream !

In the end the dreams became his whole life, and from that time his life underwent a curious change: he, as it were, slept when he was awake and kept awake when he was asleep. Anyone seeing him sitting dumbly before an empty table, or walking along the street, would have taken him for a sleep-walker, a somnambulist, or for a man ruined by drink. He stared vacantly in front of him; his natural absent-mindedness increased, until at last all feeling and emotion were completely banished from his face. He revived only at the approach of night.

Such a condition undermined his health, and his worst time came when sleep began to desert him altogether. Anxious to save the only treasure he still possessed, he did all he could to regain it. He had heard there was one unfailing remedy against insomnia: all he had to do was to take opium. But where was he to get opium? He then remembered a Persian shopkeeper he knew who sold shawls and who pestered him for a picture of a beautiful girl. He decided to go to him, thinking that the Persian would be sure to supply him with opium.

The Persian received him sitting on a divan with his legs crossed under him.

"What do you want opium for?" he asked the painter.

Piskarev told him about his insomnia.

"All right, I'll get you the opium," said the Persian, "but paint me a beautiful girl. And, mind, I want that girl to be really beautiful, with black eyebrows and eyes as big as olives, and me lie beside her smoking my pipe. She is to be beautiful, remember! She must be a real beauty!"

Piskarev promised everything. The Persian went out for a minute and came back with a little bottle with some dark liquid, poured some of it very carefully into another bottle, which he gave to Piskarev with instructions not to use more than seven drops in a tumbler of water. The painter seized the precious phial greedily and rushed straight back home. He would not have parted with that little bottle of opium for a king's ransom.

When he got home he poured a few drops into a glass of water and, swallowing it, went to bed.

Oh, what bliss! What joy! There she was! There she was again! But how different she looked! Oh, she was lovely as she sat at the window of that bright country house! How simple her dress was—a simplicity in which only a poet's fancy is clothed! And her hair. . . . How plain her coiffure was and how lovely! How it suited her! A small kerchief was thrown lightly round her slender neck; everything about her revealed a mysterious, indefinable sense of good taste. How sweetly, how beautifully she walked! How musical was the rustle of her plain dress and the sound of her footsteps! How lovely her arm encircled by a bracelet of hair!

"Do not despise me! I'm not the sort of woman you take me for. Look at me! Look at me closer. Tell me now, do you really think I'm capable of doing what you think I do?"

"No, no! Of course not! Let anyone who thinks so, only let him . . ."

But just at that moment he woke! He was deeply touched, lacerated, tortured, and his eyes were brimming with tears! "Far better you had never existed, far better you had never been born, but had merely been the creation of an inspired artist! I'd never have left the canvas; I'd have stood before it always, looking at you and kissing you! I'd have lived and breathed with you, as the most beautiful dream, and then I should have been happy! I should have had no other desires! You would have been my guardian angel, and to you I would have prayed when I went to sleep at night and when I awoke in the morning, and it would have been you I'd have waited for if ever I had to paint saintliness and godliness. But now . . . Oh, how terrible my life is! What's the good of her being alive? Is the life of a madman pleasant to the friends and relations who once loved him? O Lord, what an awful thing life is! A perpetual clash between dream and reality!"

Such thoughts occupied him almost continuously. He thought of nothing else; he hardly touched any food; and with the impatience, with the passion of a lover he waited for the evening when once more he would see the vision he longed for. The concentration of all his thoughts upon one subject at last began to exercise so powerful an influence over his whole existence as well as over his imagination that the longed-for dream came to him almost every day, but the situation in which he saw the girl he loved was always the exact opposite of reality, for his thoughts were as pure as the thoughts of a child. It was through these dreams of his that their subject seemed to become in some way purer and was so completely transformed.

The doses of laudanum inflamed his mind more than ever, and if there ever was a man in love to the last extremity of madness, violently, dreadfully, annihilatingly, rebelliously in love, that unhappy man was he!

Of all his dreams one delighted him more than any other. He dreamt that he was in his studio. He was happy, and it was with real pleasure that he was sitting at his easel with the palette in his hand. And she was there, too. She was his wife. She sat beside him, leaning her sweet little elbow on the back of his chair and watching him work. Her eyes, languid and heavy, disclosed such a huge load of bliss. Everything in the room breathed of paradise; everything was so bright, so beautifully tidy! O Lord, and now she leaned her sweet little head on his bosom! . . . Never had he dreamt a better dream. After it he got up feeling refreshed and less abstracted than before. Strange thoughts came into his head. "Perhaps," he thought, "she has been drawn into her life of vice against her own will by some terrible accident. In her heart of hearts she is perhaps anxious to repent; she is perhaps herself longing to escape from her awful position. And can I suffer her to go to her ruin with callous indifference when all I have to do is to hold out a hand to save her from drowning?" His thoughts went even further. "No one knows me," he said to himself, "and, anyway, no one dares say anything about me. If she really repents, if she expresses her genuine sorrow and contrition and agrees to change her present way of life, I will marry her. I ought to marry her and I shall probably do much better than any other man who marries his housekeeper or often the most contemptible of creatures. For my action will be wholly disinterested and it may also turn out to be great, since I shall restore to the world one of its beautiful ornaments."

Having conceived this rather rash plan, he felt the colour returning to his cheeks; and, going up to the looking-glass, he was appalled to see how hollow his cheeks had become and how pale his face was. He began dressing with great care; he washed, smoothed his hair, put on his new cut-away coat and a smart waistcoat. Then, flinging his cloak over his shoulders, he went out into the street. Inhaling the fresh air, he felt a new man, like a convalescent who decides to go out for a walk for the first time after a long illness. His heart was beating fast as he approached the street where he had not been since his first fatal meeting with the girl.

He spent a long time looking for the house, for his memory seemed to have failed him. He walked twice along the street, uncertain before which house to stop. At last one looked familiar to him. He ran quickly up the stairs and knocked at the door. The door opened and . . . who came out to meet him? Why, his ideal, his mysterious idol, the original of his dreams, his life, the sum and substance of his existence, she in whom he lived so dreadfully, so agonisingly, so blissfully—she stood before him, she herself! He trembled, hardly able to stand on his feet from weakness, so overwhelmed was he with happiness. She stood before him as lovely as ever, though her eyes looked sleepy, though a pallor had spread over her face, which was no longer as fresh as before; but still she was beautiful.

"Oh, it's you!" she said on seeing Piskarev and rubbing her eyes (it was two o'clock in the afternoon). "Why did you run away from us that evening?"

He sank into a chair, feeling too faint to stand, and looked at her.

"I've only just got up. They brought me home at seven this morning. I was dead drunk," she added with a smile.

Oh, if only she had been dumb, if only she had been unable to speak at all rather than utter such words! In a flash she had shown him her whole life. He could see it as clearly as though it had passed before him in a panorama. But, in spite of that, he decided with a heavy heart to try and see whether his admonitions would have any effect upon her. Plucking up courage, he began explaining her awful position to her in a voice that shook, but which was at the same time full of passionate conviction. She listened to him with an attentive air and with the feeling of wonder we display at the sight of something strange and unexpected. She glanced with a faint smile at her friend who was sitting in a corner and who had stopped cleaning a comb and was also listening with rapt attention to the new preacher.

"It's true I'm poor," said Piskarev at last, after a long and highly instructive homily, "but we will work, we'll do our best, both of us, to improve our position. Surely nothing can be more agreeable than the feeling that our success will be due entirely to our own efforts. I will do my painting, and you shall sit beside me and inspire me in my work. You can do some embroidering or some other kind of needlework, and we shall have all we need."

"How do you mean?" she interrupted with an expression of undisguised scorn. "I'm not a washerwoman, or a dressmaker! You don't expect me to work, do you?"

Oh, she could not have described the whole of her mean and contemptible life better than in those words! A life full of idleness and emptiness, the true companions of vice.

"Marry me !" her friend, who till then had sat silent in a corner, interjected with an impudent air. "When I'm married I will sit like this !" she declared with a stupid grimace on her pathetic face, to the great amusement of the beautiful girl.

Oh, that was too much ! That was more than he could bear ! He rushed out of the room, too stunned to feel or think. He felt dazed and wandered about all day stupidly, aimlessly, seeing nothing, hearing nothing, feeling nothing. No one knew whether he had slept anywhere that night or not, and it was only on the following day that by some blind instinct he staggered back to his room, looking terrible, haggard and pale, with his hair dishevelled and signs of madness in his face. He shut himself up in his room, let no one in and asked for nothing. Four days passed, and his locked room was not opened once. At last a week passed, and still his room remained locked. People knocked at his door and began calling him, but there was no reply; in the end they broke down the door and found his lifeless body with the throat cut. From his convulsively outspread arms and his terribly contorted face it was evident that his hand had been unsteady and that he must have suffered a long time before his sinful soul had left his body.

So perished the victim of a mad passion, poor Piskarev, the gentle, shy, modest, childishly good-natured man, who carried a spark of genius in his breast which might with time have blazed forth into a great bright flame. No one shed any tears over him; there was no one to be seen by his dead body, except the ordinary figure of the district police inspector and the bored face of the police surgeon. Quietly and without any religious service, his body was taken to Okhta, and the only man who followed it was a night watchman, an ex-soldier who did indeed weep, but only because he had had a glass of vodka too many. Even Lieutenant Pirogov did not come to pay his last respects to the poor luckless artist upon whom during his lifetime he had conferred his exalted patronage. However, he had other business to attend to, being involved in rather an extraordinary adventure. But let us turn to him. I do not like corpses and dead men and I always feel rather ill at ease when my path is crossed by a long funeral procession, and an old crippled soldier, dressed like some Capuchin, takes a pinch of snuff with his left hand because he is carrying a torch in his right. The sight of a rich catafalque and a velvet pall always depresses me terribly, but my feeling of depression is mingled with grief whenever I see the bare, pine coffin of some poor wretch being taken to the cemetery on a cart and only some old beggar woman, who had met it at the crossroads, following it because she has nothing else to do.

I believe we left Lieutenant Pirogov at the moment when he parted from Piskarev and went in pursuit of the blonde. This blonde was a very slender and an exceedingly attractive little creature. She stopped before every shop and gazed at the belts, kerchiefs, ear-rings, gloves and all sorts of pretty trifles in the shop-windows. She was never still, she kept looking in all directions, and was continually casting glances behind her. "You'll be mine, my pretty one!" Pirogov murmured complacently, as he continued to pursue her, hiding his face in the collar of his greatcoat to make sure that none of his friends recognised him. But I suppose we ought really to tell our readers a little more about Lieutenant Pirogov.

Before saying anything about Lieutenant Pirogov, however, we must say something about the circle to which he belonged. There are army officers in St. Petersburg who form a kind of middle class of their own. You will always find them at a dinner or at a party given by some State Councillor or Regular State Councillor who has achieved his rank by forty years of hard work. One or two pale daughters, colourless like St. Petersburg itself and with the first bloom of youth perhaps a little worn off, the tea-table, the piano, the improvised dances—all this is inseparable from the bright epaulette glittering in the lamplight between the refined, fair-haired young lady and the black frock-coat of her brother or of some friend of the family. To infuse a little life into those apathetic misses or to make them laugh is one of the hardest tasks in the world: one has to be a real artist to do that. But perhaps one need not be an artist at all, but merely possess the knack of saying something that is neither too clever, nor too funny. One has, in short, to be an adept in the small talk which the ladies like so much. Now the gentlemen in question must be given the credit of possessing this special gift for making these insipid beauties laugh and listen to them. "Oh, do stop! Aren't you ashamed to say such silly things!" are often their highest reward. You very rarely, indeed hardly ever, meet these gentlemen in high society. From there, alas, they are elbowed out ruthlessly by those who in those circles pass for aristocrats. On the whole however, they enjoy the reputation of being cultured and well-bred men. They are fond of discussing literature; they praise the editor Bulgarin, the poet Pushkin, and the journalist Grech, and speak with undisguised contempt of the popular writer A. A. Orlov, who is the constant butt of their wit. They never miss a public lecture, whatever its subject, whether on book-keeping or even forestry. You can rely on always finding one of them at the theatre, whatever the play, unless indeed it be some vaudeville portraying the lives of the lower classes, such as "Filatka and Miroshka—the Rivals, or Four Wooers and One Girl," which greatly offends their fastidious taste. Otherwise they are always to be found at the play. In fact, they are the best customers of a theatrical manager. They are particularly fond of fine verses in a play, and they greatly enjoy calling loudly for the actors. Many of them, by teaching in State establishments or coaching people to pass examinations for State establishments, can with time afford their own carriage and pair. Then their social circle becomes much wider and in the end they get to the stage when they marry a merchant's daughter who can play the piano and brings with her a dowry of a hundred thousand or thereabouts, in cash, and a large number of bearded relations. As a rule, however, they can never achieve such an honour till they have served long enough to have reached the rank of colonel. For the Russian bearded gentry, in spite of the fact that the smell of cabbage soup may linger about their beards, do not on any account want to see their daughters married to any man unless he is a general, or at least a colonel. Such are the main characteristics of this sort of young man. But Lieutenant Pirogov had a large number of talents which were all his own. He could, for instance, recite excellently the verses from Ozerov's *Dimitry Donskoy* and Griboyedov's *The Misfortune of Being Too Clever*, and he was an absolute master of the art of blowing smoke from his pipe in rings, so that he could string a dozen of them together, one on top of the other. He also could tell the amusing story about a cannon being one thing and a unicorn another in a most inimitable way. It is perhaps a little difficult to enumerate all the talents fate had lavished with so generous a hand upon Pirogov. He liked to talk about an actress or a dancer, but not as crudely as a young second lieutenant usually discourses on the same subject. He was very proud of his rank, to which he had only lately been promoted, and though occasionally as he lay down on the sofa he would murmur, "Vanity of vanities, all is vanity! What though I am a lieutenant?" he was, as a matter of fact, very pleased with his new dignity. He often alluded to it in conversation in a roundabout way, and once when he met some Government clerk whom he did not think sufficiently respectful to him, he stopped him at once and pointed out to him in a few trenchant words that he was a lieutenant and not some ordinary officer. He did his best to put it the more eloquently as two very good-looking ladies were passing at the time. In general Pirogov displayed a passion for the fine arts and patronised and in every possible way encouraged the artist Piskarev, which, however, might have been mainly due to his great desire to see his manly countenance portrayed on canvas. But enough of Pirogov's qualities. Man is so wonderful a creature that it is quite impossible to enumerate all his virtues, and the more you scrutinise him the more new characteristics you discover in him, and a description of all of them would go on for ever.

And so Pirogov went on pursuing the blonde, trying from time to time to attract her attention by addressing some questions to her, to which she replied rather brusquely, stiffly and inaudibly. They passed through the dark Kazan Gates and entered Meshchanskaya street, a street of tobacconists and grocery shops, of German artisans and Finnish nymphs. The blonde ran faster and darted into the gates of a rather dirty-looking house. Pirogov went after her. She ran up a narrow, dark staircase and went in at a door, through which Pirogov boldly followed her. He found himself in a big room with black walls and a soot-covered ceiling. A heap of iron screws, locksmith's tools, shining coffee-pots and candlesticks lay on the table; the floor was littered with iron and copper filings. Pirogov realised at once that it was an artisan's lodging. The fair stranger darted through a side-door into another room. For a moment Pirogov wondered what to do next, but, following the Russian practice, he decided to carry on. He found himself in a room which was quite unlike the first, a very neatly furnished room, showing that the master of the house was a German. He was struck by a really extraordinary scene.

In front of him sat Schiller, not the Schiller who wrote *Wilhelm Tell* and *The History of the Thirty Years' War*, but the well-known Schiller, the tinsmith of Meshchanskaya Street. Beside Schiller stood Hoffmann, not the writer Hoffmann, but the very excellent bootmaker of Officer Street, a great friend of Schiller's. Schiller was drunk and was sitting on a chair, stamping and shouting something in an excited voice. All this would not have surprised Pirogov. What did surprise him was the extraordinary attitude of the two men. Schiller was sitting with his head raised and his rather thick nose thrust out, while Hoffmann was holding this nose between forefinger and thumb and flourishing his cobbler's knife over it, only missing it by a fraction of an inch. Both gentlemen were talking in German, and for this reason Lieutenant Pirogov who only knew how to say *Guten Morgen* in German, could not make out what was happening. However, what Schiller was saying was this:

"I don't want a nose! I have no use for it!" he said, waving his hands. "I spend three pounds of snuff a month on my nose. And I get it in some rotten Russian shop, for a German shop does not keep Russian snuff. I pay forty copecks a pound to the dirty Russian shopkeeper, which makes one rouble and twenty copecks a month or fourteen roubles and forty copecks a year. How do you like that, Hoffmann, my dear friend? Fourteen roubles and forty copecks on my nose alone! And on holidays I usually take rappee, for I'm damned if I'm going to take that rotten Russian snuff on a holiday. In a year I use two pounds of rappee at two roubles per pound. Six and fourteen makes twenty roubles and forty copecks on snuff alone! That's sheer robbery, my dear fellow, highway robbery! Am I right, Hoffmann, dear friend of mine?" Hoffmann, who was also drunk, answered affirmatively. "Twenty roubles and forty copecks!" Schiller went on. "Damn it, man! I'm a Swabian German. I have a king in Germany! I don't want a nose! Cut off my nose! Here, take it!"

And but for the sudden appearance of Lieutenant Pirogov, Hoffmann would quite certainly have cut off Schiller's nose, for he had already placed the knife in position as though he were going to cut out a piece of leather for a sole.

Schiller was greatly annoyed that an unknown and uninvited man should have prevented him from carrying out his plan of getting rid of his expensive nose. Although he was in a blissful state of intoxication, he, besides, felt that in his present position and under such circumstances he cut rather a poor figure. Meanwhile Pirogov said with a slight bow and with his usual courtesy, "Excuse me, sir. . . ."

"Get out of here!" Schiller replied with long-drawn-out emphasis.

Pirogov felt rather disconcerted. He was not used to being spoken to in such a way. A smile which was just about to appear on his face vanished at once, and he said with a note of hurt dignity, "I'm afraid, sir—er—You evidently haven't noticed, sir, that—er—that I'm an officer!"

"An officer? What's an officer? I'm a Swabian German, I am. I can be an officer myself!" said Schiller, banging the table with his fist. "A year and a half you're a cadet, two years—a lieutenant, and tomorrow you're an officer! But I don't want to be an officer! That's what I do to an officer—phew!" and Schiller held out his open hand and blew on it.

Lieutenant Pirogov realised that there was nothing left for him to do but to withdraw, but he could not help resenting such treatment which was hardly complimentary to his rank. He stopped a few times on the stairs, as though wishing to summon enough courage and to think of a way to make Schiller feel sorry for his insolence. In the end, however, he decided that it was possible to excuse Schiller because of his quite undeniable state of intoxication. Besides, he remembered the charming blonde, and he made up his mind to forget the whole incident.

Early next morning Lieutenant Pirogov again appeared in the tinsmith's workshop. In the first room he was met by Schiller's pretty wife, who asked him in a rather severe voice, which incidentally went very well with her sweet little face, "What do you want?"

"Ah, good morning, my dear! Remember me? Oh, you sweet little rogue, what lovely eyes you've got!" said Lieutenant Pirogov, who at the same time was about to chuck her very prettily under the chin with his forefinger.

But the blonde uttered a frightened cry and asked him again very severely, "What do you want?"

"What do I want, my dear? Why, all I want is to see you, of course!" said Lieutenant Pirogov with a very charming smile, going up closer to her; but noticing that the timid blonde was about to slip through the door, he added, "I want to order some spurs, my dear. Do you think your husband could make me a pair of spurs? Not that a man wants any spur to love you, my sweet. What a man wants is a bridle rather than a spur. What lovely hands you've got!"

"I'll call my husband!" said the blonde and went out.

Lieutenant Pirogov was the perfect gentleman in declarations of that kind.

A few moments later Schiller came in looking rather sleepy, for he had only just woken up after the orgy of the previous day. Seeing Pirogov, he recalled rather vaguely the incident of the day before, that is to say, he could not remember exactly what had happened, but he had an idea that he had behaved rather stupidly, and so he gave the officer a very stern look.

"I'm afraid I can't take less than fifteen roubles for a pair of spurs," he declared, wishing to get rid of Pirogov; for, being a respectable German, he felt ashamed to look at any person who had seen him in an undignified position. Schiller liked to drink without any witnesses, with two or three friends, and at such times he used to shut himself up even from his own workmen.

"Why are you charging me so much?" Pirogov asked, politely.

"German work," said Schiller very coolly, stroking his chin. "A Russian will charge you two roubles for them."

"All right," said Pirogov. "Just to show you how much I like you and how much I desire your acquaintance, I'll pay you fifteen roubles."

Schiller thought it over for a moment. As an honest German craftsman he felt a little ashamed to have asked so much, and, wishing to put the officer off, he said that he could not possibly have them ready before a fortnight. But Pirogov agreed to that without raising a single objection.

The German considered it. He was wondering how best to do the work so that it should really be worth fifteen roubles. Meanwhile the blonde came into the workshop and began looking for something on the table, which was covered with coffee-pots. The lieutenant took advantage of the tinsmith's abstraction to go up to his wife and press her arm, which was bare to the shoulder.

Schiller did not like that at all.

"*Mein' Frau!*" he exclaimed.

"*Was wollen Sie doch?*" said the blonde to her husband.

"*Gehn Sie* to the kitchen!" said her husband.

The blonde went out.

"In a fortnight then?" said Pirogov.

"Yes, sir, in a fortnight," said Schiller, reflectively. "I'm very busy now."

"Good-bye. I'll call again."

"Good-bye, sir," replied Schiller, locking the door after him.

Lieutenant Pirogov made up his mind not to abandon his quest in spite of the fact that the German woman had quite openly rebuffed all his advances. It never occurred to him that any woman could resist him, particularly as his good manners and his brilliant rank gave him the right to expect every possible consideration from the fair sex. We feel bound, however, to state that Schiller's wife, for all her good looks, was rather a stupid woman. Not that stupidity in a pretty woman is to be despised; on the contrary, it greatly enhances her charm. At any rate, I have known many husbands who were in raptures over the stupidity of their wives, finding it the best proof of their child-like innocence. Beauty works perfect wonders. Far from producing a feeling of disgust, all her intellectual shortcomings become somehow extraordinarily attractive in a beautiful woman; even vice seems only to add to her charm. But let her beauty vanish and a woman will have to be twenty times as clever as a man to inspire respect, let alone love. Anyway, however stupid Schiller's wife was, she was faithful to her vows, and Pirogov would therefore have found it extremely difficult to succeed in his bold enterprise; but the greater the obstacles, the sweeter the victory, and he found the blonde more and more fascinating every day. He began paying frequent visits to Schiller to see how the work on his spurs was progressing, so that in the end Schiller got sick and tired of it. He did his best to finish the spurs as quickly as possible, and at last they were ready.

"Oh, what fine workmanship!" exclaimed Lieutenant Pirogov when he saw the spurs. "How wonderfully they're made! I'm sure our general himself hasn't got such fine spurs!"

Schiller felt very flattered. There was quite a merry twinkle in his eyes and he forgave Pirogov everything. "A Russian officer," he thought, "is a clever fellow!"

"I suppose you couldn't make me a sheath for a dagger or something, could you?"

"Why, of course, sir," said the German with a smile.

"Excellent! Do make me a sheath for a dagger then. I'll bring it you. I have a very fine Turkish dagger, but I'd like to have another sheath for it."

This was just like a thunderbolt to Schiller. He knit his brows, thinking, "What a fool I am!" and inwardly cursing himself for being responsible for Pirogov's second order. But he felt it would be dishonest to refuse it now, particularly as the Russian officer had been so nice about his work. So after shaking his head, he agreed to do the sheath. But the kiss which Pirogov impudently imprinted on the blonde's lips as he went out left him utterly bewildered.

146

I think it will not be out of place here to make the reader a little better acquainted with Schiller.

Schiller was a real German in the full sense of the word. Even at the age of twenty, when the Russian lives without a care for the morrow, Schiller had already planned his future in a most thorough and methodical way and never under any circumstances did he deviate from the course he had set himself. He resolved to get up at seven, to lunch at two, to be punctual in everything, and to get drunk every Sunday. He resolved to save a capital of fifty thousand in ten years, and this was as certain and irrevocable as fate itself, for a Civil Servant will sooner forget to peep into his chief's ante-room to see if he is in than a German will consent to break his word. Under no circumstances did he increase his expenses, and if the price of potatoes went up, he did not spend a penny more on them, but merely bought less potatoes, and though such a regime often resulted in his being hungry, he soon got used to it. His exactness was such that he made it a rule never to kiss his wife more than twice in twenty-four hours, and to make sure he did not kiss her three times he never put more than one teaspoonful of pepper in his soup. On Sundays, however, this rule was not so strictly observed, for then Schiller drank two bottles of beer and one bottle of cummin brandy, which he always abused. He did not drink like an Englishman, who bolts the door immediately after dinner and gets dead drunk in solitude. On the contrary, like a German, he always drank in merry company, either with Hoffmann the shoemaker or with Kuntz the carpenter, also a German and a great drunkard. Such was the character of the worthy Schiller who now found himself in a devilishly awkward fix. Although he was a German and therefore a little phlegmatic, Pirogov's behaviour aroused in him a feeling which was very much like jealousy. He racked his brains, but could not think how to get rid of this Russian officer. Meanwhile Pirogov, smoking a pipe in the company of his brother officers (for so Providence seems to have decreed that wherever there are officers there are also pipes), alluded rather self-importantly and with an agreeable smile on his lips to the little intrigue with a pretty German lady, with whom, according to him, he was on very intimate terms, though as a matter of fact he had almost given up all hope of ever having his way with her.

One day he was walking along Meshchanskaya Street, staring at the house adorned with Schiller's signboard with coffee-pots and *samovars* on it, when, to his great delight, he beheld the pretty head of Mrs. Schiller looking out of the window and watching the passers-by. He stopped, blew her a kiss and said *Guten Morgen*. The blonde bowed to him as to an old friend.

"Is your husband at home ?"

"Yes, he's at home."

"And when isn't he at home ?"

"He's never at home on Sundays," replied the foolish little blonde.

"That's not bad," thought Pirogov to himself. "I must remember that."

Next Sunday he descended like a bolt from the blue on Schiller's establishment. Schiller, as his wife had said, was not at home. His pretty wife looked rather frightened, but on this occasion Pirogov behaved with the utmost discretion, treated her with great respect, and, bowing very courteously, paraded all the elegance of his slender figure in his close-fitting uniform. He joked very agreeably and politely, but the silly little German woman replied to all his remarks only in monosyllables. At last having tried every approach he could think of and seeing that nothing seemed to amuse her, he suggested that they should dance. The pretty German woman immediately agreed, for German women are very fond of dancing. Pirogov, in fact, pinned all his hopes on that, for, in the first place, dancing was something that gave her pleasure; secondly, it gave him the opportunity of displaying his figure and dexterity; and, thirdly, he could get much closer to her in dancing, for he could put his arm round her and lay the foundations for everything that was to come; in short, he was sure that such a propitious start was bound to lead to complete success.

He chose for their first dance a gavotte, knowing that the Germans like a slow, sedate dance. The pretty German woman stepped out into the middle of the room and lifted her entrancing little foot. This attitude so enchanted Pirogov that he immediately started kissing her. Mrs. Schiller screamed, but this merely increased her charm in Pirogov's eyes, who smothered her with kisses. Suddenly the door opened and in walked Schiller with Hoffmann and Kuntz the carpenter. All these worthy artisans were as drunk as lords.

I leave it to the reader to imagine Schiller's anger and indignation.

"You're an impertinent fellow, sir !" he shouted, boiling over with indignation. "How dare you kiss my wife, sir ? You're a scoundrel, sir, and not a Russian officer ! Damn it, Hoffmann, my dear fellow, I'm a German, and not a Russian pig, aren't I ?" Hoffmann nodded. "Oh, I'm not going to be made a cuckold ! Take him by the collar, Hoffmann, there's a good fellow ! I'm not going to put up with it," he went on brandishing his arms about violently, his face the colour of his red waistcoat. "I've been living in St. Petersburg for eight years ! I have a mother in Swabia and an uncle in Nuremberg. I'm a German, I am, and not some horned beast ! Strip him, Hoffmann, my dear friend ! Off with his clothes ! Hold him by his arms and legs, *Kamarad* Kuntz !"

The Germans seized Pirogov by his arms and legs. In vain did the lieutenant try to defend himself against them; the three German artisans were the most stalwart specimens of German manhood in St. Petersburg, and they treated him with such an utter lack of ceremony and civility that I cannot find words in which to describe this highly regrettable incident.

I am sure that next day Schiller was in a high fever, that he was shaking like an aspen leaf and expecting any minute the arrival of the police, and that he would have given anything in the world if what had happened the previous day had been a dream. However, what was done could not be undone. But nothing could compare with Pirogov's anger and indignation. The very thought of so terrible an insult made him furious. Siberia and the lash seemed to him the least punishment Schiller deserved. He rushed back home so that, having dressed, he could go at once to the general and report to him in the most lurid colours the outrage committed on his person by the German artisan. At the same time he meant to send in a written complaint to the General Staff, and if the punishment should still be unsatisfactory, he resolved to take the matter further and, if need be, further still.

But the whole thing somehow petered out most strangely; on the way to the general, he went into a pastrycook's, ate two pastries, read something out of the *Northern Bee*, and left with his anger somewhat abated. The evening, moreover, happened to be particularly cool and pleasant and he took a few turns on Nevsky Avenue; by nine o'clock he calmed down completely and it occurred to him that it was hardly wise to disturb the general on a Sunday, especially as he was quite likely to be out of town. And so he went instead to a party given by one of the directors of the Auditing Board, where he found a very agreeable company of Civil Servants and army officers. There he spent a very pleasant time and so distinguished himself in the mazurka that not only the ladies but also the gentlemen were in raptures over it.

What a wonderful world we live in ! I could not help reflecting as I strolled along Nevsky Avenue the other day and as I recalled these two incidents. How strangely, how mysteriously does fate play with us ! Do we ever get what we want ? Do we ever attain what all our endeavours seem to be specially directed to ? Everything seems to happen contrary to our hopes and expectation. Fate rewards one man with a pair of splendid horses, and you see him driving about in his carriage, looking bored and paying no attention to the beauty of his trotters, while another man whose heart is consumed with a passion for horseflesh has to go on foot and get all the satisfaction he can by clicking his tongue whenever a fine trotter is led past him. One man has an excellent cook, but unhappily nature has endowed him with so small a mouth that he cannot possibly take more than two pecks, while another has a mouth as big as the arch of the General Headquarters, but, alas, he has to be content with a German dinner of potatoes. How strangely does fate play with us all !

But strangest of all are the incidents that take place on Nevsky Avenue. Oh, do not trust that Nevsky Avenue ! I always wrap myself up more closely in my cloak when I walk along it and do my best not to look at the things I pass. For all is deceit, all is a dream, all is not what it seems. Take that gentleman who is strolling about in the immaculate coat. You think he is very rich, don't you ? Not a bit of it : he carries all his wealth on his back. You may think that those two fat men who have stopped in front of the church that is being built are discussing its architecture. But you are wrong. They are merely discussing those two sitting crows facing each other so strangely. You may fancy that that enthusiast who is waving his arms about is complaining to his friend about his wife who threw a ball out of a window at an officer who was a complete stranger to him. Not at all : he is talking of Lafayette. You think those ladies . . . but the ladies are least of all to be trusted. And please don't look so often into the shop-windows : the trinkets displayed there are no doubt very beautiful, but there is a strong odour of money about them. And may the Lord save you from peeping under the hats of the ladies ! However much a cloak of a beautiful girl may flutter in the distance, I, for one, will never follow it to satisfy my curiosity. Away, away from the street lamp, for heaven's sake ! Pass it

quickly, as quickly as you can ! You'll be lucky if all you get
is a few drops of stinking oil on your new suit. But, even apart from
the lamp-post, everything is full of deceit. It lies at all times, does
Nevsky Avenue, but most of all when night hovers over it in a thick
mass, picking out the white from the dun-coloured houses, and all
the town thunders and blazes with lights, and thousands of carriages
come driving from the bridges, the outriders shouting and jogging
up and down on their horses, and when the devil himself lights all
the street-lamps to show everything in anything but its true colours.

TARAS BULBA

I

"COME ON, son, turn round! Lord, what a sight you are! What sort of clerical frocks have you got on? Do they all go about dressed like that at the Academy?"

With these words old Bulba welcomed his two sons on their return from Kiev where they had completed their course at the religious academy.

His sons had only just dismounted from their horses. They were two stalwart fellows, who wore a sullen look, like two seminarists who had recently been let out of school. Their strong, healthy faces, covered with the first down of youth, were yet untouched by the razor. They looked greatly embarrassed by such a welcome from their father and stood motionless, with downcast eyes.

"Wait! Wait! Let me have a good look at you!" Taras went on, turning them round. "Just look at their long coats! What coats! I'm sure you won't find such coats anywhere in the world! Now then, one of you, run across the yard, will you? I bet you get all tangled up in your skirts and come a cropper!"

"Don't make fun of me, Dad! Don't make fun of me!" the elder of them said at last.

"High and mighty, aren't you? Why shouldn't I make fun of you?"

"I wouldn't if I were you. You may be my father, but, by God, if you make fun of me I'll thrash you!"

"Oho! So that's the kind of son you are, eh? Thrash your own father, will you?" said Taras Bulba, retreating a few steps in surprise.

"Well, what if you are my father? I won't take an insult lying down from anyone, no matter who he is!"

"So you want to have a fight with me, do you? All right. How shall we fight? With our fists?"

"I don't care how we fight, Dad."

"Very well, let it be with our fists then!" said Taras Bulba, rolling up a sleeve. "Let's see how good you are with your fists!"

And instead of exchanging greetings after so long a separation, father and son began pommelling each other in the ribs, and the back and chest, now breaking away and watching out for an opportunity of getting in a blow, now advancing again.

"Look at him! Look at the old fool! Gone clean off his head, he has!" said their pale, thin, tender-hearted mother, who stood in the doorway and had not yet had a chance of embracing her darling boys. "The children have only just come home, we've not seen them for over a year, and all he can think of is fighting with fists!"

"Damn it, the boy fights well!" said Bulba, stopping. "He certainly fights well," he went on, recovering a little. "So well that a man had better think twice before trying it on with him! Make a fine Cossack, he will! Well, welcome home, son! Come, let's embrace!" And father and son exchanged kisses. "That's right, son. Well done. Hit everyone as hard as you hit me: don't let anyone off! But all the same, your clothes do look funny, you know. What's this rope doing here? And you, what are you standing there like a dummy for?" he said, turning to the younger son. "Why don't you thrash your old dad, you son of a dog?"

"What will he be thinking of next, I wonder," said the mother, who was meanwhile embracing her younger son. "Have you ever heard of such a thing? A child beating his own father! The poor child is so young, he has come such a long way, he is tired out (the poor child was over twenty years old and exactly seven foot tall), he should have a good rest now and something to eat, and he wants him to fight!"

"Well, I can see you're a mother's darling, son!" said Bulba. "Now listen to me. Don't pay any attention to what your mother says: she's only a woman! She knows nothing. You don't want to be pampered, do you? All the pampering you want is to be out on an open plain on a good horse! See this sabre? That's a mother for you! All that damned rubbish they've been stuffing your heads with: academies, all those books, grammars, philosophies—pshaw! I wouldn't give a brass farthing for it!"

Here Bulba imparted still greater force to his argument by using a word which never appears in print. "You know what I'm going to do? I'm going to send you this very week to the Cossack head-quarters on the Dnieper, to the *Syech*. There they'll teach you some-thing worth knowing. That's the proper school for you. It's only there you'll learn wisdom!"

"You don't mean they're going to be only one week at home?" said the frail old mother in a plaintive voice, her eyes brimming with tears. "Why, the poor boys won't have time to enjoy themselves; they won't have time to get to know their own home; and I shan't see enough of them, either!"

"Stop your howling, woman. A Cossack can't afford to waste his time with women. I dare say you'd like to hide them under your petticoat, wouldn't you? And sit on them like a brooding hen on her eggs! Go on, go on, put everything you have on the table for us. We don't want your tarts, or honey-cakes, or poppy-seed cakes, or any other of your delicacies. Fetch me a whole sheep, or a goat, and some forty-year-old mead! And, mind, let's have plenty of vodka. Real vodka, I mean. None of your fancy stuff with raisins and what not. Pure vodka that foams and bubbles and hisses like mad!"

Bulba led his sons into the large room of the cottage. Two pretty maidservants with red necklaces, who were tidying the room, rushed out of it as soon as Bulba and his sons came in. They were ap-parently alarmed at the arrival of the young masters who were not in the habit of leaving a pretty girl alone, or they might have simply wished to observe the female custom of uttering a stream and rushing away headlong at the sight of a man and then keeping their faces covered a long time with their sleeves to hide their shame. The room was furnished after the fashion of that time, a fashion of which hints have been preserved in songs and popular ballads which used to be sung in the Ukraine by blind, bearded old men to the gentle tinkling of a bandore while a large crowd gathered round to listen; for that was the custom of those hard, turbulent days when bitter battles were just beginning to be fought in the Ukraine against the Poles who tried to impose the Uniate faith upon the people. Every-thing in the room was spotlessly clean, the walls and floor coated with coloured clay. On the walls were sabres, horse-whips, bird-nets, fishing tackle, muskets, a cunningly wrought powder-horn, a gold bridle, and hobbles with silver plates. The windows in the room were small, with opaque, round glass, such as can only be found nowadays in old churches, through which it was impossible to see anything without lifting a sliding pane. The window-sills and the door-lintels were painted red. On the shelves round the corners of the room stood jugs, large bottles and flasks of green and dark-blue glass, chased silver goblets, and gilt cups of various makes: Venetian, Turkish and Circassian, that had come into Bulba's parlour by various routes after passing through three or four hands, as was common enough in those adventurous times. All round the room were birch-wood benches; an enormous table stood in the corner under the icons; a wide stove, covered with brightly coloured tiles, with little nooks and all kinds of shelves and protrusions. All this was very familiar to our two young men, who used to walk home for their summer holidays every year; they walked because at that time they had no horses, for it was not customary for students to ride on horse-back. All they had were their long tufts of hair over their foreheads, which every Cossack bearing arms had a right to pull. It was only now that they had finished their course at the Academy that Bulba had sent them a pair of young stallions from his own drove of horses.

In honour of his sons' arrival Bulba had invited to his house all the officers who were available at the time; and when two of them arrived, together with the Cossack Captain Dmitro Tovkatch, an old friend of his, he at once introduced his sons to them, saying, "See what fine fellows they are ? I'll be sending them to the *Syech* soon !" The guests congratulated Bulba, declaring in one voice that nothing could be better and that there was no finer school for a young man than the famous Cossack settlement below the Dnieper Falls.

"Well, my friends, sit down at the table ! Please sit down anywhere you like !" said Bulba. "Now, sons, first of all let's have a drink of vodka," Bulba went on. "May God bless you, my sons. To your health, sons ! To you, Ostap, and to you, Andrey ! God grant you should always be lucky in war. May you rout the infidels, the Turks and the Tartars, and the Poles, too, if they should attempt anything against our faith. Come, let me fill your cup again ! How do you like the vodka, son ? Good, eh ? And what's vodka in Latin ? Ah, there you are, son ! They were a lot of fools, those Romans: they didn't even know there was such a thing as vodka in the world. Now what's the name of the fellow who wrote Latin verses ? I'm afraid I'm not a very good scholar. Damned if I can remember his name. Horace was it ?"

"What a cunning devil Dad is!" the elder son, Ostap, thought to himself. "Knows everything, the old hound does, and just pretends to know nothing!"

"I expect your abbot did not let you have a sniff of vodka, did he?" Taras went on. "And I suppose they gave you many a good scourging at the Academy with the birch and cherry twigs on the back and on everything else that a Cossack has, didn't they? And perhaps as you seem to have grown a bit too clever, they gave you a lashing with a leather thong, too? Come on, confess! I daresay you caught it not only on Saturdays, but every Wednesday and Thursday, too!"

"Never mind that, Dad," replied Ostap. "What's gone is gone. It's all over now, isn't it?"

"Let them try now," said Andrey. "Let anybody just try to touch me now; let some Tartar rabble only get in my way! They'll soon learn what a Cossack sabre is like!"

"Well said, son, well said! And, damn it, if it comes to that, why shouldn't I come with you? Upon my soul, I will, too! What the devil is the sense of my staying here? What am I supposed to do here? Grow buckwheat, look after the house, tend the sheep and feed the swine, or keep my wife company? Away with it all! I'm a Cossack! I won't do it! What if there is no war? I'll go with you to the *Syech* just to have a good time. Damned if I won't!" And old Bulba got more and more worked up and then he lost his temper altogether, got up from the table, drew himself up to his full height, and stamped his foot. "We'll go tomorrow! Why put it off? What kind of an enemy will we hatch out here? What do we want this cottage for? What do we want these pots for?"

Saying this, he began smashing the pots and the bottles on the table and throwing them about all over the room.

His poor wife, who was accustomed to such outbursts from her husband, sat on a bench and looked on disconsolately. She dared not say anything. Bulba's decision was a great blow to her and, on hearing it, she could not refrain from tears. She looked at her children, from whom she was to be parted so soon, and—but who could describe how great her mute anguish was? It seemed to tremble in her eyes and made her convulsively compressed lips quiver.

Bulba was as stubborn as a mule. He was one of those characters who could only have sprung into existence in the turbulent days of the fifteenth century in that semi-nomadic corner of Europe. At that time the whole of southern Russia, which was still in a primitive state, had been abandoned by its princes and laid waste and burnt to ashes by the ruthless Mongol freebooters. Deprived of home and shelter, man grew dauntless. He settled on the ashes of burnt villages, in spite of the perpetual danger and in the sight of his predatory neighbours, having grown used to looking them straight in the face and forgetting that there was such a thing as fear in the world. It was then that the traditionally pacific Slav spirit became tempered in the flames of war and the Cossack brotherhood arose—an expression of the boundless, reckless exuberance of the Russian character. All the country along the Dnieper, all the fording places, all the hills and dales suitable for cultivation, were settled by the Cossacks, whose numbers no one ever knew and whose bold comrades in arms were fully justified in replying to the Sultan who wanted to know how many of them there were, "Who can tell? They are scattered all over the steppe: where there's a hillock, there's a Cossack!" It was indeed quite an extraordinary manifestation of Russian strength: it was struck out of the heart of the Russian people, like a spark out of a flint, by one national calamity after another. Instead of the former feudal dukedoms, instead of small towns filled with huntsmen, instead of petty princes who were always fighting and selling their towns, warlike settlements arose, army units of regular troops and volunteers, united by common danger and a common hatred of the non-Christian robber bands. Everyone knows from history how their incessant struggles and their restless, rough and tempestuous life saved Europe from the ruthless raids which threatened to destroy it. The Polish kings, who had replaced the hereditary princes as rulers of these vast lands, were too far away and too weak to defend them, but they realised the importance of the Cossacks and their great value as frontier troops. They therefore encouraged the Cossacks and set great store on their warlike disposition. Under their remote authority, the hetmans, elected from the ranks of the Cossacks themselves, transformed the armed settlements and districts into regiments and divisions. It was not a standing army; there were no troops to be seen anywhere; but in the event of a war and a general uprising every man appeared on his horse, fully armed, within eight days and no more, receiving only one gold rouble of pay from the king, and within a fortnight an army assembled such as no recruiting levies could have raised. When the campaign was over, each man went back to his meadows and ploughlands, to the Dnieper ferries, and caught fish, traded, brewed beer, and was a free Cossack. Foreigners in those days quite rightly marvelled at his unusual qualities. There was no craft that a Cossack did not know: distilling vodka, constructing a cart, grinding gunpowder, doing the work of blacksmiths and locksmiths, and, in addition, indulging in reckless debauchery—drinking and carousing as only a Russian can—he was equal to everything. Besides the registered Cossacks who considered it their duty to appear in war-time, it was possible at any time in an emergency to raise large detachments of volunteer cavalry; the Cossack captains had only to go about the fairs and markets of all townships and villages and, standing on a cart, shout at the top of their voices: "Hey, you beer-brewers and distillers! leave your brewing and sprawling behind the stove, feeding the flies on your fat carcasses! Come, win for yourself knightly honour and glory! You ploughmen, buckwheat sowers, shepherds, whoremongers, leave your ploughs, stop dirtying your yellow boots in the earth, stop running after wenches and wasting your knightly strength! It is time you bethought yourselves of winning Cossack glory!" And those words were like sparks falling upon dry wood. The ploughman broke his plough, the distillers and brewers left their tubs and smashed their barrels, the craftsmen and tradesmen sent their crafts and shops to the devil, smashed up the pots in the house, and everyone—whatever his trade or occupation—mounted his horse. In fact, it was here that the Russian character acquired its amplitude, its strength and breadth, its firm exterior.

Taras was one of the old regular army colonels: he was created for the alarms of war and was distinguished by the coarse directness of his character. In those days the influence of Poland was beginning to be felt among the Russian nobility. Many of them were already adopting Polish manners, living in luxury, keeping resplendent retinues of servants, hawks and hounds, giving banquets, building country mansions. Taras loathed it all. He liked the simple life of the Cossacks and quarrelled with those of his friends who were disposed to adopt the Warsaw fashions, calling them the flunkeys of the Polish gentlemen. Always active, always on his feet, he looked upon himself as the rightful defender of the Orthodox faith. Taking the law into his own hands, he would go to a village whose inhabitants complained of oppression by Government licence holders and mono-polists or of an increase in the tax on chimneys. Assisted by his Cossacks, he sat in judgment over the oppressors of the people and dealt with them according to the dictates of his conscience. He had made it an invariable rule to have recourse to the sword in three cases, namely, when the Government commissars showed the slightest lack of respect for the Cossack elders and did not take off their hats in their presence; when the Orthodox religion was held up to scorn and ancient customs were flouted; and, lastly, when the enemies were Tartars or Turks, against whom he always thought it right to take up arms for the greater glory of Christendom.

Now he was already thinking with pleasure how he would arrive with his two sons at the *Syech*, the Cossack military settlement below the Dnieper Falls, and say, "Look, what fine fellows I have brought you !" He saw himself introducing them to all his old battle-scarred friends or watching their first feats of arms or admiring their prowess in drinking, which he looked upon as one of the chief distinctions of a true knight. He had meant first to send them off alone, but, seeing what fine fellows they were, how strong and tall and handsome, his warlike spirit was aroused and he resolved to go with them himself next day, though the only necessity for doing so was his own stubborn will. He lost no time in making all the neces-sary arrangements for the journey, he issued orders, selected the horses and the harness for his young sons, looked into the stables and barns, and picked out the servants who were to go with them the next day. He handed over his authority to the Cossack Captain Tovkatch, together with a strict order to come at once with his whole regiment when he received a summons from the *Syech*. He forgot nothing, drunk though he was and his head dizzy from the fumes of strong liquor. He even ordered the horses to be watered and the best wheat to be put in their mangers, and he came back tired from his exertions.

"Well, children, to bed," he said. "Tomorrow we'll do as God pleases. No, no, don't make up a bed for us ! We don't want a bed. We shall sleep in the open air !"

Night had only just enfolded the sky in her embrace, but Bulba always retired early. He stretched himself on a rug, covered himself with a sheepskin, for the night air was rather fresh ànd, besides, he liked to wrap himself up warmly when at home. He was soon snoring, and the whole household followed his example. Every man in the different corners of the yard was whistling and snoring in his sleep, the night-watchman being the first to fall asleep, for he had drunk more than any in celebration of the homecoming of the young masters. The poor mother alone did not sleep. She bent over the pillow of her beloved sons who were lying side by side; she combed out their young curls, hanging in careless disarray from their heads, and bedewed them with her tears. She gazed at them not only with her eyes, but with the whole of her being; all her feelings seemed to be concentrated in that gaze, and she could not gaze enough on them. She had suckled them at her breast, she had reared them, she had cherished them, and now she was seeing them only for a moment. "Oh, my sons, my dear, dear sons, what's going to happen to you? What awaits you?" she murmured, and tears lingered in the wrinkles which disfigured her once lovely face. She was indeed pitiful, like every woman of that adventurous age. Too brief, all too brief was her experience of love; it lasted only one moment and it was gone, only one moment of great rapture, only one moment of the fever of youth, and her harsh lover forsook her for his sabre, his comrades, his drinking bouts. She would see her husband for two or three days in a year, and for several years she would have no news of him at all. But even when she did see him, when they did live together, it was not much of a life for her. She had to put up with insults, even with blows; the only caresses she knew were given as a favour; she was a pathetic kind of human being among this crowd of wifeless adventurers, on whom the wild life of the Cossacks in the military settlement below the Dnieper Falls had left its harsh imprint. Her youth was gone in a flash without joy or pleasure, and the bloom on her cheeks had faded without kisses, and her lovely breasts had withered, and the beautiful girl became a wrinkled old woman in the space of only a few years. All love, every emotion, all that is tender and passionate in woman, had turned in her into one feeling of maternal love. She fluttered over her children like a gull of the steppes, passionately, ardently. Her dear, dear sons were being taken from her; they were taking them away, and never would she see them any more. Who knows, perhaps in their first battle a Tartar would cut off their heads, and she would not know even where lay their abandoned bodies which some wayside bird of prey would pick clean; and for each drop of their blood she would gladly give her life. Sobbing, she looked into their eyes, heavy with sleep and on the point of closing, and thought to herself,

"Maybe when Bulba wakes he will put off their going for a day or two; maybe he thought of going so soon because he had drunk so much."

High up in the sky the moon shed its bright light for hour after hour on the courtyard filled with sleeping men, on the thick clump of willows and on the tall weeds which smothered the palisade surrounding the yard. But she still sat by the pillow of her dear sons, never for a moment taking her eyes off them, and not thinking of sleep. Already the horses, scenting the dawn, left off grazing and lay down in the grass. The leaves on the topmost branches of the willows began rustling, and little by little a faint ripple ran down the trees till it reached the lowest branches. But she stayed there till daylight, not a bit tired and inwardly praying for the night to go on for ever. From the steppe came the loud neighing of a colt; the sky was overspread with gleaming red bars of light. Bulba suddenly awoke and leapt to his feet. He remembered very well the order he had given the day before.

"Wake up, lads! It's time, it's time! Water the horses! And where's the old woman? (This was his usual name for his wife.) Hurry up, old woman. We want something to eat. We have a long journey before us!"

The poor old lady, deprived of her last hope, dragged herself wearily into the cottage. While she was preparing breakfast and weeping quietly all the time, Bulba was giving his last orders and busying himself in the stables, picking out the best trappings for his sons himself.

The students were suddenly transformed. Instead of their muddy boots, they had boots of red morocco leather with silver-shod heels; breeches as wide as the Black Sea itself, with thousands of folds and pleats drawn in with a golden cord; long straps with tassels and various appurtenances for the pipe were attached to the cord. A Cossack coat of scarlet cloth, bright as fire, was girt at the waist with a gay-coloured sash; a pair of chased Turkish pistols were stuck into the sash, and a sabre rattled at their sides. Their faces, still scarcely sunburnt, looked handsomer and whiter; their young black moustaches seemed to bring out more lustrously the whiteness of their skin and their healthy bloom of youth; they looked very dashing under their black lambskin caps with gold tops.

When she saw them in their resplendent dress, their poor mother could not utter a word; her eyes became misted over with tears.

"Well, sons, everything's ready! No use wasting our time!" Bulba said at last. "Let's all sit down before the journey, according to the Christian custom."

All sat down, including the servants who had been standing respectfully at the door.

"Now bless your children, Mother," said Bulba. "Pray to God that they may fight bravely, that they may always defend the honour of knighthood, that they may always champion the Christian faith, and, if they don't, that they may perish utterly and that nothing may be left of them in the world. Go up to your mother, children! A mother's prayer brings succour on land and sea."

The mother, weak as a mother, embraced them and, bringing out two small icons, put them, sobbing, round their necks.

"May the Blessed Virgin keep and preserve you. . . . Don't forget your mother, my dear sons. . . . Don't forget to write to me. . . . Just a few words. . . ." She could say no more.

"Well, come along, children!" said Bulba.

Saddled horses were standing at the front steps. Bulba leapt on to his Devil, which shied wildly, feeling Bulba's sixteen stone on his back, for the old Cossack colonel was very stout and heavy.

When the mother saw her sons already in the saddle, she rushed up to the younger one, in whose features there was more of tenderness, grasped his stirrup, clung to his saddle, and, with despair in her eyes, would not let him go. Two sturdy Cossacks took her carefully and carried her off into the cottage. But when they rode out of the gate, she ran out with the nimbleness of a wild goat, which was so unusual in a woman of her age, and with a force that was hardly credible she stopped the horse and embraced one of her sons with a kind of blind, frenzied fervour. She was again carried away.

The young Cossacks rode on, feeling sad, and restraining their tears for fear of their father, who, for his part, was also feeling a little upset, though he tried not to show it.

It was a dull day; the green foliage glistened brightly; the birds seemed to twitter discordantly. Having ridden some distance, they looked back. Their farmstead seemed to have sunk into the earth and nothing could be seen above it but the two chimneys of their little cottage and the tops of the trees, which they used to climb like squirrels. Before them there still stretched the same meadow that could have recalled to them the whole story of their lives, from the time when they used to roll about in its dewy grass to the time when they used to wait in it for the blackbrowed Cossack girl who fled timidly across it on her swift, sturdy legs. Now all they could see was the pole over the well with the cartwheel fastened to the top and sticking out forlornly against the sky, and now the plain they had just ridden across looked in the distance like a high hill and hid everything behind it.

Farewell, O happy, happy days of childhood! Farewell to play! Farewell to everything! . . .

II

All three horsemen rode in silence. Old Taras was thinking of his past, of his youth that was gone for ever, of the years that would never, never return, the years a Cossack always mourns, for he would like his whole life to be one long protracted youth. He was wondering which of his old comrades he would meet at the *Syech*. He tried to remember which were dead and which were still living. A tear, a big, round tear, gathered slowly in his eye, and his grey old head drooped mournfully.

His sons were occupied with other thoughts. But we must say more about those sons of his. They had been sent to the Kiev Academy in their twelfth year, for all people of quality in those days thought it necessary to give their children an education, though it was done with the intention that they should forget it completely afterwards. When they first came to school, they were, like the other new scholars, wild creatures who had been allowed to grow up in freedom, and it was at school that the boys received a certain polish and acquired some common characteristics which made them resemble one another. The elder boy, Ostap, began his academic career by running away in his first year. He was brought back, given a dreadful flogging, and set down to his books. Four times he buried his reading book in the ground, and four times, after being mercilessly whipped, he was bought a new one. He would quite certainly have done it a fifth time, had not his father given him his solemn word that, unless he finished his course at the Academy, he would be kept in a monastery as a lay brother for twenty years, adding the further threat, fortified by a solemn oath, that Ostap would never see the famous Cossack military headquarters below the Dnieper Falls. It is interesting that this was said by the same

Taras who abused learning and, as we have seen, advised his sons to have nothing to do with it. From that time Ostap began to apply himself diligently to his tedious studies and was soon among the best scholars at the Academy. The kind of education in vogue at that time was entirely divorced from life. Those scholastic, grammatical, rhetorical and logical niceties had no relation whatever to the times in which they lived and were never of any practical use to them in life. Indeed, the learning they acquired at school could not be applied to anything afterwards, and that was true even of those subjects which were less scholastic. The most learned men in those days were also the most ignorant, for they altogether lacked experience of life. Moreover, the republican organisation of the school and the presence of so large a number of big and healthy young fellows was bound to arouse in them an interest in activities that had no connexion whatever with their studies. Their poor fare, the frequent punishments by hunger, the many cravings that are born in a young, strong, healthy lad, awakened in them that spirit of adventure which afterwards found its proper outlet at the Cossack military settlement below the Dnieper Falls. The hungry students prowled about the streets of Kiev and compelled every one to be on his guard. Immediately they caught sight of a student, the women stallholders in the market put their hands on their pies, their bread rings, and their pumpkin seeds, guarding them as eagles do their fledglings. The prefect, whose duty it was to keep an eye on the schoolfellows under his charge, had such enormous pockets in his breeches that he could easily have put the entire stall of a bemused market woman in them. The students of the Academy formed a world of their own: they were not admitted to the higher circles of society which consisted of Polish and Russian noblemen. Adam Kissel, the governor of the city, in spite of his patronage of the Academy, never introduced them into society, and he gave orders that they should be kept under the strictest possible control. This injunction, however, was quite superfluous, for the rector and the monk-professors did not believe in sparing the rod or the lash, and often the lictors by their orders flogged their prefects so unmercifully that the poor fellows rubbed their breeches for weeks afterwards. Many of them did not seem to mind it very much. The flogging to some of them seemed hardly more stinging than vodka spiced with pepper; others on the other hand were sick and tired of the incessant scourgings and they ran away to the Cossack military headquarters below the Dnieper Falls, if they could find the way there or were not themselves intercepted on the road. Ostap, though he now began applying himself very diligently to his studies of logic and even theology, did not escape the pitiless birch. It was natural that this should in a way harden the character and lend it that firmness that has always characterised the Cossacks. Ostap was always looked upon as one of the best comrades. He did not often take the lead in daring enterprises, such as the plundering of an orchard or a kitchen garden, but he was always one of the first to follow the lead of an adventurous student, and never under any circumstances did he betray his comrades. No rod or leather thong could make him do that. He set his face sternly against any allurements other than fighting and wild carousing; at least he scarcely ever thought of anything else. He was frank with his equals. He was kind-hearted so far as that was compatible with such a character and in those days. He was genuinely touched by the tears of his poor mother, and it was that alone that troubled him and made his head droop pensively.

His brother Andrey was of a much livelier disposition and his feelings were in some ways also more developed. He applied himself to his studies more willingly and with less effort than a stronger and sterner character usually devotes to them. He had more initiative than his brother and he took the lead more frequently in some dangerous enterprise, and, thanks to his resourceful wit, he sometimes managed to escape punishment, while his brother Ostap slipped off his coat without thinking twice about it and lay down on the floor, never dreaming of asking for mercy. He, too, was burning with the desire to distinguish himself in battle, but his soul was at the same time accessible to other feelings. He was overcome by a strong yearning for love after he had reached his eighteenth year and woman figured more and more frequently in his ardent dreams. As he listened to some debate on philosophy, he saw her before him every minute in his mind's eye, fresh, black-eyed, sweet; her dazzling, firm breasts, her lovely, delicate bare arm haunted him incessantly; the very dress that clung about her virginal yet strong limbs was invested in his dreams with some inexpressibly exciting voluptuousness. He carefully concealed from his friends these passionate stirrings of his youthful soul, for in those days it was considered dishonourable and shameful for a Cossack to think of woman and love before he had seen any fighting. Of late years he had generally taken part less frequently as leader of some student gang; more often he had prowled about alone in some secluded Kiev lane smothered in cherry orchards, between little houses that peeped out alluringly into the street. Sometimes he would even wander into the quarter of the aristocrats, into what is now old Kiev, where the Ukrainian and Polish nobles lived and where the houses were all built in a certain fanciful style.

One day as he walked along one of these streets lost in dreams, a nobleman's coach nearly knocked him down and the coachman, a man with an enormous moustache, caught him a terrific blow across the back with his whip. The young student flew into a rage. Without a moment's thought he recklessly seized one of the back wheels in his powerful hands and stopped the coach. But the coachman, afraid of a severe chastisement, whipped up the horses, which dashed forward, while Andrey, who luckily had just time to snatch away his hand, fell face downward in the mud. A loud peal of melodious laughter resounded above him. He raised his eyes and saw standing at a window one of the loveliest creatures he had ever seen in his life, with a pair of sparkling black eyes and a skin white as snow tinted by the rosy hues of the morning sun. She was laughing heartily and her laughter lent an added brilliance to her dazzling beauty. He was struck dumb. He looked at her completely disconcerted, absent-mindedly rubbing the dirt off his face, but only succeeding in smearing it more and more over it. Who could this beautiful girl be ? He tried to find out from the servants, a crowd of whom, all dressed in handsome liveries, were standing at the gate listening to a young bandore-player. But seeing his dirty appearance, the servants laughed at him and did not vouchsafe an answer. At last he found out that she was the daughter of the governor of Kovno who was on a visit to Kiev. The very next night, with an impudence characteristic of an Academy student, he got through the palisade into the garden, climbed up a tree whose branches spread over the roof of the house, clambered on to the roof and through the chimney of the open fireplace made his way straight into the bedroom of the beautiful girl who was at the time sitting in front of a candle and taking the costly ear-rings out of her ears. The young Polish girl was so frightened to see an unknown man suddenly confronting her that she could not utter a sound; but when she saw that the student was standing with downcast eyes, too shy to move a hand, and when she recognised him as the same student who had fallen in the mud before her eyes, she was overcome with laughter again. Besides, it was not as if there were anything the matter with Andrey's looks; on the contrary, he was a very handsome fellow indeed. The girl went on laughing merrily and for some time amused herself at his expense. She was frivolous as all Polish girls are, but her eyes, those wonderful, piercingly bright eyes of hers, looked at him with a gaze that was as steady as constancy itself. The student could not stir a limb, and when the governor's daughter went up boldly to him, he felt as though he were tied up in a sack. She put her glittering diadem on his head, hung ear-rings on his lips, and threw over him her transparent muslin blouse with frills embroidered with gold thread. She dressed him up and played all sorts of silly pranks with him, with the careless abandon of a child, so characteristic of frivolous Polish women, and this threw the poor student into even greater confusion. He certainly cut a most ridiculous figure as he stood staring into her dazzling eyes with an open mouth. A sudden noise behind the door of her bedroom alarmed the girl. She told him to hide under the bed, and when all was quiet again she called her maid, a captive Tartar woman, and ordered her to take him out into the garden and see that he got safely over the fence. But this time the student was not so lucky: the awakened watchman caught him fair and square across the legs with his truncheon, and the governor's servants, who came running at the watchman's cries, gave him a good trouncing in the street, but he eventually got away, saved by his swift legs. It was very dangerous for him to go near the governor's house after this, for the Kovno governor had brought with him a large retinue of servants. But Andrey met the girl once again in the Catholic cathedral; she saw him, too, and smiled very charmingly at him, as though at an old friend. He caught one more glimpse of her on another occasion, but soon afterwards the Kovno governor left Kiev, and instead of the beautiful black-eyed Polish girl an unknown fat face stared at him out of the window. . . .

This was what Andrey was thinking of as he rode along with lowered head and eyes fixed on the mane of his horse.

Meanwhile the steppe had long since received them in its green embrace, and the high grass, hemming them in on all sides, hid them from view, only their black Cossack caps showing among its spikes.

"Cheer up, lads! Why are you so silent and woebegone?" Bulba said at last, rousing himself from his reverie. "You're not monks, are you? Now then, to the devil with your melancholy

167

thoughts ! Let's light our pipes, clap spurs to our horses and gallop faster than any bird !"

The Cossacks, bending low over their horses, disappeared in the grass. Now even their black caps could not be seen; only the waving grass, as they crushed it under their horses' hoofs, showed the track of their swift career.

The sun had for some time been shining from a clear sky, flooding the steppe with its bright, warm light. In a trice the Cossacks shook off their gloomy thoughts and their hearts fluttered like birds.

The further they rode, the more beautiful did the steppe become. In those days all the south, all that vast territory known today as New Russia, up to the shores of the Black Sea, was one green, virgin wilderness. No plough ever passed across its measureless waves of wild plants. Only the horses, which were lost in them as in a wood, trampled them. Nothing in nature could be more beautiful; the whole surface of the earth was like a vast ocean of green and gold besprinkled with millions of different flowers. Between the high slender stalks of grass light-blue, dark-blue and purple cornflowers stirred; the yellow broom raised aloft its pyramid-shaped head; white yarrow speckled the surface with its parasol-like plumes; an ear of wheat brought from heaven knows where ripened in the dense thicket of grass. Beneath their slender stems partridges darted about, craning their necks. The air was filled with a thousand different bird calls. Hawks hovered motionless in the sky with outspread wings, their eyes fixed immovably on the sea of grass. The cries of a large flock of wild geese moving aslant the sky re-echoed from heaven knows what far-away lake. A gull rose from the grass, flapping her wings slowly, and bathed luxuriously in the blue waves of the air, now melting away in the blue sky and becoming only a black spot, now turning over, her wings flashing in the sun. . . . Oh, how beautiful they are, the steppes, the devil take them ! . . .

Our travellers only halted for a few minutes for dinner. The troop of ten Cossacks who accompanied them dismounted and untied the wooden kegs of vodka and the pumpkin rinds they used instead of bowls. All they ate was bread and dripping or flat cakes, and they only drank one cupful of vodka to keep up their strength—for Taras Bulba never permitted drinking on the road—and they continued their journey until nightfall.

In the evening the whole steppe was completely transformed. Its entire variegated expanse blazed up with the last bright gleam of sunshine and gradually darkened, so that a shadow could be seen creeping over it, and the steppe grew dark-green. The exhalations rose more thickly from it; every flower, every blade of grass exhaled a fragrance, and the whole steppe exuded a sweet perfume. Broad bars of rose-tinted gold stretched across the dark-blue sky, as if daubed on it with a gigantic brush; light, transparent wisps of white cloud drifted across it from time to time, and the freshest imaginable breeze, as enchanting as the waves of the sea, scarcely stirred the tops of the grass and brushed faintly against the cheek. All the music which had resounded during the day was hushed and replaced by another. Striped pouched marmots crept out of their holes, sat on their hind paws and filled the steppe with their whistling. The chirring of the grasshoppers became louder. Sometimes the cry of a swan came floating from afar and rang like silver in the air.

The travellers, halting for the night in the middle of the steppe' selected a camping place, built a fire and, putting a cauldron on it. cooked a stew; the steam from the cauldron rose slantingly in the air, Having supped, the Cossacks lay down to sleep, leaving their horses hobbled in the grass. They stretched themselves on their coats. The bright stars shone down upon them. They heard the countless myriads of insects that filled the grass, their whistling, buzzing and chirring resounding clearly in the stillness of the night, growing clearer in the fresh air and lulling the drowsy ear. If one of them rose and stood up for a short time, he saw the whole steppe dotted with the gleaming sparks of glow-worms. Sometimes the sky was lighted up here and there with the glow from dry reeds—which were being burnt in the meadows and along the banks of the streams, and a dark string of swans, flying northward, would suddenly gleam with a silvery-pink light, and it looked as if red kerchiefs were flying across the dark sky.

The travellers rode on without any adventures. Nowhere did they come across any trees; before them stretched the boundless, free and beautiful steppe. Only from time to time did they catch a glimpse of the blue ridge of the distant woods which stretched along the bank of the Dnieper. Only once did Taras point out to his sons a little black speck far away in the grass. "Look, boys," he said, "that's a Tartar galloping there !" A little head with a moustache fixed its narrow eyes straight on them in the distance, sniffed the air like a blood-hound, and, seeing thirteen Cossacks, vanished like a mountain goat.

"Well, boys, why don't you try to overtake the Tartar? Oh dear, no. It's no use trying, for you'll never catch him: his horse is swifter than my Devil."

Still, Bulba thought it wiser to take precautions now, fearing that an ambush might be concealed somewhere. They galloped up to the Tatarka, a small tributary of the Dnieper, plunged with their horses into the water and for a long time swam along with the current to conceal their tracks, then scrambled out on to the bank and continued their journey.

Three days later they were not far from their destination. There was a sudden chill in the air; they felt the proximity of the Dnieper. Then they saw it sparkling in the distance, separated from the horizon by a dark line. A chill wind blew from its cold waves, and it stretched nearer and nearer till at last it covered half the surface of the land. They had reached that part of the Dnieper where the river, no longer hemmed in by the rapids, at last asserts itself and, roaring like the sea, flows freely on its course. It is there that the islands in midstream force it still farther out of its banks and its waters spread far and wide over the earth, meeting neither rocks nor hills to impede their flow. The Cossacks dismounted, embarked on a ferry, and after three hours' sailing reached the shores of the island of Hortiga, where the Cossack military camp was situated at the time, the *Syech*, which so often changed its quarters.

A crowd of people on the shore were engaged in a heated argument with the ferrymen. The Cossacks got their horses ready. Taras drew himself up with dignity, threw out his chest, tightened his belt, and passed a hand proudly across his moustache. His young sons, too, spruced themselves up, feeling strangely alarmed, but at the same time also experiencing a vague sensation of pleasure. They rode together into the suburb of the Cossack settlement which was about half a mile from the *Syech* proper. As they rode in, they were deafened by the clatter of fifty blacksmiths' hammers striking in twenty-five smithies, dug into the ground and covered with turf. Strong tanners were sitting under the awnings on the front steps of their cottages and were kneading the hides of oxen with their huge hands; traders were sitting in their tents beside heaps of flints, tinder and gunpowder; an Armenian had hung out costly kerchiefs; a Tartar was roasting a sheep's head dipped in batter on a spit; a Jew, craning his neck, was drawing vodka out of a barrel. But the first man they came across was a Dnieper Cossack who lay asleep in the middle of the road with outstretched arms and legs. Taras Bulba could not help stopping and admiring him.

"Look at him ! How grandly he lies in the middle of the road !" he said, stopping his horse. "Damn it, what a grand figure !"

It was indeed an extremely picturesque scene: the Cossack was stretched out in the road like a lion, his long tuft of hair tossed proudly back and covering almost half a yard of ground; his wide breeches of costly scarlet cloth were smeared with tar to show the utter indifference with which their owner regarded them. Having admired him, Bulba made his way farther along the narrow street, which was jammed with artisans of every description, who carried on their trades in the street itself, and men of all nations who filled this suburb of the *Syech* to overflowing; the suburb indeed was like a fair which fed and clothed the Cossacks of the military settlement who were only concerned with making merry and letting off their guns.

At last they passed the suburb and saw a few scattered Cossack barracks, covered with turf, or, Tartar-fashion, with felt. Some of them had a row of cannons in front. There were no fences, nor any of the little low houses with awnings on small wooden posts which were to be seen in the suburb. A small rampart and a barricade of felled trees, left entirely unguarded, revealed a terrible want of the most elementary precautions. A few stalwart Cossacks, lying right in the road with their pipes between their teeth, looked at them unconcernedly and did not dream of making way for them. Taras rode between them carefully with his sons. "Good day to you, gentlemen," he said. "Good day to you, sir," they replied. Picturesque groups of people were dotted all over the plain. From their tanned faces it could be seen that they had all been hardened in battle and had suffered all sorts of hardships.

So this was the *Syech* ! This was the nest from which so many lion-hearted and proud fighters came ! This was the source whence freedom and Cossack chivalry flowed all over the Ukraine !

The travellers came out into a large square where the assemblies of the Cossacks were usually held. On a big upturned tub sat a Cossack. He had taken off his shirt and was mending it. Their way was barred again by a crowd of musicians, in the middle of which a young Cossack was cutting capers, his cap tilted jauntily on one side and his hands raised over his head. "Faster ! Faster ! Play faster ! And you, Foma, don't stint vodka to orthodox Christians !"

And Foma, a Cossack with a black eye, dispensed a huge mugful of vodka to every man who approached him. Beside the young Cossack, four old warriors set their feet working at a tremendous pace, spun round sideways like a whirlwind almost at the head of the musicians and then, dropping to the ground all of a sudden, flung their feet out quickly and stamped the firmly beaten ground vigorously and sharply with their silver-shod heels. All over the vast space the earth resounded dully to the thud of flying feet, and the rhythmic beat of the silver-shod heels filled the air with a noise that could be heard for miles. One Cossack let out loud, ear-splitting yells as he flew after the others in the dance. His long tuft of hair waved in the wind, his powerful chest was exposed and, as he was wearing a warm winter sheepskin, sweat poured from him as from a bucket.

"Take off your sheepskin, man !" Taras said at last. "Why, you're all steaming hot !"

"Can't !" shouted the Cossack in reply.

"Why not ?"

"Can't do it ! Shall lose it if I do. Lose everything I take off. That's the kind of man I am. If I take a thing off, I spend it on drink !"

The young fellow had neither cap, nor belt round his coat, nor embroidered kerchief: all had gone long ago to pay for his drinks. The crowd grew larger; other Cossacks joined the dancers. It was impossible to watch the dance without being thrilled by the wild abandon with which they all flung themselves into this most free and most furious dance the world has ever seen, a dance called *Kazachok* from its mighty originators.

"Oh," cried Taras, "if it weren't for my horse I'd join in the dance myself !"

Meanwhile old Cossacks with grey tufts of hair on their shaven heads appeared in the crowd, men who had been elders more than once and whose great services had won them general recognition in the *Syech*. Taras soon met a large number of old acquaintances. Ostap and Andrey heard nothing but greetings: "Hullo, Petcheritza !" "Good day, Kosolup !" "Where have you sprung from, Taras ?" "How did you get here, Doloto ?" "How are you, Kirdyaga ?" "Glad to see you, Goosty !" "Never thought of meeting you again, Remen !" And the old warriors, who had met here from all over the turbulent world of eastern Russia, embraced and kissed each other and overwhelmed each other with questions : "What's happened to Kassyan ?" "What's Borodavka doing ?" "What about Kolopyor ?" "Any news from Pidsyshok ?" And all Taras Bulba heard in reply was that Borodavka had been hanged in Tolopan, that Kolopyor had been flayed alive at Kizirmen, and that Pidsyshok's head had been pickled in a barrel and sent to Constantinople.

Old Bulba bowed his head and murmured thoughtfully, "Ah, they were good Cossacks, every one of 'em !"

III

Taras and his two sons had been living for about a week at the *Syech*. Ostap and Andrey did little military schooling. The *Syech* scorned military exercises which it considered a waste of time. The young Cossacks were trained and instructed in the art of warfare by experience alone, experience gained in the heat of battles, which for that reason were almost continuous. The intervals between the fighting the Cossacks considered too precious to be spent on learning the discipline of war, with the exception perhaps of an occasional target shoot and, less frequently, horse racing and hunting wild game in the meadows and the steppes; the rest of the time was given up completely to junketing—a sign of a high exuberance of spirits. The whole military settlement presented an extraordinary spectacle : it was a kind of never-ending feast, a ball that began noisily and somehow forgot to end. There were some Cossacks who were occupied in a craft, and a few more who kept shops and engaged in trade; but the majority drank and danced and made merry from morning till evening, while there was still a pleasant jingle in the pocket and while the gold and valuables they had won in battle had not yet passed into the hands of hucksters and inn-keepers. This general banqueting had something spell-binding about it. It was not a gathering of drunkards who spent their last penny on drink to drown their sorrows; it was just one wild riot of high spirits. Every one who came here cast himself adrift from his old life and forgot all his former troubles and joys. He, as it were, bade a lasting farewell to his past life and threw himself gaily into the free-and-easy life of his comrades, carefree revellers like himself, for, like his comrades, he had neither kindred, nor a roof over his head, nor a family, nothing in fact but the open sky and the everlasting banquet of his soul. It was this that produced that wild gaiety which could not have arisen from any other source. The tales and idle talk heard among the crowds that gathered in the square and sat about lazily on the ground were often so amusing and revealed so natural a gift for vivid story-telling that you had to possess the imperturbable, placid exterior of a Dnieper Cossack to keep a straight face without even a twitch of the moustache—a characteristic feature that even today distinguishes the southern Russian from the rest of his countrymen. The gaiety was drunken and clamorous, but for all that this was not a grim drinking den where men seek oblivion in a brutish kind of gaiety. It was an intimate circle of schoolfellows, the only difference being that instead of sitting at a desk and listening to the dreary rambling of the schoolmaster they went out on a raid of five thousand horse, and, instead of a field to play ball in, they had vast, unguarded frontiers which no enemy could cross with impunity, in the sight of which the Tartar never dared to show his quick head, and beyond which the Turk in his green turban gazed, stern and motionless. The difference was that instead of being kept at school against their will, they had of their own free will forsaken their fathers and their mothers and run away from their homes; that there were men there who had had the noose round their necks and who, instead of pale death, saw life again, and life in all its riotous gaiety; that there were men there who regarded it as a point of honour never to keep a penny in their pockets; that there were men there to whom a gold rouble had always been a fortune and whose pockets, thanks to the Jewish tax-farmers and innkeepers, could be turned inside out without any fear of losing anything. There, too, were all the students of the Kiev Academy who had found the academic birch too much of a good thing and who did not bring a single letter of the alphabet with them from school; but among them were also those who knew something of Horace, Cicero and the Roman Republic. There were many of the officers there who afterwards distinguished themselves in the royal armies; there were hundreds of experienced partisans there who cherished the honourable conviction that it did not matter where a man fought so long as he fought and that it was dishonourable for a gentleman not to engage in warfare. There were also many there who had come to the *Syech* in order to be able to say afterwards that they had been at the *Syech* and were therefore veteran fighters. But who was not there? This strange republic was one of the necessities of the age. Lovers of military life, lovers of gold goblets, rich brocades, ducats and reals could find employment here at any time; only the lovers of women could find nothing here, for no woman dared show herself even in the suburb of the *Syech*.

It seemed exceedingly strange to Ostap and Andrey that hundreds of people arrived at the *Syech* almost daily and it never occurred to anyone to ask them where they came from, who they were, or what were their names. They came there as though returning to their own homes which they had only left an hour before. The newcomer merely went to see the general, who usually said:

"Hullo! Do you believe in Christ?"

"I do," the man replied.

"Do you believe in the Holy Trinity?"

"I do."

"Do you go to church?"

"Yes, sir."

"Well then, cross yourself!"

The man crossed himself.

"All right," the general said, "now you can go to any detachment you like."

And that was the end of the ceremony.

All the *Syech* prayed in one church and they were ready to defend it to the last drop of their blood, though they would not hear of fasting or abstinence. Only Jews, Armenians, and Tartars, greedy of gain, ventured to live and trade in the suburb, for the Cossacks never liked bargaining and paid as much money as their hand happened to pull out of their pocket. However, the fate of these avaricious hucksters was most pitiable: they were like the people who live at the foot of Vesuvius, for as soon as the Cossacks ran out of money they smashed their stalls and helped themselves to everything they liked without payment.

The *Syech* was composed of sixty separate military units or "houses," each very much like an independent republic, but still more like a boarding school where the children are provided with all the necessities. No one owned anything, or kept anything to himself; everything was in the hands of the commander of the detachment who for that reason was usually referred to as "the old man." He kept their money, their clothes, all their provisions, the flour and fats for their thin broth, their porridge, and their fuel; the Cossacks even entrusted him with their money for safe-keeping. Very often disputes arose between different "houses," and this invariably led to a free for all. The detachments swarmed all over the square and fought each other with their fists until one or the other party gained the upper hand, and then both indulged in an orgy of drinking. Such was the *Syech*, which provided so many attractions to young men.

Ostap and Andrey threw themselves into this sea of wild gaiety with all the ardour of youth, and instantly forgot their father's house, their school, and all that had interested them before; they gave themselves up entirely to their new life. Everything fascinated them: the riotous customs of the *Syech* and its uncomplicated justice and its laws which seemed to them rather severe in so freedom-loving a republic. If a Cossack was caught stealing from another Cossack, even if the thing he had stolen was of no value, it was regarded as a slur on the good name of all the Cossacks: he was bound to the whipping-post as a common thief and a cudgel was laid beside him, and every passer-by was obliged to deal him a blow with it until he was in this way beaten to death. If a man did not pay his debts, he was chained to a cannon where he had to remain until one of his friends took pity on him and set him free by paying his debt for him. But what impressed Andrey most was the terrible punishment meted out for murder. A pit was dug in his presence, the murderer lowered alive into it and the coffin with the body of the murdered man placed on top of him, and then both were covered with earth. Andrey was for weeks haunted by this terrible form of capital punishment and for a long time he could not get out of his mind the awful picture of the man buried alive in the same grave with the dreadful coffin of the man he had murdered.

It did not take the two young men very long to become popular with the Cossacks. They frequently went hunting with men of their own detachments and occasionally with the whole of their detachment and some of the neighbouring detachments as well, and shot large numbers of steppe birds, stags and wild goats, or went on the lakes, rivers and streams, each stretch of water assigned by lot to a different detachment, and cast nets and sweep-seines and drew out large hauls of fish to provide food for their entire "house." Although there was nothing there to test a Cossack's fitness for battle, they had already made a mark among the other young men by their initiative and daring and the luck that seemed to attend all their efforts. They were excellent shots, rarely missing their target, and they could swim across the Dnieper against the current, a feat for which a Cossack was accorded a triumphant reception in Cossack circles.

But Taras was preparing a different kind of activity for them. Such an idle life was not to his taste: what he wanted was real action. He was always trying to think of some way to rouse the *Syech* to some bold enterprise where a Cossack knight would have plenty of scope to show his mettle. At last one day he went to see the general and, without beating about the bush, said to him:

"Well, General, it's about time the Cossacks had some real work to do."

"There isn't any work for them at present," replied the commanding officer, removing his small pipe from his mouth and spitting.

"What do you mean? Couldn't they go on an expedition against the Turks or the Tartars?"

"No, sir. They can make war neither on the Turk nor on the Tartar," the general replied coolly, replacing the pipe in his mouth.

"Why not?"

"Because they can't. We promised the Sultan peace."

"But he's an infidel. Both God and the Holy Scripture command us to draw the sword against the infidel."

"We have not the right to do it. If we had not sworn by our faith, then perhaps we might have done it, but I'm afraid it's quite out of the question now."

"Out of the question, is it? What do you mean, we have not the right to do it? I have two sons, young men both of them. Neither has ever been in battle, and all you say is we haven't the right. Do you mean the Cossacks mustn't go to war?"

"What I mean is that they can't go to war now."

"Then according to you it is right that the Cossacks should waste their strength, that a man should perish like a dog without fighting for the good cause, without being of any use to his country or to Christendom in general? If that is so, then what the devil are we living for? What's the use of our life? Tell me that. You're a clever man; you weren't chosen commander-in-chief for nothing, were you? Well then, tell me what we are living for?"

The general made no reply to this. He was an obstinate Cossack, and after a short pause he just said, "There won't be any war, all the same."

"So there won't be any war?" asked Taras.

"No, sir."

"And it's no use even thinking about it, is it ?"

"No use at all."

"You wait, you stubborn old devil," thought Bulba to himself. "I'll show you !" and he made up his mind then and there to revenge himself on the commanding officer.

Having talked the matter over with a few of his friends, Taras invited all the Cossacks to a drink and it was not long before several drunken Cossacks went straight to the square and made for the post to which the kettle-drums, used to summon the Cossacks to a general assembly, were fastened. Not finding the drumsticks, which were always kept by the drummer, they each seized a log and began beating the drums. The first to come running at the noise was the drummer, a tall man with only one eye, and that one, too, very sleepy.

"Who dares beat the drums ?" he shouted.

"Hold your tongue ! Take your drumsticks and get on with it when you are told !" replied the tipsy elders.

The drummer immediately took the drumsticks out of his pocket, for he had taken the precaution of bringing them with him, knowing too well how such incidents ended. The kettle-drums rolled, and soon dark groups of Cossacks began to swarm, like bees, on the square. They all gathered into a ring, and after the third drum-roll the elders at last put in an appearance: the commander-in-chief with his mace, the badge of his office, in his hand; the judge with the official army seal; the clerk with his ink-horn; and the captain with his rod. The commanders and the elders took off their caps and bowed in all directions to the Cossacks, who stood proudly with arms akimbo.

"What's the meaning of this assembly, gentlemen ? What do you want ?" asked the general, but the shouts and the imprecations hurled at him made it impossible for him to continue with his speech.

"Put down your mace ! Put down your mace, you son of Satan !" Cossacks shouted from the crowd.

Some of the detachments that remained sober were, it seemed, ready to resist the demand, and a fight immediately broke out between the sober and the drunken Cossacks. The shouting and the uproar became general.

The commander tried to speak, but knowing very well that the infuriated, undisciplined crowd might beat him to death, which almost always happened on such occasions, he bowed very low to the Cossacks, put down his mace, and disappeared into the crowd.

"Is it your wish, gentlemen, that we, too, put down our badges of office?" said the judge, the clerk and the captain, making ready at once to put down the ink-horn, the army seal and the rod.

"No, no! You can remain!" the crowd shouted. "The general is an old woman. That's why it was necessary to turn him out. We want a man for our general!"

"Whom will you choose for your general now?" asked the elders.

"Kukúbenko! We want Kukúbenko!" shouted some.

"We don't want Kukúbenko!" shouted others. "Too soon for him. The milk isn't dry on his lips."

"Let Shilo be our chief!" still others shouted. "Let's make Shilo our general!"

"To hell with Shilo!" the crowd began to curse. "The son of a bitch is a worse thief than a Tartar! Tie him up in a sack, the drunken devil!"

"Borodáty! Let Borodáty be our general!"

"We don't want Borodáty! To the devil with Borodáty!"

"Shout Kirdyaga," whispered Taras to several Cossacks.

"Kirdyaga! Kirdyaga!" shouted the crowd. "Borodáty! Borodáty! Kirdyaga! Kirdyaga! Shilo! To hell with Shilo! Kirdyaga!"

All the candidates, hearing their names called, at once left the crowd, so as to give no excuse to anyone for saying afterwards that they had taken a personal part in their election.

"Kirdyaga! Kirdyaga!" The shouts became stronger. "Borodáty!"

The supporters of each candidate came to blows, and the supporters of Kirdyaga triumphed in the end.

"Go and fetch Kirdyaga!" the crowd shouted.

About a dozen Cossacks, some of them hardly able to stand on their feet, so befuddled were they, went at once to tell Kirdyaga about his election.

Kirdyaga, a rather elderly but clever Cossack, had been sitting for some time in his "house" and pretended not to know what was taking place.

"Well, gentlemen," he said, "what can I do for you?"

"Come along; you've been elected general!"

"Really, gentlemen, I'm sure I don't deserve such an honour," said Kirdyaga. "What sort of general will I make ? Why, I'm not clever enough for such a responsible post ! Couldn't you have found a better man in the whole army ?"

"Come along ! Come along !" shouted the Cossacks.

Two of them took him by the arms and, in spite of his resistance, he was at last dragged to the square, the Cossacks who had been sent to fetch him swearing at him, punching him on the back and kicking him.

"Don't you try running back, damn you !" they exhorted him. "Accept the honour, you cur, when it's been offered to you !"

In this way Kirdyaga was at length led into the circle of the Cossacks.

"Well, men," those who brought him shouted at the top of their voices, "are you agreed that this Cossack should be our general ?"

"Agreed ! Agreed !" the crowd roared, and all the plain resounded with their cry.

One of the elders then picked up the mace and offered it to the newly elected commander. Kirdyaga, as was the custom, at once refused it. The elder offered it to him a second time, and again Kirdyaga refused; but when it was offered to him a third time, he accepted it immediately. A roar of approval rang through the crowd, and again the plain resounded far and wide with the Cossacks' cry. Then four of the oldest Cossacks with grey moustaches and grey tufts of hair (there were not any really old men in the *Syech*, for no Dnieper Cossack died a natural death) stepped forth out of the crowd, and, each taking up a handful of earth, which had been turned to mud by the recent rain, placed it on Kirdyaga's head. The wet earth ran down his head and trickled over his cheeks and moustache, and his whole face was covered with mud. But Kirdyaga never stirred, and thanked the Cossacks for the honour shown him.

It was in this way that the noisy assembly came to an end to the great gratification of Bulba, whatever the feelings of the rest of the Cossacks might have been, for that was how he had revenged himself on the former commander. Besides, Kirdyaga was an old friend of his and had been with him on many campaigns on land and sea, sharing the toils and hardships of war.

The crowd began dispersing at once and the Cossacks were soon celebrating the elections of a new general by an orgy such as Ostap and Andrey had not yet seen. The inns in the suburb were smashed, and the Cossacks helped themselves to mead, vodka and beer without payment, the innkeepers being too glad to escape with their lives. The whole night was spent in shouting and the singing of songs extolling Cossack feats of arms, and for many hours the rising moon gazed upon the crowds of musicians, marching through the streets with bandores, drums and round balalaikas, and upon the choristers kept in the *Syech* to sing in the church and to glorify the heroic deeds of the Dnieper Cossacks. At last drink and exhaustion laid low even the strongest heads, and here and there a Cossack could be seen sinking to the ground, and while friend was embracing friend and shedding sentimental tears over him, he would roll over and both would tumble down to the ground together. In one place a whole crowd of drunken Cossacks were lying in a heap; in another a Cossack reeled drunkenly for some time, trying to choose a more comfortable place to lie down and ending up by sprawling over a block of wood. The last and strongest of them all went on babbling incoherently for some time, but at last he, too, was felled by the power of drink, and all the *Syech* was asleep.

IV

Next day Taras was already conferring with the new general about how to rouse the Dnieper Cossacks to some warlike action. Kirdyaga was a clever and crafty Cossack who knew his men inside out, and at first he said: "It's quite impossible to break our oath! Quite impossible!" But, after a short pause, he added, "Well, I suppose it could be done without breaking our oath. We'll have to think of something. Some way could be found, I'm sure. Let's first get the people together, not at my command, you understand, but of their own accord. I expect you could manage that, couldn't you? As soon as you get them out on the square, the elders and I will come along, too, just as if we knew nothing about it."

Scarcely an hour after their talk, the kettle-drums began beating a tattoo. There were plenty of drunken and reckless Cossacks about. Thousands of Cossack caps covered the square. A hubbub of voices arose. "What's up? What's the matter? What's the meaning of this meeting?" Nobody knew. At last first in one corner, then in another, people were heard saying, "There's no war! Our Cossack strength is being wasted! Our commanders don't seem to care a damn! Grown too fat, the swine! There's no justice in the world!" The other Cossacks listened at first, and then they, too, began saying, "There's no justice in the world! Indeed, there isn't!" The elders seemed to be astonished at such speeches. At last the general stepped forward and said, "My friends, may I say a few words to you?"

"Speak! Speak!"

"What I wanted to talk to you about, my friends, and I daresay you know it as well as I do, is that many Cossacks have run up big debts with the Jewish innkeepers and with their own friends, too, so that they couldn't raise a penny from the devil himself at present. Then there is of course the further consideration that there are many young men among us who have never been to war and don't know what war is like, and I need hardly tell you that a young man cannot exist without war. What kind of a Dnieper Cossack will he make, I ask you, if he has not even once beaten the infidel?"

"He speaks well," thought Bulba.

"Now, friends, please do not think that I'm saying this because I want to break the peace. God forbid! I am saying this because, after all, it's true, isn't it? Then there is our church. . . . Yes, my friends, we have a church all right, and I hope I'm not committing any sin by telling you frankly that our church is a disgrace. A disgrace to *us*, I mean. Here, by the grace of God, our *Syech* has been in existence for many years, and to this very day not only the outside of our church but even the icons are without ornaments. Someone might at least have thought of providing silver frames for them! But all that our church has ever received by way of adornments is what some Cossack left it in his will, and what he left, my friends, isn't very much, either, for the poor devil had squandered everything on drink in his lifetime. So, you see, I'm saying all this not because I want to start a war against the Moslems. No! We have promised peace to the Sultan and it would be a great sin if we broke our promise, for we have taken an oath in accordance with our laws."

"What the devil is he driving at?" thought Bulba.

"So you see, my friends, we just can't start a war; our knightly honour forbids such a thing. But we might, in my humble opinion, do this: let us send our young men on a trip across the Black Sea and let them pick up a few baubles on the coasts of Anatolia. What do you say, friends?"

"Let's all go! Take us all!" the crowd shouted. "We're ready to lay down our lives for our faith!"

The general was alarmed. The last thing he wanted was to raise the entire Dnieper Cossack force; to break the peace seemed in the present circumstances to be utterly wrong to him.

"Will you allow me to say a few more words, my friends?" he said.

"No! No!" the Cossacks shouted. "You'll not improve on what you've said already!"

"Well, friends, if that is how you want it, I can't do anything to stop you. I'm only your servant. It's well known, and we have it also from the Scripture, that the voice of the people is the voice of God. There can't be anything wiser than what the whole people decides to do. But I'd like to tell you this. As you know, the Sultan will hardly allow our young men's little escapade to go unpunished. So in the meantime we'll get ready. Our forces will be fresh and we need fear no one. Moreover, if we all went now, the Tartars might fall upon the *Syech*! Those Turkish curs will not dare show themselves, let alone pay a visit to the house while the master is at home, but directly our backs are turned they'll fall upon us from behind and bite us hard! And as I am now speaking quite frankly to you, I may as well add that we have not enough boats in reserve, nor enough powder ground for us all to go. As for me, my friends, I'd be only too glad to do as you like, for I'm your servant and am ready to do whatever you decide."

The crafty chieftain fell silent. The Cossacks began discussing the matter in groups, while the detachment commanders consulted together. Fortunately few of them were drunk, and so they decided to listen to wiser counsel.

A number of people set off at once to the other side of the Dnieper where the army treasury and some of the weapons taken from the enemy were hidden in inaccessible places under the water and in the reeds. The rest immediately rushed to overhaul the boats and get them ready for the expedition. In a twinkling the bank of the river was covered with men. Several carpenters arrived with axes in their hands. Old, sunburnt, broad-shouldered, strong-legged Cossacks, some with grizzled and some with black moustaches, rolled up their trousers and stood knee-deep in the water, hauling the boats from the bank with stout ropes. Others dragged ready-made, dry timber and trees of all sorts. In one place men were nailing boards to the boats; in another they had turned a boat upside down and were caulking and tarring it; in a third they were binding long bundles of reeds to the sides of the boats, as was the custom among the Cossacks, to prevent them from being sunk by the waves of the sea. Further up all along the shore camp-fires had been built and tar was being boiled in huge copper cauldrons for tarring the vessels. Old and experienced Cossacks were instructing the young. The tapping of hammers and the shouts of the workmen resounded all over the neighbourhood; the whole of the riverside sprang to life and began throbbing with activity.

Just at that time a large ferry-boat was approaching the bank. A group of people on board waved their hands frantically while still at a distance. They were Cossacks in torn coats. Their tattered clothes (many had nothing but the shirt on their backs and the pipe between their teeth) showed that they had either escaped from some disaster or had been drinking so well they had squandered all they had on them. A thick-set, broad-shouldered Cossack of about fifty left the group and stood in front. He shouted louder and waved his arms about more vigorously than the rest; but the hammering and the shouts of the workmen drowned his words.

"What's your news?" asked the general when the ferry-boat reached the bank.

All the workmen stopped their work, and, raising their axes and chisels, looked on expectantly.

"Bad news, sir!" the thick-set Cossack shouted from the ferry.

"What's wrong?"

"Will you give me leave to speak, gentlemen?"

"Speak!"

"Or would you rather call an assembly?"

"Speak, we're all here!"

They all pressed together, forming one huge crowd.

"Have you heard nothing of what's going on in the hetman's land?"

"Well, what is going on there?" asked one of the detachment commanders.

"What indeed! Has the Tartar stopped up your ears with wads of hemp that you've heard nothing?"

"Well, tell us what is happening there."

184

"What's happening there no man born and baptised has ever seen in his life."

"Tell us what's happening there, you son of a bitch!" someone shouted from the crowd, having evidently lost all patience.

"We're now living in such times, friends, that even our holy churches aren't ours any longer."

"Not ours? What do you mean?"

"What I mean is that they've all been leased out to the Jews. If you don't pay the Jew beforehand, no mass can be celebrated."

"What are you talking about?"

"And if the mean scoundrel of a Jew does not put a mark on the Holy Easter Cake with his unclean hand, it cannot be consecrated."

"He's lying, friends! Who ever heard of such a thing? An unclean Jew putting a mark on the Holy Easter Cake!"

"Listen, gentlemen, listen to me. I have something worse to tell you. Catholic priests are now driving all over the Ukraine in their two-wheeled carriages. But it isn't the carriages that matter; what matters is that they are not putting horses to their carriages, but orthodox Christians. Listen! There's something worse still I have to tell you. I have heard people say that Jewish women are making themselves petticoats out of our priests' chasubles. These are the things that are going on in the Ukraine, gentlemen. And you sit here and enjoy yourselves! The Tartar, it seems, has given you such a fright that you have neither ears nor eyes and you don't hear or see what's going on in the world."

"Wait a minute," said the general, who had been standing with his eyes fixed upon the ground as is the habit of Dnieper Cossacks who, when important matters are at stake, never give way to their first impulse, but keep quiet and let the terrible force of their indignation accumulate in silence. "Wait a minute; let me say something, too. What were you doing while all this was going on? What were you—may the devil beat your father black and blue!— what were you doing, I say? Where were your sabres? Or didn't you have any? How came you to permit such lawlessness?"

"So you want to know how we came to allow such lawlessness, do you? What did you expect us to do with fifty thousand Poles about? And—why deny it?—there were many traitors among our people, too, who preferred to adopt their religion."

"And what about your hetman? What about your colonels? What were they doing?"

"What were our colonels doing? God grant we may never have to do the same!"

"What do you mean?"

"What I mean is, sir, that our hetman is now lying in Warsaw, roasted in a copper bull, and the arms and heads of our colonels are being carried about from fair to fair and displayed to the people. That's what our colonels have done!"

The crowd was deeply stirred. At first a dead silence fell upon the riverside like the stillness before a violent storm, then all at once people burst into speech and the whole bank of the river seemed to be talking.

"What's that? Jews letting out Christian churches? Catholic priests putting orthodox Christians between shafts? Are we going to tolerate such indignities on Russian soil at the hands of cursed infidels? Let them treat the hetman and the colonels like that? Never! Such things shall never be!"

Such words flew from mouth to mouth. The Dnieper Cossacks were in an uproar and they became conscious of their strength. This was not an outburst by a fickle mob. Grave and strong-minded people who were not easily roused, but who, once roused, kept up their indignation at white heat subbornly and for a long time, were also deeply stirred.

"Hang all the Jews!" someone in the crowd shouted. "Don't let them make petticoats for their Jewesses out of our priests' vestments! Don't let them make marks upon the Holy Easter Cake! Let's drown the rascals in the Dnieper!"

These words were like a spark in a powder magazine, and the crowd rushed to the suburb with the intention of cutting the throats of all the Jews.

The poor sons of Israel, losing what little courage they had, hid in empty vodka barrels and ovens and even crept under the skirts of their wives, but the Cossacks fished them out from everywhere.

"Gracious lords," cried one Jew, tall and thin as a rake, thrusting his wretched face, contorted with panic, from a group of his companions, "gracious lords, a word, I pray you; let me say only one word to you! We've something very important to tell you, something of very great importance, something you've never heard before!"

"All right, let him say it," said Bulba, who always liked to hear what an accused had to say for himself.

"Noble lords," said the Jew, "such noble lords the world has never seen ! Such good, kind, brave gentlemen !" His voice faltered and shook with terror. "How could we think evil of the Dnieper Cossacks ? Those leaseholders in the Ukraine do not belong to our people at all ! I swear to you they're not our people; they're not Jews at all ! The devil knows what they are. Something to spit on and throw away. They'll tell you the same. Isn't that so, Solomon, or you, Samuel ?"

"It's true ! It's true !" Solomon and Samuel replied from the crowd, both in torn skull-caps and pale as death.

"We have never had any dealings with your enemies," the lanky Jew went on, "and we certainly don't want to have anything to do with the Catholics; may they dream of nothing but the devil ! Why, we're like brothers to the Cossacks. . . ."

"What's that ? You want the Cossacks to be your brothers ?" someone in the crowd of Cossacks shouted. "You won't live long enough for that to happen, you damned Jews ! Into the Dnieper with them, friends ! Let's drown the dirty rascals !"

These words were the signal. The Cossacks seized the Jews by the arms and began flinging them into the river. Their pitiful cries rang out on all sides, but the Cossacks merely laughed at the sight of a pair of Jewish legs in shoes and stockings kicking in the air. The poor orator, who had brought the trouble upon his own head, slipped out of his long coat by which he had been seized and in his close-fitting striped vest flung himself at Bulba's feet, clutching at his knees and beseeching him in a piteous voice, "My lord, my lord, my noble lord, I knew your late brother Dorosho ! Oh, what a fine soldier he was, sir ! A real ornament to all the Cossack knighthood ! I gave him eight hundred sequins that he might be ransomed from the Turks !"

"You knew my brother ?" asked Bulba.

"Yes, sir. I knew him, sir. Oh, he was such a generous gentleman !"

"And what's your name ?"

"Yankel, sir."

"All right," said Bulba, and after a moment's reflection he turned to the Cossacks and said, "There'll always be time to hang the Jew, if need be, but give him to me today."

Having said this, Taras led the Jew to his own carts, beside which his Cossacks were standing. "Crawl under a cart, lie there and don't move ! And you, lads, don't let the Jew go."

He then set off to the square, for the Cossacks had been flocking there for some time. Everyone had immediately left the bank of the river and the equipment of the boats, for now that they were going on a campaign by land and not by sea they did not want ships and Cossack canoes, but carts and horses. Now they all wanted to go, old and young, all of them, on the advice of their elders, their detachment commanders and their general and by the will of the entire Cossack army resolved to march straight against Poland to avenge all the wrongs and indignities against their faith and the Cossack good name, collect booty from the cities, set fire to the villages and the crops, and spread the glory of Cossack arms from one end of the steppe to the other. All of them were making ready on the square, putting on their belts and arming. The general seemed to have grown several feet taller. He was no longer the humble slave of every whim of a free people; he was a dictator, a despot, whose word was law. The headstrong and unruly warriors stood shoulder to shoulder in their ranks, their heads lowered respectfully, not daring to raise their eyes when the general was giving his orders: he issued them quietly, unhurriedly, and without raising his voice, pausing now and again, like an old and experienced Cossack, who was not for the first time putting his carefully thought out plans into execution.

"Inspect everything," he said. "See that you leave nothing undone. Make sure your carts are in good order, and your pails full of tar. Test your weapons thoroughly. Don't take too much clothing with you: one shirt and two pairs of breeches for each Cossack, one pot of broth and one of crushed millet—no one is to take more than that. We shall have all the provisions we need in our carts. Every Cossack is to take two horses with him. And we shall have to take about four hundred oxen, for we shall want them at the fords and in the marshes. And remember, gentlemen, discipline must be maintained above everything. I know there are some among you who, if God should put anything in their way that rouses their greed, will at once start tearing up a piece of nankeen cloth or expensive velvet to wrap round his legs. Give up that damnable habit of yours ! Don't touch petticoats or dresses; take weapons only, if good, and gold pieces, or silver, for these won't take up much room and may come in useful in any eventuality. And I'm afraid there's one thing more I must warn you about : anyone getting drunk on the campaign can expect no mercy. I shall order him to be tied like a dog by the neck to a cart, whoever he may be, even though he be the most valiant Cossack of the whole army; he will be shot like a dog on the spot and his body left without burial for the birds to pick clean, for a man drunk on a campaign does not deserve a Christian burial. Young men, obey your elders in everything! If you get grazed by a bullet, or scratched by a sabre on the head or anywhere else, do not pay much attention to such a trifle: mix a charge of powder in a tankard of weak vodka, drink it off at a gulp, and all will be well, there will be no fever even; and on the wound, if it is not too big, simply put a little earth, first mixing it with spittle in the palm of your hand, and the wound will dry up. Now then, lads, to work, to work, and do everything without haste and thoroughly and well!"

So spoke the general, and as soon as he had finished all the Cossacks set to work. The whole *Syech* was sober, and not a single drunken man could be found anywhere, as though there had never been any drunkards among the Cossacks. Some were mending the felloes of the wheels and changing the axles in the carts; others were carrying sacks with provisions to the carts or piling weapons on them; others still were rounding up the horses and oxen. From every side came the tramp of horses' hoofs, the firing of guns that were being tested, the rattle of sabres, the bellowing of oxen, the creaking of carts that were being placed in position, loud cries and urging on of horses and oxen—and soon the Cossack army stretched for miles over the plain, and if you wanted to run from the head to the tail of it you would have had to run a very long way. In the little wooden church the priest conducted a service and sprinkled all with holy water; and everyone kissed the cross. When the Cossack army set off, moving out of the *Syech* in a long line, all the Cossacks looked back, saying almost in the same words, "Farewell, our mother! May the Lord keep and preserve you from all misfortune!"

As he was riding through the suburb, Taras Bulba saw his Jew Yankel who had already pitched some kind of a tent with an awning and was selling flints, powder, and various kinds of medicaments and provisions which the troops might need on the road, including even white and black loaves of bread. "How do you like this damned Jew?" thought Taras to himself.

"You fool," he said, riding up to him, "what are you doing here? Do you want to be shot like a sparrow?"

In reply, Yankel went up closer to him and made a sign with both hands, as though he wished to confide some secret.

"Don't breathe a word about it to anyone, sir," he said, "but among the Cossack carts there is one that belongs to me. I'm carrying all sorts of stores for the Cossacks, and on the way I shall let them have provisions at a cheaper price than any Jew has ever sold. So help me, sir!"

Taras Bulba shrugged his shoulders, marvelling at the irrepressible nature of the Jews, and rode off to join the Cossack troops.

V

Soon all the south-west of Poland became a prey to panic. Everywhere rumours spread: "The Dnieper Cossacks! The Dnieper Cossacks are on the march!" All who could save themselves saved themselves; all who could leave their homes fled and ran in different directions after the manner of that unsettled, happy-go-lucky age when neither fortresses nor castles were built and man put up his thatched hut anyhow and only for a short time. "Why waste money and labour on a cottage," he thought to himself, "when in his next raid the Tartar will anyway raze it to the ground?" All the countryside was in confusion. Some exchanged their oxen and plough for a horse and a gun and went to join the regiments; others fled to a place of safety, driving away their cattle and carrying away with them whatever could be carried away. There were also those on the roads who met the invader with arms in their hands; but mostly people preferred to flee while there was still time. Everyone knew how hard it was to deal with that violent and warlike crowd known under the name of the Dnieper Cossack army, whose external unruly disorderliness was merely a cloak for the disciplined orderliness that was best adapted for times of war. The horsemen rode without overstraining or overheating their horses; those on foot marched soberly behind the carts; and the whole army moved only by night, resting by day and choosing for their camp wastelands, uninhabited places and woods which in those days were still plentiful. Spies and scouts were sent on ahead to spy out the land and bring news of the whereabouts of the enemy forces, their disposition and strength. Very often they appeared suddenly in places where they were least expected—and then everything took leave of life: the villages went up in flames, the cattle and horses that were not driven off with the army were slaughtered on the spot, and it really looked as though the Cossacks were feasting rather than conducting a military operation. Today the evidence of brutality which the Cossacks left behind them everywhere in that semi-savage age would make people's hair stand on end: slaughtered babes, women with breasts cut off, men set free with their skin torn from their feet and legs to their knees—in short, the Cossacks paid off old scores with interest. The prelate of one monastery, hearing of their approach, sent two monks to tell the Cossacks from him that they were not behaving as they should, that there was an agreement between the Polish Government and the Cossacks, that they were violating their oath of fealty to the king and that by doing so they were also violating every national law. "Tell the bishop from me and from all the Dnieper Cossacks not to worry," replied the Cossack general. "The Cossacks have so far only been lighting their pipes." And soon the majestic abbey was a blazing heap of ruins and its huge Gothic windows were gaping caverns amid the leaping flames. The fleeing crowds of monks, Jews, and women soon filled to overflowing the cities which offered the slightest hope of safety because of their garrisons and the citizens' defence forces. The belated help sent occasionally by the Government and consisting mostly of cavalry battalions either could not find the Cossacks or were afraid to attack them, and, at the first encounter, turned tail and fled on their swift horses. Now and then it also happened that a number of Polish commanding officers who had been victorious in many battles in the past decided to join forces and offer joint resistance to the Dnieper Cossacks.

It was in those engagements that our two young Cossacks showed their mettle, for they shunned plunder, easy gain and a helpless enemy and were anxious to win their spurs before the eyes of their older comrades by engaging in single combat with the high-spirited and boastful Pole, flaunting on his mettlesome steed with his rich cloak flying in the breeze. That sort of training had its lighter moments; they had picked up a great many rich trappings, costly sabres and guns. In one month the callow fledglings had grown up and were completely transformed; they were men now, and their features in which till now a certain softness could be perceived looked strong and stern now. Old Taras was glad to see his two sons among the foremost. Ostap seemed to have been born for battle and the hard discipline of war. Never at a loss and never flustered by any unforeseen development, he could, with a coolness that was almost unnatural in a young man of twenty-two, instantly gauge the whole danger of any given situation and find a way of evading it, but only with the intention of overcoming it the more surely afterwards. All his movements were already beginning to be distinguished by a confidence that was born of experience, and it was impossible not to perceive in them the qualities of a future leader of men. His whole body conveyed the impression of great strength, and there was something of the tremendous power of a lion in the way in which he displayed his knightly prowess in the field. "He'll make a fine colonel one day," old Taras used to say. "A damned fine colonel ! Shouldn't be at all surprised if he proved himself to be a better man than his father !"

Andrey fell completely under the spell of the enchanting music of the bullets and the swords. He did not know what it meant to stop and consider or calculate and gauge beforehand his own and his enemy's strength. A battle filled him with rapture and delight : it was a festival to him, a gay carnival, especially in those minutes when his head was aflame and everything danced and capered before his eyes, when heads were flying and horses crashing thunderously to the ground, while he dashed along, like one intoxicated, amid the whistling bullets and flashing swords, dealing out blows right and left and hardly feeling those he received himself. Many a time his father could not help admiring Andrey, too, seeing how, urged on by his fiery enthusiasm alone, he hurled himself into the thick of battle where no cool-headed and prudent fighter would ever venture and merely by the fury of his onslaught achieved wonders that left veteran warriors gaping with surprise. Old Taras marvelled and murmured, "He's a good soldier, too. I only hope the enemy does not capture him one day. He's not Ostap, but he's a good soldier, a very good soldier !"

The Cossack army decided to march straight on the city of Dubno, which, according to rumours, had many wealthy inhabitants and much of the Polish king's treasure. In a day and a half the march was accomplished and the Cossacks appeared before the city. The inhabitants decided to defend themselves to the last and to put up with every hardship a long siege might entail. They preferred to die in the squares and streets of their city, on the thresholds of their own homes, rather than admit the enemy into them. The city was surrounded by a high mound of earth, and where the rampart was lower a stone wall jutted out, or a house, converted into a battery, or an oak palisade. The garrison was strong and was fully conscious of the importance of its task. At first the Dnieper Cossacks attempted to take the city by storm and tried to scale the rampart, but they were met with volley after volley of grapeshot. It seemed that the tradesmen and inhabitants of the city had no intention of remaining idle, either, and a crowd of them could be seen standing on the rampart. In their eyes could be read a desperate determination to resist the enemy at all costs. The women, too, decided to take part in the fighting, and they hurled stones, barrels and pots on the heads of the Cossacks, following it up with boiling water and, finally, with sacks of sand, which blinded the attackers.

The Dnieper Cossacks did not like to have anything to do with fortresses: laying siege to a city was not their way of conducting war. The general ordered a retreat. "Don't worry, men," he said; "let us withdraw. But may I be an accursed Tartar and not a Christian if we let a single one of them out of the city! Let the dogs die of hunger!" The troops withdrew and surrounded the whole city, and having nothing better to do, began laying waste the surrounding countryside, burning the neighbouring villages, setting fire to the shocks of corn in the fields, turning their droves of horses into the cornfields which had not been touched by the reaping hook and where, as luck would have it, heavy ears of corn swayed in the wind, the result of an exceptionally good harvest which that year had generously rewarded the husbandman. The inhabitants of the beleaguered city watched with horror the destruction of their means of subsistence. Meanwhile the Dnieper Cossacks, having formed a double ring round the city with their carts, settled down, as though they were in the *Syech*, in detachments, smoked their pipes, exchanged captured weapons, played leap-frog and odd-and-even, and every now and then looked with cold indifference at the starving city. At night they lighted camp-fires; the cooks in each detachment cooked porridge in huge copper cauldrons; wakeful sentries mounted guard by the fires which burnt all night. But very soon the Dnieper Cossacks began to weary of their life of inactivity and prolonged abstinence, unattended as it was by any fighting. The general even ordered the issue of a double ration of vodka, a concession occasionally made to the troops when no hard fighting was in progress or any difficult marches ahead. The young men, and Ostap and Andrey in particular, disliked such a life. Andrey was quite plainly bored.

"What a silly fellow you are," said Taras to him. "Remember the proverb, Be patient, Cossack, and you'll be chieftain one day ! It is not enough that a man's spirits should never fail him in a tight corner. That doesn't make him a good soldier. For a good soldier is a man who in times of inaction never allows weariness to get the better of him, but puts up cheerfully with everything and, whatever you do to him, will have his own way in the end."

But a fiery youth will never agree with an old man : their characters are different and they look with different eyes on the same thing.

Meanwhile Taras Bulba's regiment arrived, led by Tovkatch ; with him were two other captains, a clerk and other officers ; there were over four thousand Cossacks in it, including not a few volunteers who had joined of their own free will and without any special summons as soon as they heard what was afoot. The captains brought Bulba's sons a blessing from their mother, who sent them each an icon of cypress wood from the Mezhigorsky Monastery in Kiev. The two brothers put the two holy icons round their necks and fell into thought as they remembered their old mother. What did that blessing portend ? What did it tell them ? Was it a blessing for victory over the enemy, followed by a merry homecoming with booty and glory, immortalised in the songs of bandore-players, or . . . But the future remains for ever unknown and it stands before a man like the autumn mist that rises from the marshes : the birds fly about in it wildly, with a flutter of wings, not seeing or recognising one another, the dove not seeing the hawk, and the hawk not seeing the dove, and none knowing how far he is from his doom. . . .

Ostap was attending to his duties and had long since gone off to the detachments ; but Andrey felt (he hardly knew why) something weighing heavily on his heart. The Cossacks had long finished their evening meal. The last gleam of sunset had long died in the sky, and the air was full of the loveliness of a July night ; but he had not gone back to the detachments, nor did he go to sleep, but seemed to have become unconsciously absorbed in the contemplation of the scene before him. Myriads of stars twinkled with a bright and sharp gleam in the sky. The plain was covered for miles around with carts, scattered all over it, each cart with its pail of tar hanging from it, each cart loaded with provisions and possessions of all sorts taken from the enemy. Beside the carts, under the carts, and at a little distance from the carts—everywhere in fact—Cossacks could be seen stretched on the grass. They were all sleeping in picturesque attitudes: one with a large sack under his head, another with a cap, a third simply using his comrade's side for a pillow. A sabre, a matchlock, a short pipe with copper mountings, a metal pipe cleaner, and a bag of flints and tinder were always within reach of every Cossack. The heavy oxen lay with their legs bent under them and their huge, whitish bulks might from a distance have been mistaken for grey boulders scattered on the slopes of the plain. From every side there rose from the grass the heavy snoring of the sleeping fighting men, answered from the fields by the resounding neighing of the horses, protesting against their hobbled feet. Meanwhile something grand and awe-inspiring was added to the beauty of the July night. This was the glow from the still smouldering fires of the burnt-down villages and buildings in the neighbourhood. In one place the flames still spread calmly and majestically across the sky; in another, meeting something inflammable, they suddenly blazed up, hissing and leaping like a whirlwind to the very stars, and torn, ragged balls of fire flickered out far, far away at the very edge of the horizon. There the black mass of a gutted monastery towered menacingly, like a grim Carthusian monk, revealing its gloomy grandeur every time its ruins reflected the flames. Yonder the monastery garden was burning, and the trees, it seemed, could be heard hissing amid the spirals of smoke, and every time a flame leapt out it threw a phosphorescent purplish-red light on the clusters of ripe plums or transformed the pears, which were here and there turning yellow, into red gold, and right in the midst of them there loomed the dark outline of the body of a poor Jew or monk, hanging on the wall of the building or the branch of a tree, and being consumed with the rest of the building in the flames. In the distance birds could be seen soaring over the fire, and they looked like a heap of dark tiny little crosses upon a fiery field. The beleaguered city seemed to have fallen asleep; its spires, roofs, palisade, and walls fitfully reflected the faint glow of the distant conflagrations.

Andrey walked round the Cossack lines. The camp-fires, by which the guards were sitting, were on the point of going out any minute, and the guards themselves were asleep, having consumed their stew and the dumplings with true Cossack appetite. He was surprised at such carelessness, thinking, "It's a good thing there is no powerful enemy near and there's nothing to fear." At last he, too, went up to one of the carts, clambered into it and lay down on his back with his hands clasped under his head. But he could not go to sleep and he lay a long time gazing at the sky: it all lay open before him, the air was clear and transparent, the conglomeration of stars that compose the Milky Way and lie in a wide belt athwart the sky shone with unusual brightness. At times Andrey seemed to doze off, a light mist of drowsiness shutting out the sky from him for a moment, and then it grew clear again and everything was once more visible.

It was during one of those moments of forgetfulness that he seemed to have caught a glimpse of some strange human face. Thinking that he must be dreaming, he opened his eyes and saw a real human face, a wan, emaciated face, bending over him and looking straight into his eyes. Long coal-black hair, unkempt and dishevelled, crept from under the dark veil flung over the head; the strangely glittering eyes and the deathly pallor of the dark face, each feature of it standing out sharply, might well have made him think that it was an apparition rather than a human being. He put his hand on his musket instinctively and said in a strangled voice, "Who are you? If you're a spirit from hell, then vanish out of sight; but if you're a human being, you've chosen a bad time for a joke: I'll shoot you dead on the spot!"

In reply the apparition put its finger to its lips and seemed to implore him to keep silent. He dropped his hand and began to peer closer. From the long hair, the neck and half-bared bosom, he saw that it was a woman. But she was not a native of those parts. Her face was swarthy and wasted with illness; her broad cheekbones protruded above her sunken cheeks; her narrow slits of eyes slanted upwards. The more he scrutinised her features, the more they seemed somehow familiar to him. At last he could not restrain himself and asked, "Tell me who you are. I seem to know you. Have I seen you somewhere?"

"Two years ago in Kiev."

"Two years ago in Kiev?" Andrey repeated, racking his brains for some surviving memory from his old student life. He looked at her intently once more and suddenly cried at the top of his voice, "You're the Tartar woman! The maid of the Polish young lady! The governor's daughter!"

"Hush! . . . ." said the Tartar woman, putting her hands together imploringly. She trembled all over and turned her head round quickly to see whether anyone had been wakened by Andrey's loud cry.

"Please tell me how you got here and why you are here," Andrey said in a whisper, breathlessly, his voice breaking at every word with pent-up emotion. "Where's your mistress? She's still alive, isn't she?"

"She's here, sir. In the city."

"In the city?" he almost cried again at the top of his voice, feeling a sudden rush of blood to his heart. "Why is she in the city?"

"Because my master himself is in the city. He's been governor of Dubno for the past sixteen months."

"Well, is she married? Tell me, tell me how she is! Why do you look so strangely at me?"

"She has had nothing to eat for two days. . . ."

"What?"

"None of the inhabitants of the city has had a bite of bread for a long time, sir. They've been eating nothing but earth for days."

Andrey was dumbfounded.

"My mistress saw you with the other Cossacks from the city rampart, sir. She said to me, 'Go and tell the knight to come to me if he still remembers me, but if he doesn't, let him give you a piece of bread for my old mother, for I don't want to see my mother die before my eyes. Let me die first and her after me! Go and ask him, fall at his feet, clutch him by the hands! He, too, has an old mother—let him give you some bread for her sake!'"

Many different emotions awoke and blazed up in the youthful heart of the Cossack.

"How did you get here? Which way did you come?"

"By an underground passage."

"Is there such an underground passage?"

"Yes, sir."

"Where?"

"You won't betray us, sir?"

"I swear by the Holy Cross!"

"You have to go down into the ravine, sir, and then cross the stream. It's just where the reeds are. . . ."

"And does it come out in the city?"

"Yes, sir. Straight by the city monastery."

"Let's go. Let's go at once!"

"But, sir, what about the bread? Just a piece of bread, sir, in the name of Christ and the Blessed Virgin!"

"All right, you shall have your bread. Stay here by the cart, or, better still, lie down in it. Nobody will see you; they're all asleep. I shan't be long."

He went off to the carts where the stores of provisions belonging to his detachment were kept. His heart was pounding. All his past, everything that had been submerged by his present Cossack bivouack existence and the stern realities of war, floated to the surface again, drowning, in turn, the present. Again the proud girl rose up before his mind's eye, as though from the fathomless depths of the ocean: her lovely hands, her eyes, her laughing lips, her thick nut-brown hair that fell in curls over her bosom; all the supple, harmonious lines of her girlish figure flashed through his memory. They had never really died, they had never vanished from his heart, they had merely made way for other powerful emotions which had for a time overwhelmed him; but often, very often, had the young Cossack's deep sleep been troubled by them, and often had he lain awake for hours unable to understand the cause of his sleeplessness.

He walked on while his heart was beating more and more violently at the mere thought that he would see her again. His knees trembled. When he reached the carts he seemed to forget what he had come for: he put his hand to his forehead and stood rubbing it a long time, trying to remember what he had to do. At last he gave a start and was all filled with dread: he suddenly remembered that she was dying of hunger. He rushed to a cart and put under his arm a number of large loaves of black bread; but immediately it occurred to him that that kind of food which was good enough for a stalwart and far from fastidious Cossack was too coarse and entirely unsuitable for her delicate constitution. Then he remembered that only the day before the general had reprimanded the cooks for having used up the whole of the buckwheat flour for their broth when there was enough of it for three whole meals. Fully confident of finding enough thin porridge in the cauldrons, he pulled out his father's small army kettle and went with it to the cook of his own detachment who was asleep by the two ten-gallon cauldrons under which the embers were still glowing. Looking into them, he was amazed to see that both were empty. It required superhuman powers to eat it all, especially as there were fewer men in his detachment than in the others. He looked into the cauldrons of the other detachments, but there was nothing anywhere. He could not help recalling the saying, "The Dnieper Cossacks are like children: if they haven't enough, they'll eat it all; and if they have too much, they won't leave anything, either." What was he to do? Then he remembered that on one of the carts of his father's regiment there was a sack with loaves of white bread which they had found when plundering the bakery of a monastery. He went straight to his father's cart, but the sack was not there: Ostap had taken it for a pillow and, stretched on the ground, was snoring for the whole plain to hear. Andrey seized the sack with one hand and pulled it away so violently that Ostap's head fell on the ground and he sat up in his sleep and, with his eyes closed, shouted at the top of his voice, "Hold him! Hold the damned Pole! Get his horse! Get his horse!"

"Shut up or I'll kill you!" Andrey cried in alarm, swinging the sack at him.

But Ostap stopped talking anyway. He lay down quietly and was soon snoring away with such vigour that his breath set the grass quivering. Andrey looked round apprehensively to see whether Ostap's outcry in his sleep had wakened any Cossack. One shaven head with a long tuft of hair was raised in the nearest detachment, but after looking round it fell back on the ground again. After waiting a minute or two, Andrey at last retraced his steps with the sack slung over his shoulder. The Tartar woman was lying in the cart, scarcely daring to breathe.

"Get up," said Andrey. "Let's go! Don't be afraid. They're all asleep. Can you take just one of these loaves, if I can't carry them all?"

Without waiting for a reply, he slung the sacks over his back, pulled another sack of millet off a cart, as he passed it, took under his arms even the loaves he had meant to give the Tartar woman to carry and, stooping a little under the weight, walked boldly between the rows of sleeping Cossacks.

"Andrey!" said old Bulba as his younger son passed him.

Andrey's heart sank. He stopped and, trembling all over, asked softly, "What?"

"Andrey, there's a woman with you! Take care, sir! I'll thrash you within an inch of your life when I get up! Mark my words, women will be the ruin of you!"

Saying this, Taras propped up his head on his hand and began scrutinising intently the Tartar woman, who was muffled in her veil.

Andrey stood more dead than alive, and did not have the courage to look his father in the face. But when he raised his eyes at last and glanced at his father, he saw that old Bulba was asleep, his head resting on the open palm of his hand.

He crossed himself. The panic which had gripped his heart disappeared even more quickly than it came. When he turned round to glance at the Tartar woman, he saw her standing motionless like a statue of black granite, all muffled up in her veil, and the glow from a distant fire which suddenly blazed up was reflected only in her eyes, which were glazed like the eyes of a corpse. He pulled her by the sleeve and they set off together, continually looking back, until at last they went down the slope to a low-lying dell, almost a ravine, in some places called a creek, at the bottom of which a stream overgrown with sedge and covered with small mounds trickled lazily. Having reached the bottom of the dell, they were completely hidden from the view of the whole plain on which the Cossacks had pitched their camp. At any rate, when Andrey looked round, he saw the slope rising up behind him like a steep wall above the height of a man. A few blades of grass waved on the crest of the slope and above them the moon was rising in the sky in the shape of an inverted sickle of brightly shining gold. The fresh breeze that blew from the steppe showed that dawn was not far off: but no distant crowing of cocks could be heard, for neither in the sacked villages nor in the city itself was there a single cock left. They crossed the stream over a small tree-trunk; the opposite bank looked much higher than the bank behind them and was much more precipitous. This place was apparently considered one of the most impregnable and safest natural strongholds in the city fortifications; at all events the rampart was much lower here and no sentries could be seen behind it. At the same time, a little farther away, there rose up the thick wall of the monastery. The steep bank was all overgrown with wild plants and grasses and the little dell between it and the stream was covered with reeds, almost as high as a man. At the top of the steep bank the remains of a wattle fence could be discerned, showing that at one time there had been a kitchen garden there; in front of it grew broad burdock leaves and behind it rose goose-foot, wild orach and prickly thistle, and a sun-flower raised its head above them all. Here the Tartar woman took off her shoes and walked barefoot, pulling up her skirt a little, for the place was soggy and muddy. Making their way through the reeds, they stopped in front of a heap of brushwood and faggots, and, moving aside the brushwood, they found a vaulted entrance to a sort of a cave, an opening not bigger than the opening of a bread oven. The Tartar woman, stooping, went in first; Andrey followed her, bending down as low as he could to be able to get through with his sacks, and soon they found themselves in complete darkness.

VI

Andrey moved very slowly in the dark and narrow underground passage, following the Tartar woman and carrying the sacks of bread. "We shall soon be able to see," said his guide. "We're getting near the place where I left a candlestick." And, sure enough, the dark earthen walls soon became dimly visible. They reached a small subterranean chamber which seemed to have been used as a kind of a chapel, at least there was a little narrow table, in the shape of a communion table, placed against one wall, and an almost completely faded and discoloured picture of a Catholic Madonna could be descried above it. A little silver lamp hung before the Madonna, throwing a faint glimmer on it. The Tartar woman bent down and picked up from the floor a copper candlestick she had left there, a candlestick with a small, slender stem and a pair of snuffers, a long pin for trimming the light and an extinguisher, all hanging on little chains round it. She picked it up and lighted it from the little lamp. The light grew brighter, and as they walked on together, now in the full glare of the light thrown by the candle, now hidden in the coal-black shadows, they looked like a painting by Gherardo della Notte. The fresh, handsome face of the young Cossack knight, brimming over with health and youth, contrasted strikingly with the pale, wan face of his companion. The passage grew a little wider and Andrey found that he could now walk upright. He examined these earthen walls with interest for they reminded him of the Kiev catacombs. Just as in the Kiev catacombs, there were recesses in the walls, in which here and there coffins stood; occasionally they even came across human bones which had grown so soft that they had disintegrated into white powder. It was plain that here, too, there had been holy men who had sought refuge from the storms of life, from human sorrows and temptations. In places the passage was very damp, and sometimes they had to walk through puddles of water. Andrey had to stop frequently to let his companion rest, for she was continually overcome by weariness. The small morsel of bread she had swallowed gave her a pain in the stomach, unaccustomed to food and unable to digest it, and she had frequently to stop and stand still for several minutes in one place.

At last they came to a little iron door. "Thank God we have arrived," said the Tartar woman in a faint voice, and she raised her hand to knock at the door, but she had not the strength to do it. Andrey struck a violent blow on the door instead of her, and the sound reverberated behind the door, showing that there was a big space there, and changed in tone, apparently on meeting a high vaulted roof. After a few minutes there was a rattle of keys and someone could be heard coming down a staircase. At length the door was unlocked and they saw a monk, standing on a narrow staircase with a bundle of keys and a candle in his hands. Andrey involuntarily stopped dead at the sight of the Catholic monk, for the monks aroused hatred and contempt in the Cossacks who treated them more inhumanly than Jews. The monk, too, stepped back a little, but a word uttered softly by the Tartar woman reassured him. He held up the candle for them, locked the door, and led them up the stairs. Andrey found himself beneath the lofty, dark arches of the monastery church. A priest was kneeling at one of the altars on which stood tall candlesticks and candles, and was praying in a low voice. On each side of him two young clerics in purple vestments and white lace stoles knelt with censers in their hands. The priest prayed that a miracle might be wrought: that the city should be saved; that the failing spirit of the people should be fortified and patience vouchsafed to them; that the tempter, who incited the people to murmur and provoked them to give way to mean-spirited, cowardly lamentations over their earthly misfortunes, should be utterly confounded. A few women, looking like ghosts, knelt in different corners of the church, their weary heads resting or lying lifelessly on the backs of the chairs and the dark wooden benches in front of them; a few men knelt mournfully, propped up against the columns and pilasters on which the vaulted roof of the aisles rested. The stained-glass window above the altar gleamed with the rosy tints of morning, and large circular blobs of light, blue, yellow, and of different other colours, fell from it on the floor and in a trice illumined the whole church. The entire altar and the deep recess in which it was placed seemed suddenly bathed in radiance; the smoke from the censers hung in the air in a bright, iridescent cloud. From his dark corner Andrey gazed, not without amazement, at this miracle wrought by the light. At that moment the majestic strains of the organ suddenly filled the church and, growing richer and richer, swelled and turned into peals of thunder; then, as suddenly, they were transformed into heavenly music, and their sweet sounds, soaring higher and higher under the arched roof, resembled the thin clear voices of young girls, and finally they changed once more into a deep roar and peals of thunder, and then died away. But for a long time the peals of thunder reverberated through the church, quivering beneath the vaults of the roof, and Andrey, with a gaping mouth, marvelled at the majestic music.

At that time he felt someone give him a pull by the skirt of his coat. "Come, sir," said the Tartar woman. They crossed the church, unperceived by a soul, and went out into the square in front of it. The sky had for some time been red with the dawn: everything proclaimed the rising sun. The square was completely deserted; in its centre there were still some little wooden tables which showed that perhaps a week before there had been a food market there. The road which in those days was never paved, was just a heap of dry mud. The square was built round with little stone and clay houses of one story, with wooden beams and pillars all the way up their walls and with crossed timber ties, in the manner in which the inhabitants usually built their houses in those days, as may still be seen in some parts of Poland and Lithuania. All of them had high gables, with large numbers of dormer windows and flues. On one side of the square, almost next door to the church, rose a higher building constructed in quite a different style from the rest, probably the town hall or some government office. It was of two stories and on top of it was a belvedere, built in two arches, and a sentry was standing inside it; a huge clockface was let into the roof.

The square seemed dead, but Andrey thought he heard a faint moan. Looking more closely, he noticed on the other side of the square a group of two or three people, lying almost motionless on the ground. He gazed at them more intently, wondering whether they were asleep or dead, and at that moment he stumbled over something lying at his feet. It was the dead body of a woman, apparently a Jewess. She seemed to have been quite young, though from her contorted and emaciated features it was impossible to tell her age. Her head was covered by a red silk kerchief; the lappets over her ears were adorned with two rows of pearls or beads; two or three long strands of hair, all in curls, fell from under them on her withered neck with its rigid veins. Beside her lay a baby, convulsively clutching her wasted breast with its fingers and twisting it in an access of blind fury, having found no milk in it. The child did not scream or cry, and it was only from its faintly rising and falling stomach that it could be seen that it was not yet dead, or at any rate that it had not yet breathed its last. They turned into the streets and were suddenly stopped by a raving lunatic who, seeing Andrey's precious load, sprang at him like a tiger and caught hold of him, shouting, "Bread!" But his strength was not equal to his frenzy; one push from Andrey and he toppled to the ground. Moved by pity, Andrey flung him a loaf, and he fell upon it like a mad dog, gnawing and biting it, and a moment later he died there in the street in terrible convulsions, no longer able to digest his food. Almost at every step they came across the terrible victims of famine. It seemed as if many of them, unable to bear their tortures within doors, had rushed out on purpose into the street in the vain hope of obtaining some nourishing balm from the air. At the gate of a house sat an old woman and it was impossible to say whether she was asleep or dead or simply lost in thought; at any rate she heard nothing and saw nothing and sat motionless in one and the same place with her head sunk on her breast. A stiffened, wasted body was hanging in a noose from the roof of another house. The poor wretch had not been able to endure the pangs of hunger any more and had preferred to hasten his death by suicide.

At the sight of these gruesome signs of starvation, Andrey could not help asking the Tartar woman, "Couldn't they really find some way of keeping body and soul together? Surely a man in his last extremity ought to eat anything, even what he had been too fastidious to touch before; he should even eat the animals forbidden by law; everything eatable ought to be eaten at such a time."

"Everything has been eaten, sir," replied the Tartar woman. "All the cattle, every horse and dog. You won't even find a mouse in the whole city. You see, sir, we used to get everything here from the villages."

"But how can you go on defending the city when you're dying so horrible a death?"

"The governor, sir, had already made up his mind to surrender the city, but yesterday the colonel in Buzhany sent a hawk into the city with a message not to surrender as he was setting out with his regiment to relieve the city and was only waiting for another colonel so that they might come together. Now they're expected to arrive any minute. . . . But here we are, sir. This is our house."

Andrey had noticed already from a distance a house which was quite different from the other houses and seemed to have been designed by an Italian architect: it was a two-storied house built of fine, thin bricks. The windows of the first floor were set in high, jutting granite cornices; the top story consisted entirely of small arches, forming a gallery; between the arches were tablets with armorial bearings, and at the corners of the house were more tablets. A wide outer staircase of coloured brick descended into the square. At the foot of the staircase were two sentries, one on each side, who picturesquely and symmetrically leant with one hand on a halberd standing beside them and with the other propped up their drooping heads, and in this pose looked more like carved figures than living men. They were neither asleep nor dozing, but they seemed to be utterly unconscious of everything, and did not even notice who went up the steps. At the top of the staircase they came upon a richly attired officer, armed from head to foot, who held a prayer book in his hand. He was about to raise his weary eyes to look at them, but the Tartar woman said something to him and he dropped them again on the open pages of his prayer book. They went into the first room, rather a spacious one, which was either a waiting-room or just a vestibule; it was crowded with people sitting in different attitudes round the walls: soldiers, servants, huntsmen, cup-bearers and other members of the retinue regarded as indispensable for a Polish nobleman of high rank, who was both a soldier and a landowner. A candle went out and a wisp of pungent smoke rose with a faint sputter to the ceiling; two other candles were still burning in two enormous candlesticks which stood in the middle of the room, though the morning light had for some time been pouring through the large latticed window. Andrey was about to go straight through a wide oak door decorated with a coat of arms and many other carved ornaments, but the Arab woman pulled him by the sleeve and pointed to a little door in the side wall. They went through the door into a corridor and then into a room, which he examined closely. The light, coming through a crack in the shutter, fell upon a few things: a crimson curtain, a gilt cornice, and a painting on the wall. The Tartar woman asked him to wait there, opened the door into another room, from which there came the gleam of a candle. He heard a whisper and a soft voice which shook him to the core.

Through the open door he caught a glimpse of the graceful figure of a woman with long, beautiful hair which fell on her raised arm. The Tartar woman came back and told him to go in.

He hardly remembered how he went in or how the door closed behind him. Two candles were burning in the room and a little lamp glimmered before a holy image; under it, according to Catholic custom, there stood a high table with steps to kneel on during prayer. But this was not what his eyes were seeking. He turned round and saw a woman who seemed to have become frozen into immobility or turned to stone as she was about to make some quick movement. It seemed as though her whole figure had yearned to rush to meet him and had suddenly stopped dead. And he, too, stood before her in the same startled pose. He had never dreamt that she would look like that; this woman before him had nothing in common with the girl he had known before; there was nothing in her that was even remotely like that girl, but she was twice as beautiful and twice as lovely as she had been before; at that time there was something unfinished, something incomplete about her, but now she was like a work of art to which the artist has given the last finishing touch. That girl was a charming, frivolous creature; this one was a great beauty, a woman in all the perfection of her loveliness. In her raised eyes he could read real feeling, not fragments or hints of feelings, but feeling in all its depth and amplitude. Tears still glistened in them, and that made them shine with an added brilliance that seemed to go through his heart. The lines of her bosom, neck and shoulders were now perfectly formed; the hair, which before fell in light curls over her face, was now a heavy, luxuriant mass, part of which was done up, while the rest fell over the full length of her arm in long, delicate, beautifully curling strands, and over her bosom. Every one of her features seemed to have been completely transformed. In vain did he try to find in them one of those he had preserved in his memory: there was none. However great her pallor was, it did not dim her exquisite beauty; on the contrary, it endowed it with something overpoweringly impetuous, something irresistibly triumphant. And Andrey was suddenly overcome by a feeling of reverent awe, and stood motionless before her.

The Polish girl, too, seemed to have been greatly struck by the looks of the Cossack, who appeared before her in all the beauty and strength of his youthful manliness, and who by the very immobility of his limbs revealed the ease and freedom of his movements. His eyes flashed with bright resolution; his velvety eyebrows rose in a bold arch; his sunburnt cheeks glowed with all the brilliance of a chaste flame; and his youthful black moustache shone like silk.

"No, there is nothing I can do that would repay you for your generosity, sir," she said, the silvery notes of her voice trembling. "God alone can reward you, not I, a weak woman. . . ."

She dropped her eyes, and her sweet, delicately-hued eyelids, fringed with lashes long as arrows, hid them, and her beautiful face was bowed and a faint flush spread over it.

Andrey did not know what to say to this; he wanted to open up his heart to her, to tell her all he felt for her and with all the passion with which he felt it, but he could not. Something seemed to seal his lips; his words were robbed of sound; he felt that it was not for him who was bred in the Academy and the rough life of the camp, to answer such speeches, and he felt furious with his Cossack nature.

At that moment the Tartar woman came into the room. She had had time to cut the loaf brought by the young Cossack knight into slices, and she brought them on a golden dish which she set before her mistress. The beautiful girl glanced at her and at the bread, and then raised her eyes to Andrey—and oh, how eloquently her eyes spoke! The tender look which showed how helpless, how utterly powerless she was to express the feelings that overwhelmed her was easier for Andrey to understand than any words. His heart grew suddenly light; everything within him relaxed, and he felt so buoyant! His feelings, hitherto violently restrained, as though someone was pulling them in by a harsh bridle, were now set free, unrestrained, and he was about to pour them out in a torrent of words. But suddenly the beautiful girl turned to the Tartar woman and asked her anxiously, "What about mother? Have you taken her some food?"

"She's asleep, ma'am."

"And Father?"

"I did take him some. He said he'd come himself to thank the knight."

She took the bread and raised it to her lips. With a feeling of intense delight Andrey watched her breaking it with her lovely fingers and eating; but suddenly he remembered the man who, frenzied with hunger, had died before his eyes after swallowing a piece of bread. He turned pale and, seizing her by the arm, cried,

"That's enough ! Please don't eat any more ! You've had nothing to eat for so long that the bread will be poison to you now !" And she dropped her hand, put the bread on the dish and, like an obedient child, looked into his eyes. Oh, if it were possible to convey the meaning of that look in words ! But no sculptor's chisel, nor painter's brush, nor the all-powerful word, can express what is sometimes seen in the eyes of a fair maid, nor the feeling of tenderness that overwhelms a man who gazes into them.

"My queen !" cried Andrey, his heart and soul overflowing with emotion. "Tell me what you want and I shall do it ! Set me any task, however hazardous or impossible, and I shall fly to perform it ! Command me to do what no man can do, and I will do it even if I die in the attempt ! Yes, even if I should die, for to die for you —I swear it by the Holy Cross !—would make me so happy that . . . but I can't tell you how happy it would make me, for no words can describe it. I have three farms ; half of my father's droves are mine ; all that my mother brought my father, what she even conceals from him—all that is mine ! No one of the Cossacks has such weapons as I have : for the handle of my sabre alone I could get the best drove of horses and three thousand sheep. And I shall renounce it all, I shall give it all up, throw it all away, burn it, drown it all, if you say only one word, or just raise that sweet, black eyebrow of yours ! But perhaps I shouldn't be speaking like this to you. I know that I'm talking foolishly and also inopportunely and out of place, that it is not for me who have spent my life at the Kiev Academy and at the Cossack settlement below the Dnieper Falls to talk as men talk who are accustomed to move in the company of kings, princes and the noblest knights in the kingdom. I know all that. . . . And I know you're different from all of us and that all the other noblemen's wives and daughters are far beneath you. We're not even worthy to be your slaves ; only the heavenly angels can serve you !"

The sweet maid listened to his frank and sincere words with ever growing amazement ; she did not miss a single word of his speech, for in his words, as in a mirror, his young, strong spirit was reflected ; and every simple word of that speech, spoken in a voice that came straight from the heart, was invested with great power. Her lovely face bent forward, she tossed back her unruly hair, and gazed at him with parted lips. Then she was about to say something, but suddenly stopped short, for she remembered that the Cossack knight was moved by different considerations, that his father, his brother and all his countrymen stood behind him like relentless avengers; that the Cossacks who were besieging the city were merciless and that all in the city were doomed to a terrible death . . . and her eyes suddenly filled with tears. She quickly snatched up a silk embroidered handkerchief and buried her face in it, and in a trice it was all wet with her tears; and for a long time she sat with her lovely head thrown back, biting her sweet lower lip with her dazzlingly white teeth, as though she had suddenly felt the sting of a poisonous snake; and she did not remove her handkerchief from her face that he might not see her great sorrow.

"Please say something to me! Just one word!" Andrey entreated her, taking her by the hand, which was as smooth as satin. His blood went racing through his veins at this touch, and he pressed the hand that lay lifelessly in his, but she made no reply, remaining motionless and without removing the handkerchief from her face. "Why are you so sad? Tell me, why are you so sad?"

She flung away the handkerchief, tossed back the long hair that kept falling over her eyes, and overwhelmed him with pitiful words, speaking in a soft voice, in a voice that was like the light breeze that, rising on a beautiful evening, suddenly goes rustling through the dense thicket of reeds on the bank of a stream—they murmur and they stir and, all of a sudden, a thousand mournful sounds are heard, and the wayfarer stops to listen to them, overcome by a strange sadness and paying no heed to the glory of the sunset or to the jocund songs of the labourers returning from their work in the cornfields, nor to the distant rumble of some passing cart.

"Tell me, don't you think I deserve to be pitied as long as I live? Don't you think my mother is one of the unhappiest women in the world to have given birth to a luckless creature like me? Think how cruel my destiny has been! How pitiless my fate! The common hangman is not as pitiless as that! The foremost noblemen, the wealthiest gentlemen of the land, men belonging to the most illustrious families of my country, counts and foreign barons—they were all at my feet, and every one of them would have thought himself the happiest man on earth if I had loved him. I had only to lift a finger and the handsomest man of them all, the most accomplished and the noblest, would have been my husband. But my cruel fate has not given my heart to any of them. Not to the fairest and bravest of my country, but to a stranger, to an enemy of my people,

209

does my heart belong ! Why, O Blessed Mother of God, do you persecute me so ? For what sins, for what terrible crimes do you persecute me so heartlessly, so mercilessly ? My whole life has been spent in luxury and riches. The costliest dishes and the best wines were my daily food and drink. And what was it all for ? To what purpose ? So that my end should be more cruel than that of the poorest beggar in the kingdom ? But it seems that it is not enough that I should be condemned to so horrible an end ! It is not enough that before my end I must watch my father and my mother, for whom I'd gladly have suffered a thousand deaths, die in terrible agonies—all this is not enough : it seems that before I die I must experience love such as I have never experienced, and hear words such as I have never heard. It seems that my heart must be torn to pieces by his words, so that my bitter fate should be a hundred times more bitter, so that I should be a hundred times sorrier for myself, so that my death should appear a hundred times more dreadful to me, and so that with my last breath I should reproach you, O cruel fate, and you, too—forgive my transgression !—O Holy Mother of God !"

And when she fell silent a feeling of utter hopelessness was reflected in her face, each feature of which told of gnawing pain, and everything—from her mournfully drooping brow and downcast eyes to the tears which lingered and dried on her flushed cheeks—seemed to say, "There is no happiness on this face !"

"It is unheard of," cried Andrey ; "it cannot be ; it shall not be that the fairest and the best of women should suffer so bitter a fate when she was born to be adored by all that is best in the whole world. No, no. You shall not die. No, it is not you who will die. I swear to you by my birth and by all that is dear to me in the world—you shall not die ! But should it so fall out that neither force, nor prayer, nor courage can turn aside your bitter fate, we will die together, and I will die first, I will die before you, at your lovely feet, and never will they part me from you, never while there's still breath in my body !"

"Do not deceive yourself and me, sir," she said, gently shaking her beautiful head. "I know and, to my great sorrow, I know it too well, that you must not love me. I know where your sacred duty lies : your father, your comrades, your country are calling you ! And we are your enemies !"

"What do I care for my father, my comrades, and my country ?"

said Andrey with a toss of his head and drawing himself up to his full height, his erect figure looking like a black poplar beside a stream. "If that is what is worrying you, then let me tell you this: I have no one, no one, no one !" he repeated in that voice and with that gesture with which an impetuous and indomitable Cossack expresses his determination to perform something which no man in the world has ever performed. "Who says that my country is the Ukraine ? Who gave it to me for my country ? A man's country is what his soul most desires, what is most dear to it. Yes, here is my country ! And I shall carry this country of mine in my heart; I shall carry it there while I live—and let any Cossack try to tear it out ! I shall sell, give away and destroy everything, everything there is, for such a country !"

Petrified for an instant, she gazed into his eyes like a beautiful statue; then suddenly she burst into tears, and with the glorious impetuosity of which only an extravagantly generous woman created for noble impulses of the heart is capable, she threw herself on his neck, flung her lovely, snow-white arms about him, and broke into sobs. At that moment there came from the street confused cries accompanied by the blowing of trumpets and the beating of drums, but he heard nothing. All he heard was the fragrant breath of her sweet lips on his face; all he saw was the tears that rolled down her cheeks in a flood; and all he felt was the touch of her perfumed hair that fell from her head, entangling him as with dark and glittering silken threads.

At that moment the Tartar woman ran in with a joyful cry. "Saved ! Saved !" she cried, beside herself. "Ours have entered the city ! They've brought bread, millet, flour and Cossack prisoners !" But neither of them heard who the "ours" were who had entered the city, what they had brought with them, or what Cossacks were taken prisoner. Full of feelings such as it is not given to man to taste on earth, Andrey kissed the fragrant lips that had clung to his cheek, and those fragrant lips did not remain unresponsive; they replied in the same manner, and in that moment of ecstasy when their lips had met and joined in one long, passionate kiss, they experienced what it is given to man to experience only once in a lifetime.

So did the Cossack perish ! So was he lost to all the Cossack knighthood ! Never will he see the Cossack camp below the Dnieper Falls again, nor his father's farms, nor the church of God.

Neither will the Ukraine ever see one of her bravest sons who undertook to defend her! Old Taras will tear the grey hair from his head and curse the day when he begot such a son to his eternal shame and dishonour.

VII

The Cossack camp was in an uproar. At first no one seemed able to explain how the Polish troops had succeeded in entering the city. It was only after some time that it became known that the men of the Pereyaslav detachment, stationed in front of the side gates of the city, had been dead drunk; it was small wonder then that half of them were killed and the other half taken prisoner before they knew what was happening. While the next detachments, awakened by the noise, were snatching up their arms, the Polish troops were already entering the gates and their rearguard had opened fire upon the sleepy and half-drunken Cossacks who rushed pell-mell after them.

The general gave the order for them all to assemble, and when they had all drawn up in a circle and, taking off their caps, fallen silent, he said:

"So that's what happened last night, my friends. That is what drunkenness has brought us to. That is how the enemy has snapped his fingers at us. It seems it is your way, if given a double portion of vodka, to get so blind drunk that the enemy of Christ's army will not only take the breeches off you, but sneeze in your face, and you won't know anything about it."

The Cossacks stood with bowed heads, realising too well that it was their own fault; only Kukúbenko, commander of the Nezamaykov detachment, raised his voice in protest.

"Just a moment, sir," he said. "It may not be seemly to protest when the general is addressing the whole army, but if the facts warrant it one must say it. Your reprimand, sir, is not altogether just. The Cossacks would have been guilty, and indeed deserved to die, if they had been drunk on the march or in the field or while engaged on some hard task. But we had nothing at all to do; we were just wasting our time before this city. There was no fast, nor any other Christian reason for abstinence, so is it any wonder, sir, that, being idle, a man should take to drink? There is no sin in that. What we had better do now, sir, is to show them what it means to fall upon people who through no fault of their own are taken by surprise and are unable to defend themselves. Before we beat them hard, but now let us beat them so that there won't be any of them left to run away."

The speech of the detachment commander pleased the Cossacks. They raised their heads, which they had hardly hoped to be able to do, and many nodded approval, saying, "Well said, Kukúbenko! Good old Kukúbenko!" And Taras Bulba, who stood not far from the general, said, "Well, General, it seems that Kukúbenko has spoken the truth! What have you to say to this?"

"What have I to say to this? Why, I say, Blessed is the father who begot such a son! It does not require great wisdom to utter a word of reprimand, but it does require a great deal of wisdom to utter a word which, while not offending a man who is in trouble, will cheer him up and raise his spirits, as the spur gives courage to a horse, refreshed by a drink of water. I myself meant to say a word of comfort to you afterwards, but Kukúbenko forestalled me."

"Well said, General! Good old General!" A murmur passed through the ranks of the Cossacks. "Aye, aye," others caught up the cry, "he spoke well!" And the oldest of them all, who stood there like grey-headed pigeons, nodded and, twitching their grey moustaches, muttered softly, "A well-spoken word!"

"Now listen, friends; listen carefully," said the general. "To take a fortress by storm, to scale walls, and to tunnel under them as foreign engineers from Germany do, is—the devil take it!—neither decent nor worthy of a Cossack. But to judge by what has happened, the enemy has certainly not entered the city with large stores of provisions; they do not seem to have had many carts with them. Now the people in the city are very hungry and it is ten to one that they will eat everything up at once, and there's the hay for the horses. . . . Well, I don't know, maybe one of their saints will drop it to them from heaven, though I doubt it, somehow, for all their priests are good at words, not miracles. Anyway, for one reason or another, they're quite sure to come out of the city. You will therefore divide your forces into three parts, each occupying the three roads before the three gates. Before the main gates five detachments, before each of the other gates three detachments. The Dyadykív and the Korsun detachments into ambush! Colonel Taras and his regiment into ambush! The Tytarev and the Timoshev detachments in reserve on the right flank, and the Shcherbínov and the Styeblikív detachments on the left flank ! And those of you who have sharp tongues in your heads step out of the ranks to taunt the enemy. The Poles are a feather-brained lot and they can't stand abuse, so that they may even come out of the gates this very day. Detachment commanders ! Each of you carry out a careful inspection of your detachment ! If you are short of men, fill up your ranks from what remains of the Pereyaslav detachment. Check everything again ! Every Cossack to be given a cupful of vodka and a loaf of bread to take off the effects of last night's debauch, though I expect all of them had enough yesterday to last them for some time, for to be quite frank you've all gorged yourselves so much that I'm surprised no one burst from overeating in the night. And one last warning: if any Jewish innkeeper sells a Cossack even one tankard of weak vodka I'll nail a sow's ear to the dog's forehead and hang him up by the legs ! Now to work, men, to work !"

Such were the orders given by the general, and all the Cossacks bowed low to him and went bareheaded to their carts and encampments, and it was only when they were a long way off that they put on their caps. All began getting ready for battle. They tested their sabres and broadswords, filled their powder flasks with gunpowder from sacks, rolled the carts back and put them in position, and picked out their horses.

On his way back to his regiment Taras could not help wondering what had become of Andrey: was he bound while asleep and taken prisoner with the rest ? That seemed hardly likely, for Andrey was not one of those who would let himself be taken alive. But he was not to be found among the slain Cossacks, either. Sunk in thought, Taras was walking in front of his regiment, which was waiting to be led into ambush, and he did not hear that someone had been calling him by name for some time.

"Who wants me ?" he said at last, coming to himself.

The Jew Yankel stood before him.

"Sir, sir !" the Jew was saying in a hurried and broken voice, as though he had a matter of the utmost importance to impart to him. "I've been in the city, sir !"

Taras looked at the Jew and wondered how he had managed to get into the city.

"How the devil did you get there ?" he asked.

"I'll tell you at once, sir," said Yankel. "As soon as I heard the uproar at dawn and the Cossacks began firing, I seized my coat and

214

ran there without putting it on, getting my arms in my sleeves on the way, for I wanted to find out as quickly as I possibly could what was the reason of the uproar and why the Cossacks should be firing at daybreak. I reached the gates just when the last Polish troops were entering the city. And who do you think, sir, did I see riding in front of a detachment of horse? Why, standard-bearer Galyandóvich, an old acquaintance of mine: he has owed me a hundred gold pieces for the last three years. I went after him as though intending to get my money back and entered the city together with them."

"You mean you entered the city and wanted to get your money back as well?" asked Bulba. "Didn't he have you hanged on the spot like a dog?"

"Well, sir," replied the Jew, "it is quite true he wanted to hang me, and his servants had already got hold of me and were about to put the rope round my neck, but I implored the Polish gentleman to spare my life, telling him that I didn't mind waiting for the money he owed me as long as he liked and promising him to lend him more if he'd help me to collect my debts from the other gentlemen. For you see, sir, standard-bearer Galyandóvich has not a single gold piece in his pocket, though he has farms and estates and four castles and steppe-land right up to Shklov; but like a Cossack he has no money at all, not a penny. And even now he would have had nothing to go to the war in if the Breslau Jews had not equipped him. He did not attend the last meeting of the Seym because . . ."

"What did you do in the city? Seen any of us?"

"Of us, sir? Why, of course, I saw lots of us: Isaac, Rakhum, Samuel, Khayvalokh, the Jewish contractor. . . ."

"Confound them, the rascals!" Taras exclaimed, flying into a rage. "What are you thrusting those scurvy knaves of your kindred into my face for? I'm asking you about our Dnieper Cossacks."

"No, sir, I didn't see our Dnieper Cossacks. I only saw your son Andrey, sir."

"You saw Andrey?" cried Bulba. "Well, where did you see him? In a dungeon? A pit? Dishonoured? Bound?"

"Good gracious, sir, who would dare to bind such a fine gentleman as Andrey? Oh, he's such a great knight, sir! Upon my soul, I hardly recognised him. Wears gold shoulder-pieces, and his arm-guards are of gold, too, and his cuirass is of gold, and his helmet is of gold, and there's gold on his belt—everything he wears is of gold, sir; there's gold everywhere. Just like the sun in the spring, sir, when every little bird chirps and sings in the garden and every wild flower smells sweet, so he is all shining in gold ! And the governor, sir, has given him one of the best horses to ride : I should think the horse alone must have cost two hundred gold pieces."

Bulba was dumbfounded. "Why has he put on someone else's accoutrements ?"

"Why, sir ? Because it is better ! He rides about, and the others ride about; he's instructing them, and they're instructing him. Like the richest Polish gentleman, sir !"

"But who has forced him to do it ?"

"Forced him to do it, sir ? I never said that anyone had forced him. Don't you know, sir, that he's gone over to them of his own free will ?"

"Who's gone over ?"

"Why, your son Andrey, sir."

"Gone over ? Where ?"

"Gone over to their side, sir. To the Poles. He's one of them now."

"You're lying, you scoundrel !"

"Why should I be lying, sir ? Am I such a fool as to tell you a lie ? Don't I know that a Jew will be hanged like a dog if he tells a lie to a gentleman ?"

"So according to you he has sold his country and his faith, has he ?"

"I never said he had sold anything, sir. I only said he had gone over to them."

"You lie, you damned Jew ! Such a thing has never happened in a Christian country ! You must be mistaken, you cur !"

"May the grass grow on the threshold of my house, sir, if I'm lying. May everyone spit on the tomb of my father, and my mother, and my father-in-law, and my father's father, and my mother's father, if I am mistaken. If you wish, sir, I can even tell you why he went over to them."

"Why ?"

"Because the governor of the city, sir, has a beautiful daughter. My goodness, what a beauty ! What a beauty !" Here the Jew tried his best to show how beautiful the governor's daughter was by spreading out his arms, screwing up his eyes, and twisting his mouth, as though tasting some titbit.

"Well, what's that got to do with it ?"

"Why, sir, it is for her sake that he's done it all. You see, sir, if a man falls in love he's like the sole of a shoe that's been soaked in water: you can bend it any way you like."

Bulba pondered deeply. He remembered how great is the power of a weak woman, how many strong men she has ruined, and how highly susceptible Andrey's nature was where women were concerned, and he stood there rooted to the ground for a long time.

"Listen, sir, I'll tell you everything," said the Jew. "As soon as I heard the uproar and saw the Polish troops going through the gates of the city, I snatched up a string of pearls, just in case. . . . For you see, sir, there are many noble and beautiful ladies in the city, and I said to myself, They're sure to want to buy pearls even if they have nothing to eat. So when the standard-bearer's servants let me go, I ran to the governor's courtyard to sell the pearls. I found everything out from their Tartar maid. 'There'll be a wedding soon,' she said. 'As soon as they drive off the Cossacks.' Your son Andrey, sir, seems to have promised them to drive off the Cossacks."

"And didn't you kill him on the spot, the damned traitor?"

"Why should I have killed him? He's gone over of his own will, hasn't he, sir? How can you blame him? He's better off there, so he's gone over there!"

"And you saw him face to face?"

"Why, of course I did, sir. Face to face! What a splendid soldier he is, sir! The most splendid soldier of them all! Bless my soul, he recognised me at once, and when I went up to him he said to me. . . ."

"What did he say?"

"He said . . . But as a matter of fact, sir, he first of all beckoned to me with his finger and then he said, 'Yankel,' he said, and I said, 'Sir,' I said. 'Yankel,' he said, 'tell my father, tell my brother, tell the Cossacks, tell 'em all, that my father is no father to me, my brother no brother, and my comrades no comrades, and that I will fight them all, I will fight with all of them!'"

"You're lying, you damned Judas!" Taras shouted, losing control of himself. "You're lying, you cur! Didn't you crucify Christ, too, you man accursed of God? I'll kill you, you Satan, you! Run, run as fast as you can, or I'll kill you on the spot!"

With these words Taras drew his sabre, and the terrified Jew took to his heels and ran as fast as his thin, spare legs would carry him. He ran for a long time without looking back through the Cossack camp and for miles over the open plain, though Taras never thought of pursuing him, reflecting that it was unfair to vent his anger on the first man who happened to cross his path.

He now remembered that on the previous night he had seen Andrey walking through the camp with some woman, and he bowed his grey head; but he still refused to believe that such a disgraceful thing could have happened to him and that his own son should have sold his faith and soul.

At last he led his regiment into ambush and disappeared with it behind a wood, the only wood that had not been burnt by the Cossacks. Meanwhile the Dnieper Cossacks, foot and horse, were taking up their positions across the three roads before the three gates. One after another the different detachments marched by: the Uman, the Popovich, the Kanev, the Styeblikiv, the Nezamáykov, the Gurguiziv, the Týtarev and the Timoshev. The Pereyaslav detachment alone was missing: its Cossacks had drunk deep and drunk away their lives and freedom. Some of them awoke bound in the hands of their enemies; some of them without waking passed in their sleep into the damp earth; and Khlib, their commander, found himself in the Polish camp without his breeches and his coat of mail.

The movement of the Cossack troops was heard in the city. Everybody hastened to the rampart, and the Cossacks beheld a picturesque scene: the Polish knights, one more handsome than the other, stood on the rampart. Their copper helmets shone like suns, plumed with feathers white as swans. Others wore blue and pink light caps, with the tops bent on one side. Their doublets had wide, loose-hanging sleeves and were embroidered with gold or adorned with rows upon rows of little cords. Some wore swords and weapons in sumptuous settings, which must have cost the Polish gentlemen a great deal of money, and there were many more accoutrements of all sorts. Foremost stood the Buzhany colonel, looking haughtily about him, in his red cap trimmed with gold. The colonel was a corpulent man, taller and stouter than any other Polish officer, and his wide, costly coat barely met round him. On the other side of the rampart, almost at the side gates, stood the other colonel, a small, dried-up man; but his keen little eyes looked out sharply from under his beetling eyebrows, and he turned quickly in all directions, pointing smartly with his thin, sinewy hand and giving orders; it was plain that, in spite of his frail body, he was well versed in the art of war. Not far from him stood the standard-bearer, a tall, lanky man with a thick moustache, and his face did not seem to lack colour: the Polish gentleman, it was evident, dearly loved strong mead and a merry feast. And behind them were hundreds of Polish nobles of every description, some of them equipped at their own expense, others at the expense of the king's treasury, others again on money borrowed from the Jews, having pledged all that was left in their ancestral castles. There were also quite a few senatorial darlings there, men who, invited to banquets because their illustrious names shed a certain lustre upon their hosts, did not hesitate to help themselves to silver goblets from the tables and sideboards, and who, after being thus honoured one day, found themselves sitting on the box of some grandee's carriage the next in the humble role of his lordship's coachman. There were all sorts and conditions of men there. Some of them could not afford a drink, but they had all put on their best attire for the war.

The Cossack ranks stood quietly before the walls. There was no gold on any of them; only here and there did it gleam on the hilt of a sabre and the mountings of a musket. The Cossacks did not like to dress up in costly coats for battle: they wore plain coats of mail and long garments of plain cloth, and their black, red-topped sheepskin caps stretched for miles over the plain.

Two men rode out in front of the ranks of the Dnieper Cossacks. One quite young, the other older; both were renowned for the rich vocabulary of taunts, and both not such bad Cossacks in action, either. Okhrim Nash and Mikita Golokopýtenko were their names. After them rode out Nemid Popovich, a thick-set Cossack, who had been in and out of the *Syech* for many years. He had been at the siege of Adrianople, and had suffered many hardships in his day; was nearly burnt alive and escaped to the *Syech* with his head singed and his moustache burnt off. But Popovich had put on fat, grown a new tuft of hair on top of his shaven head of so prodigious a length that it went round his ear, grown large and bushy moustaches, black as pitch—and a biting, caustic tongue had Popovich.

"Look at their red coats," he cried. "They look fine in them, don't they? The whole damned army in red coats! But what I'd like to know is whether there's any red blood under those red coats of theirs!"

"I'll show you!" the stout colonel shouted from above. "I'll have you all trussed up! Hand over your horses and your muskets, you villains! Have you seen how I've trussed up those friends of yours? Bring the Cossacks out on the rampart! Let them have a look at their friends!"

And they led the captured Cossacks out on the rampart, with their hands tied tightly behind their backs. Ahead of all walked detachment commander Khlib, without his breeches and coat of mail, just as they had captured him drunk. The Cossack commander hung his head, ashamed of his nakedness before his comrades and even more ashamed of having allowed himself to be caught in his sleep, like a dog. His head had turned grey in a single night.

"Don't worry, Khlib! We'll get you out of this!" the Cossacks shouted to him from below. "It isn't your fault they took you naked; accidents will happen to anyone. It is they who ought to be ashamed of themselves for having brought you out without decently covering up your nakedness, to humiliate you!"

"Seems to me you're a brave enough army when it comes to fighting men who're asleep," Golokopýtenko said, looking up at the rampart.

"You wait, we'll shave off your long locks!" the Poles shouted from above.

"I'd like to see you shave off our long locks!" said Popovich, turning round on his horse to show them the long tuft of hair behind his ear, and then, glancing at his own comrades, he said, "Who knows? Maybe these damned Poles are right; if that big-bellied one brings them out, they won't have anything to worry about!"

"Why won't they have anything to worry about?" asked the Cossacks, knowing that Popovich had some scathing answer on the tip of his tongue.

"Why, because their whole damned army can hide behind that belly of his and you'll never be able to reach any of them with a spear!"

All the Cossacks burst out laughing, and long afterwards many of them kept shaking their heads and saying, "What a fellow that Popovich is, to be sure! Only let him start poking fun at a man and well . . ." But what they meant by "well" the Cossacks did not say.

"Fall back from the walls! Quick!" the general shouted, for the Poles seemed to have been cut to the quick by Popovich's last sally, and the colonel waved his hand.

No sooner had the Cossacks moved aside than there came a volley of grapeshot from the rampart. A commotion arose on the wall.

The grey-haired governor himself appeared on his horse. The gates were opened and the Polish army marched out. In front, in straight lines, rode the hussars in their embroidered coats, behind them came men in coats of mail, then cuirassiers with lances, then soldiers in copper helmets, then the Polish nobles, each accoutred in his own fashion and each riding apart from the rest. The proud gentlemen did not wish to mingle with the others in the ranks, and those of them who were not in command of the regular troops rode apart with their retinues of servants. After the nobles came more lines of soldiers, followed by the standard-bearer; then still more lines of soldiers, followed by the stout colonel; and in the rear of the whole army rode the short colonel.

"Attack them ! Attack them at once ! Don't let them form into ranks !" the general shouted. "All detachments press upon them at once ! Leave all the other gates ! Týtarev detachment attack on the flank ! Dyadkiv detachment attack on the other flank ! Kukúbenko and Palývoda attack them in the rear ! Harrass them, harrass them ! Keep them apart !"

And the Cossacks attacked on all sides, broke up their lines and threw them into confusion and were themselves thrown into confusion. They did not give the enemy time to fire ; the battle developed into a fight of sword against sword and lance against lance. Their ranks got all mixed up, and every man had a chance to show his mettle.

Demid Popovich speared three common soldiers and unseated two of the finest Polish nobles, saying, "Oh, what lovely horses ! I've wanted such horses for myself a long time !" And he drove the horses far out into the plain, shouting to the Cossacks who were standing there to catch them. Then he forced his way again into the thick of the fray, once more attacked the two Polish nobles he had thrown from their horses, killed one and threw his lasso round the neck of the other, fastened the rope to the saddle and dragged him across the whole plain, having first taken off his sword with its costly handle and untied from his belt a purse full of gold pieces.

Kobíta, a stout Cossack and quite a young man still, engaged in combat with one of the bravest warriors of the Polish army. They fought a long time. Both were unseated and both went on fighting on foot, hand to hand, and the Cossack was almost on the point of winning, having knocked his enemy down and driven a sharp

Turkish dagger into his chest, but he did not escape himself: he fell on top of his dead enemy, struck on the temple by a hot bullet. The man who killed him was one of the most illustrious of Polish knights, the handsomest gentleman of them all, the scion of an ancient princely family. Like a slender poplar, he dashed along on his dun-coloured steed. And many acts of great bravery had he accomplished already. Two Cossacks had he cut in pieces; he had thrown Fyodor Korzh, a gallant Cossack, to the ground, together with his horse, fired at the horse and killed the Cossack with his lance from behind the horse; many a head and many an arm had he severed; and now it was the turn of Kobíta, whom he felled with a bullet in the head.

"That's the man I'd be glad to try my strength with!" shouted Kukúbenko, commander of the Nezamaykov detachment.

Spurring on his horse, he fell straight upon him from the rear with so loud and piercing a whoop that all who were near shuddered at the unnatural sound. The Pole wanted to turn his horse round and meet his enemy face to face, but the horse refused to obey. Frightened by the terrible shout, it shied to one side, and Kukúbenko hit the Pole with a bullet from his musket. The hot bullet struck him between the shoulder blades, and he fell from his horse. But even then the Pole would not yield, and he tried to deal a blow at his foe with his sword, but hand and sword sank powerlessly to the ground. Taking his heavy broadsword in both his hands, Kukúbenko drove it straight into his pale lips. The sword knocked out two teeth, white as sugar, cleft the tongue in twain, smashed the neck-bone and penetrated deep into the earth: so he pinned him there to the damp earth for ever. The noble blood welled out of his body, deep-red as the guelder-rose over the bank of the stream, staining his gold-embroidered coat all red. Kukúbenko left him at once, rushing into the midst of another large enemy force with his Nezamaykov Cossacks.

"Fancy leaving such rich trappings!" said Borodáty, commander of the Uman detachment, and he left his followers and rode up to the place where the Polish nobleman slain by Kukúbenko lay. "I killed seven Polish squires with my own hand, but such trappings I have not yet seen on any!"

And overcome by greed, Borodáty bent down to take the costly armour off the dead man. Already he had taken off a Turkish dagger set with precious stones, untied a purse of gold pieces from the belt, taken off his chest a knapsack containing fine linen, costly silver and a maid's curl, carefully treasured in remembrance. Borodáty did not hear the red-nosed standard-bearer, whom he had once thrown from the saddle and given a good knock for luck, rush at him full tilt from the rear. The standard-bearer swung his sword and smote the stooping Cossack across the back of the neck. The Cossack's greed was his undoing: the mighty head flew off and the headless body fell to the ground, bedewing the earth with blood far and wide. The Cossack's stern soul flew up into the high heavens, frowning and indignant and also marvelling that it had so soon flown from so mighty a body. The standard-bearer had scarcely time to seize the commander's head by its long forelock to tie it to his saddle before a grim avenger was upon him.

As a hawk, soaring in the sky and circling round and round on powerful wings, suddenly hovers motionless in the air over one spot and then drops like an arrow upon the quail calling for its mate at the edge of some country road, so did Ostap, Taras Bulba's son, suddenly swoop down on the standard-bearer and fling a noose about his neck. The standard-bearer's red face grew purple as the cruel rope tightened about his throat. He grasped his pistol, but his hand clawed the air convulsively, and the shot went wide of the mark. Swiftly Ostap untied from the standard-bearer's saddle the silken cord, which the Pole carried for binding prisoners, bound him hand and foot with his own cord, fastened one end of it to the saddle and dragged him across the plain, calling to the Cossacks of the Uman detachment in a loud voice to come and pay their last honours to their slain commander.

When the men of the Uman detachment heard that their commander Borodáty was dead, they left the battlefield and hurried to take up his body, and they began discussing there and then whom they should choose to succeed him. At last they said, "Why discuss it at all? We could not find a better commander than Ostap Bulba. It's true he's younger than any of us, but he has the understanding of an old man."

Taking off his cap, Ostap thanked all his Cossack comrades for the honour done him. He did not plead either his youth or his in-experience, knowing that in war-time there were more important things to think of, but at once led them against a large force of the enemy and showed them that they had not done amiss in choosing him for their commander.

The Poles soon realised that things were getting too hot for them and they retreated, racing across the plain to rally at the other end of it. The short colonel waved to the four companies of fresh troops, each a hundred strong, who were standing apart at the very gates of the city, and a volley of grapeshot was immediately fired from there at the Cossacks: the bullets struck the Cossack oxen that were staring wildly at the battle. The panic-stricken oxen bellowed and raced off towards the Cossack encampments, smashing the carts and trampling many underfoot. But Taras, who rushed out of the ambush with his regiment at that very moment, galloped off with a loud shout to head them off. The whole maddened herd, frightened by his shout, turned back and stampeded the Polish regiments, scattering the cavalry and trampling and dispersing them all.

"Oh, thank you, thank you, oxen!" the Dnieper Cossacks shouted. "In the past you've served us faithfully on the march, and now you've done your bit of active service, too !" And they attacked the enemy with renewed force. Many enemies did they slay in that attack and many Cossacks showed their mettle: Metélitza, Shilo, the two Pisarénkos, Vovtúzenko, and not a few others. The Poles saw that things were going badly with them, so they raised a banner and began shouting for the city gates to be opened. The iron-studded gates opened with a creak, and, like sheep returning to their fold, the spent and dust-covered horsemen crowded through the gates. Many Cossacks wanted to pursue them, but Ostap stopped his Uman men, saying, "Keep back ! Keep back, friends ! Don't go too close to the gates !" And he was right, for they opened up a murderous fire on the Cossacks from the walls with everything they could lay their hands on, and many were struck. At that moment the general rode up and commended Ostap, saying, "Here's a new commander, but he leads his troops like an old one !" Old Bulba turned round to have a look who the new commander might be, and he saw Ostap on his horse at the head of the Uman detachment, with his cap tilted rakishly on one side and the commander's staff in his hand. "Well, I'll be damned !" the old man said, looking at Ostap, and he was overjoyed and he thanked the men of the Uman detachment for the honour shown his son.

The Cossacks withdrew once more, in readiness to go back to their encampments, while the Poles appeared on the city ramparts again, this time in tattered cloaks. Many costly coats were stained with gore, and the fine copper helmets were thick with dust.

"Well, did you bind us?" the Dnieper Cossacks shouted to them from below.

"See this?" the fat colonel shouted from above, showing them a rope. "I've got it all ready for you!" and the dusty, exhausted warriors went on uttering threats, and the more defiant on both sides hurled taunts at one another.

At last all dispersed. Some went to rest, worn out with the fighting; others were scattering some earth on their wounds and tearing into bandages kerchiefs and costly garments taken from the slain enemy; and those who were not so tired went to collect their dead and pay them the last honours: they dug graves with their broadswords and spears, scooped the earth out with their caps and the skirts of their coats, laid out the Cossack bodies honourably and covered them up with fresh earth, so that no crow or eagle or other bird of prey might claw out their eyes. But the bodies of the Poles, gathered anyhow in bundles of ten or more, they bound to the tails of wild horses and, setting them loose on the plain, they kept chasing them for hours, lashing them across the flanks with their whips. The frenzied horses galloped over fields and hillocks, across ditches and streams, and the dead bodies of the Poles were battered against the earth, covered with blood and dust.

Then all the Cossack detachments sat down in rings to supper, and for hours they went on recounting the share each of them had taken in the day's battle and the acts of heroism that had fallen to the lot of each, a tale to be told and re-told a hundred times to strangers and posterity. They did not lie down to sleep for a long time, but old Taras was awake longer, for he was wondering all the time why Andrey had not been seen among the enemy. Had the Judas been ashamed to take up arms against his own comrades, or had the Jew deceived him and had Andrey simply been taken prisoner by the enemy? But then he recalled that Andrey's heart had always been exceedingly susceptible to women's speeches, and he was overcome with grief and vowed vengeance against the Polish girl who had bewitched his son. And he would have carried out his vow. He would have paid no heed to her beauty; he would have dragged her out by her thick, luxuriant hair; he would have pulled her along all over the plain among the Cossacks. Her lovely breasts and shoulders, gleaming like the never-melting snow on the summits of high mountains, would have been crushed on the earth and covered with blood and dust. He would have torn to pieces her lovely, sweet body. But Bulba knew not what God had in store for man on the morrow, and slumber began to assert its sway over him, and at last he fell asleep. But the Cossacks still talked among themselves, and all through the night the sentries, wide awake and sober, stood watch by the camp-fires, peering keenly in all directions.

VIII

The sun had not yet gone half across the sky when all the Dnieper Cossacks gathered in circles. News had come from the *Syech* that in the absence of the Cossacks the Tartars had plundered everything in it, dug up the treasures the Cossacks had secretly buried in the earth, slain or taken prisoner all who were left behind, and with all the captured herds of cattle and droves of horses set off straight for Perekop. Only one Cossack, Maxim Golodúkha, had succeeded in escaping from the Tartars on the way. He had stabbed the *Mirza*, taken off his bag of sequins and ridden away from his pursuers on a Tartar horse and in Tartar dress for a day and a half and two full nights. He had ridden the horse to death, mounted another on the road, ridden that one to death, too, and arrived at the Cossack camp on a third, having learnt on the way that the Cossacks were laying siege to Dubno. He could only tell them the bare facts of the disaster, but how it had happened—whether the Cossacks had drunk too deep according to their custom and had let themselves be carried off into captivity while drunk, or how the Tartars had found out where the army treasury had been buried—of that he could say nothing. The Cossack was too worn out, he was all swollen, his face scorched by the sun and weather-beaten; he sank down and immediately fell fast asleep.

In such a case it was the accepted rule among the Dnieper Cossacks to set off at once in pursuit of the raiders, with the idea of overtaking them on the road; for otherwise the prisoners might find themselves in the bazaars of Asia Minor, Smyrna, or the island of Crete, and indeed no one could tell in what places their Cossack heads with the long tufts of hair might not be seen. This was why the Cossacks had assembled. They all had their caps on, for they had not come to receive the orders of their officers, but to consult together as equals.

"Let the old men speak first ! We want to hear their advice !" some shouted.

"The general! Let the general speak! We want to hear his advice!" others shouted.

The general took off his cap and thanked all the Cossacks for the honour, not as their commanding officer, but as their comrade.

"There are many among us," he said, "who are old and wise in counsel, but since you've done me the honour, my advice is not to lose time, friends, but to go in pursuit of the Tartars. For you all know what a Tartar is: he will not wait for us to overtake him with his plunder, but will dispose of it instantly, and we shall never be able to recover it. So my advice is: let's go! We've had good sport here. The Poles now know what the Cossacks are. We have avenged our faith as much as we could, and there's precious little gain to be had from a starving city. So my advice is: let's go!"

"Let's go! Let's go!" loud cries were raised in the different Cossack detachments.

Bulba did not relish these words and he lowered still more over his eyes his grizzled, beetling eyebrows, like bushes growing on the high crest of a mountain and thickly sprinkled with the sharp northern frost.

"No, General, your counsel is not right," he said. "You are wrong. You seem to have forgotten that we are leaving our men in the hands of the Poles. You would, it seems, have us dishonour the first sacred duty of comradeship and leave our comrades behind to be flayed alive or to be quartered and their dismembered bodies put up for show in every city and village, as they did to the hetman and to the best soldiers in the Ukraine. Have they not done enough mischief? Have they not desecrated and dishonoured all that we hold sacred? What kind of people are we, I ask you. What kind of a Cossack is he who abandons his comrade in dire need, abandons him like a dog, to perish in an alien land? If it has come to this that there is not one among us who cares for Cossack honour any more, if it has come to this that you don't mind if people spit in your faces and call you all manner of names, then no one shall treat me like that. I will stay here alone."

Bulba's words made a deep impression on the assembled Cossacks, who visibly wavered.

"But have you forgotten, brave and gallant colonel," said the general, "that our comrades are prisoners in the hands of the Tartars also? That if we do not come to their rescue now they'll be sold into lifelong slavery among the heathens, which is much worse than the most cruel death? Have you forgotten that they have now all our treasure, won by Christian blood?"

The Cossacks pondered deep and did not know what to say. Not one of them was anxious to earn a bad name for himself. Then Kassyan Bovdyúg, the oldest man in the Cossack army, stepped forward. He was held in great honour by all the Cossacks. Twice had he been elected general, and he had also acquitted himself well on the battlefield, but for many years now he had been too old to take part in any campaign, or give advice to anybody. What the old soldier liked best was lying on his side in a Cossack ring and listening to the tales of adventure and Cossack campaigns. He never took part in their talk, but just listened, pressing down with his finger the ash in his short pipe which he hardly ever removed from his mouth. He would sit there for hours, his eyes screwed up a little, and the Cossacks found it hard to say whether he was asleep or still listening. He had stayed at home during all the recent campaigns, but this time the old man for some reason could not bear being left behind. With a wave of his hand, after the manner of the Cossacks, he had said, "Oh, well, I suppose I'd better be coming along, too. Who knows, maybe I shall be of some use to the Cossacks yet!"

All the Cossacks fell silent when he stepped forth before the assembly, for it was long since they had heard him speak. Every one wanted to know what Bovdyúg would say.

"It is now my turn to say a word to you, friends," he began. "Listen to an old man, children. Our general has spoken wisely, and, as the head of the Cossack army, he is in duty bound to look after it and to take care of the army treasury, and he could not therefore have spoken more wisely. Ay, that's the first thing I should like to say to you. And now listen to what I have to say next. What I have to say is that Colonel Taras (God grant him long years and may there be many more colonels like him in the Ukraine!) has also spoken the truth. The first duty and obligation of a Cossack is to observe the rules of comradeship. In all my long life I have never heard of a Cossack who has at any time or in any way deserted or betrayed a comrade. They are all our comrades, whether there are more or less of them with the Poles or the Tartars makes no difference. They are all our comrades and they are all dear to us. So this is what I'd like to say to you: those of you who have at heart the fate of our comrades taken prisoner by the Tartars, go after the Tartars, and those who have at heart the fate of the prisoners seized by the Poles, remain here. The general, as indeed is his duty, will go with the half of the army in pursuit of the Tartars, while the other half will choose its commander here, and no man, if you do not mind taking the advice of an old man whose head has turned white, is more worthy of being in command of the remaining Cossack forces than Taras Bulba. There is no man among us who is his equal in valour."

So spoke Bovdyúg and fell silent; and all the Cossacks were glad that the old man had in this way showed them what they had to do. They threw their caps in the air and shouted, "Thank you, thank you, sir ! For years you were silent, and now you have spoken at last. You said you would be useful to the Cossacks, and you were right !"

"Well, are you agreed to do this ?" asked the general.

"Agreed ! Agreed !" shouted the Cossacks.

"Is the assembly at an end then ?"

"Yes, the assembly's at an end !"

"Then listen to my orders now, friends," said the general, stepping forward and putting on his cap, while all the Cossacks to a man took off their caps and stood bareheaded and with downcast eyes, as was the custom among the Cossacks whenever a commanding officer addressed them. "Now, friends, you must separate. Those who want to go, line up on the right, and those who want to remain, on the left; where the greater part of a detachment goes, there goes also their commander, and the men left over from a detachment will join other detachments."

And they all began crossing over, some to the right and some to the left. Whichever side the majority of a detachment joined, there its commander went also; and if only a small part of a detachment went over to one side or the other, it joined forces with another detachment; and the forces on either side were more or less equal in strength. Among those who decided to remain were almost the whole of the Nezamáykov detachment, the larger part of the Popóvich detachment, the entire Uman detachment, the entire Kanev detachment, the greater part of the Steblikív detachment, and the greater part of the Timoshev detachment. All the others volunteered to go in pursuit of the Tartars. There were many brave and stalwart Cossacks on both sides. Among those who decided to go after the Tartars was Chereváty, the good old Cossack Pokotípolye, Lemish, Khoma Prokopóvich; Demid Popóvich also joined them, for he was a Cossack of an incorrigible character who hated to stay too long in one place: he had already tried his strength with the Poles and now he wanted to try his strength with the Tartars. The detachment commanders of that force included Nostyugán, Pókrysha, Nevylýchky, and many other brave and renowned Cossacks wished to measure swords with the Tartars. There were not a few splendid fighters among the Cossacks who chose to remain: the detachment commanders Demitróvich, Kukúbenko, Vertýkhvist, Balabán and Ostap Bulba. There were many other famous and stalwart Cossacks, too: Vovtúzenko, Cherevichénko, Stepan Guska, Mikola Goostý, Zadorózhny, Metélitza, Ivan Zakrutýguba, Mossy Shilo, Degtyarénko, Sidorénko, Pisarénko, as well as Pisarénko the Second and Pisarénko the Third, and many other good Cossacks. All were men of great experience who had taken part in many campaigns. They had marched on the shores of Anatolia; on the salt marshes and the steppes of the Crimea; along the rivers, great and small, which fall into the Dnieper; along all the inlets, bays and islands of the Dnieper. They had been in Moldavia, Wallachia, and Turkey. They had sailed all over the Black Sea in their double-ruddered Cossack canoes; in fifty such canoes all in a row they had attacked the tallest and richest ships. Many a Turkish galley had they sent to the bottom of the sea, and they had fired much powder in their day. Many a time had they torn up expensive brocades and rich velvets to wrap round their feet and legs. Many a time had they stuffed the purses fastened to a cord round their waists with sequins of the purest gold. And incalculable is the wealth each of them had squandered on drink and revelry, as much as could have lasted another man a lifetime. They had spent it all in true Cossack fashion, treating everybody and hiring musicians that everybody in the world might be merry. Even now it was rare to come across any of them who had not some treasure buried somewhere: beakers, silver pitchers and bracelets, under the reeds on the Dnieper islands, that the Tartar might not find them, if by some unlucky chance he should succeed in launching a surprise attack on the *Syech*. But the Tartar might have found it hard to discover it, anyway, for the owner himself was no longer sure where he had buried it. Such were the Cossacks who had decided to remain and take vengeance on the Poles for their faithful comrades and the Christian faith ! The old Cossack Bovdyúg also decided to remain. "I'm too old now to run after the Tartars," he said. "Long have I prayed to God that, when my time comes, I may end my life in a war for a holy and Christian cause. And so it has come to pass. There could be no more glorious end anywhere for an old Cossack."

When they had all separated and stood drawn up in two lines facing each other, the general passed between them and said:

"Well, dear friends, is one side satisfied with the other?"

"We're all satisfied, sir," replied the Cossacks.

"Well, then, embrace and take leave of one another, for God knows if we shall ever meet again in this life. Obey your commander and do what you know yourselves to be best: for you know very well what Cossack honour bids you."

And all the Cossacks, large as their numbers were, kissed one another. The first to bid farewell were the two commanders. After stroking their grey moustaches, they kissed each other on each cheek, then, clasping hands and gripping them firmly, each wanted to ask the other, will, friend, shall we see one another again?" but they said nothing, they were silent, the two grey-headed soldiers sank into thought. All the Cossacks said a last farewell to one another, well knowing that there was much work in store for both the forces. They decided not to separate until darkness hid from the enemy the reduction in the numbers of the besieging army. Then they went off to dinner in their separate detachments.

After dinner all those who had the journey before them lay down to rest, and they slept well and soundly, as though feeling that it might be the last time they would enjoy undisturbed sleep. They slept till sunset, and when the sun had gone down and dusk had fallen they began tarring their carts. Having got everything ready, they let their carts go on ahead and, after taking leave of their comrades once again, they set off quietly after their carts, the cavalry sedately, with never a shout or a whistle to the horses, tramping lightly after the foot-soldiers, and soon they disappeared in the darkness. All that could be heard was the hollow sounds of horses' hoofs and the creaking of some wheel which was not yet running smoothly or which had not been well tarred because of the darkness. The comrades they had left behind went on waving their hands to them for a long time from a distance, though nothing could be seen; and when they turned at last and went back to their places, when they saw by the light of the brightly twinkling stars that half of the carts were gone and that many, many comrades were no longer with

231

them, sadness stole into the heart of every one of them, and they grew thoughtful and bowed down their reckless heads.

Taras saw how troubled the Cossack ranks had become and how despondency, so unseemly in a brave soldier, was slowly spreading among the Cossacks. But he kept silent, for he wanted to give them time to get used to everything, even to the dejection caused by the leave-taking. Meanwhile he was making preparations in silence to rouse them suddenly and at one stroke by uttering the Cossack battle cry, and in this way to make sure that courage would come anew and with greater force than ever into the heart of every one of them—a transformation of which only the Slav race is capable; the great and mighty Slav race which compared with any other is as the ocean to a shallow stream: in a storm it roars and thunders, raising mountainous, foam-flecked billows as no impotent river can; but on a calm, windless day it spreads its boundless, mirror-like surface far and wide, clearer and serener than any river, a never-ending delight to the eye.

And Taras ordered his servants to unload one of his carts that stood apart. It was larger and stronger than any other cart in the Cossack camp; its mighty wheels were rimmed with double bands of iron; it was heavily laden, covered with horse-cloths and strong ox-hides, and bound with taut tarred ropes. In the cart were barrels and kegs of fine old wine, which had lain for many years in Bulba's cellars. He had brought it along with him, intending to keep it in reserve, so that if the great moment came when a decisive battle had to be fought, a battle worthy to be handed down to posterity, every single Cossack might taste of that precious wine and be filled with great courage in keeping with so great an occasion. Hearing the colonel's command, the servants rushed to the carts, cut the strong ropes with their broadswords, removed the stout ox-hides and horse-cloths and unloaded the kegs and barrels from the cart.

"Take all of you anything you can lay hands on," Bulba said to the Cossacks, "a jug or the bucket with which you water your horse, your gauntlet or your cap, and if you have nothing else just hold out your hands."

And all the Cossacks took whatever they could lay their hands on: one a jug, another the bucket with which he watered his horse, a third a gauntlet, a fourth a cap, and a fifth just held out his hands. Walking slowly along the ranks, Bulba's servants poured out from the barrels and kegs for all. But Taras bade them not to drink until he gave them a sign to drink together. It was plain that he wanted to say something to them. Taras knew that however strong good old wine was by itself, and however suitable to fortify the spirit of man, the wine's power and the man's spirit would be twice as strong if strengthened by the right kind of speech.

"I'm treating you, friends," said Bulba, "not in honour of your having made me your commander, great as such an honour is, and not to commemorate our leave-taking from our comrades: at another time either would have been seemly and proper, but now we are confronted with quite a different task. We are confronted with a task, friends, that will require the utmost exertion from all of us, a task that will put our great Cossack valour to the test. And so, friends, let us all drink, together; let us drink, first of all, to the holy orthodox faith, to the time when it will at last spread all over the world and everywhere will be only one holy faith, and all the Moslems on earth will become Christians ! And, at the same time, let us drink to the *Syech*, that long may it stand to the utter undoing of the whole Moslem world, and that every year it should send out young warriors, each better than the last, each handsomer than the last. And let us also drink to our glory, so that our grandsons and the sons of our grandsons may tell that once there were men who never dishonoured their comradeship or betrayed their own people. So to our faith, dear friends, to our faith !"

"To our faith !" all who stood in the front ranks cried in deep voices. "To our faith !" those further away took up the cry—and all the Cossacks, old and young, drank to their faith.

"To the *Syech* !" said Taras, raising his hand high above his head.

"To the *Syech* !" boomed the deep voices in the front ranks. "To the *Syech* !" the old men repeated softly, twitching their grey moustaches, and with a flutter like young falcons the young Cossacks repeated the toast, "To the *Syech* !" And far, far away the plain heard how the Cossacks were honouring their *Syech*.

"Now the last drink, friends, to the glory of all the Christians in the world !"

And every single Cossack drank his last draught to the glory of all the Christians in the world. And for a long time the toast was repeated among the detachments: "To the glory of all Christians in the world !"

The pitchers were empty, but still the Cossacks stood with their hands raised; though the eyes of all, bright with the wine, looked merry, they were wrapt in deep thought. They were not thinking of easy gain or the spoils of war; they were not wondering which of them would have the luck to collect great numbers of gold pieces, costly weapons, embroidered coats, and Circassian stallions. They were scanning the future like eagles perched on the summit of a rocky mountain, a high, precipitous mountain, from which the boundless sea, dotted with galleys like small birds, ships and all manner of vessels, can be seen stretching far into the distance; the sea, bounded on two sides with faintly visible thin lines of coast, with towns on the shore, like midges, and woods, drooping like fine grass. Like eagles they gazed all over the plain, as though trying to catch a glimpse of their darkly looming fate. Aye, the whole plain with its untilled fields and roads will all too soon be covered with their bleaching bones; soon, all too soon, will it be drenched in their Cossack blood and strewn with shattered carts and broken swords and splintered spears; their heads with tangled and gory tufts of hair and drooping moustaches will be scattered far and wide, and soon, all too soon, will the eagles swoop down and claw at and peck out their eyes. But from a death-bed so spacious and so wide great good will arise ! Not one noble action will perish, and Cossack glory will not be lost like a tiny grain of powder from the barrel of a musket. The time will come when a bandore-player with a grey beard covering his chest, or perhaps a white-haired old man still full of vigour, a man prophetic in spirit, will utter a mighty and resounding word about them. And their glory will spread like a whirlwind all over the world, and generations still unborn will talk of them. For a mighty word is carried far and wide, being like the booming copper of a church-bell into which the bell-founder has blended much pure, precious silver that its lovely peal may ring out far over cities and villages, over hovels and palaces, summoning all alike to prayer.

IX

No one in the city knew that half of the Cossack army had gone in pursuit of the Tartars. From the tower of the town hall the sentries saw that some of the carts were moving out behind the wood, but it was thought that the Cossacks were preparing to lay an ambush, and the French engineer was of the same opinion. Meanwhile the general's words were coming true, and the city began to suffer from a shortage of food; as often happened in the old days the troops had underestimated the amount of food they would need. They tried to make a sortie, but one half of the bold men who took part in it were slain by the Cossacks on the spot and the other driven back into the city with nothing to show for their pains. The Jews, however, took advantage of the sortie to nose everything out: why and where the Cossacks had gone, and under which leaders, and what detachments and how many, and how many of them had been left, and what they were thinking of doing. In short, within a few minutes everything was known in the city. The two colonels plucked up courage and prepared to give battle. Taras saw what was happening from the commotion and the movement in the city, and he promptly took all the necessary measures, made the best dispositions of his troops, issued orders and instructions, divided his detachments into three camps, surrounding them with the carts by way of bulwarks, a battle formation in which the Cossacks were invincible. He ordered two detachments to lie in ambush, covered part of the plain with sharp stakes, broken weapons and fragments of spears, with the intention of driving the enemy cavalry there at the first favourable opportunity. And when everything had been done as well as could be, he addressed his troops, not because he wanted to encourage them or refresh their spirits (he knew very well that their spirits needed no refreshing), but simply to tell them all that was in his heart.

"I want to tell you, dear friends," he said, "what comradeship is. You have heard from your fathers and your grandfathers how greatly honoured our country was once by all men: she made her influence felt among the Greeks, she collected gold pieces as tribute from Constantinople, and her cities were wealthy cities, and her temples were rich temples, and her princes were princes of Russian descent and not Catholic infidels. All that was taken by the heathens; all was lost. We were left orphaned and defenceless. Just as a widow is left defenceless after the death of her strong husband, so were we, too, and so was our country. It was at such a time, friends, that we clasped each other's hands in brotherhood: this is what our comradeship is founded on! And there are no bonds more sacred than the bonds of comradeship. The father loves his child, the mother loves her child, and the child loves its father and mother; but, my friends, this is not the same: a wild beast, too, loves its young! But to become kindred in spirit, though not in blood, is what only man can do. There have been comrades in other lands, too, but such comrades as in Russia there have never been. More than one of you, I know, has had to live for many years in foreign lands: you could see that there are also men, God's creatures like you, and you talk with them just as you do with your own people; but when it comes to hearing a word uttered straight from the heart, then—no !—you feel at once that it isn't the same thing. They are clever people, but not the same; they are men like us, but not the same ! No, my friends, to love as a Russian heart can love, to love not with your mind or with your heart, but with all that God has given you, with everything you have . . . ah !" Taras said, and with a wave of the hand, a twitch of the moustache and a shake of his grey head he added, "No, no one can love like that ! I know that abominable infamy and shameful villainy have struck deep roots in our country. All the people seem to be concerned about is that their barns should be full of grain, that there should be plenty of hayricks in their fields, that they should have large droves of horses, and that their sealed casks of mead should be safe in their cellars; they ape the devil alone knows what heathen customs; they despise their own tongue; they do not care to talk to their own folk; they sell their own countrymen as people sell a soulless beast in the market. The favour of an alien king, and not of a king only, but the paltry favour of some Polish grandee who strikes them in the face with his yellow boot, is dearer to them than any brotherhood. But even the most villainous knave of them all, whatever he may be, even though he has all his life been grovelling in dirt and bending the knee, even such a man, my friends, has a grain of Russian feeling; and one day it will awaken and, poor wretch, he will smite his breast and tear his hair and curse in a loud voice this rotten life of his, ready to expiate by tortures his shameful acts. Let them therefore all know what comradeship means in Russia. If die we must, not one of them will ever die as we shall. No, not one, not one ! They're too chicken-hearted for that !"

So spoke the commander, and when he finished his speech, he went on shaking his head, which had grown silvery in the service of the Cossack cause. All who had stood there listening to him were deeply moved by his speech, which went straight to their hearts. The eldest in the ranks stood motionless, their grey heads bowed, a tear quietly gathering in their old eyes, and slowly they wiped it away with their sleeves; and then, as though by common consent, they waved their hands at the same instant and shook their veteran heads. Without a doubt old Taras had recalled to their minds much of what is familiar and best in the heart of man who has grown wise through sorrow, hard work, great bravery and all the vicissitudes of life, as well as in the heart of those who are too young to have gained such experience, but who have divined much with their pure, youthful souls to the abiding joy of the aged parents who begot them.

Meanwhile the enemy forces were already marching out of the city to the beating of drums and the blowing of trumpets, and the Polish nobles, arms akimbo, rode forth, surrounded by their innumerable servants. The stout colonel was issuing orders. And they began to advance in serried ranks against the Cossack encampments with flashing eyes and glittering copper trappings, uttering threats and taking aim with their harquebuses. As soon as the Cossacks saw that they had come within gunshot, they fired their long harquebuses all together, and they went on firing without ceasing. The loud reports resounded far and wide through the surrounding meadows and cornfields, mingling into one continuous roar. The whole plain was covered with smoke, but the Cossacks went on firing without a moment's pause. Those in the rear kept loading the guns and passing them across to those in front, causing consternation in the ranks of the enemy who could not understand how the Cossacks could fire without reloading their guns. By now nothing could be seen for the great smoke which hid the two contending armies; it was impossible to see who was hit and who was still on his feet, but the Poles felt that the bullets were flying thick and that things were getting a little too hot; and when they fell back to move out of the smoke and look about them, they saw that many were missing from their ranks, while among the Cossacks perhaps two or three were killed out of a hundred. And the Cossacks went on firing without ceasing. Even the foreign engineer was astonished, having never before seen such tactics, and he could not refrain from saying aloud before them all, "What brave fellows the Cossacks are! That's the way to fight! Everyone ought to take an example from them!" And he advised the Poles to turn their cannon at once upon the Cossack camp. Loud was the roar from the wide throats of the iron cannons; the earth shook and trembled a long way off as it re-echoed the sound of the gunfire, and twice as much smoke rolled over the plain. Men smelt the gunpowder in the squares and streets of near and distant cities. But the

Polish gunners aimed too high, and the red-hot cannon-balls described too high an arc: they flew through the air with a terrible whine, passed over the heads of all the Cossack forces, and plunged deep into the ground, throwing up the black earth high into the air. The French engineer tore his hair at such incompetence and began sighting the guns himself, paying no heed to the hail of bullets from the Cossacks.

Taras saw from a distance that the Nezamáykov and the Steblikív detachments were in danger of being wiped out, and he shouted in a resounding voice, "Get out quick from behind the carts ! Mount your horses ! All mount your horses !" But the Cossacks could not have carried out either command if Ostap had not rushed into the very midst of the Polish artillery-men and struck the linstocks out of the hands of six gunners; he was driven off by the Poles before he had time to deal in the same way with the remaining four. Meanwhile the foreign captain himself took a linstock in his hand to fire off the biggest cannon the Cossacks had ever seen. Terribly it gaped with its huge throat, and a thousand deaths seemed to lurk there. And when it was fired, and after it the three others, making the earth shake four times as it re-echoed hollowly the thunder of the cannonade—great was the havoc they wrought ! Many an old mother will weep bitter tears for her Cossack son, smiting her withered breasts with her bony hands; many a widow will be left in Glukhov, Nemirov, Chernigov and other cities. She will run out to the market every day, poor woman, stopping every passer-by, gazing into everybody's eyes to see whether the one dearer to her than all the world is not among them; but hundreds of soldiers will pass through the city, and never will she find among them the one who is dearer to her than all the world.

Half of the Nezamáykov detachment had been wiped out: it seemed as though they had never existed. As a field, where every ear of corn glitters and is heavy with grain like a new, shining gold piece, is suddenly beaten down by hail, so were they beaten down and laid low.

Oh, how furious the Cossacks were ! How they all attacked together ! How Detachment Commander Kukúbenko boiled with rage when he saw that more than half of his men were gone ! With his remaining Cossacks he made his way into the midst of the enemy forces. In his wrath he made mincemeat of the first Pole he came across, hurled many horsemen from their saddles, killing both horse and rider, fought his way to the gunners and captured one cannon. And he saw that the Uman detachment commander, too, was busy, and Stepa Gusska had captured the chief cannon. He left those Cossacks to carry on and led his men against another enemy throng: where the Nezamáykov Cossacks passed, they left a wide street, and where they turned, there was a lane. The ranks of the Poles could be seen dwindling and their dead were piling up in stacks. Vovtúzenko by the carts, Cherevíchenko in front, Degtyarénko by the furthest carts, and beyond Detachment Commander Vertýhvist. Degtyarénko had already raised two Poles upon his spear, but the third he attacked was not so easy to overcome. The Pole was an agile and a stalwart man, adorned with rich harness and surrounded by a retinue of no less than fifty servants. He pressed Degtyarénko hard, flung him to the ground and, swinging his sword over him, shouted to the Cossacks, "None of you, dogs, can hold his own against me !"

"Here's one who can !" said Mossy Shilo, stepping forward.

A mighty Cossack was Shilo. More than once had he been in command on sea, and many hardships had he suffered. The Turks had captured him and his men at Trebizond and placed them all aboard their galleys as slaves, putting iron chains on their hands and feet, giving them no millet for whole weeks together and only loathsome sea-water to drink. The poor prisoners suffered and endured all, and no torture could make them renounce their orthodox faith. But Mossy Shilo, their commander, gave in at last. He trampled underfoot the holy law, wound a vile turban round his wicked head, gained the confidence of the Pasha, became the steward on the Turkish ship and chief overseer over all the galley-slaves. It was a grievous blow to the unhappy captives, for they knew that if any of their own people turned traitor to his faith and went over to their oppressors he would persecute them more mercilessly than any infidel; and so indeed it came to pass. Shilo put them all into new chains, three in a row, bound them with ropes that cut their flesh to the bone, and rained blows upon them with his fists. But when the Turks, glad to have procured such a servant, began feasting and, forgetting their own law, all got drunk, he produced the sixty-four keys and gave them to the galley-slaves that they might free themselves and cast their chains into the sea and take up sabres instead and cut down the Turks. The Cossacks took much booty then and returned to their country covered with glory, and long after the bandore-players glorified Mossy Shilo. They would have chosen him general, but he was a most eccentric Cossack. Sometimes he would perform some really amazing feat, such as would never have occurred to the wisest of them, but at other times he was guilty of the most foolish and irresponsible actions. He spent everything he had on drink and gay revelry, was in debt to everyone in the *Syech* and, in addition, was caught stealing like some petty thief. One night he abstracted the entire Cossack harness belonging to another detachment and pledged it with an innkeeper. For so shameful an act he was tied to the whipping-post in the market-place and a cudgel was placed beside it that every Cossack might deal him a blow according to his strength; but not one man could be found among the Dnieper Cossacks who would lift the cudgel against him, for they all remembered his services in the past. Such was the Cossack Mossy Shilo.

"There are still men who can beat curs like you!" he said, advancing against the Polish nobleman.

Oh, how stoutly they fought. The shoulder-pieces and breastplates of both were dented by their mighty blows. The villainous Pole cut through Shilo's coat of mail, inflicting a wound on his body with his blade: the Cossack's coat of mail became red with blood, but Shilo paid no heed to it, and, swinging his sinewy arm (terribly strong was his stout arm!), hit him on the head with all his might and stunned him. The copper helmet was shivered and the Pole staggered and fell heavily upon the ground. Shilo began raining blows upon his stunned enemy, slashing him mercilessly with his sword. Cossack, take care! Do not dispatch your enemy! Turn round! But the Cossack did not turn round, and one of the servants of the slain nobleman stabbed him in the neck with a knife. Shilo turned and was about to lay his hand on the bold fellow, but he lost him in the smoke of battle. From all sides came the cracking of matchlocks. Shilo staggered. He felt that his wound was mortal. As he fell to the ground, he put his hand upon it and said, turning to his comrades, "Farewell, dear friends. Long may the holy Russian land stand and may its glory never pass!" And he closed his weary eyes, and his Cossack soul flew out of his dour body.

By then Zadorózhny had ridden forth with his men, Detachment Commander Vertýkhvist was harrying the Polish ranks, and Balabán was attacking them.

"Well, men," said Taras, calling to the commanders of detachments, "have you enough powder in your flasks? Is there strength left in the Cossack arm? Are the Cossacks standing fast?"

"Yes, sir, we have enough powder in our flasks! The Cossack arm is still strong! The Cossacks are standing fast!"

And the Cossacks pressed their foes hard, and the Polish ranks were thrown into utter confusion. The short colonel sounded a rally and ordered eight painted standards to be raised to gather his men who were scattered all over the plain. The Poles rushed to their standards, but they had hardly time to form into ranks again when Detachment Commander Kukúbenko launched another attack with his Nezamáykov men, hurling himself into their midst and riding full tilt against the big-bellied colonel. The colonel wilted under this sudden attack and, turning his horse round, fled at a gallop. Kukúbenko pursued him all across the plain, preventing him from joining his regiment.

Seeing this chase from a detachment on the flank, Stepan Gusska galloped to intercept the Polish colonel with a lasso in his hand, his head bent low over his horse's mane, and at the first opportunity cast the noose round the colonel's neck with one throw. The colonel's face turned purple, and he clutched at the rope with both hands, trying to tear it apart; but Gusska hurled his spear with terrific force, driving it straight through his belly, and there he was left, nailed to the ground. But now it was Gusska's turn. The Cossacks had scarcely time to look round when they saw Gusska raised on four spears! The poor fellow had just time to say, "May all our enemies perish and may Russia rejoice for ever!" and then he gave up the ghost.

The Cossacks looked round, and there on the flank Metélitza was having good sport with the Poles, smiting them hip and thigh, while on the other flank Detachment Commander Nevelýchky was pressing the foe hard with his men; and at the carts Zakrutýguba was pitching into the Poles and putting them to flight, while at the distant carts Pisarénko the Third had driven off a whole horde of them; at the other carts hand-to-hand fighting was going on, the Cossacks and the Poles engaged in mortal combat on top of the carts.

And Taras rode out in front of all and called to the commanders, "Well, men, is there enough powder in your powder flasks? Is there strength left in the Cossack arm? Are the Cossacks standing fast?"

"Yes, sir, we've still powder in our flasks! The Cossack arm is still strong! The Cossacks are still standing fast!"

But Bovdyúg had already fallen from the cart, struck by a bullet under the very heart. The old man rallied his last strength and said, "I'm not sorry to leave this world. May all men die like that! May Russia be glorious to the end of time!" And Bovdyúg's soul flew straight into heaven to tell the old men long since dead how gallantly men can fight in Russia and, what is better still, how they can die for their holy faith.

Very soon after that, Detachment Commander Balabán was flung to the ground. He had received three mortal wounds from a spear, from a bullet, and from a heavy broadsword. One of the bravest of Cossacks, he had been in command of many sea expeditions, most famous of all being his raid on the coasts of Anatolia. They had collected many sequins at that time, rich Turkish possessions of all sorts, precious fabrics and all kinds of accoutrements. But on their way home disaster overtook them: the poor fellows came under Turkish fire. When the Turkish man-of-war fired a volley at them, it scored a direct hit and half the boats spun round and capsized and many a Cossack was drowned; but the reeds fastened to the sides of the boats prevented them from sinking. Balabán rowed away as fast as he could, placed his boat straight against the sun and so became invisible to the Turkish ship. They spent the whole of the following night baling out the water with their caps and pitchers and stopping up the holes. They cut up their wide Cossack breeches into sails, and so sailed away, making good their escape from the fastest Turkish ship. And not only did they arrive at the *Syech* without any further trouble, but they brought with them a gold embroidered chasuble for the bishop of the Mezhigorsk Monastery in Kiev and a setting for an icon of pure silver for the Church of the Intercession at the *Syech*. And the bandore-players went on glorifying the good luck of the Cossacks for many years. But now Balabán bowed his head, feeling the agonies of death upon him, and said quietly, "It seems to me, dear friends, I'm not dying such a bad death after all: I have cut down seven with my sword, I have slain nine with my spear, I have trampled many more under my horse, and I can't remember the number I have killed with my bullet. May Russia flourish for ever!" and his soul flew away.

Cossacks! Cossacks! Do not let down the flower of your

army ! By now Kukúbenko was surrounded, seven men only remained of the Nezamáykov detachment, and they were finding it
hard work to beat off the attacks of the enemy. Their commander's
clothes were already stained with blood. Taras himself, seeing the
plight he was in, hastened to his rescue. But the Cossacks were too
late: before the enemies who had encompassed him were driven off,
a spear had pierced his heart. Slowly he sank into the arms of the
Cossacks, who caught him as he fell, and his young blood gushed
out of his wound, like the precious wine brought by careless
servants in a glass vessel from the cellar: they slip, and the costly
jar is smashed, the wine is spilt on the ground and the master, who
comes running at the noise, tears his hair, for he has carefully kept
the wine for one of the happiest moments of his life when, if God so
willed, he should meet a friend of his youth in his old age that they
might together recall the good old days when men knew how to
make merry in a different and better fashion. Kukúbenko looked
round and said, "I thank God that I've had the good fortune to die
before your eyes, dear friends ! May men have a happier life after us,
and may our country, dearly beloved of Christ, flourish for ever
and ever !" And the young soul flew out of the body and the angels
received it in their arms and carried it into heaven: it will be well
with him there. "Sit on my right hand, Kukúbenko," Christ will
say to him. "You haven't been false to your brotherhood ; you have
been guilty of no dishonourable deed ; you have never deserted a
man in trouble ; you have always guarded and preserved My Church."

Everyone was greatly grieved by Kukúbenko's death. The Cossack
ranks were beginning to dwindle fast. Many, many a brave man had
fallen, but the Cossacks still stood fast.

"Well, men," Taras shouted to the remaining detachments, "have
you enough powder in your flasks ? Are not your sabres blunted ?
Is your strength giving out ? Are the Cossacks still standing
fast ?"

"We've still enough powder, sir ! Our sabres are sharp enough !
The Cossack arm is still strong ! The Cossacks are still standing
fast !"

And once more the Cossacks threw themselves into the fray, as
though they had never suffered any losses. Only three detachment
commanders were still alive ; streams of blood ran red over the plain
and across them the bridges made of the bodies of the Cossacks and
the enemy rose higher and higher. Taras glanced at the sky and he

saw a long string of gerfalcons flying across it. Well, someone at least was going to have a good time ! Here Metelitza was lifted on a spear, there the head of Pisarénko the Second had been severed from the body and rolled on the ground, and yonder Okhrim Gusska staggered and crashed to the ground, cut into four pieces. "Now !" said Taras and waved his handkerchief. Ostap understood the signal and, dashing out of ambush, he bore down upon the enemy cavalry. The Poles could not hold out against his furious attack and turned tail, while he continued to pursue them, chasing them straight to the place where the stakes and broken spears were driven into the ground. The horses began to stumble and fall, and the Poles were flung headlong over their heads. At the same time the Cossacks of the Korsun detachment, seeing that the enemy was within range, opened up a murderous fire upon them with their matchlocks.

The Poles were overwhelmed and thrown into confusion, and the Cossacks recovered their spirits. "We've won ! We've won !" shouts were raised on every side, and trumpets were sounded and a banner of victory was unfurled. The beaten Poles were running in all directions, looking for cover.

"No," said Taras, glancing at the gates of the city, "it's a bit too soon to shout victory !" And he spoke the truth.

The gates were opened and a regiment of hussars, the flower of all the Polish cavalry regiments, galloped out into the plain. All the riders were mounted on dun-coloured Caucasian stallions, and foremost rode a knight, bolder and handsomer than any of them all. His black hair streamed from under his copper helmet ; a rich scarf embroidered by the hand of a peerless beauty was wound round his arm and waved in the wind. Taras was struck dumb when he recognised Andrey. Meanwhile, seized by the excitement and the heat of battle and eager to be worthy of the gift tied to his arm, Andrey raced along like a young wolfhound, the youngest, handsomest, swiftest in the pack. At the first halloo of the expert huntsman he races off, his legs flying in a straight line, his whole body sloping sideways, throwing up lumps of snow and ten times outstripping the hare in his headlong career. Old Taras stopped and watched his son scattering the Cossacks, clearing a path in their midst, and raining blows right and left. And Taras could not restrain himself any longer and shouted, "What ? Your own people ? Killing your own people, you damned villain ?" But Andrey did not even see who was before him, whether friend or foe. He saw nothing. All he saw was curls,

244

long, long curls, and a bosom like the breast of a swan on a stream, and a snow-white neck and shoulders, and all, all that is created for passionate kisses.

"Hey, there, lads! Get him into the wood! Entice him to the wood for me!" shouted Taras.

And at once thirty of the swiftest Cossacks volunteered to entice Andrey to the wood. Setting their high caps firmly on their heads, they galloped right across the plain to intercept the hussars. They struck the front ranks on the flank and threw them into confusion, separated them from those behind, distributed a few presents here and there, while Golokopýtenko dealt Andrey a blow with the flat of his sword across the back, and straightway the Cossacks galloped away from them as fast as they could. Andrey was wild with fury! His young blood boiled with rage! Clapping his sharp spurs to his horse, he dashed off at a gallop after the Cossacks, without looking back, without seeing that only twenty of his men were following him. The Cossacks went on galloping at full speed and made straight for the wood. Andrey was close on their heels and in another minute he would have overtaken Golokypýtenko, when suddenly a strong hand grasped his horse's bridle. Andrey looked round: Taras was before him! He trembled all over and grew suddenly pale; so does a schoolboy who rashly picks a quarrel with one of his schoolfellows and receives a blow with a ruler on the forehead for his pains, blaze up like a flame and, jumping from the bench, run after his frightened friend, ready to tear him limb from limb, when suddenly he runs into the master as he is entering the classroom: in an instant his blind fury evaporates and his impotent rage melts away. So Andrey's anger was gone in an instant, as though it had never been. And he saw before him only his terrible father.

"Well, what shall we do now?" said Taras, looking him straight in the face.

But Andrey could say nothing in reply and he stood there without uttering a word, his eyes fixed on the ground.

"Well, son, have your Poles done you any good?"

Andrey was silent.

"So it's treachery, is it? Treachery! You'd betray your faith! Betray your own folk? Very well, get off your horse!"

Obediently, like a child, Andrey got off his horse and stood before Taras more dead than alive.

"Stand still and don't move ! I begot you, and I will kill you !" said Taras and, stepping back, he took the gun from his shoulder.

Andrey was white as a sheet; only his lips moved faintly as he uttered someone's name. But it was not the name of his country, nor of his mother, nor of his brother that he uttered—it was the name of the beautiful Polish girl.

Taras fired.

Like a sheaf of corn, cut by the sickle, like a lamb that feels the deadly steel at its heart, Andrey hung his head and fell upon the sward without uttering a word.

The murderer of his son stood still and gazed long at the lifeless body. Andrey was beautiful even in death. His manly face, so recently full of vigour and irresistible fascination to women, was still marvellously beautiful; his black eyebrows, like sombre velvet, set off his blood-drained features.

"What a fine Cossack he'd have made !" said Taras. "Tall and black-browed, and a face like the face of a nobleman, and his arm was mighty in battle—and now he has perished, perished ingloriously, like a vile dog !"

"What have you done, Father ? Did you kill him ?" asked Ostap, who had just at that moment ridden up.

Taras nodded.

Ostap looked intently into the dead man's eyes. He was sorry for his brother and said at once, "Let's give him an honourable burial, Father. Don't let us leave him here to be dishonoured by his enemies or to be torn to pieces by the birds of prey !"

"They'll bury him without us," said Taras. "He'll have many women weeping and mourning over him !"

And for a minute or two he still wondered whether to throw his son's body to the wolves or take pity on his knightly honour, which a gallant soldier was bound to respect in any man. But at that moment Golokopýtenko galloped up to him.

"Bad news, sir. The Poles have been reinforced. Fresh troops have just arrived to their aid."

Before Golokopýtenko had finished speaking, Vovtúzenko galloped up.

"Bad news, sir. More fresh troops are coming to their aid !"

No sooner had Vovtúzenko spoken than Pisarénko came running on foot.

"Where are you, sir ?" he cried. "The Cossacks are looking for

246

you. Detachment Commander Nevylýchky is slain, Zadorózhny is slain, Chervichénko is slain, but the Cossacks are still standing fast. They don't want to die without a last look at you, sir. They want you to see them, too, before the hour of death."

"To horse, Ostap!" said Taras, and he hurried that he might see his Cossacks, that he might yet look upon them for the last time, and that they, too, might see their general before they died.

But before they had time to ride out of the wood, the enemy had already surrounded it on all sides, and riders appeared between the trees with drawn swords and spears.

"Ostap, Ostap, don't let them take you!" shouted Taras, drawing his sabre and striking at the enemy right and left.

Six men had suddenly fallen upon Ostap, but it seemed they had attacked him in an unlucky hour: for the head of the first flew off, the second slipped and turned head over heels, the third was hit in the ribs with a spear, the fourth, braver than the others, was just in time to miss a bullet in the head, but his horse was hit in the chest and, rearing, the frenzied animal fell to the ground and crushed his rider under him.

"Well done, son! Well done, Ostap!" shouted Taras. "Hold on! I'm coming!"

And all the time he was beating off the enemy who pressed upon him from every side. He fought and slashed away, handing out presents upon the head of many a Pole, and all the time he kept looking ahead of him at Ostap. Then he saw at least eight men attacking Ostap all at once.

"Ostap, Ostap, don't let them take you!"

But Ostap was already overpowered. One man had flung a noose round his head, and now they were binding him. . . . Ostap was captured.

"Oh, Ostap, Ostap!" cried Taras, forcing his way towards his son and cutting down mercilessly every one who stood between him and Ostap. "Oh, Ostap, Ostap!"

But just then Taras himself was hit on the head as though with a huge stone: everything spun round dizzily before his eyes. For a split second there flashed before him in a confused mass heads, spears, smoke, the gleam of a fire, branches covered with leaves that seemed to brush past his very eyes. Then he crashed to the ground like a felled oak, and a mist spread over his eyes.

X

"Must have been asleep a long time," said Taras, waking up as though from a heavy, drunken sleep and trying to recognise the objects around him.

A terrible weakness overpowered his limbs. He could make out only faintly the walls and corners of an unfamiliar room. At last he perceived that Tovkatch was sitting before him, apparently listening to every breath he took.

"Aye," said Tovkatch to himself, "you might have been asleep for ever !" but he said nothing, only shaking a finger at him and motioning him to be silent.

"But tell me where am I ?" asked Taras again, racking his brains and trying to remember what had happened.

"Keep quiet !" his comrade shouted sternly at him. "What more do you want to know ? Can't you see that you've been badly mangled ? For the past fortnight we've been galloping without stopping, and you've been in a high fever all the time and talking wildly. This is the first time you've had a quiet sleep. Don't talk if you don't want to do yourself an injury."

But Taras kept on trying to collect his thoughts and to remember what had happened. "But wasn't I surrounded and almost captured by the Poles ? I couldn't possibly have got away from that crowd, could I ?"

"Keep quiet, will you ?" shouted Tovkatch gruffly, like a nurse driven frantic by a naughty child. "What do you want to know how you got away for ? Will it do you any good ? Is it not enough that you did get away ? There were men who would not leave you in the lurch : let that be enough for you ! We've still many a night's ride before us. You don't think you could pass for a common Cossack, do you ? No, sir. They have placed a price of two thousand gold pieces on your head !"

"And Ostap ?" Taras cried suddenly, and he tried hard to rise, for all at once he remembered that Ostap had been seized and bound before his eyes and that he was now in the hands of the Poles. He was overwhelmed with grief. He tore off the bandages on his wounds and flung them away from him. He tried to say something in a loud voice, but instead he started rambling again. He relapsed into a delirium, and senseless, confused words poured from his lips. His

248

loyal comrade stood before him, swearing and heaping countless harsh and reproachful words upon him. At last he seized him by the hands and feet, swaddled him like a baby, carefully replacing all his bandages, wrapped him in an ox-hide, put him in splints, and, fastening him with cords to the saddle, set off again at a fast gallop.

"Dead or alive, but I'll bring you home ! Never will I let the Poles dishonour your Cossack birth, tear your body to pieces and fling it into the water. If an eagle is to claw out your eyes, let it at least be one of our eagles of the steppe, and not one that comes flying from the land of the Poles. I'll bring you to the Ukraine, though I bring you there dead !"

So spoke his loyal comrade. He galloped without rest for many days and nights, and he brought him unconscious to the *Syech* below the Dnieper Falls. There he applied himself tirelessly to nursing him back to health with herbs and embrocations. He found a wise old Jewish woman who for a whole month gave him many different potions to drink, and at last Taras began showing signs of recovery. Whether it was the medicine or his own iron constitution that gained the day, it is hard to say, but within six weeks he was on his legs again ; his wounds healed and only the scars left by the sabres showed how dangerously the old Cossack had been wounded. But he never recovered his high spirits : he looked sad and gloomy. Three deep lines furrowed his brow and never left it. He gazed about him : everything was new to him at the *Syech*. All his old comrades were dead. Not one was left of those who had stood up with him for the just cause, for faith and brotherhood. And those who had gone with the general in pursuit of the Tartars, even those had long passed away. All of them had laid down their lives ; all of them had perished. Some had been killed honourably in battle ; some had died of hunger and thirst amid the Crimean salt marshes ; some had died in captivity, unable to endure the disgrace of slavery. And their former general himself had been dead a long time. Not one of his old comrades had been left alive ; gone was the Cossack might, once so irresistible, and grass had been growing over it a long, long time. All he had been able to gather was that there had been a great, noisy feast : all the drinking vessels had been smashed, not a drop of wine was left ; the guests and the servants had carried off all the costly goblets and rich jars, and the master of the house stood bewildered, wondering if it had not been much better for the feast not to have taken place at all. In vain did they try to divert and to cheer Taras; in vain did the grey-headed, bearded bandore-players come in twos and threes and glorify his Cossack deeds ! He looked upon the world with harsh indifference, and on his unmoved face unquenchable sorrow was graven deep, and with a bowed head he would murmur, "Ostap, my son, my son !"

The Dnieper Cossacks were making preparations for an expedition by sea. Two hundred boats were lowered into the Dnieper, and Asia Minor saw them with shaven heads and long tufts of hair, putting her flourishing coasts to fire and sword; she saw the turbans of her Moslem inhabitants strewn on the earth like her innumerable flowers, on her blood-drenched fields, and floating along her coasts; she saw hundreds of Dnieper Cossacks, their wide breeches smeared with tar and black whips in their hands. The Cossacks laid waste the vineyard and fed upon its grapes; they left heaps of dung in the mosques; they used costly Persian shawls to wind round their legs or girt round their soiled coats. Long afterwards their short pipes could be picked up in those parts. They sailed back in high spirits. A Turkish man-of-war with ten cannon pursued them and dispersed their flimsy canoes with one volley from all her guns. A third of their number found a grave in the depths of the sea, but the rest assembled again and reached the mouth of the Dnieper with twelve barrels full of sequins. But Taras remained unmoved by it all. He went off into the meadows and the steppes, as though to hunt; but the charge in his musket remained unfired, and, laying it down, he would sit on the sea-shore, full of gnawing grief. He would sit there like that for hours, with bowed head, murmuring, "Ostap, my son, my son !" Before him stretched the Black Sea, sparkling in the sun; in the distant reeds a sea-gull called; his white moustache gleamed like silver, and tears rolled down upon it one by one.

At last Taras could endure it no longer. "Whatever happens, I must go and find out whether he is still alive or in his grave, or whether there is anything left of him in the grave. I will find out, come what may !"

And a week later he was in the city of Uman, armed and on horseback, with spear and sabre, a travelling bag strapped to his saddle, a pot of porridge, a powder horn and bullets, a hobble for his horse, and other equipment. He rode straight up to a dirty, ill-kept little house, with small, grimy windows that could scarcely be seen, thick with dirt as they were; the chimney was stopped up with a rag and the roof was full of holes and covered with sparrows; a heap of refuse lay before the very door A Jewish woman in a cap and with discoloured pearls looked out of the window.

"Is your husband at home?" said Bulba, dismounting from his horse and tying the reins to the iron hook near the door.

"Yes, sir, he's at home," said the woman, and she hurried out immediately with some wheat in a bucket for the horse and a beaker of beer for the rider.

"Where's your Jew?"

"He's in the other room, saying his prayers," said the woman, curtsying and wishing Bulba good health as he lifted the beaker to his lips.

"Stay here and see to my horse—he wants some fodder and water—while I go and speak with him alone. I have business with him."

This Jew was our old friend Yankel. He had been there for some time, renting some land and keeping an inn, and gradually he had got all the nobles and squires in the neighbourhood into his hands, had gradually drained them of almost all their money and left a deep mark of his Jewish presence in that country. For a distance of three miles in every direction there was not a single cottage left in good repair: everything was tumbling down and falling into decay, everything was being spent on drink, nothing but poverty and rags remained; the whole countryside lay waste as after a fire or a pestilence. And if Yankel had stayed there another ten years he would most likely have laid waste the whole province.

Taras entered the room. The Jew was saying his prayers, covered with his rather dirty praying-shawl and, as was the custom of his faith, he turned to spit for the last time when he suddenly saw Bulba standing behind him. The first thought that flashed across the mind of the Jew was the reward of two thousand gold pieces placed on Bulba's head; but he was ashamed of his greed and did his best to suppress the everlasting thought of gold which twines like a worm round the soul of a Jew.

"Look here, Yankel," said Taras to the Jew, who first bowed to him and then locked the door carefully that they should not be seen. "I saved your life once. The Dnieper Cossacks would have torn you to pieces like a dog, if I had not stopped them. Now it's your turn to do me a service."

The Jew made a wry face. "What sort of service, sir? If it's some service I can do for you, I shall of course be glad to do it."

"Ask no questions. Take me to Warsaw!"

"To Warsaw? How do you mean, to Warsaw, sir?" said Yankel, his eyebrows and shoulders raised in astonishment.

"Don't ask any questions. Take me to Warsaw. Whatever happens, I must see him again, say just one word to him."

"To whom, sir?"

"To him. To Ostap, my son."

"But haven't you heard, sir, that . . ."

"I know, I know everything. They've offered two thousand gold pieces for my head. The fools! They know what it's worth, don't they? I'll give you five thousand, two thousand now (Bulba emptied two thousand gold pieces from his leather purse) and the rest when I come back."

The Jew immediately seized a towel and covered the money with it.

"Oh, what lovely money, what lovely money!" he said, turning a gold coin over in his hand and trying it with his teeth. "I expect the man you took these lovely pieces of gold from did not live another hour. Must have gone straight to the river and drowned himself. For who would like to lose such lovely gold coins, sir?"

"I wouldn't have asked you. I might perhaps have found the way to Warsaw myself, but I'm afraid those damned Poles might somehow recognise me and seize me. For to tell you the truth I'm not much good at clever tricks. It's just what you Jews have been created for. You can cheat the devil himself: you know all the tricks! That's why I've come to you. Besides, I couldn't have done much in Warsaw by myself. So get your cart out at once and take me there."

"So you think it's as simple as that, sir? Put your mare to your cart and gee-up Bess! Do you really think, sir, I could take you to Warsaw without taking good care to hide you first?"

"All right, hide me, if you must. Where will you hide me, though? Not in an empty barrel?"

"Oh dear, in an empty barrel indeed! Do you suppose, sir, you could be hidden in a barrel? Don't you realise, sir, that every man we meet on the road will at once jump to the conclusion that there must be vodka in the barrel?"

"Well, let him think there's vodka in it."

"Do you really mean it, sir ? Let him think there's vodka in it ?" said the Jew, catching hold of his side-curls and then throwing up his hands in dismay.

"What are you so alarmed about ?"

"But don't you know, sir, that God created vodka so that every man might taste it ? In that country they're all fond of a good thing; they're all after vodka. A Polish gentleman will run five miles after a barrel, pierce a hole in it, and, finding nothing in it, he'll at once say to himself, 'A Jew will never carry an empty barrel. There's something wrong here. Seize the Jew ! Take all the money away from the Jew ! Throw the Jew into jail !' For the Jew, sir, is blamed for everything that goes wrong. It's all the Jew's fault ! Everyone regards the Jew as a dog. Everyone thinks that if he's a Jew he's not a human being at all !"

"All right, put me in a cart with fish then."

"Oh dear, oh dear, that isn't possible, either, sir. All over Poland the people are now as hungry as dogs; they'll filch the fish and discover you under it."

"Well, carry me on the devil himself for all I care, only take me there !"

"Now listen to me, sir; listen to me !" said the Jew, tucking up the cuffs of his sleeves and approaching him with outstretched hands. "This is what we'll do. Fortresses and castles are being built all over Poland now, French engineers have arrived from Germany specially for that purpose, so lots of bricks and stones are being carted along the road. If you don't mind, sir, I'll put you at the bottom of the cart and cover you up with bricks. You look very strong and healthy, sir, and I don't suppose you'd mind it very much if it should feel a little heavy. I'll make a hole in the bottom of the cart, sir, and I shall feed you through that."

"All right, do as you like, only take me !"

And an hour later a cart-load of bricks left Uman, drawn by two mares. On one of them sat the tall Jew Yankel, and his long, curly side-locks fluttered in the wind from under his Jewish skull-cap, and he jogged up and down on the horse, looking as thin as a rake and as long as a mile-post by the wayside.

XI

At the time when the events described here took place there were on the frontiers as yet neither customs officers nor customs guards, those veritable terrors of men of enterprise, and therefore anyone could take across the frontiers anything he liked. And even if a search or inspection was sometimes made, it was mostly done for the special delight of the official, particularly if the things in the cart exercised a powerful attraction on his eye and if his own arm was of sufficient weight and strength. But bricks aroused no interest and were allowed to be taken through the main gates of the city without interference. In his narrow cage Bulba could only hear the noises of the road and the shouts of the drivers. Yankel jogged up and down on his short-shanked, dusty trotter and, after going round in a circle a few times, turned into a dark, narrow street known as Dirty Street or Jewish Street, for in that street almost all the Jews of Warsaw were to be found. This street was very much like a back-yard turned inside out. The sun seemed never to peep into it at all. The completely blackened wooden houses with large numbers of poles stretched from one side of the street to the other greatly increased the general gloom. Only very rarely did one catch a glimpse of a red-brick wall between them, and even that had turned completely black in many places. Only here and there the stucco top of a wall caught the sunlight and gleamed with a whiteness that dazzled the eye. Here everything seemed made up of sharp contrasts: pipes, rags, shells of all sorts, broken pots, and discarded bins. Everyone flung into the street everything he had no further use for, giving the passers-by every opportunity of regaling every sense with all this rubbish. A man on horseback could easily reach with his hand the poles which were stretched across the street from one house to the other, and which were hung with Jewish stockings, short breeches and a smoked goose. Sometimes the rather attractive face of a Jewish girl, adorned with begrimed beads, could be seen looking out of a dilapidated window. Scores of Jewish children, dirty and in rags, screamed and played about in the filth. A red-haired Jew, with freckles all over his face that made him look like a sparrow's egg, peeped out of a window and immediately addressed Yankel in his incomprehensible lingo, and Yankel at once drove into the yard. Another Jew came down the street, stopped, and also

254

entered into conversation, and when at last Bulba scrambled out from under the load of bricks he was met by the sight of three Jews who were engaged in a very heated discussion.

Yankel turned to him and said that everything would be done, that his son Ostap was kept in the city dungeon, and that though it would be difficult to persuade the guards, he hoped to arrange a meeting.

Bulba then went with the three Jews into the house.

The Jews again began talking in their incomprehensible language. Taras looked at each of them and it seemed as though he were suddenly deeply moved by something: a consuming flame of hope, the hope which sometimes visits a man in the utmost depths of despair, suddenly lit up his harsh, apathetic face. His old heart began beating violently, as though he were a young man.

"Listen, Jews," he said, and there was a note of exaltation in his voice, "you can do everything you like in the world, you can dig a thing up from the bottom of the sea, and there is an old saying that a Jew can even steal himself, if he wants to. Get my Ostap out of jail; give him a chance to escape from their diabolic hands ! Here, I have promised this man twelve thousand gold pieces; I will add another twelve, I'll sell everything I possess, all costly goblets and the buried gold, my cottage, my last shirt, and will make a contract with you for the rest of my life to share whatever I obtain in war equally with you !"

"But I'm afraid it can't be done, sir ! It can't be done !" said Yankel with a sigh.

"No, it can't be done," said another Jew.

All the three Jews exchanged glances.

"We might try," said the third Jew with a timid look at the other two. "With God's help we may carry it off !"

The three Jews began talking in German. But however much he strained his ears, Bulba could not make out anything; all he heard was the often repeated word "Mordecai," and that was all.

"Listen, sir," said Yankel, "we shall have to ask the advice of a man, the like of whom there has never been in this world. Oh, oh, oh ! He's as wise as Solomon, and if he can do nothing, no one in the world can do it. Stay here, sir, lock the door and don't let anyone in."

The Jews went out into the street.

Taras locked the door and looked through the little window at the filthy Jewish thoroughfare. The three Jews had stopped in the middle of the street and begun talking rather excitedly. They were soon joined by a fourth and finally by a fifth. He heard the same name repeated again: "Mordecai! Mordecai!" The Jews kept looking towards one side of the street; at last from behind some dingy house at the end of it there appeared a foot in a Jewish shoe and the fluttering skirts of a coat. "Ah! Mordecai! Mordecai!" the Jews all cried with one voice. A lean Jew, a little shorter than Yankel and far more wrinkled, with an enormous upper lip, drew near the impatient group; and all the Jews vied with each other in hurriedly telling him the story while Mordecai glanced several times at the small window, and Taras guessed that they were talking about him. Mordecai waved his arms about, listened, interrupted the conversation, often turned away to spit, lifting the skirts of his coat, thrust his hand into his pocket and took out some trinkets, incidentally displaying a pair of very shabby trousers. At length all the Jews raised such a clamour that another Jew who seemed to be standing on the look-out signalled to them to be silent. Taras was beginning to feel anxious about his own safety, but remembering that Jews cannot discuss anything except in the street and that Satan himself could not understand their language, he felt reassured.

A few minutes later the Jews came into his room all together. Mordecai went up to Taras, patted him on the shoulder, and said, "When God and we, sir, make up our minds to do a thing, everything will be all right."

Taras looked at this Solomon, the like of whom had never been seen in the world, and his hopes revived a little. And indeed his appearance could inspire a certain amount of confidence: his upper lip was really quite terrifying and its thickness had undoubtedly been increased by external circumstances. Solomon's beard had only fifteen hairs—and those on the left side; and his face bore so many marks of blows he had received for his pluck that he had doubtless lost count of them long ago and grown used to regarding them as birth-marks.

Mordecai went away with his companions, who were full of admiration for his wisdom. Bulba was left alone. He found himself in a strange and quite unusual situation: for the first time in his life he was conscious of anxiety. His mind was in a state of feverish excitement. He was no longer as he used to be: unbending, inflexible, steadfast as an oak. He was timid; he was weak. He started at the slightest noise, at the appearance of every fresh Jewish figure at the end of the street. In this condition he spent the whole day, without eating or drinking, and never for a moment did he take his eyes off the little window looking on to the street. At last, late in the evening, Mordecai and Yankel appeared. Taras Bulba's heart sank.

"Well, any luck?" he asked with the impatience of a wild horse.

But before the Jews had plucked up courage to reply, Taras noticed that one of Mordecai's side-locks which, though rather untidily, had hung down in ringlets from under his skull-cap, was no longer there. He seemed to wish to say something, but what he did at last say made so little sense that Taras could make nothing of it. As for Yankel, he kept putting his hand to his mouth as though he were suffering from a cough.

"It's quite impossible, sir," said Yankel. "It's out of the question now. Upon my soul, it's impossible! Such a vile people, sir, that nothing could be viler. Let Mordecai tell you. Mordecai did more than anyone in the world could have done, but it seems God did not want it to happen. Three thousand soldiers are guarding the prisoners, and tomorrow they are to be taken out to their execution."

Taras looked straight into the eyes of the Jews, but no longer with any impatience or anger.

"And if you want to see your son, sir, it must be done very early tomorrow morning, before sunrise. The sentries have agreed and their officer has promised his help. Oh, may they have no happiness in the next world! Oh dear, what a greedy people! I assure you, sir, you won't find such greedy people even among us: fifty gold pieces I gave to each of them, and to the officer. . . ."

"All right, take me to him!" said Taras firmly, recovering all his self-possession.

He agreed to Yankel's proposal to dress up as a foreign count who had arrived from Germany. The far-sighted Jew had already procured the clothes for the purpose. By now it was night. The master of the house, the red-haired, freckled Jew, pulled out a light mattress covered with some kind of matting and spread it on a bench for Taras. Yankel lay down on the floor on a similar mattress. The red-haired Jew helped himself to a glass of some liquid, threw off his coat, and, looking like a lean chicken in his socks and slippers, betook himself with his wife to a sort of cupboard. Two Jewish children lay down on the floor beside the cupboard like two little puppies. But Taras did not sleep; he sat motionless, drumming softly with his fingers on the table. He kept his pipe in his mouth and smoked, making the Jew sneeze in his sleep and pull the blanket over his face. As soon as a faint glimmer of light appeared in the sky, Taras poked Yankel with his foot.

"Get up, Jew," he said, "and let's have the count's dress!"

In a few minutes he was dressed. He blackened his moustache and eyebrows, put a little dark cap on the crown of his head, and not one among his closest friends could have recognised him. He did not look more than thirty-five. His cheeks glowed with health and the scars on his face helped to give him a commanding air. The gold-embroidered dress looked well on him.

The streets were still asleep. Not a single street merchant had yet appeared in the city with his basket on his arm. Bulba and Yankel came to a building which looked like a sitting heron. It was low, wide, huge and grimy, and on one side of it a long, slender tower rose like the neck of a stork, with a projecting piece of roof on top. This building was used for a number of different purposes: for barracks, a jail, and even a court of justice. Our visitors went in at the gate and found themselves in the middle of a spacious hall or covered courtyard. About a thousand men were asleep there. Directly opposite the entrance was a low door before which two sentries were sitting, playing a kind of game which consisted in one of them striking the other on the palm of the hand with two fingers. They took little notice of the newcomers and only turned their heap when Yankel said, "It's us! Do you hear, gentlemen, it's us!"

"Go in," said one of them, opening the door with one hand while he held out the other to his companion to receive his blows.

They went into a dark and narrow passage, which brought them again to a similar hall with small windows near the ceiling.

"Who goes there?" shouted several voices, and Taras saw quite a large number of soldiers, all fully armed. "Our orders are to admit no one!"

"But it's us!" Yankel cried. "It's us, gentlemen!"

But no one paid the slightest attention to him. Luckily there walked in at that moment a fat man who seemed to be their commanding officer, for he swore louder than any of them.

"It's us, sir. You know us, don't you? The count will be very obliged to you, sir."

"Let 'em go in, blast and damn you! And don't let anyone

258

else in, and don't take your swords off, either, and don't make such a bloody mess on the floor. . . ."

The rest of his eloquent orders the visitors did not hear.

"It's us! It's me! It's your friends!" Yankel kept saying to everyone he met.

"Well, can we go in now?" he asked one of the guards, when they had at last reached the end of the corridor.

"I suppose so, but I don't know whether they'll admit you right into the jail. Yan isn't there now. There's another man on guard there," replied the sentry.

"Damn," said the Jew softly; "that's bad, sir."

"Let's go," said Taras stubbornly.

The Jew obeyed.

At the arched door leading to the dungeons stood a soldier with a three-tiered moustache: one tier turned backwards, the second straight forward, and the third downwards, which made him look uncommonly like a tom-cat.

The Jew sidled up to him cringingly. "Your excellency. . . . My lord. . . ."

"Are you speaking to me, Jew?"

"Yes, my lord, I'm speaking to you."

"Ha! I'm just a common soldier!" said the man with the three-tiered moustache, with a merry twinkle in his eyes.

"Dear, dear, and I thought you were the governor himself! Dear, dear, dear. . . ." Yankel wagged his head and spread out his fingers. "Oh, how splendid you look, sir! Just like a colonel, a regular colonel! Another finger's breadth and you would be a colonel. All you want, sir, is to be mounted on a horse, a real thoroughbred, sir, as swift as an arrow, and I'm sure you could drill a regiment!"

The soldier stroked the lower tier of his moustache and his eyes positively beamed.

"Oh, there's nothing in the world to beat a soldier!" the Jew went on. "Lord, what fine fellows! What splendid galloons! What lovely little decorations! How beautifully they gleam, just like the sun itself! And the ladies, sir. . . . Dear me, dear me. . . . The moment they see a soldier. . . . Oh dear, oh dear. . . ." Yankel wagged his head again.

The soldier twirled the upper tier of his moustache and let out a sound that was not unlike the neighing of a horse.

"I'd like to ask you to do me a service, sir," said Yankel. "This prince here has come from abroad and he wants to have a look at the Cossacks. He has never seen a Cossack in his life."

The arrival of foreign counts and barons was a fairly common occurrence in Poland; they were often drawn there solely by curiosity to see this almost semi-Asiatic corner of Europe. They looked upon Muscovy and the Ukraine as parts of Asia. For this reason the soldier, making rather a low bow, thought fit to add a few words from himself.

"I don't know what you want to see them for, your excellency," he said. "They're dogs, not men, and their religion is such that everyone despises it."

"You lie, you damned rascal!" said Bulba. "You're a dog yourself! How dare you say that our religion is despised! It's your heretical faith that is despised!"

"Oho!" said the soldier. "I know who you are, my friend: you're one of the same lot I have in prison. Just a minute, I'll call our men here!"

Taras saw that he had made a bad slip, but his stubbornness and annoyance prevented him from thinking of something to mend matters. Luckily Yankel immediately came to his help.

"My lord, how is it possible that a count should be a Cossack? And if he really were a Cossack, how do you suppose he'd have come to be dressed like that? Why, doesn't he look a count?"

"Tell me another!" said the Polish soldier, about to open his big mouth and give a shout.

"Your royal highness, not a sound, please! For God's sake, not a sound!" cried Yankel. "If you keep quiet, we shall pay you as you've never been paid before: we'll give you two gold pieces!"

"Two gold pieces, eh? Two gold pieces is nothing to me! I pay the barber that for shaving only half of my chin. A hundred gold pieces, Jew!" Here the soldier gave a twirl to the upper tier of his gigantic moustache. "And if you don't give me the hundred pieces, I'll raise the alarm at once!"

"Why so much?" the Jew murmured mournfully, turning pale and untying his leather purse.

But he was glad there was no more money in his purse and that the soldier could not count beyond a hundred.

"Come on, sir, let's go quickly! You see what a disgusting

lot they are !" said Yankel, noticing that the soldier was fingering the money as though regretting he had not asked for more.

"What do you mean, you damned Pole," said Bulba. "You've taken the money and you don't intend to show them to me ? You must show them to me. Now that you've got your money, you've no right to refuse."

"Go to the devil, both of you ! Go on or I'll raise the alarm this very minute and then you'll. . . . Take yourselves off quick, I say !"

"Come on, sir, let's go !" cried poor Yankel. "To the devil with them ! May they have such bad dreams that . . ."

Slowly and with bowed head Bulba turned and retraced his steps, followed by reproaches from Yankel, whose heart bled at the thought of the wasted gold pieces.

"Why did you have to provoke him ? Let the dog curse ! Those fellows can't help cursing ! O Lord, the luck of some people ! A hundred gold pieces just for turning us out ! And one of our people will have his side-locks pulled out and his face slapped so hard that you couldn't look at him without a shudder, but he won't be given a hundred gold pieces. Oh dear ! no, O Lord, O merciful Lord !"

But their failure had a far greater effect on Bulba, which could be seen from the blazing fire in his eyes.

"Come on," he said suddenly, as though rousing himself, "let's go to the square. I want to see how they will torture him."

"But why go there, sir ? We can't help him by going there, can we ?"

"Come along !" Taras said obstinately, and the Jew trailed after him, sighing like a nurse.

It was not difficult to find the square where the executions were to take place: crowds of people were converging on it from all sides. In that savage age a public execution was one of the greatest attractions not only to the ignorant, but also to the upper classes. Numbers of old women of great piety, numbers of girls and young women who were so timid that all night afterwards they dreamed of bloodstained corpses and cried out in their sleep as loudly as a hussar, never missed a chance of satisfying their curiosity. "Oh, how horrible !" many of them cried hysterically, closing their eyes and turning away. "What dreadful tortures !" But they remained there all the same for quite a long time. One man stood gaping with his hands thrust forward, as though he meant to jump on the heads of the crowd to get a better view. A butcher poked his face out of the mass of narrow, small and ordinary heads, observing the whole proceedings with the air of a connoisseur and talking in monosyllables with a gunsmith whom he addressed familiarly because he had once been drinking with him in the same ale-house. Some engaged in heated discussions, others were even laying bets, but the majority belonged to the class of people who gape at everything that takes place in the world and go on picking their noses. In the front row, close to the city guards with their huge moustaches, a young gentleman, or at any rate one who looked like a gentleman, was standing. He was dressed in a military uniform and looked as if he had put on absolutely everything he had, leaving nothing in his lodging but a torn shirt and an old pair of boots. Round his neck he wore two chains, one on top of the other, with some kind of gold coins on them. He was standing with his sweetheart and kept glancing round all the time for fear someone should soil her silk dress. He explained everything to her, leaving nothing that could possibly be added. "All these crowds, my sweet," he told her, "all the people you can see here, have come to look at the execution of the criminals. And this man, darling, the one who's holding an axe and other instruments in his hand, is the executioner, and he will put them to death. And when he begins to break a criminal on the wheel and inflict other tortures on him, he will still be alive, but when his head is cut off, then, my sweet, he'll die at once. At first he'll scream and move, but directly his head is cut off he won't be able to scream, or eat, or drink, because he won't have any head, darling." And the girl heard it all with an expression of mingled horror and excitement on her face.

The roofs of the houses were black with people. Grotesque faces with moustaches and something that looked like women's night-caps peered from dormer windows. The aristocracy sat on balconies under awnings. The pretty little hand of a laughing lady, gleaming white as sugar, lay on the railings. Illustrious noblemen, rather portly, looked on with an air of great dignity. A footman in a gorgeous livery with long, flowing sleeves was handing round various drinks and refreshments. Sometimes a playful young miss with a pair of sparkling black eyes would take a cake or some fruit in her lovely little hand and throw it to the crowd. A throng of hungry knights held out their caps to catch it, and a tall Polish gentleman in a faded red doublet with rows of tarnished golden cords, whose head towered above the crowd, was the first to catch it, thanks to his long arms, and he kissed the prize, pressed it to his heart and then put it in his mouth. A falcon, hanging in a gilt cage under the balcony, was also a spectator; with his beak on one side and one claw raised, he, too, gazed attentively at the people. But suddenly a hubbub arose in the crowd and voices were heard on all sides, "They're bringing them ! They're bringing them ! The Cossacks !"

They walked bareheaded, with long tufts of hair over their foreheads; their beards had been left to grow. They walked, looking neither afraid nor sullen, but with a kind of quiet dignity; their garments of costly cloth were threadbare and hung in rags about them. At the head of them all came Ostap.

What were old Taras Bulba's feelings when he saw his son Ostap ? Oh, what he must have felt in his heart then ! He looked at his son from the crowd and not one movement of his escaped him. Now the Cossacks drew near the scaffold. Ostap stopped. He was the first to drain that bitter cup. He looked at his comrades, raised his hand and said in a loud voice, "O God, grant that none of the heretics standing here may hear how a true Christian suffers and that none of us may utter a sound !" After this he went up to the scaffold.

"Well done, son ! Well done !" Bulba murmured, and he bowed his grey head.

The hangman tore off Ostap's old rags; then they bound his arms and legs in specially made frames and . . . But we will not harrow the feelings of our readers with a description of the fiendish tortures, which would make their hair stand on end. They were the product of that coarse and savage age when man's whole life seemed to be steeped in violence and blood and his heart was so hardened that he felt no pity. In vain did some people, the few who were the exception in those days, oppose these dreadful acts. In vain did the king and many nobles, enlightened in mind and heart, argue that such cruel punishments could only inflame the vengeance of the Cossack nation. For the influence of the king and those who shared his enlightened views was of no avail beside the unbridled violence and arrogant spirit of the Polish grandees whose thoughtlessness, incredible lack of foresight, childish vanity and absurd pride turned the Seym into a travesty of government. Ostap bore the tortures and endured the agonies like a hero. Not a cry, not a moan was heard even when the bones of his arms and legs were being broken, when the awful cracking sound they made was heard amid the dead silence of the crowd, even by the remotest spectators, when the Polish ladies turned away their eyes—nothing resembling a moan escaped his lips, nor did his face falter. Taras stood in the crowd with a bowed head, but, at the same time, he murmured approvingly, raising his eyes proudly, "Well done, son ! Well done !"

But when Ostap was subjected to his last mortal agonies, it seemed as though his strength was beginning to give way. He looked round. O Lord, there was not a single face he knew ! Oh, if only one of his kindred were present at his death ! He would not have cared to hear the sobs and lamentations of a weak mother or the frenzied cries of a wife, tearing her hair and smiting her white breasts ; all he wished now was to see a resolute man who might have strengthened and comforted him with a wise word at his end. And his heart failed him and he cried out in the weakness of his spirit, "Father, where are you ? Do you hear ?"

"I hear !" a voice rang out amid the general silence, sending a shudder through the thousands of people who packed the square. A detachment of cavalry immediately forced their way through the crowd, carefully inspecting the people. Yankel turned pale as death, and when the mounted soldiers moved some distance away from him, he turned round fearfully to glance at Taras, but Taras was beside him no longer: he had disappeared.

XII

Taras had reappeared. An army of one hundred and twenty thousand Cossacks mustered on the frontiers of the Ukraine. This was no small body of men or some detachment bent on plunder or out in pursuit of the Tartars. No, the whole nation had risen, for the patience of the people was at an end; they had risen to avenge the flouting of their rights, the humiliating disrespect shown to their customs, the insults heaped upon the faith of their forefathers and their sacred traditions, the desecration of their churches, the wild excesses of alien overlords, the oppression, the forced allegiance to the Pope, the shameful domination of the Jews in a Christian land, everything that had helped to store up and deepen for years and years the fierce hatred of the Cossack people. The young but intrepid hetman Ostranitza was in command of this vast Cossack army. At his side was Gunya, his aged and experienced counsellor and friend. Eight colonels led regiments of twelve thousand each. Two staff captains and one keeper of the badge of the hetman's office—a painted staff topped by a white horse-hair plume tied with red cords—rode after the hetman. The chief standard-bearer carried the principal banner; many more banners and standards fluttered in the distance; the assistants of the Keeper of the Hetman's Staff bore other badges of office. There were many other regimental ranks, officers in charge of transport and commissariat, regimental clerks and, with them, infantry and cavalry detachments; there were as many volunteers and partisans as there were regular army Cossacks. From all over the Ukraine the Cossacks had risen, from Chigirin, from Pereyaslav, from Baturin, from Glukhov, from the Lower Dnieper and from all the districts and islands of the Upper Dnieper. Horses without number and countless lines of carts trailed over the fields. And among all those Cossacks, among the eight regiments, one regiment was the best of all, and that crack regiment was under the command of Taras Bulba. Everything seemed to have combined to give him an advantage over the others: his age, his experience, his skill in manœuvring his troops, and his hatred of the enemy, which was far more bitter than anyone's. His ruthless ferocity and cruelty seemed excessive even to the Cossacks. His grey head knew only one punishment: the fire and the gallows; and in the councils of war he had only one plan—total annihilation.

No need to describe all the battles in which the Cossacks had excelled themselves, nor the whole course of the campaign: all that is recorded in the pages of the Chronicles. Everybody knows what a war in defence of the faith is like in Russia: no force is stronger than faith. It is as firm and as terrible as the rock, unwrought by the hand of man, in the midst of the turbulent and ever-changeful sea. From the fathomless depths of the ocean it raises to the skies its indestructible walls, fashioned out of sheer rock. It can be seen from all sides and fearlessly does it challenge the waves as they dash themselves against it and roll past. And woe to the ship that is driven on it ! Her weak masts and rigging are shivered, and everything aboard her is smashed and sinks beneath the wave; and the startled air is rent with the piteous cries of her doomed crew.

The pages of the Chronicles contain detailed descriptions of the flight of the Polish garrisons from the liberated cities; of the hanging of the unscrupulous Jewish contractors; of the weakness of the royal hetman Nicholas Potocki with his numerous army against the invincible Cossack force; of his defeat and pursuit and the loss of the best part of his troops in a small stream; of the siege by the relentless Cossack army of the little township of Polonnoye where he had fled with the remnants of his forces; and of his solemn oath, when finally driven into a corner, of full satisfaction on the part of the king and his government and the restoration of all their former rights and privileges. But the Cossacks were not so foolish as to be taken in by that: they knew very well what a Polish oath was worth. And Potocki would no longer have been prancing about on his six-thousand-rouble Caucasian stallion, the cynosure of the eyes of all the great ladies and the envy of the nobles, he would not have cut such a figure at the Diets, entertaining the Polish senators to sumptuous banquets, if he had not been saved by the Russian clergy of that little town. When all the priests came out to welcome the Cossacks in their bright gold chasubles, bearing icons and crosses, with their bishop at the head in his pastoral mitre and cross in hand, all the Cossacks bowed their heads and took off their caps. They would have shown no respect to anyone at that time, not even to the king himself; but they dared not do anything against their own Christian church and they showed respect to their own clergy. The hetman together with the colonels agreed to let Potocki go, taking from him a solemn oath to leave the Christian churches their full freedom, to forswear all ancient enmities, and to respect the honour of the Cossack army. Only one colonel would not consent to such a peace. That colonel was Taras. He tore a tuft of hair from his head and exclaimed:

"Hetman and colonels, do not act like old women! Don't trust the Poles; they'll betray you yet, the curs!"

When the regimental clerk presented the peace treaty for signing and the hetman put his authoritative hand to it, Taras took off his costly Turkish sabre of the finest steel, drew out the flashing blade and broke it, like a reed, in two, throwing the parts in different directions and saying, "Farewell, gentlemen! As the two parts of that sword can never be united and form one sword again, so shall we, comrades, never meet in this world! So remember my farewell words (as he said this, his voice swelled, rose higher, gathering unwonted strength—and all were abashed at his prophetic words): in the hour of your death you will think of me ! You believe you've purchased peace and quiet, do you ? You think every one of you is going to live like a lord, do you ? You'll live like lords all right, only not the way you think: they'll tear the skin off your head, hetman, stuff it with chaff, and for years it will be seen all at the fairs ! As for you, gentlemen, you won't keep your heads on your shoulders, either. In damp dungeons will you perish, immured within stone walls, if you are not boiled alive in cauldrons like sheep ! And you, lads," he went on, turning to his followers, "which of you wants to die a soldier's death ? Not by the stove or on comfortable beds, not drunk under the fence of an ale-house, like any other carrion, but an honourable Cossack death, all in one bed, like a bridegroom and his bride ! Or do you prefer to go back to your homes, turn infidel and carry the Polish priests on your backs ?"

"We go with you, Colonel ! We go with you !" cried all who were in Bulba's regiment, and many others ran over to their side.

"Well, if it is with me you want to go, then follow me !" said Taras and, pushing his cap down on his head, he looked defiantly at all who stayed behind, straightened himself on his horse and shouted to his men, "Never fear; no man will reproach us or blame us ! Away now, men ! Let's pay a call on the Catholics !"

He whipped his horse, and one hundred carts with provisions and supplies moved off after him, and with them there were a great many Cossacks on horse and on foot, and, turning round, he again looked menacingly at those who stayed behind—and full of wrath was his look. No one dared to stop them. The regiment marched off in sight of the whole army, and Taras kept turning round and looking menacingly at them.

The hetman and the colonels were greatly disconcerted: they pondered deep and were silent for a long time as though oppressed by dark forebodings. Taras did not prophesy in vain: everything came true as he had predicted. A short time after the treacherous act at Kanev, the hetman's head was impaled on a stake, and the same fate was shared by many of the foremost men in the country.

And what did Taras do ? He roamed at large all over Poland with his regiment, burnt eighteen small towns and about forty

Catholic churches, and was already approaching Krakow. He had slain hundreds of Polish squires of all sorts, sacked some of the finest and richest castles; his Cossacks unsealed and spilt on the ground barrels of mead and wine hundreds of years old, carefully preserved in the cellars of Polish noblemen, cut to pieces and burnt costly cloths and garments, and smashed the vessels they found in cupboards and store-houses. "Spare nothing!" Taras kept repeating. Nor did the Cossacks spare the young, black-browed Polish ladies, white-bosomed and bright-eyed; even at the altars they could not save themselves: Taras burnt them together with altars. Not one pair of snow-white arms was raised from the flames to the skies, and their piteous cries would have made the damp earth itself trouble with pity and the tall steppe grass bend low. But the cruel Cossacks paid no heed to anything and, picking up the babes from the streets on their spears, they flung them into the flames, too. "That's for you in memory of Ostap!" was all Taras would say. And he celebrated Ostap's memory in this way in every town and village until the Polish Government realised that Taras Bulba's actions were something more than acts of brigandage, and the same Potocki was put at the head of five regiments and ordered to capture Taras without fail.

For six days the Cossacks retreated from their pursuers along country lanes. They fled so quickly that their horses could hardly stand the pace and just managed to save the Cossacks. But this time Potocki was equal to the task imposed upon him: he pursued them relentlessly and overtook them on the bank of the Dniester, where Bulba stopped for a rest in an abandoned, dilapidated fortress.

The fortress stood at the very edge of the precipitous bank of the river Dniester, with its shattered rampart and ruined remnants of walls. The top of the cliff was strewn with rubble and broken bricks and seemed about to topple over into the river. It was there that the royal hetman Potocki surrounded Taras Bulba's forces on the two sides that looked out on the open plain. For four days the Cossacks fought hard against the Polish troops, using bricks and stones to keep the attackers at bay. But as their supplies had run out and their strength was exhausted, Taras decided to fight his way through the enemy ranks. The Cossacks would have fought their way through and their swift horses would perhaps have served them well once more, had not Taras suddenly stopped in full flight and shouted,

"Halt ! I've dropped my pipe and tobacco. I won't leave even my pipe to those damned Poles !" And the old Cossack commander bent down and began looking in the grass for his pipe with tobacco, which had been his inseparable companion by land and by sea, on the march and at home. Meanwhile a whole band of the enemy swooped down on him and seized him by his powerful shoulders. He strained every muscle in his body in an attempt to shake them off, but this time the Polish soldiers did not scatter on the ground as they did in the past. "Oh, old age, old age !" the stout old Cossack muttered and burst into tears. But old age was not to blame: force prevailed against force. Nearly thirty men were hanging on to his arms and legs.

"Caught you at last !" the Poles shouted. "Now all that remains to be done is to decide what honour to bestow on the dog !"

And with the hetman's permission, they decided to burn him alive in the sight of all.

A dead tree whose top had been struck by lightning stood only a few yards away from the place where they had captured him. They fastened him with iron chains to the trunk of the tree, nailed his hands to it, and having raised him up higher so that he could be seen from every side, they began to build a fire under the tree. But Taras did not look on the pile of wood, nor did he think of the fire in which they were going to burn him: the poor fellow gazed in the direction where the Cossacks were keeping up a steady fire against their pursuers. He could see everything plainly from his height. "Quick, men, occupy the hill !" he shouted. "The hill behind the wood ! They can't get you there !" But the wind did not carry his words. "Oh, they're lost ! They're lost !" he cried in despair and glanced below where the waters of the Dniester sparkled. A gleam of joy came into his eyes. He saw the sterns of four boats protruding from behind the scrub, and he shouted at the top of his voice, "To the river bank ! To the river bank, lads ! Take the cliff path on your left ! There are boats on the bank ! Bo-o-ats ! Take 'em all ! They won't be able to pursue you !"

This time the wind blew from the other direction, and the Cossacks heard every word he said. But for such advice he received a blow on the head with the back of an axe, and everything went black before his eyes.

The Cossacks rode full speed down the hill path with their pursuers hot on their trail. But the path twisted and turned too much, and, halting for an instant, they all said, "Come on, boys, we've nothing to lose! Down we go!" And they raised their whips and whistled. Their Tartar horses rose from the ground, flattened out in the air like snakes, leapt over the ravine and plunged straight into the Dniester. Only two of them did not jump far enough to fall into the river, and they hurtled down from the top of the cliff on to the rocks below and perished there with their horses without even uttering a cry. All the rest of the Cossacks were swimming in the river with their horses and unmooring the boats. The Poles stopped at the brink of the precipice, marvelling at the incredible feat of the Cossacks and wondering whether to jump or not.

One colonel, a hot-blooded, impetuous young man, the brother of the beautiful Polish girl who had bewitched poor Andrey, did not hesitate long, but leapt with his horse after the Cossacks. He turned over three times in the air with his horse and crashed upon the sharp rocks. He was torn to pieces by the sharp stones and perished at the bottom of the precipice, his brains mingled with his blood, bespattering the shrubs which grew on the rugged walls of the chasm.

By the time Bulba recovered from the blow and looked at the Dniester, the Cossacks were in their boats and rowing away; bullets were showered upon them from above, but did not reach them. And the eyes of the old Cossack flashed with joy.

"Farewell, comrades!" he shouted to them from above. "Remember me and come here again next spring, and have a merry time! Well, who won, you damned villains? Do you think there's anything in the world a Cossack is afraid of? You wait, the time's coming when you'll learn what the orthodox Russian faith is! Already the nations of the world, far and near, are beginning to feel that a Czar will arise in Russia so mighty that there will be no power on earth that will not submit to him! . . ."

By now the fire was rising above the heap of dry wood, the flames were enveloping his legs, and in another minute they spread all over the tree. . . . But are there any fires or any tortures or indeed any force in the whole world that can prevail against Russian force?

The Dniester is no small river, and it has creeks, dense sedges, sandbanks and deep pools without number; the surface of the river, smooth as a mirror, sparkles and glitters, ringing with the loud call of swans, and the proud golden-eye skims swiftly over its waves, and there are many snipe, buff-breasted sandpipers and other wild fowl among its reeds and on its banks. The Cossacks rowed swiftly in the narrow, double-ruddered boats; they rowed like one man, carefully avoiding the sandbanks, rousing the birds, which took wing—and they talked of their commander.

THE OVERCOAT

I N THE department . . . but perhaps it is just as well not to say in which department. There is nothing more touchy and ill-tempered in the world than departments, regiments, government offices, and indeed any kind of official body. Nowadays every private individual takes a personal insult to be an insult against society at large. I am told that not so very long ago a police commissioner (I don't remember of what town) sent in a petition to the authorities in which he stated in so many words that all Government decrees had been defied and his own sacred name most decidedly taken in vain. And in proof he attached to his petition an enormous volume of some highly romantic work in which a police commissioner figured on almost every tenth page, sometimes in a very drunken state. So to avoid all sorts of unpleasant misunderstandings, we shall refer to the department in question as *a certain department*.

And so in *a certain department* there served *a certain Civil Servant*, a Civil Servant who cannot by any stretch of the imagination be described as in any way remarkable. He was in fact a somewhat short, somewhat pockmarked, somewhat red-haired man, who looked rather short-sighted and was slightly bald on the top of his head, with wrinkles on both cheeks, and a rather sallow complexion. There is nothing we can do about it : it is all the fault of the St. Petersburg climate. As for his rank (for with us rank is something that must be stated before anything else), he was what is known as a perpetual titular councillor, the ninth rank among the fourteen ranks into which our Civil Service is divided, a rank which, as every one knows, has been sneered at and held up to scorn by all sorts of writers who have the praiseworthy habit of setting upon those who cannot hit back. The Civil Servant's surname was Bashmachkin. From this it can be clearly inferred that it had once upon a time originated from the Russian word *bashmak*, to wit, shoe. But when, at what precise date, and under what circumstances the meta-morphosis took place, must for ever remain a mystery. His father, grandfather, and, why, even his brother-in-law as well as all the rest of the Bashmachkins, always walked about in boots, having their soles repaired no more than three times a year. His name and patronymic were Akaky Akakyevich. The reader may think it a little odd, not to say somewhat *recherché*, but we can assure him that we wasted no time in searching for this name and that it happened in the most natural way that no other name could be given to him, and the way it came about is as follows:

Akaky Akakyevich was born, if my memory serves me right, on the night of 23rd March. His mother of blessed memory, the wife of a Civil Servant and a most excellent woman in every respect, took all the necessary steps for the child to be christened. She was still lying in bed, facing the door, and on her right stood the godfather, Ivan Ivanovich Yeroshkin, a most admirable man, who was a head clerk at the Supreme Court, and the godmother, Arina Semyonovna Byelobrúshkina, the wife of the district police inspector, a most worthy woman. The mother was presented with the choice of three names, namely, Mokkia, Sossia, or, it was suggested, the child might be called after the martyr Khozdazat. "Oh dear," thought his late mother, "they're all such queer names!" To please her, the calendar was opened at another place, but again the three names that were found were rather uncommon, namely, Trifily, Dula and Varakhassy. "Bother," said the poor woman, "what queer names! I've really never heard such names! Now if it had only been Varadat or Varukh, but it would be Trifily and Varakhassy!" Another page was turned and the names in the calendar were Pavsikakhy and Vakhtissy. "Well," said the mother, "I can see that such is the poor innocent infant's fate. If that is so, let him rather be called after his father. His father was Akaky, so let the son be Akaky, too." It was in this way that he came to be called Akaky. The child was christened, and during the ceremony he began to cry and pulled such a face that it really seemed as though he had a premonition that he would be a titular councillor one day. Anyway, that is how it all came to pass.

We have told how it had come about at such length because we are anxious that the reader should realise himself that it could not have happened otherwise, and that to give him any other name was quite out of the question.

When and at what precise date Akaky had entered the department, and who had appointed him to it, is something that no one can remember. During all the years he had served in that department many directors and other higher officials had come and gone, but he still remained in exactly the same place, in exactly the same position, in exactly the same job, doing exactly the same kind of work, to wit, copying official documents. Indeed, with time the belief came to be generally held that he must have been born into the world entirely fitted out for his job, in his Civil Servant's uniform and a bald patch on his head. No particular respect was shown him in the department. Not only did the caretakers not get up from their seats when he passed by, but they did not even vouchsafe a glance at him, just as if a common fly had flown through the waiting-room. His superiors treated him in a manner that could be best described as frigidly despotic. Some assistant head clerk would just shove a paper under his nose without even saying, "Please copy it," or "Here's an interesting, amusing little case!" or something in a similarly pleasant vein as is the custom in all well-regulated official establishments. And he would accept it without raising his eyes from the paper, without looking up to see who had put it on his desk, or whether indeed he had any right to put it there. He just took it and immediately settled down to copy it. The young clerks laughed and cracked jokes about him, the sort of jokes young clerks could be expected to crack. They told stories about him in his presence, stories that were specially invented about him. They joked about his landlady, an old woman of seventy, who they claimed beat him, or they asked him when he was going to marry her. They also showered bits of torn paper on his head and called them snow. But never a word did Akaky say to it all, as though unaware of the presence of his tormentors in the office. It did not even interfere with his work; for while these rather annoying practical jokes were played on him he never made a single mistake in the document he was copying. It was only when the joke got too unbearable, when somebody jogged his arm and so interfered with his work, that he would say, "Leave me alone, gentlemen. Why do you pester me?" There was a strange note in the words and in the voice in which they were uttered: there was something in it that touched one's heart with pity. Indeed, one young man who had only recently been appointed to the department and who, following the example of the others, tried to have some fun at his expense, stopped abruptly at Akaky's mild expostulation, as though stabbed through the heart; and since then everything seemed to have changed in him and he saw everything in quite a different light. A kind of unseen power made him keep away from his colleagues whom at first he had taken for decent, well-bred men. And for a long time afterwards, in his happiest moments, he would see the shortish Civil Servant with the bald patch on his head, uttering those pathetic words, "Leave me alone! Why do you pester me?" And in those pathetic words he seemed to hear others: "I am your brother." And the poor young man used to bury his face in his hands, and many a time in his life he would shudder when he perceived how much inhumanity there was in man, how much savage brutality there lurked beneath the most refined, cultured manners, and, dear Lord, even in the man the world regarded as upright and honourable. . . .

It would be hard to find a man who lived so much for his job. It was not sufficient to say that he worked zealously. No, his work was a labour of love to him. There, in that copying of his, he seemed to see a multifarious and pleasant world of his own. Enjoyment was written on his face; some letters he was particularly fond of, and whenever he had the chance of writing them, he was beside himself with joy, chuckling to himself, winking and helping them on with his lips, so that you could, it seemed, read on his face every letter his pen was forming with such care. If he had been rewarded in accordance with his zeal, he would to his own surprise have got as far as a state councillorship; but, as the office wits expressed it, all he got for his pains was a metal disc in his button-hole and a stitch in his side. Still it would be untrue to say that no one took any notice of him. One director, indeed, being a thoroughly good man and anxious to reward him for his long service, ordered that he should be given some more responsible work than his usual copying, that is to say, he was told to prepare a report for another department of an already concluded case; all he had to do was to alter the title at the top of the document and change some of the verbs from the first to the third person singular. This, however, gave him so much trouble that he was bathed in perspiration and kept mopping his forehead until at last he said, "No, I can't do it. You'd better give me something to copy." Since then they let him carry on with his copying for ever. Outside this copying nothing seemed to exist for him. He never gave a thought to his clothes: his uniform was no longer green, but of some nondescript rusty white. His collar was very short and narrow so that his neck, though it was not at all long, looked as if it stuck a mile out of the collar, like the necks of the plaster kittens with wagging heads, scores of which are carried about on their heads by street-vendors of non-Russian nationality. And something always seemed to cling to his uniform: either a straw or some thread. He possessed, besides, the peculiar knack when walking in the street of passing under a window just at the time when some rubbish was tipped out of it, and for this reason he always carried about on his hat bits of water-melon or melon rind and similar trash. He had never in his life paid the slightest attention to what was going on daily in the street, and in this he was quite unlike his young colleagues in the Civil Service, who are famous as observers of street life, their eagle-eyed curiosity going even so far as to notice that the strap under the trousers of some man on the pavement on the other side of the street has come undone, a thing which never fails to bring a malicious grin to their faces. But even if Akaky did look at anything, he saw nothing but his own neat lines, written out in an even hand, and only if a horse's muzzle, appearing from goodness knows where, came to rest on his shoulder and blew a gale on his cheek from its nostrils, did he become aware of the fact that he was not in the middle of a line, but rather in the middle of the street.

On his arrival home, he would at once sit down at the table, quickly gulp down his cabbage soup, eat a piece of beef with onions without noticing what it tasted like, eating whatever Providence happened to send at the time, flies and all. Noticing that his stomach was beginning to feel full, he would get up from the table, fetch his inkwell and start copying the papers he had brought home with him. If, however, there were no more papers to copy, he would deliberately make another copy for his own pleasure, intending to keep it for himself, especially if the paper was remarkable not so much for the beauty of its style as for the fact of being addressed to some new or important person.

Even at those hours when all the light has faded from the grey St. Petersburg sky, and the Civil Service folk have taken their fill of food and dined each as best he could, according to his salary and his personal taste; when all have had their rest after the departmental scraping of pens, after all the rush and bustle, after their own and other people's indispensable business had been brought to a conclusion, and anything else restless man imposes upon himself of his own free will had been done, and even much more than is necessary:

when every Civil Servant is hastening to enjoy as best he can the remaining hours of his leisure—one more enterprising rushing off to the theatre, another going for a stroll to stare at some silly women's hats, a third going to a party to waste his time paying compliments to some pretty girl, the star of some small Civil Service circle, while a fourth—as happens in nine cases out of ten—paying a call on a fellow Civil Servant living on the third or fourth floor in a flat of two small rooms with a tiny hall or kitchen, with some pretensions to fashion—a lamp or some other article that has cost many self-denying sacrifices, such as doing without dinners or country outings; in short, even when all the Civil Servants have dispersed among the tiny flats of their friends to play a stormy game of whist, sipping tea from glasses and nibbling a penny biscuit, or inhaling the smoke of their long pipes and, while dealing the cards, retailing the latest high society scandal (for every Russian is so devotedly attached to high society that he cannot dispense with it for a moment), or, when there is nothing else to talk about, telling the old chestnut about the fortress commandant who was told that the tail of the horse of Falconnetti's statue of Peter I had been docked—in short, even while every government official in the capital was doing his best to enjoy himself, Akaky Akakyevich made no attempt to woo the fair goddess of mirth and jollity. No one could possibly ever claim to have seen him at a party. Having copied out documents to his heart's content, he went to bed, smiling in anticipation of the pleasures the next day had in store for him and wondering what the good Lord would send him to copy. So passed the peaceful life of a man who knew how to be content with his lot on a salary of four hundred roubles a year; and it might have flowed on as happily to a ripe old age, were it not for the various calamities which beset the lives not only of titular, but also of privy, actual, court and any other councillors, even those who give no counsel to any man, nor take any from anyone, either.

There is in St. Petersburg a great enemy of all those who receive a salary of four hundred roubles a year, or thereabouts. This enemy is none other than our northern frost, though you will hear people say that it is very good for the health. At nine o'clock in the morning, just at the hour when the streets are full of Civil Servants on their way to their departments, he starts giving such mighty and stinging filips to all noses without exception, that the poor fellows simply do not know where to put them. At a time when the foreheads of even those who occupy the highest positions in the State ache with the frost, and tears start to their eyes, the poor titular councillors are sometimes left utterly defenceless. Their only salvation lies in running as fast as they can in their thin, threadbare overcoats through five or six streets and then stamping their feet vigorously in the vestibule, until they succeed in unfreezing their faculties and abilities, frozen on the way, and are once more able to tackle the affairs of State.

Akaky had for some time been feeling that the fierce cold seemed to have no difficulty at all in penetrating to his back and shoulders, however fast he tried to sprint across the legal distance from his home to the department. It occurred to him at length that his overcoat might not be entirely blameless for this state of affairs. On examining it thoroughly at home, he discovered that in two or three places, to wit, on the back and round the shoulders, it looked like some coarse homespun cotton; the cloth had worn out so much that it let through the wind, and the lining had all gone to pieces. It must be mentioned here that Akaky's overcoat, too, had been the butt of the departmental wits; it had been even deprived of the honourable name of overcoat and had been called a *capote*. And indeed it was of a most peculiar cut: its collar had shrunk in size more and more every year, for it was used to patch the other parts. The patching did no credit to the tailor's art and the result was that the final effect was somewhat baggy and far from beautiful. Having discovered what was wrong with his overcoat, Akaky decided that he would have to take it to Petrovich, a tailor who lived somewhere on the fourth floor up some back stairs and who, in spite of the disadvantage of having only one eye and pock marks all over his face, carried on a rather successful trade in mending the trousers and frock-coats of government clerks and other gentlemen whenever, that is to say, he was sober and was not hatching some other scheme in his head.

We really ought not to waste much time over this tailor; since, however, it is now the fashion that the character of every person in a story must be delineated fully, then by all means let us have Petrovich, too. To begin with, he was known simply by his Christian name of Grigory, and had been a serf belonging to some gentleman or other; he began calling himself Petrovich only after he had obtained his freedom, when he started drinking rather heavily every holiday, at first only on the great holidays, and thereafter on any

278

church holiday, on any day, in fact, marked with a cross in the calendar. So far as that went, he was true to the traditions of his forebears and in his altercations with his wife on this subject he would call her a worldly woman and a German. Having mentioned his wife, we had better say a word or two about her also; to our great regret, however, we know very little about her, except that Petrovich had a wife, who wore a bonnet, and not a kerchief; there appears to be some doubt as to whether she was good-looking or not, but on the whole it does not seem likely that she had very much to boast of in that respect; at any rate, only guardsmen were ever known to peer under her bonnet when meeting her in the street, twitching their moustaches and emitting a curious kind of grunt at the same time.

While ascending the stairs leading to Petrovich's flat—the stairs which, to do them justice, were soaked with water and slops and saturated with a strong spirituous smell which irritates the eyes and which, as the whole world knows, is a permanent feature of all the backstairs of St. Petersburg houses—while ascending the stairs, Akaky was already wondering how much Petrovich would ask for mending his overcoat, and made up his mind not to give him more than two roubles. The door of Petrovich's flat was open because his wife had been frying some fish and had filled the whole kitchen with smoke, so that even the cockroaches could no longer be seen. Akaky walked through the kitchen, unnoticed even by Mrs. Petrovich, and, at last, entered the tailor's room where he beheld Petrovich sitting on a large table of unstained wood with his legs crossed under him like a Turkish pasha. His feet, as is the custom of tailors when engaged in their work, were bare. The first thing that caught his eye was Petrovich's big toe, which Akaky knew very well indeed, with its deformed nail as thick and hard as the shell of a tortoise. A skein of silk and cotton thread hung about Petrovich's neck, and on his knees lay some tattered piece of clothing. He had for the last minute or two been trying to thread his needle and, failing every time, he was terribly angry with the dark room and even with the thread itself, muttering under his breath, "Won't you go through, you beast? You'll be the death of me yet, you slut!" Akaky could not help feeling sorry that he had come just at the moment when Petrovich was angry: he liked to place an order with Petrovich only when the tailor was a bit merry, or when he had, as his wife put it, "been swilling his corn-brandy, the one-eyed devil!" When in such a state, Petrovich was as a rule extremely amenable and always gave in and agreed to any price, and even bowed and thanked him. It was true that afterwards his wife would come to see Akaky and tell him with tears in her eyes that her husband had been drunk and had therefore charged him too little; but all Akaky had to do was to add another ten-copeck piece and the thing was settled. But now Petrovich was to all appearances sober as a judge and, consequently, rather bad-tempered, intractable and liable to charge any old price. Akaky realised that and was about, as the saying is, to beat a hasty retreat, but it was too late: Petrovich had already screwed up his only eye and was looking at him steadily. Akaky had willy-nilly to say, "Good morning, Petrovich!" "Good morning, sir. How are you?" said Petrovich, fixing his eye on Akaky's hands in an effort to make out what kind of offering he had brought.

"Well, you see, Petrovich, I—er—have come—er—about that, you know . . ." said Akaky.

It might be as well to explain at once that Akaky mostly talked in prepositions, adverbs, and, lastly, such parts of speech as have no meaning whatsoever. If the matter was rather difficult, he was in the habit of not finishing the sentences, so that often having begun his speech with, "This is—er—you know . . . a bit of that, you know . . ." he left it at that, forgetting to finish the sentence in the belief that he had said all that was necessary.

"What's that you've got there, sir?" said Petrovich, scrutinising at the same time the whole of Akaky's uniform with his one eye, from the collar to the sleeves, back, tails and buttonholes, which was all extremely familiar to him, since it was his own handiwork. Such is the immemorial custom among tailors; it is the first thing a tailor does when he meets one of his customers.

"Well, you see, Petrovich, I've come about this here, you know . . . this overcoat of mine. The cloth, you know. . . . You see, it's really all right everywhere, in fact, excellent. . . . I mean, it's in fine condition here and—er—all over. Looks a bit dusty, I know, and you might get the impression that it was old, but as a matter of fact it's as good as new, except in one place where it's a bit—er—a bit, you know. . . . On the back, I mean, and here on the shoulder. . . . Looks as though it was worn through a bit, and on the other shoulder too, just a trifle, you see. . . . Well, that's really all. Not much work in it. . . ."

Petrovich took the *capote*, first spread it on the table, examined it for a long time, shook his head, and stretched out his hand to the window for his round snuff-box with a portrait of some general, though which particular general it was impossible to say, for the place where the face should have been had been poked in by a finger and then pasted over with a square bit of paper. Having treated himself to a pinch of snuff, Petrovich held the overcoat out in his hands against the light and gave it another thorough examination, and again shook his head; he then turned it with the lining upwards and again shook his head, again took off the lid with the general pasted over with paper, and, filling his nose with snuff, replaced the lid, put away the snuff-box and, at last, said, "No, sir. Impossible to mend it. There's nothing left of it."

Akaky's heart sank at those words. "Why is it impossible, Petrovich?" he said, almost in the imploring voice of a child. "It's only on the shoulders that it's a bit worn, and I suppose you must have bits of cloth somewhere. . . ."

"Oh, I've got plenty of bits of cloth, sir, lots of 'em," said Petrovich. "But you see, sir, you can't sew 'em on. The whole coat's rotten. Touch it with a needle and it will fall to pieces."

"Well, if it falls to pieces, all you have to do is to patch it up again."

"Why, bless my soul, sir, and what do you suppose the patches will hold on to? What am I to sew them on to? Can't you see, sir, how badly worn it is? You can't call it cloth any more: one puff of wind and it will be blown away."

"But please strengthen it a bit. I mean, it can't be just—er—really, you know . . ."

"No, sir," said Petrovich firmly, "it can't be done. Too far gone. Nothing to hold it together. All I can advise you to do with it, sir, is to cut it up when winter comes and make some rags to wrap round your feet, for socks, sir, are no damned good at all: there's no real warmth in 'em. It's them Germans, sir, what invented socks to make a lot of money (Petrovich liked to get in a word against the Germans on every occasion). As for your overcoat, sir, I'm afraid you'll have to get a new one."

At the word "new" a mist suddenly spread before Akaky's eyes and everything in the room began swaying giddily. The only thing he could still see clearly was the general's face pasted over with paper on the lid of Petrovich's snuff-box.

"How do you mean, a new one?" he said, still as though speaking in a dream. "Why, I haven't got the money for it."

"Well, sir, all I can say is that you just must get yourself a new one," said Petrovich with callous indifference.

"Well, and if . . . I mean, if I had to get a new one . . . how much, I mean . . ."

"How much will it come to, sir?"

"Yes."

"Well, sir, I suppose you'll have to lay out three fifty-rouble notes or more," said Petrovich, pursing his lips significantly.

He had a great fondness for strong effects, Petrovich had. He liked to hit a fellow on the head suddenly and then steal a glance at him to see what kind of a face the stunned person would pull after his words.

"One hundred and fifty roubles for an overcoat!" cried poor Akaky in a loud voice, probably raising his voice to such a pitch for the first time in his life, for he was always distinguished by the softness of his voice.

"Yes, sir," said Petrovich. "And that, too, depends on the kind of coat you have. If you have marten for your collar and a silk lining for your hood, it might cost you two hundred."

"Now look here, Petrovich . . ." said Akaky in a beseeching voice, not hearing, or at any rate doing his best not to hear, what Petrovich was saying, and paying no attention whatever to the effect the tailor was trying to create. "Please, my dear fellow, just mend it somehow, so that I could still use it a bit longer, you know. . . ."

"No, sir, it will merely mean a waste of my work and your money," said Petrovich.

After such a verdict Akaky left Petrovich's room feeling completely crushed, while the tailor remained in the same position a long time after he had gone, without going back to his work, his lips pursed significantly. He was greatly pleased that he had neither demeaned himself nor let down the sartorial art.

In the street Akaky felt as though he were in a dream. "So that's how it stands, is it?" he murmured to himself. "I really didn't think that it would turn out like that, you know. . . ." Then after a pause he added, "Well, that's that. There's a real surprise for you. . . . I never thought that it would end like that. . . ." There followed another long pause, after which he said, "So that's how it is ! What a sudden . . . I mean, what a terrible blow ! Who could have . . . What an awful business !"

Having delivered himself thus, he walked on, without noticing it, in quite the opposite direction from his home. On the way a chimney-sweep brushed the whole of his sooty side against him and blackened his shoulder; from the top of a house that was being built a whole handful of lime fell upon him. But he was aware of nothing, and only when some time later he knocked against a policeman who, placing his halberd near him, was scattering some snuff from a horn on a calloused fist, did he recover a little, and that, too, only because the policeman said, "Now then, what are you pushing against me for ? Can't you see where you're going ? Ain't the pavement big enough for you ?" This made him look up and retrace his steps.

But it was not until he had returned home that he began to collect his thoughts and saw his position as it really was. He began discussing the matter with himself, not in broken sentences, but frankly and soberly, as though talking to a wise friend with whom it was possible to discuss one's most intimate affairs.

"No, no," said Akaky, "it's pretty clear that it is impossible to talk to Petrovich now. He's a bit, you know . . . Been thrashed by his wife, I shouldn't wonder. I'd better go and see him next Sunday morning, for after all the drink he'll have had on Saturday night he'll still be screwing up his one eye, and he'll be very sleepy and dying for another drink to help him on his feet again, and his wife won't give him any money, so that if I come along and give him ten copecks or a little more he'll be more reasonable and change his mind about the overcoat, and then, you know . . ."

So Akaky reasoned with himself, and he felt greatly reassured.

Sunday came at last and, noticing from a distance that Petrovich's wife had left the house to go somewhere, he went straight in. To be sure, Petrovich did glower after his Saturday night's libations, and he could barely hold up his head, which seemed to be gravitating towards the floor, and he certainly looked very sleepy; and yet, in spite of this condition, no sooner did he hear what Akaky had come for than it seemed as if the devil himself had nudged him.

"Quite impossible, sir," he said. "You'll have to order a new one." Akaky immediately slipped a ten-copeck piece into his hand. "Thank you very much, sir," said Petrovich. "Very kind of you, I'm sure. I'll get a bit o' strength in me body and drink to your health, sir. But if I were you, sir, I'd stop worrying about that overcoat of yours. No good at all. Can't do nothing with it. Mind, I can promise you one thing, though: I'll make you a lovely new overcoat. That I will, sir."

Akaky tried to say something about mending the old one, but Petrovich would not even listen to him and said, "Depend upon it, sir, I'll make you a new one. Do my best for you, I will, sir. Might even while we're about it, sir, and seeing as how it's now the fashion, get a silver-plated clasp for the collar."

It was then that Akaky at last realised that he would have to get a new overcoat, and his heart failed him. And how indeed was he to do it? What with? Where was he to get the money? There was of course the additional holiday pay he could count on; at least there was a good chance of his getting that holiday bonus. But supposing he did get it, all that money had already been divided up and disposed of long ago. There was that new pair of trousers he must get; then there was that long-standing debt he owed the shoemaker for putting new tops to some old boots; he had, moreover, to order three shirts from the sempstress as well as two pairs of that particular article of underwear which cannot be decently mentioned in print—in short, all the money would have to be spent to the last penny, and even if the director of the department were to be so kind as to give him a holiday bonus of forty-five or even fifty roubles instead of forty, all that would remain of it would be the veriest trifle, which in terms of overcoat finance would be just a drop in the ocean. Though he knew perfectly well, of course, that Petrovich was sometimes mad enough to ask so utterly preposterous a price that even his wife could not refrain from exclaiming, "Gone off his head completely, the silly old fool! One day he accepts work for next to nothing, and now the devil must have made him ask more than he is worth himself!"—though he knew perfectly well, of course, that Petrovich would undertake to make him the overcoat for eighty roubles, the question still remained: where was he to get the eighty roubles? At a pinch he could raise half of it. Yes, he could find half of it all right and perhaps even a little more, but where was he to get the other half? . . .

But first of all the reader had better be told where Akaky hoped to be able to raise the first half.

Akaky was in the habit of putting away a little from every rouble he spent in a box which he kept locked up and which had a little hole in the lid through which money could be dropped.

At the end of every six months he counted up the accumulated coppers and changed them into silver. As he had been saving up for a long time, there had accumulated in the course of several years a sum of over forty roubles. So he had half of the required sum in hand; but where was he to get the other half? Where was he to get another forty roubles?

Akaky thought and thought and then he decided that he would have to cut down his ordinary expenses for a year at least: do without a cup of tea in the evenings; stop burning candles in the evening and, if he had some work to do, go to his landlady's room and work by the light of her candle; when walking in the street, try to walk as lightly as possible on the cobbles and flagstones, almost on tiptoe, so as not to wear out the soles of his boots too soon; give his washing to the laundress as seldom as possible, and to make sure that it did not wear out, to take it off as soon as he returned home and wear only his dressing-gown of twilled cotton cloth, a very old garment that time itself had spared. To tell the truth, Akaky at first found it very hard to get used to such economy, but after some time he got used to it all right and everything went with a swing; he did not even mind going hungry in the evenings, for spiritually he was nourished well enough, since his thoughts were full of the great idea of his future overcoat. His whole existence indeed seemed now somehow to have become fuller, as though he had got married, as though there was someone at his side, as though he was never alone, but some agreeable helpmate had consented to share the joys and sorrows of his life, and this sweet helpmate, this dear wife of his, was no other than the selfsame overcoat with its thick padding of cotton-wool and its strong lining that would last a lifetime. He became more cheerful and his character even got a little firmer, like that of a man who knew what he was aiming at and how to achieve that aim. Doubt vanished, as though of its own accord, from his face and from his actions, and so did indecision and, in fact, all the indeterminate and shilly-shallying traits of his character. Sometimes a gleam would appear in his eyes and through his head there would flash the most bold and audacious thought, to wit, whether he should not after all get himself a fur collar of marten. All these thoughts about his new overcoat nearly took his mind off his work at the office, so much so that once, as he was copying out a document, he was just about to make a mistake, and he almost cried out, "Oh dear!" in a loud voice, and crossed himself. He went to see Petrovich at least once a month to discuss his overcoat, where it was best to buy the cloth, and what colour and at what price, and though looking a little worried, he always came back home well satisfied, reflecting that the time was not far off when he would pay for it all and when his overcoat would be ready.

As a matter of fact the whole thing came to pass much quicker than he dreamed. Contrary to all expectations, the director gave Akaky Akakyevich not forty or forty-five, but sixty roubles! Yes, a holiday bonus of sixty roubles. Whether he, too, had been aware that Akaky wanted a new overcoat, or whether it happened by sheer accident, the fact remained that Akaky had an additional twenty roubles. This speeded up the whole course of events. Another two or three months of a life on short commons and Akaky had actually saved up about eighty roubles. His pulse, generally sluggish, began beating fast. The very next day he went with Petrovich to the shops. They bought an excellent piece of cloth, and no wonder! For the matter had been carefully discussed and thought over for almost six months, and scarcely a month had passed without enquiries being made at the shops about prices, so as to make quite sure that the cloth they needed was not too expensive; and the result of all that foresight was that, as Petrovich himself admitted, they could not have got a better cloth. For the lining they chose calico, but of such fine and strong quality that, according to Petrovich, it was much better than silk and was actually much more handsome and glossy. They did not buy marten for a fur collar, for as a matter of fact it was rather expensive, but they chose cat fur instead, the best cat they could find in the shop, cat which from a distance could always be mistaken for marten. Petrovich took only two weeks over the overcoat, and that, too, because there was so much quilting to be done; otherwise it would have been ready earlier. For his work Petrovich took twelve roubles—less than that was quite out of the question: he had used nothing but silk thread in the sewing of it, and it was sewn with fine, double seams, and Petrovich had gone over each seam with his own teeth afterwards, leaving all sorts of marks on them.

It was . . . It is hard to say on what day precisely it was, but there could be no doubt at all that the day on which Petrovich at last delivered the overcoat was one of the greatest days in Akaky's life. He brought it rather early in the morning, just a short time before Akaky had to leave for the department. At no other time would the overcoat have been so welcome, for the time of rather sharp frosts had just begun, and from all appearances it looked as if the severity of the weather would increase. Petrovich walked in with the overcoat as a good tailor should. His face wore an expression of solemn gravity such as Akaky had never seen on it before. He seemed to be fully conscious of the fact that he had accomplished no mean thing and that he had shown by his own example the gulf that separated the tailors who merely relined a coat or did repairs from those who made new coats. He took the overcoat out of the large handkerchief in which he had brought it. (The handkerchief had just come from the laundress: it was only now that he folded it and put it in his pocket for use.) Having taken out the overcoat, he looked very proudly about him and, holding it in both hands, threw it very smartly over Akaky's shoulders, then he gave it a vigorous pull and, bending down, smoothed it out behind with his hand; then he draped it round Akaky, throwing it open in front a little. Akaky, who was no longer a young man, wanted to try it on with his arms in the sleeves, and Petrovich helped him to put his hands through the sleeves, and—it was all right even when he wore it with his arms in the sleeves. In fact, there could be no doubt at all that the overcoat was a perfect fit. Petrovich did not let this opportunity pass without observing that it was only because he lived in a back street and had no signboard and because he had known Akaky Akakyevich so long that he had charged him so little for making the overcoat. If he had ordered it on Nevsky Avenue, they would have charged him seventy-five roubles for the work alone. Akaky had no desire to discuss the matter with Petrovich and, to tell the truth, he was a little frightened of the big sums which Petrovich was so fond of tossing about with the idea of impressing people. He paid him, thanked him, and left immediately for the department in his new overcoat. Petrovich followed him into the street where he remained standing a long time on one spot, admiring his handiwork from a distance; then he purposely went out of his way so that he could by taking a short-cut by a side-street rush out into the street again and have another look at the overcoat, this time from the other side, that is to say, from the front.

Meanwhile Akaky went along as if walking on air. Not for a fraction of a second did he forget that he had a new overcoat on his back, and he could not help smiling to himself from time to time with sheer pleasure at the thought of it. And really it had two advantages:

one that it was warm, and the other that it was good. He did not notice the distance and found himself suddenly in the department. He took off the overcoat in the hall, examined it carefully and entrusted it to the special care of the door-keeper. It is not known how the news of Akaky's new overcoat had spread all over the department, but all at once every one knew that Akaky had discarded his *capote* and had a fine new overcoat. They all immediately rushed out into the hall to have a look at Akaky's new overcoat. Congratulations and good wishes were showered upon him. At first Akaky just smiled, then he felt rather embarrassed. But when all surrounded him and began telling him that he ought to celebrate his acquisition of a new overcoat and that the least he could do was to invite them all to a party, Akaky Akakyevich was thrown into utter confusion and did not know what to do, what to say to them all, or how to extricate himself from that very awkward situation. He even tried a few minutes later with the utmost good humour to assure them, blushing to the roots of his hair, that it was not a new overcoat at all, that it was just . . . well, you know . . . just his old overcoat. At last one of the clerks, and, mind, not just any clerk, but no less a person than the assistant head clerk of the office, wishing to show no doubt that he, for one, was not a proud man and did not shun men more humble than himself, said, "So be it ! I will give a party instead of Akaky Akakyevich. I invite you all, gentlemen, this evening to tea at my place. As a matter of fact, it happens to be my birthday." The Civil Servants naturally wished him many happy returns of the day and accepted his invitation with alacrity. Akaky tried at first to excuse himself, but everybody told him that it was not done and that he ought to be ashamed of himself, and he just could not wriggle out of it. However, he felt rather pleased afterwards, for it occurred to him that this would give him a chance of taking a walk in the evening in his new overcoat.

That day was to Akaky like a great festival. He came home in a most happy frame of mind, took off his overcoat, hung it with great care on the wall, stood for some time admiring the cloth and lining, and then produced his old overcoat, which had by then gone to pieces completely, just to compare the two. He looked at it and could not help chuckling out loud : what a difference ! And he kept smiling to himself all during dinner when he thought of the disgraceful state of his old overcoat. He enjoyed his dinner immensely and did no copying at all afterwards, not one document did

sure that his host would not detain him on one pretext or another, he stole out of the room and found his overcoat in the hall. The overcoat, he noticed not without a pang of regret, was lying on the floor. He picked it up, shook it, removed every speck of dust from it and, putting it over his shoulders, went down the stairs into the street.

It was still light in the street. A few small grocers' shops, those round-the-clock clubs of all sorts of servants, were still open; from those which were already closed a streak of light still streamed through the crack under the door, showing that there was still some company there, consisting most probably of maids and men-servants who were finishing their talk and gossip, leaving their masters completely at a loss to know where they were. Akaky walked along feeling very happy and even set off running after some lady (goodness knows why) who passed him like a streak of lightning, every part of her body in violent motion. However, he stopped almost at once and went on at a slow pace as before, marvelling himself where that unusual spurt of speed had come from. Soon he came to those never-ending, deserted streets, which even in daytime are not particularly cheerful, let alone at night. Now they looked even more deserted and lonely; there were fewer street lamps and even those he came across were extinguished: the municipal authorities seemed to be sparing of oil. He now came into the district of wooden houses and fences; there was not a soul to be seen anywhere, only the snow gleamed on the streets, and hundreds of dismal, low hovels with closed shutters which seemed to have sunk into a deep sleep, stretched in a long, dark line before him. Soon he approached the spot where the street was intersected by an immense square with houses dimly visible on the other side, a square that looked to him like a dreadful desert.

A long way away—goodness knows where—he could see the glimmer of a light coming from some sentry-box, which seemed to be standing at the edge of the world. Akaky's cheerfulness faded perceptibly as he entered the square. He entered it not without a kind of involuntary sensation of dread, as though feeling in his bones that something untoward was going to happen. He looked back, and then cast a glance at either side of him: it was just as though the sea were all round him. "Much better not to look," he thought to himself, and, shutting his eyes, he walked on, opening them only to have a look how far the end of the square was. But what he saw was a couple of men standing right in front of him, men with moustaches, but what they were he could not make out in the darkness. He felt dazed and his heart began beating violently against his ribs. "Look, here is my overcoat!" one of the men said in a voice of thunder, grabbing him by the collar. Akaky was about to scream, "Help!" but the other man shook his fist in his face, a fist as big as a Civil Servant's head, and said, "You just give a squeak!" All poor Akaky knew was that they took off his overcoat and gave him a kick which sent him sprawling on the snow. He felt nothing at all any more. A few minutes later he recovered sufficiently to get up, but there was not a soul to be seen anywhere. He felt that it was terribly cold in the square and that his overcoat had gone. He began to shout for help, but his voice seemed to be too weak to carry to the end of the square. Feeling desperate and without ceasing to shout, he ran across the square straight to the sentry-box beside which stood a policeman who, leaning on his halberd, seemed to watch the running figure with mild interest, wondering no doubt why the devil a man was running towards him, screaming his head off while still a mile away. Having run up to the police constable, Akaky started shouting at him in a gasping voice that he was asleep and did not even notice that a man had been robbed under his very nose. The policeman said that he saw nothing, or rather that all he did see was that two men had stopped him (Akaky) in the middle of the square, but he supposed that they were his friends; and he advised Akaky, instead of standing there and abusing him for nothing, to go and see the police inspector next morning, for the inspector was quite sure to find the men who had taken his overcoat.

Akaky Akakyevich came running home in a state of utter confusion. His hair, which still grew, though sparsely, over his temples and at the back of his head, was terribly tousled; his chest, arms and trousers were covered with snow. His old landlady, awakened by the loud knocking at the door, jumped hurriedly out of bed and with only one slipper on ran to open the door, modestly clasping her chemise to her bosom with one hand. When she opened the door and saw the terrible state Akaky was in, she fell back with a gasp. He told her what had happened to him, and she threw up her arms in dismay and said that he ought to go straight to the district police commissioner, for the police inspector was quite sure to swindle him, promise him all sorts of things and then leave him in the lurch;

it would be much better if he went to the district police commissioner who, it seemed, was known to her, for Anna, the Finnish girl who was once her cook, was now employed by the district commissioner of police as a nurse, and, besides, she had seen him often as he drove past the house, and he even went to church every Sunday and always, while saying his prayers, looked round at everybody very cheerfully, so that, judging from all appearances, he must be a kind-hearted man.

Having listened to that piece of advice, Akaky wandered off sadly to his room, and how he spent that night we leave it to those to judge who can enter into the position of another man. Early next morning he went to see the district police commissioner, but they told him that he was still asleep. He came back at ten o'clock and again they said he was asleep. He came back at eleven o'clock and was told that the police commissioner was not at home. He came back at lunch-time, but the clerks in the waiting-room would not admit him on any account unless he told them first what he had come for and what it was all about and what had happened. So that in the end Akaky felt for the first time in his life that he had to assert himself and he told them bluntly that he had come to see the district commissioner of police personally, that they had no right to refuse to admit him, that he had come from the department on official business, and that if he lodged a complaint against them, they would see what would happen. The clerks dared say nothing to this and one of them went to summon the commissioner.

The police commissioner took rather a curious view of Akaky's story of the loss of his overcoat. Instead of concentrating on the main point of the affair, he began putting all sorts of questions to Akaky which had nothing to do with it, such as why he was coming home so late, and was he sure he had not been to any disorderly house the night before, so that Akaky felt terribly embarrassed and went away wondering whether the police were ever likely to take the necessary steps to retrieve his overcoat.

That day (for the first time in his life) he did not go to the department. Next day he appeared looking very pale and wearing his old *capote*, which was in a worse state than ever. Many of his colleagues seemed moved by the news of the robbery of his overcoat, though there were a few among them who could not help pulling poor Akaky's leg even on so sad an occasion. It was decided to make a special collection for Akaky, but they only succeeded in collecting a trifling sum, for the clerks in his office had already spent a great deal on subscribing to a fund for a portrait of the director and also on some kind of a book, at the suggestion of one of the departmental chiefs, who was a friend of the author. Anyway, the sum collected was a trifling one. One Civil Servant, however, moved by compassion, decided to help Akaky with some good advice at any rate, and he told him that he should not go to the district police inspector, for though it might well happen that the district police inspector, anxious to win the approbation of his superiors, would somehow or other find his overcoat, Akaky would never be able to get it out of the police station unless he could present all the necessary legal proofs that the overcoat belonged to him. It would therefore be much better if Akaky went straight to a certain Very Important Person, for the Very Important Person could, by writing and getting into touch with the right people, give a much quicker turn to the whole matter.

Akaky Akakyevich (what else could he do?) decided to go and see the Very Important Person. What position the Very Important Person occupied and what his job actually was has never been properly ascertained and still remains unknown. Suffice it to say that the Very Important Person had become a Very Important Person only quite recently, and that until then he was quite an unimportant person. Moreover, his office was not even now considered of much importance as compared with others of greater importance. But there will always be people who regard as important what in the eyes of other people is rather unimportant. However, the Very Important Person did his best to increase his importance in all sorts of ways, to wit, he introduced a rule that his subordinates should meet him on the stairs when he arrived at his office; that no one should be admitted to his office unless he first petitioned for an interview, and that everything should be done according to the strictest order: the collegiate registrar was first to report to the provincial secretary, the provincial secretary to the titular councillor or whomsoever it was he had to report to, and that only by such a procedure should any particular business reach him. In Holy Russia, we are sorry to say, every one seems to be anxious to ape every one else and each man copies and imitates his superior. The story is even told of some titular councillor who, on being made chief of some small office, immediately partitioned off a special room for himself, calling it "the presence chamber," and placed two commissionaires in coats with red collars and galloons at the door with instructions to take hold of the door handle and open the door to any person who came to see him, though there was hardly room in "the presence chamber" for an ordinary writing-desk.

The manners and habits of the Very Important Person were very grand and impressive, but not very subtle. His whole system was based chiefly on strictness. "Strictness, strictness, and *again* strictness !" he usually declared, and at the penultimate word he usually peered very significantly into the face of the man he was addressing. There seemed to be no particular reason for this strictness, though, for the dozen or so Civil Servants who composed the whole administrative machinery of his office were held in a proper state of fear and trembling, anyhow. Seeing him coming from a distance they all stopped their work immediately and, standing at attention, waited until the chief had walked through the room. His usual conversation with any of his subordinates was saturated with strictness and consisted almost entirely of three phrases : "How dare you, sir ? Do you know who you're talking to, sir ? Do you realise who is standing before you, sir ?" Still, he was really a good fellow at heart, was particularly pleasant with his colleagues, and quite obliging, too; but his new position went to his head. Having received the rank of general, he got all confused, was completely nonplussed and did not know what to do. In the presence of a man equal to him in rank, he was just an ordinary fellow, quite a decent fellow, and in many ways even a far from stupid fellow; but whenever he happened to be in company with men even one rank lower than he, he seemed to be lost; he sat silent and his position was really pitiable, more particularly as he himself felt that he could have spent the time so much more enjoyably. A strong desire could sometimes be read in his eyes to take part in some interesting conversation or join some interesting people, but he was always stopped by the thought : would it not mean going a little too far on his part ? Would it not be mistaken for familiarity and would he not thereby lower himself in the estimation of everybody ? As a consequence of this reasoning he always found himself in a position where he had to remain silent, delivering himself only from time to time of a few monosyllables, and in this way he won for himself the unenviable reputation of being an awful bore.

It was before this sort of Very Important Person that our Akaky presented himself, and he presented himself at the most inopportune moment he could possibly have chosen, very unfortunate for himself, though not so unfortunate for the Very Important Person.

At the time of Akaky's arrival the Very Important Person was in his private office, having a very pleasant talk with an old friend of his, a friend of his childhood, who had only recently arrived in St. Petersburg and whom he had not seen for several years. It was just then that he was informed that a certain Bashmachkin wanted to see him. "Who's that?" he asked abruptly, and he was told, "Some Civil Servant." "Oh," said the Very Important Person, "let him wait. I'm busy now."

Now we believe it is only fair to state here that the Very Important Person had told a thumping lie. He was not busy at all. He had long ago said all he had to say to his old friend, and their present conversation had for some time now been punctuated by long pauses, interrupted by the one or the other slapping his friend on the knee and saying, "Ah, Ivan Abramovich!" or "Yes, yes, quite right, Stepan Varlamovich!" However, he asked the Civil Servant to wait, for he wanted to show his friend, who had left the Civil Service long ago and had been spending all his time at his country house, how long he kept Civil Servants cooling their heels in his anteroom. At last, having talked, or rather kept silent as long as they liked, having enjoyed a cigar in comfortable arm-chairs with sloping backs, he seemed to remember something suddenly and said to his secretary, who was standing at the door with a sheaf of documents in his hand, "Isn't there some Civil Servant waiting to see me? Tell him to come in, please."

Seeing Akaky's humble appearance and old uniform, he turned to him and said shortly, "What do you want?" in an abrupt and firm voice, which he had specially rehearsed in the solitude of his room in front of a looking-glass a week before he received his present post and the rank of general.

Akaky, who had long since been filled with the proper amount of fear and trembling, felt rather abashed and explained as well as he could and as much as his stammering would let him, with the addition of the more than usual number of "wells" and "you knows," that his overcoat was quite a new overcoat, and that he had been robbed in a most shameless fashion, and that he was now applying to his excellency in the hope that his excellency might by putting in a word here and there or doing this or that, or writing to the Commissioner of Police of the Metropolis, or to some other person, get his overcoat back. For some unknown reason the general considered such an approach as too familiar. "What do you mean, sir?" he said in his abrupt voice. "Don't you know the proper procedure? What have you come to me for? Don't you know how things are done? In the first place you should have sent in a petition about it to my office. Your petition, sir, would have been placed before the chief clerk, who would have transferred it to my secretary, and my secretary would have submitted it to me. . . ."

"But, your excellency," said Akaky, trying to summon the handful of courage he had (it was not a very big handful, anyway), and feeling at the same time that he was perspiring all over, "I took the liberty, your excellency, of troubling you personally because —er—because, sir, secretaries are, well, you know, rather unreliable people. . . ."

"What? What did you say, sir?" said the Very Important Person. "How dare you speak like this, sir? Where did you get the impudence to speak like this, sir? Where did you get these extraordinary ideas from, sir? What's the meaning of this mutinous spirit that is now spreading among young men against their chiefs and superiors?" The Very Important Person did not seem to have noticed that Akaky Akakyevich was well over fifty, and it can only be supposed, therefore, that if he called him a young man he meant it only in a relative sense, that is to say, that compared with a man of seventy Akaky was a young man. "Do you realise, sir, who you are talking to? Do you understand, sir, who is standing before you? Do you understand it, sir? Do you understand it, I ask you?"

Here he stamped his foot and raised his voice to so high a pitch that it was not Akaky Akakyevich alone who became terrified. Akaky was on the point of fainting. He staggered, trembled all over, and could not stand on his feet. Had it not been for the door-keepers, who ran up to support him, he would have collapsed on the ground. He was carried out almost unconscious. The Very Important Person, satisfied that the effect he had produced exceeded all expectations and absolutely in raptures over the idea that a word of his could actually throw a man into a faint, glanced at his friend out of the corner of his eye, wondering what impression he had made on him; and he was pleased to see that his friend was rather in an uneasy frame of mind himself and seemed to show quite unmistakable signs of fear.

Akaky could not remember how he had descended the stairs, or how he had got out into the street. He remembered nothing. His hands and feet had gone dead. Never in his life had he been so hauled over the coals by a general, and not his own general at that. He walked along in a blizzard, in the teeth of a howling wind, which was sweeping through the streets, with his mouth agape and constantly stumbling off the pavement; the wind, as is its invariable custom in St. Petersburg, blew from every direction and every side street all at once. His throat became inflamed in no time at all, and when at last he staggered home he was unable to utter a word. He was all swollen, and he took to his bed. So powerful can a real official reprimand be sometimes !

Next day Akaky was in a high fever. Thanks to the most generous assistance of the St. Petersburg climate, his illness made much more rapid progress than could have been expected, and when the doctor arrived he merely felt his pulse and found nothing to do except prescribe a poultice, and that only because he did not want to leave the patient without the beneficent aid of medicine; he did, though, express his opinion then and there that all would be over in a day and a half. After which he turned to the landlady and said, "No need to waste time, my dear lady. You'd better order a deal coffin for him at once, for I don't suppose he can afford an oak coffin, can he ?"

Did Akaky Akakyevich hear those fateful words and, if he did hear them, did they produce a shattering effect upon him ? Did he at that moment repine at his wretched lot in life ? It is quite impossible to say, for the poor man was in a delirium and a high fever. Visions, one stranger than another, haunted him incessantly: one moment he saw Petrovich and ordered him to make an overcoat with special traps for thieves, whom he apparently believed to be hiding under his bed, so that he called to his landlady every minute to get them out of there, and once he even asked her to get a thief from under his blanket; another time he demanded to be told why his old *capote* was hanging on the wall in front of him when he had a new overcoat; then it seemed to him that he was standing before the general and listening to his reprimand, which he so well deserved, saying, "Sorry, your excellency !" and, finally, he let out a stream of obscenities, shouting such frightful words that his dear old

298

landlady kept crossing herself, having never heard him use such words, particularly as they seemed always to follow immediately upon the words, "your excellency." He raved on and no sense could be made of his words, except that it was quite evident that his incoherent words and thoughts all revolved about one and the same overcoat. At length poor Akaky Akakyevich gave up the ghost.

Neither his room nor his belongings were put under seal because, in the first place, he had no heirs, and in the second there was precious little inheritance he left behind, comprising as it did all in all a bundle of quills, a quire of white Government paper, three pairs of socks, a few buttons that had come off his trousers, and the *capote* with which the reader has already made his acquaintance. Who finally came into all this property, goodness only knows, and I must confess that the author of this story was not sufficiently interested to find out. Akaky Akakyevich was taken to the cemetery and buried. And St. Petersburg carried on without Akaky, as though he had never lived there. A human being just disappeared and left no trace, a human being whom no one ever dreamed of protecting, who was not dear to anyone, whom no one thought of taking any interest in, who did not attract the attention even of a naturalist who never fails to stick a pin through an ordinary fly to examine it under the microscope; a man who bore meekly the sneers and insults of his fellow Civil Servants in the department and who went to his grave because of some silly accident, but who before the very end of his life did nevertheless catch a glimpse of a Bright Visitant in the shape of an overcoat, which for a brief moment brought a ray of sunshine into his drab, poverty-stricken life, and upon whose head afterwards disaster had most pitilessly fallen, as it falls upon the heads of the great ones of this earth ! . . .

A few days after his death a caretaker was sent to his room from the department to order him to present himself at the office at once: the chief himself wanted to see him ! But the caretaker had to return without him, merely reporting that Akaky Akakyevich could not come, and to the question, "Why not ?" he merely said, "He can't come, sir, 'cause he's dead. That's why, sir. Been buried these four days, he has, sir." It was in this way that the news of his death reached the department, and on the following day a new clerk was sitting in his place, a much taller man, who did not write letters in Akaky's upright hand, but rather sloping and aslant.

But who could have foreseen that this was not the last of Akaky Akakyevich and that he was destined to be the talk of the town for a few days after his death, as though in recompense for having remained unnoticed all through his life. But so it fell out, and our rather poor story quite unexpectedly acquired a most fantastic ending.

Rumours suddenly spread all over St. Petersburg that a ghost in the shape of a Government clerk had begun appearing near Kalinkin Bridge and much farther afield, too, and that this ghost was looking for some stolen overcoat and, under the pretext of recovering this lost overcoat, was stripping overcoats off the backs of all sorts of people, irrespective of their rank or calling: overcoats with cat fur, overcoats with beaver fur, raccoon, fox and bear fur-coats, in fact, overcoats with every kind of fur or skin that men have ever made use of to cover their own. One of the departmental clerks had seen the ghost with his own eyes and at once recognised Akaky Akakyevich; but that frightened him so much that he took to his heels and was unable to get a better view of the ghost, but merely saw how he shook a finger at him threateningly from a distance. From all sides complaints were incessantly heard to the effect that the backs and shoulders, not only of titular councillors, but also of court councillors, were in imminent danger of catching cold as a result of this frequent pulling off of overcoats. The police received orders to catch the ghost at all costs, dead or alive, and to punish him in the most unmerciful manner as an example to all other ghosts, and they nearly did catch it. A police constable whose beat included Kiryushkin Lane had actually caught the ghost by his collar on the very scene of his latest crime, in the very act of attempting to pull a frieze overcoat off the back of some retired musician who had once upon a time tootled on a flute. Having caught him by the collar, the policeman shouted to two of his comrades to come to his help, and when those arrived he told them to hold the miscreant while he reached for his snuff-box which he kept in one of his boots, to revive his nose which had been frostbitten six times in his life; but the snuff must have been of a kind that even a ghost could not stand. For no sooner had the policeman, closing his right nostril with a finger, inhaled with his left nostril half a handful of snuff than the ghost sneezed so violently that he splashed the eyes of all three. While they were raising their fists to wipe their eyes, the ghost had vanished completely, so that they were not even sure whether he had actually been in their hands. Since that time policemen were in such terror of the dead that they were even afraid to arrest the living, merely shouting from a distance, "Hi, you there, move along, will you?" and the ghost of the Civil Servant began to show himself beyond Kalinkin Bridge, causing alarm and dismay among all law-abiding citizens of timid dispositions.

We seem, however, to have completely forgotten a certain Very Important Person who, as a matter of fact, was the real cause of the fantastic turn this otherwise perfectly true story has taken. To begin with, we think it is only fair to make it absolutely clear that the Very Important Person felt something like a twinge of compunction soon after the departure of poor Akaky Akakyevich, whom he had taken to task so severely. Sympathy for a fellow human being was not alien to him; his heart was open to all kinds of kindly impulses in spite of the fact that his rank often prevented them from coming to the surface. As soon as the friend he had not seen for so long had left, he felt even a little worried about poor Akaky, and since that day he could not get the pale face of the meek little Government clerk out of his head, the poor Civil Servant who could not take an official reprimand like a man. In fact, he worried so much about him that a week later he sent one of his own clerks to Akaky to find out how he was getting on, whether his overcoat had turned up, and whether it was not really possible to help him in any way. When he learnt that Akaky had died suddenly of a fever he was rather upset and all day long his conscience troubled him, and he was in a bad mood. Wishing to distract himself a little and forget the unpleasant incident, he went to spend an evening with one of his friends, where he found quite a large company and, what was even better, they all seemed to be almost of the same rank as he, so that there was nothing at all to disconcert him. This had a most wonderful effect on his state of mind. He let himself go, became a very pleasant fellow to talk to, affable and genial, and spent a very agreeable evening. At dinner he drank a few glasses of champagne, which, as is generally acknowledged, is quite an excellent way of getting rid of gloomy thoughts. The champagne led him to introduce a certain change into his programme for that night, to wit, he decided not to go home at once, but first visit a lady friend of his, a certain Karolina Ivanovna, presumably of German descent, with whom he was on exceedingly friendly terms. It should be explained here that the Very Important Person was not a young man, that he was a good husband and a worthy father of a family. Two sons, one of whom was already in Government service, and a very sweet sixteen-year-old daughter, whose little nose was perhaps a thought too arched, but who was very pretty none the less, came every morning to kiss his hand, saying, "*Bonjour, papa*." His wife, who was still in the prime of life and not at all bad-looking, first gave him her hand to kiss and then, turning it round, kissed his hand. But the Very Important Person, who was very satisfied indeed with these domestic pleasantries, thought it only right to have a lady friend in another part of the town for purely friendly relations. This lady friend was not a bit younger or better-looking than his wife, but there it is: such is the way of the world, and it is not our business to pass judgment upon it. And so the Very Important Person descended the stairs, sat down in his sledge, said to his coachman, "To Karolina Ivanovna," and, wrapping himself up very snugly in his warm overcoat, gave himself up completely to the enjoyment of his pleasant mood, than which nothing better could happen to a Russian, that is to say, the sort of mood when you do not yourself have to think of anything, while thoughts, one more delightful than another, come racing through your head without even putting you to the trouble of chasing after them or looking for them. Feeling very pleased, he recalled without much effort all the pleasant happenings of the evening, all the witty sayings, which had aroused peals of laughter among the small circle of friends, many of which he even now repeated softly to himself, finding them every bit as funny as they were the first time he heard them, and it is therefore little wonder that he chuckled happily most of the time. The boisterous wind, however, occasionally interfered with his enjoyment, for, rushing out suddenly from heaven knew where and for a reason that was utterly incomprehensible, it cut his face like a knife, covering it with lumps of snow, swelling out his collar like a sail, or suddenly throwing it with supernatural force over his head and so causing him incessant trouble to extricate himself from it. All of a sudden the Very Important Person felt that somebody had seized him very firmly by the collar. Turning round, he saw a small-sized man in an old, threadbare Civil Service uniform, and it was not without horror that he recognised Akaky Akakyevich. The Civil Servant's face was white as snow and looked like that of a dead man. But the horror of the Very Important Person increased considerably when he saw that the mouth of the dead man became twisted and, exhaling the terrible breath of the grave, Akaky's ghost uttered the following words, "Aha! So here you are! I've—er—collared you at last! . . . It's your overcoat I want, sir! You didn't care a rap for mine, did you? Did nothing to get it back for me, and abused me into the bargain! All right, then, give me yours now!" The poor Very Important Person nearly died of fright. Unbending as he was at the office and generally in the presence of his inferiors, and though one look at his manly appearance and figure was enough to make people say, "Ugh, what a Tartar!" nevertheless in this emergency he, like many another man of athletic appearance, was seized with such terror that he began, not without reason, to apprehend a heart attack. He threw off his overcoat himself and shouted to his driver in a panic-stricken voice, "Home, quick!" The driver, recognising the tone which was usually employed in moments of crisis and was quite often accompanied by something more forceful, drew in his head between his shoulders just to be on the safe side, flourished his whip and raced off as swift as an arrow. In a little over six minutes the Very Important Person was already at the entrance of his house.

Pale, frightened out of his wits, and without his overcoat, he arrived home instead of going to Karolina Ivanovna's, and somehow or other managed to stagger to his room. He spent a very restless night, so that next morning at breakfast his daughter told him outright, "You look very pale today, Papa!" But Papa made no reply. Not a word did he say to any one about what had happened to him, where he had been and where he had intended to go.

This incident made a deep impression upon the Very Important Person. It was not so frequently now that his subordinates heard him say, "How dare you, sir? Do you realise who you're talking to, sir?" And if he did say it, it was only after he had heard what it was all about.

But even more remarkable was the fact that since then the appearance of the Civil Servant's ghost had completely ceased. It can only be surmised that he was very pleased with the general's overcoat which must have fitted him perfectly; at least nothing was heard any more of people who had their overcoats pulled off their backs. Not that there were not all sorts of busybodies who would not let well alone and who went on asserting that the ghost of the

Civil Servant was still appearing in the more outlying parts of the town. Indeed, a Kolomna policeman saw with his own eyes the ghost appear from behind a house; but having rather a frail constitution—once an ordinary young pig, rushing out of a house, had sent him sprawling, to the great delight of some cabbies who were standing round and whom, for such an insult, he promptly fined two copecks each for snuff—he dared not stop the ghost, but merely followed it in the dark until, at last, it suddenly looked round and, stopping dead in its tracks, asked, "What do *you* want?" at the same time displaying a fist of a size that was never seen among the living. The police constable said, "Nothing," and turned back at once. This ghost, however, was much taller; it had a pair of huge moustachios, and, walking apparently in the direction of Obukhov Bridge, it disappeared into the darkness of the night.